UNPLANNED PLAY

NASHVILLE PLAYERS
BOOK 1

CHELLE SLOAN

DEDICATION

To every woman who has ever thought your life is over after thirty, especially ones finding themselves without a partner, this is for you.

Life isn't over. It's just beginning. And remember the famous lyrics, some men like their girls a little bit older.

CHAPTER 1
MADDOX

There is one universal similarity among every young kid who grew up playing football in America. And that's at one point in your life, you not only thought about, but you also likely acted out, winning the biggest game of your career on the grandest stage in professional football.

The practiced touchdown run. The dance that would immediately ensue. The postgame interview. What song you would sing after the game in celebration.

It's "Livin' On A Prayer" by Bon Jovi, for those who are wondering.

But no one talks about what it's like waiting on the sideline for the minutes and seconds to count down in that championship game. What it's like to have to sit and watch your offense try to score the biggest touchdown of the team's season. Maybe no one talks about it because it's the most nerve-racking, panic-inducing, out-of-control feeling you'll ever have as a professional athlete.

I should know. I'm living it right now.

As a part of the defense for the Nashville Fury, we did our job tonight, especially in the fourth quarter. I had an interception that I brought back for a touchdown in the second. Our defense has only given up two other touchdowns and a field goal.

As for our offense, they've kept right with them. But we are the two best teams in the league. Everyone knew this was going to come down to who had the ball last.

Now, we just need to make this count.

Six seconds on the clock.

Tie ballgame.

For all the marbles and the right to call ourselves the best in the league.

I feel one of my teammates grab my hand, but I don't look to see who it is. All I can do is watch and stare at the play starting to unfold.

This isn't my first time waiting for the clock to expire with a championship ring on the line. Yes, this is my fourth year in the league, and every one of those years I've been to the biggest game of the season, which is rare as hell. Yet, every ending has been different. The first two we were soundly in the lead, so the celebration started about midway through the fourth quarter. Last year, when we lost, it was a feeling neither I nor the rest of my teammates ever wanted to feel again.

And then there's this year, the definition of a nail-biter.

Having a chance to win three championships in my first four years in the league is absolutely absurd. There are guys who have played in this league for ten-plus years who have never gotten to this game. And they aren't slouches. These are good players—future Hall of Famers even—who will never have the chance to get a ring and can call themselves the best in the world. Never have the chance to yell "I'm going to Disneyland!" into the camera with confetti raining down on them.

Then there's me—about to be twenty-five years old, drafted by the Nashville Fury in the fifth round of the draft with every pundit and expert saying I was too young and too small to play defensive back in professional football. That sure, I was a great college player—I won the top award for defensive players in my third year of college before going pro early—but my skill set wouldn't translate to the big show.

But like I have my entire life, I proved them wrong. I made the Fury's fifty-two-man roster. I was a starter by midseason. Fast forward to now, I'm on a team that's in the middle of building a dynasty, I finished the year leading the league in interceptions, and I have the second-highest jersey sales on the team.

Suck on that, experts. This is what dreams are made of.

That is, if we can score one more touchdown.

The clap of my offensive teammates' hands from the huddle shifts my focus back to the game. I'm not exactly sure of the play call, but I have to think our coaches are trying to get the ball to our tight end—and my best friend—Linc Kincaid. Not only has he been our go-to offensive weapon all season, he's the best tight end in the league. If Miami doesn't think that the ball is going to him, then they don't deserve to be here.

"Are they really only putting one guy on him?" I ask myself, and yup, they are. They are only lining up one defensive back against him. Fucking dumbasses. Do they realize they've just handed us the game? This is what I call fuck around and find out in real time.

Before Miami can change anything else, our quarterback, Bryce Donald, starts calling out his cadence. One of our receivers starts going into motion. Miami's defense locks in.

Here we fucking go…

I suck in a breath as our league MVP quarterback drops back. He's trying not to give away that he's looking for Linc, but I know this play, and that's exactly what he's doing.

I stop blinking as my head turns to the end zone, Bryce's pass sailing through the air. It's a short pass, but I swear time has nearly stopped and this whole play is happening in slow motion.

The cornerback defending Linc is staying tight on him, but

Linc has the positioning and the height advantage. Plus, Bryce and Linc have practiced this play a hundred times. I know that because many times I've been the guy doing everything I can to deflect the ball away. Like this cornerback, I also don't have the height advantage. I'm not short, but Kincaid is six-foot-five with a wing span of a passenger jet. Bryce knows where to put it, and Linc knows how to catch it. And unless the defender can swat it away, we're about to win this game.

And there it is.

No swat.

Perfect catch.

Feet down.

No fumble.

Touchdown Fury.

Ballgame.

Those are my last calm thoughts before I throw my helmet in the air and scream as I run onto the field, straight toward Linc. The noises leaving my mouth can only be described as the combination of banshee and a four-year-old on a Mountain Dew high. My arms are waving around like the inflatable tube men outside of a used car dealership. I'm pretty sure I am becoming a running meme as we speak. But I'll wear it with a badge of honor knowing what me and my teammates just did.

We made history.

Three championships in four years.

"Holy shit! We fucking won!" I scream as I jump on Linc's back, nearly taking him down. "You fucking did it, bro! You're a fucking beast."

Linc laughs as I detangle myself from his back. "Thanks, but we were able to get that last drive because of the defense. You guys played your asses off tonight."

We bring each other in for a huge hug, slapping each other on the backs, knowing that it was, in fact, a total team effort tonight.

"Tonight's celebration is going to be fucking epic!" I yell. "I have a feeling I'm going to remember it for the rest of my life!"

Linc laughs and shakes his head at me as the confetti starts pouring from the ceiling of the stadium we're playing at in Las Vegas. "Celebrating this kind of win in Vegas, it's the stuff guys dream about."

I slap his pads. "Hell, yeah, it is. You're coming, right?"

Linc gives me a reassuring nod. "Wouldn't miss it for the world."

I knew he wouldn't. Linc might be in love now—and I mean really, really, in love—but he knows a night like this might be the only one of his career. The man's been through it in his life; the fact that he's playing football at all is an achievement. I know he wants to be with his girl, but he also wants to be with us.

Plus, Ainsley's a good time. I'm sure wherever we end up we're all going to have a night we're never going to forget.

Speaking of, we should probably figure out where we're going tonight. And as the self-appointed president of the Nashville Fury After Party Committee, I feel that it's my duty to make these plans. Which is what I do mentally as I continue to hug my teammates, grab championship hats and T-shirts from our staff, and do the few on-field interviews I'm pulled in for.

We should probably hit up the stereotypical Las Vegas night club. Some spot that plays primarily EDM that's going to give me a headache for six days on top of the headache I'm going to have for the copious amount of champagne I'm about to consume tonight. I mean, it's Las Vegas, and we just won the fucking bowl. Of course there's going to be a DJ and champagne.

But what I really have in mind is something a little bit more us. A little more Fury.

A little more karaoke.

It's the right way for this team to celebrate. It's what we do. So, yes, we're going to put in our time at the club. Make our faces seen. Then, when it's appropriate, we're going to head to the real party.

I have three songs ready to go right now.

God, it's going to be fucking epic. The last few times we won, the parties were fucking sick. Bottles. Dancing. Women. Most at the same time. And those games weren't in Las Vegas, and they were still out of control.

I can only imagine what tonight's going to bring.

CHAPTER 2
GABI

'm thirty-five.

It's a Sunday night in Vegas, and I've already been drunk for three days.

I'm dehydrated, my back hurts, and I really want a bath with Epsom salt for my feet.

I'm tired as all hell.

But are any of those reasons stopping me from wearing a revenge dress and heels that I have no business wearing? Absolutely the fuck not.

Why? Oh, because I'm finally fucking divorced.

"To freedom!"

"To no more bad sex!"

"To divorce!"

"You'll never have to ask me twice to cheer to that toast," my best friend Shelby says as she holds up her shot glass. "To your new chapter in life. One with fun, hope, and without his tiny fucking dick."

"To big dicks!" This comes from my other best friend, Hannah, who, bless her heart, hasn't drank since giving birth to her two-year-old. My girl has been hammered all weekend from two drinks.

"To all of that," I say as we clink our shot glasses together and throw back the vodka. Sure, the kids these days might think that green tea shots are the way to go, but millennial women know the true way to get fucked up is a lemon drop.

They never miss.

"I still can't believe it finally happened," Hannah says as I take a sip of my vodka soda.

"Emphasis on finally," Shelby adds.

"Same here," I say. And that's not an understatement.

Because after two years of negotiation and mediation, and a year before that when I knew our marriage was over because the man I thought I was spending the rest of my life with was cheating on me with his secretary, I'm *finally* fucking divorced.

Never in a million years did I think that it would've taken twenty-two months of mediation. Then again, I never thought my ex-husband would keep insisting that I owed him money in spousal support—yes, the doctor who makes six figures a year was telling me, a former accountant turned bakery manager— that I owed him alimony. The back and forth was taking forever. Thank goodness we didn't have children, because I can only imagine what the fight would've been like if child support had to be figured out.

I knew it wasn't going to be an easy divorce, because Justin had turned into a slimy excuse for a man after thirteen years of marriage, and I'd had it. But no one was more fed up than Shelby LeBlanc. My best friend flew in from Las Vegas and plopped her ass in the chair in the waiting room of the media-tor's office so she was the first thing he saw when he walked in and he had to look at her, or clearly look away from her, with every step he took into the conference room where we were meeting. She didn't say a thing. She just stared at him, giving a look that could kill. I watched him swallow a bullfrog in his throat multiple times.

Justin had been scared of Shelby since we started dating in high school—which I get. Most people in our school were. She didn't back down from anyone. She let everyone—and that didn't exclude teachers, administrators, or asshole parents—know what she thought of them and didn't mince words. She also wasn't afraid to use her golf club as a weapon if needed. A boy cheated on Hannah our sophomore year, and his car window became intimately familiar with her seven-iron.

Justin also likely remembers that Shelby's great-aunt makes no secret of her love for all things voodoo.

Sometimes I love being from Louisiana.

Apparently Shelby's mere presence—and his knowledge that she can hit a golf ball nearly three hundred yards—was all that was needed, because that was the last mediation session we had. We finally divided the assets: I was awarded the alimony I was seeking, I let him have the house because it wasn't worth it for me to fight him on that, and, most importantly, every tie we had together was officially severed.

I'm now officially single for the first time since I was in high school. I've taken my maiden name back. And now, a month later, I'm celebrating that freedom with my two best friends during a weekend that has been dubbed the official kickoff of Gabi 2.0.

"I still wish I could've seen Justin's face when he saw Shelby there," Hannah muses. "I bet the man pissed himself."

"It was the gulp heard 'round Nashville," Shelby says. "Never in a million years did he think I'd be there. God, I love fucking with mediocre men."

"I saw a shirt the other day that said, 'I could be meaner.' I almost got it for you."

I laugh as Shelby's jaw drops. "You didn't? Come on, Hannah! At least find me the link because that sounds fucking perfect."

I laugh at my two best friends, wondering how kindergarten me got so lucky to have these women in my life. Especially because as we grew older, we've realized that we are nothing alike. We sometimes joke that if we met now, no way we'd be friends. But there's something to be said about friendships that have withstood the test of time, heartbreaks, and bad fashion trends.

Please God never let me see a pair of low-rise jeans ever again. And if you ever see me going out in a business casual look, tell me to go home.

Hannah is our prim and proper southern belle. I don't think she wore pants to school until sixth grade. The amount of dresses that were in her closet growing up rivaled a major department store. She's now a stay-at-home mom and loves every minute of raising a family in our Louisiana hometown.

Shelby was, and in many ways still is, our tomboy. She's one of the top-ranked American professional women's golfers in the world, bringing in a purse two years ago just shy of two million dollars before having to sit out last season with a shoulder injury. Because of her status, and having to do some red carpets, her tomboy ways have settled. Mostly. She still bitches when she has to wear a dress. Even tonight, when we declared that we were going out with a bang in Vegas, that meant sleek pants and a halter neckline blouse.

And then there's me. The head cheerleader who dated the captain of the football team. Member of National Honor Society and volunteer at the children's hospital. Homecoming queen and student body president. Graduated in the top ten of my class and followed said captain of the football team to Vanderbilt for college. I mean, how else were the high school sweethearts supposed to live happily ever after?

Or so they thought.

The three of us have been together through thick and thin, and when I called Shelby and Hannah to let them know it was officially over, they demanded to take me on a divorce-party girls weekend. Little did we know that we were planning it on one of the busiest weekends in Vegas. Though, I don't know if it would've changed our plans. This really was the only weekend I could feel comfortable shutting down the bakery, Hannah could make sure her husband and mother-in-law could watch her two children, and Shelby wasn't off playing or practicing somewhere.

But even though the crowds have been insane and the city is clearly being overtaken by football fans along with the normal partygoers, this has been a weekend to remember. We've gambled, seen a show—one where I got pulled up on stage by half-naked men giving me a new appreciation for a song I've known for years—and drank every night. We've laid in the sun each day and talked, something the three of us haven't done in years. It's been the perfect weekend, and I must say, a divorce party for the ages.

Even though I felt guilty leaving my bakery for three days, I know I needed this trip. The years of separation, mediation, fights, and stress have nearly broken me. But that's now all in the past. Now I can truly start moving on, becoming the version of Gabrielle Devereaux I want to be. Free of putting my dreams on hold. Actually enjoying *my* life for *me*. Doing what *I* want to do.

And in this moment, I want to do a shot.

"Who's ready for another?" I say, giving my hands a clap.

"Another?" Hannah echoes with wide eyes. "We just did one."

"Oh come on," Shelby goads her. "Remember what you said earlier. Tomorrow you're back to the land of normal, with peanut butter sandwiches and butt wiping. Live it up now."

Hannah thinks about it for not even a second. "You're right! I do go back tomorrow! Let's do a shot!"

"Oh, girl… I'm so glad you haven't changed," I say before polishing off my drink and grabbing my purse. "I'll go order a round of shots and drinks. You two pick our karaoke song."

"Are we not singing 'Goodbye Earl?' I thought that was a given?"

"It is. But you know, scan for any other ones we might've

forgotten about. And find one where I can see if these pipes still work."

This brings a huge smile to both of my best friends, but none more than Shelby. "Oh, I have many ideas."

"I'm sure you do," I say as I walk toward the bar. I loved to sing. I still do. I think. Singing was one of those many hobbies that over the years fell to the wayside in adulthood and marriage. Though, I know why it did—Justin wasn't a fan. It's not that I don't have a good voice. I do. I never had grand delusions of moving to Nashville and a producer finding me singing in a bar like this, but I can carry a tune. I sang at Hannah's wedding. Shelby was always my biggest fan and front-row center for every musical I ever performed in during high school. But… I don't know… Justin never supported me in it. He'd always asked me why I was singing, or did I have to sing every song that came on the radio. I loved my husband—emphasis on the past tense—and me singing wasn't worth getting in fights about. At first, I made sure to do it when I was alone, and, somewhere along the line, I stopped.

But no more. And that's why this place was the perfect choice for my, as Hannah put it, rebrand party. Because nothing says getting part of me back than doing something I used to love.

As I wait for our drinks at the bar, I feel a buzz of energy shifting. I look around to see what's going on, because every single person in this place is starting to lose their shit.

"What the hell?" I mutter as I try and stand taller to see what the commotion is about. I can't get too high—this dress doesn't allow for a lot of different levels—but I can't get a view. Every angle I try to see is blocked by a cell phone. Is it a celebrity? Oh, that would be fun. Maybe one of the boy band guys we couldn't get tickets for. Now that would make this a trip to remember.

"Ladies and gentlemen, please welcome in the winners of tonight's big game… winning their third championship in four years… a dynasty in the making… let's give it up for the champions… the Nashville Fury!"

Cheers erupt in the bar. I actually think it starts shaking for a minute. People are screaming and the karaoke has paused for "We Are the Champions" to start playing. I don't know if everyone here is a Nashville Fury fan, or just likes being a part of the party, but if I didn't know better, I'd think this crowd and bar was on the dead center of Broadway.

I laugh to myself as I turn back to the bar, seeing that the bartender is handing me a tray full of my drinks. I've lived in Nashville since college, and never once in those seventeen years have I ever been to a Fury game. If one of the players was standing next to me in line at the grocery store, I don't know if I'd realize it. I surely can't name any one of them now sauntering through the bar.

But you know who could? Justin. And while I've been trying not to think about my ex, I can't help but get a little chuckle out of the fact that I'm now in a bar with a bunch of football players who just won the game that I mostly watched for the concert at halftime. Justin might not be a Fury fan—his allegiance always lay with our home state team—but he's a football fan boy, and he'd be freaking out right now. Petty me wants to take a picture, post it on my social media, and let his new girlfriend show him. I know she monitors—*more like stalks*—me on a few apps. The mature part of me needs to put that thought away and have a great last night with my two best friends.

Mature me is winning right now. Though we'll see if that holds up after we take these shots.

"Here we go!" I say as I finally make my way back to the table. "Drinks and shots. We should be good for a while."

"That's what I'm talkin' about!" Shelby yells as she passes us each a packet of sugar.

"What are we toasting to this time?" Hannah asks as she carefully opens the packet to pour it on her lemon.

I raise my shot glass and the other two follow suit. "To the last night of the best vacation ever."

"To strong drinks and no hangovers," Shelby adds.

"And to an epic start to the next chapter."

With Hannah's words we all tap our glasses and throw back the shots. The normal shiver that would go down my spine is faint, which means I'm well on my way past being tipsy and will probably be certifiably drunk by the time I polish off this cocktail.

The responsible Gabi who normally exists in my body would tell me to ease up, but luckily, I left her at home. I know this is my last night where I can truly not care about the divorce, or my responsibilities, and have fun. And dammit, after years of being married to that man, where fun was only what he deemed it to be, I'm determined to make this a night to remember.

"Woo!" Hannah yells, giving her head a shake as the shot settles in. I think she's about to say something when I watch her eyes double in size.

"What is it?" I ask.

"Hot."

I laugh and turn to where her eyes haven't moved. "Hannah? Are you gawking at a bunch of football players? You're a married woman."

I glance back to see her nod slowly. "I can look. No touchy. But look? Looking is good…"

"Very good…"

You know they must be hot when Shelby's making note of it. Between living in Vegas and being a professional athlete herself —which means being around other athletes more than most— she's basically desensitized to their good looks.

"Vegas! How we doin' tonight?"

The crowd roars in response to one of the players on stage. And… hot damn… they didn't make them like that when I was his age…

I know that's possibly the oldest thing I could say, but it's the truth. No way this man is above the age of twenty-five—and I'm judging that solely by his permed haircut that I know is in style these days with the younger generation that no way a millennial man can pull off. Sure, I wasn't frequenting college bars at that age. Hell, I was celebrating my three-year wedding anniversary around then, but I still know that in no way, shape, or form, do I ever remember seeing anyone like that a decade ago.

He's wearing a fitted T-shirt that shows every one of his defined muscles. He's not overly built for his six-foot frame, but it's the definition that has my head tilting for a better angle. He's paired the outfit with well-fitting jeans and tennis shoes that I have a feeling cost an arm and a leg.

Sure, all of that is a hell of a package, but it's more than that. It's the dimple in his cheek so pronounced I can see it from the audience—which also makes him look even younger than I'm guessing he is. It's the genuine smile on his face as he interacts with the crowd. It's the way he carries himself like he owns the stage. This isn't karaoke for him, this is his personal concert that we were all invited to.

And nothing is sexier than a confident man.

"All right now, I heard this song earlier and I can't get it out of my head, so I'm going to have to sing it, if that's okay with you guys?" The crowd explodes in cheers because who's going to tell this man no right now? "The problem is, I need some help with this song. Who's going to help me?"

"She is!" Hannah yells, pointing to me even though there are dozens of girls—and guys—jumping up and down, raising their hands like they want to be called on stage as the song begins.

"Girl, what are you doing?" I ask with a laugh.

"You're going to go up there and help him!" she yells. "Remember that video I showed you today? That's what you need to do!"

I think back through the six drinks I've had tonight to figure out which video she sent me, because Hannah shows me a lot of videos. But then I remember— it showed one of our favorite actresses from when we were children on stage, dancing with the band and singer who originated this song. The crowd went nuts as she danced around the stage, living her best life.

And that's what I want to do, live my best fucking life.

I want to be the woman I used to be, and an even better version of it. I used to love to sing and dance. I was free. Extroverted. Not afraid to be in front of a crowd. Would dance on a stage on a dare.

Married me shrunk into myself. I forgot that I had a part of me that wasn't tied into being Justin's wife. That I was more than a breadwinner, and a housekeeper, and a once-a-month sex haver.

And it was shitty once-a-month sex.

But no more not taking risks. No more being a shell of myself. No more not living life.

And no more bad sex.

"Fuck it!" I yell as I slam another one of the lemon drops that's sitting on the table. "I'm going!"

"Hell yeah, you are!" I hear Shelby yell, but I don't turn around to see her or Hannah's reaction.

No, I focus on the stage.

On the lights.

On the fact that I'm actually dancing my way through the crowd, not giving a fuck about anything.

On the man I'm now making eye contact with as I make my way up the stairs.

On Gabi 2.0.

CHAPTER 3
MADDOX

I have no idea who this woman is, but I'm pretty sure I'm in love.

Where'd she come from? One minute I'm doing what the song tells me to do, and that's asking the crowd where my Sally's at tonight, and next thing you know, I see her dancing through the swarm of people, eyes trained on me, not giving a fuck as she works her way through a crowd that never stood a chance against her.

Fuck, yeah, gorgeous. Get up here. Come and dance with me.

When I heard this song earlier today, I knew I had to put it on the celebration request sheet. I mean, it's a catchy-as-fuck song guaranteed to draw the right kind of attention from the right kind of company. But never in my wildest dreams did I expect *her* to come up on stage.

I'm grinning like a fool as I keep singing, and thank God I know all the words or I'd be a blabbering idiot right now. I might know all the lyrics, but I have a feeling she doesn't. In fact, I can tell she doesn't— nor has she seen the viral videos with this song —because at this point everyone always does something to their head signaling a headache. But this woman? Nope. She's dancing around, living in the moment. Doing her own fucking thing.

It's hot as hell.

Of course it is, because her energy is matching her looks in every way. Her dark reddish-brown hair is shining under the lights of the stage. Her face is a little flushed, making her porcelain skin rosy. Her body is perfectly proportioned, with delicious curves in all the right places—and each of those is being hugged by a sparkly little black dress that I'm pretty sure was made to put men in a coma.

Me. I'm men.

But what does me in is her smile. The way I can clearly tell she doesn't give a flying fuck about anything right now. She's literally glowing as she dances around on stage. That's a turn-on if I've ever seen one.

"Sing with me!" I yell to the crowd as the last chorus of the song plays. I never ask for crowd participation unless the song explicitly calls for it. But this time I'll take all the help I can get, because if I'm not singing, that means I can pull this beauty in and dance with her. It's nothing explicit—the last thing I need is for the Fury's PR department having to deal with photos coming out tomorrow of me inappropriately dancing with strangers in Vegas—but I do take her hand and pull her in. I settle my leg between hers, letting me pull her in close as I channel my inner Johnny Castle as we both feel the music. My hand is resting on the small of her back, and in this moment, our eyes are locked. There's no one else in this bar except us. I can tell the song is coming to an end, so I take her hand and spin her out, before pulling her back in as the final note of the song plays.

"I don't know where you came from, but please don't leave yet."

Our chests are touching, and our eyes are locked. I had no idea what tonight was going to entail. If I know anything from Vegas trips in the past, is that you can never fully prepare for the night.

And I know for a fucking fact I wasn't prepared for her.

"I wasn't planning on it."

Her voice is breathy as we each come down from the adrenaline rush. But her eyes are wide as they blink rapidly; I'm guessing she's realizing what happened up here. I smile, and resist the sudden urge to kiss her, as I step away, remembering that I'm still on stage with hundreds of people in the crowd. Luckily, the DJ comes up on stage and saves the day.

"Ladies and gentlemen! Put your hands together for the Fury's starting safety, Maddox Gallagher!"

I wave to the crowd and bring the mic back up.

"Thank you all! But don't just give it up for me. Let's give a round of applause to…"

Shit. How do I not know my future wife's name?

"What's your name?" I ask as I lean in, her soft, floral perfume hitting my senses.

"Gabi."

"Let's give it up for Gabi!" I hold up her hand like she won a prize fight as every patron of the bar goes wild, cheering for both of us as we take our bows. I still have hold of her hand as we make our way down the small stairs, my other hand on the small of her back as I lead her down to the floor.

"Thanks for not kicking me off stage," she says with a laugh. "That was fun."

"Kick you off? Did you think I was going to?"

She shrugs but also at the same time gives me the most gorgeous smile I've ever seen in my life. The fact that it's highlighted by a red lip makes it just as sexy as it is sweet. "I was a strange woman inviting myself on stage with a man I've never met. You totally had the right to."

I shake my head and take a step closer. "I believe in a world with multiple universes and timelines. And in none of those worlds, or in any of those timelines, would I have ever kicked you off that stage."

Her jaw drops slightly at my statement—which is the most

truthful thing I've maybe ever said—as… something passes between us. Does she feel it? Or is it just me taking in every exciting and thrilling emotion that this night has had to offer?

"Are you here with anyone?" I ask, and I hope she can't hear the nervousness in my voice.

She nods, our eyes still locked in the hold that something has over us. "Yes. It's a girls' weekend. They dared me to go on stage with you."

I don't know how many friends she's here with, but I need to buy them drinks for the rest of the night. "What would they say if I invited you and them to come party with me and my teammates?"

That seems to surprise her. "Really? All three of us? What's the catch?"

"No catch," I say as I try to put her at ease, not even thinking, but probably should have, that I'm still a stranger asking her to come hang out with other strangers. "I'd never want to break up a girls' trip. I have a sister. I know those are sacred. But I really, really, want to keep talking to you, Gabi. And if I'm lucky, maybe later there can be an encore performance?"

I didn't mean the double entendre. I really did mean singing with her again. But the way her eyes darken at my words makes me think that maybe, if I'm lucky enough, there can be an additional victory in my hotel room.

"I'm okay with it," she says before looking over to a table where two women are watching with rapt attention. "But they have to sign off on it."

I smile and put my hand on the small of her back. "Then lead the way."

Gabi gives me one more glance, making sure that I'm serious before walking toward the two women who are looking us over closer than the TSA. I laugh as their eyes linger on where my hand is placed. They're owning their gawking. I can appreciate that.

"Ladies, I've been told this is the best table in the house. Mind if I join you?"

"Mind? We absolutely don't mind!" one of her friends squeals, pulling me in for a hug. "I'm Hannah. This is Shelby. And well, you know Gabi."

Not as well as I hope to. "Nice to meet all of you. I'm Maddox Gallagher."

"Oh, we know," Shelby says, giving me a knowing eye. "Nice interception you had tonight."

"Thank you," I say. "Did you three watch the game?"

"Kind of hard to miss it," Shelby says. "But, the more important question is, what brings you over here, Maddox Gallagher? And why aren't you on stage with your teammates?"

By the look of Shelby's smile, and the mischievous look in her eye, I can already tell this woman is being the ultimate wing woman.

"For starters, they don't need me for this song." As if on cue, all of them join in for an epic part of the bridge for this iconic boyband song. "Second, I was hoping that I could invite the three of you to come over and celebrate with us."

I don't expect an answer right away; in fact, what's happening I knew was going to. They're having a silent council meeting, all of them having some weird conversation with their eyes about what they're supposed to say. I've seen this before. My sister also had two best friends, and I swear half of their communication was telepathic. I can only hope as I watch this that whatever talk they're having is favorable for the outcome that keeps Gabi in my orbit a little bit longer.

"I have a few questions first," Gabi says, though I catch a glimpse of both Hannah and Shelby, who look like—unless I royally fuck up this quiz—the answer is going to be yes.

"Shoot. I'm an open book."

"For starters, are we going to be the only women there? Because I've listened to that podcast and it usually doesn't bode well for the females."

I shake my head. "Absolutely not. There are plenty of wives and girlfriends with us. Some are drinking with us, some are sober to make sure we act right."

"Good to know. Are there going to be more stage performances?"

"I hope so," I say. "Never in my life have I come to sing karaoke and only gone on stage once. I just hope you're going to come up there with me."

Gabi's trying to fight her smile, but Hannah and Shelby? They're clearly Team Maddox. Love this for me.

"Will you let me pick the songs?"

"You picking the songs in exchange for you and your friends hanging out with me for the night? Gabi, I'd sing 'Barbie Girl' on repeat if that meant I could spend tonight celebrating with you."

"Well then, that settles it!" Shelby yells as she picks up her purse and stands from the table. "Let's combine these celebrations!"

Hannah lets out a scream of excitement, following Shelby when the words she uses hit me. "Celebrate? What are you celebrating?"

Hannah and Shelby are headed toward the obvious VIP area where the Fury players are gathered when Gabi turns to me, taking a deep breath before she says the words I wasn't ready for. "My divorce."

"Oh." The sound is out of my mouth before I can stop it. Divorce? Sure, I wondered if she had a boyfriend, and I saw she wasn't wearing a ring... but divorce?

"Is that a problem?"

Her body suddenly goes stiff, and her eyes turn worried. Me? I'm just confused.

"Yeah," though I realize again how that sounds as I quickly shake my head. "I mean no."

Now I've confused her. "Then what do you mean?"

"I mean I'm baffled that someone was lucky enough to marry you and let you get away."

Our eyes are locked as I watch my words hit her. I know the second she realizes what I said, because they double in size. But they're true. I've known this woman for a total of twenty minutes, and unless her grand plan tonight is to take me to a hotel and harvest an organ, I don't think I'd ever divorce her if I was lucky enough to have my ring on her finger.

"I… oh… um…" I've officially left her speechless. She's shuffling her feet back and forth, and if I didn't know better, I'd think I made her a little nervous, which is a shift from the confident woman that was just on stage with me. Then again, if that was a dare, I have a feeling this is Gabi. And seeing both sides of her, I now want to know everything about her.

"How could you possibly know that?"

I give her a slight shrug and take a risk by reaching for her hand. I relax when she doesn't shove it away. "Call it a special talent."

She lets out a slight laugh, her eyes looking up at me again, but this time in a little wonder. Like she really can't believe the words I'm saying, or that I'm holding her hand. Her eyes are bouncing around as if she's trying to assess my bullshit level.

"So you can sing. You apparently can read people after knowing them for thirty seconds," Gabi lists as I watch in real time the spark come back in her green eyes. "I watched enough of the game tonight to know you're pretty good at football. Are there any other talents I should know about?"

The smirk that hits my face lets her know that there are so many things I want to say that are not limited to, but including, make her come with only my tongue and/or through nipple play; make her so wet she'd need to change her panties from a few dirty words; and, of course, fucking her until she's speaking in tongues and not able to walk the next day.

But I don't. Because I'm a fucking gentleman.

"Oh Gabi… there are so many for you to discover," I say, figuring that's the safe way for me to flirt without also coming across like a fucking douchebag. "But there will be plenty of time to learn about those later."

"Oh, will there?"

"Yes, there will," I say, putting my hand on the small of her back as I lead her toward our VIP area. "If this is truly a celebration, there's something drastically missing."

"What's that?"

"Unlimited champagne."

CHAPTER 4
GABI

h Gabi…what are you getting yourself into?

I've asked myself that question no less than ten times since Maddox sweet-talked me and the girls into coming over here, but as I sit here, surrounded by football players and their partners, I have to ask myself again, because… what in the actual hell have I got myself into?

Sure, from the outside this looks innocent enough. It's me and my two best friends, surrounded by a bunch of football players and their partners. Shelby has been in a very deep, and flirtatious, conversation with one of the coaches who recognized her. Hannah has become besties with one of the player's girl-friends named Ainsley.

Then there's me. Again, from the outside, things seem inno-cent enough. I'm sitting next to Maddox, my legs crossed into him because that's the way I like to cross my legs. It's not signaling anything. It's not me trying to be closer to him. Sure, it's helping me lean in closer, but only because the music is loud and I'm trying to hear him better. I'm also *not* thinking about other special talents that he referred to having.

Nope. None of those are true.

Except they are… because what the hell am I getting myself

into, and why do I want a Vegas rebound with a twenty-some-thing football player?

"So, Gabriella, where are you from?"

I laugh. "It's Gabrielle. But no one calls me that."

"Fair enough. Okay, Gabi, same question. Where are you from?"

I smile at the simple question. "Are you actually trying to get to know me?"

"Of course," he says, like my question is a crazy one. "I want to know as much about you as I possibly can."

I don't know if it's the vodka, the closeness, or the way his eyes have not wandered from me once, but I believe him. I assumed that if he was interested in me that it would just be for a potential hookup tonight. Which, I don't think I'm opposed to. Emphasis on think. It would be a fun, Vegas divorce-party story to say I hooked up with a hot football player on the night he won the championship. Then again, I've never really been a hookup girl—that's what you get for getting married at twenty-two to your high school sweetheart—but I didn't think small talk was part of it. Then again, what do I know?

"Originally outside of Baton Rouge. Now I live in Nashville."

His eyes double in size at my revelation. "We live in the same city?"

I can't help but laugh at his excitement. "I do. I'm on the west side. And let me guess, you're in some posh condo downtown?"

"Guilty as charged. In my defense, it makes my work commute very easy."

"I can see that," I say. "Though I'm taking your word for it. I've never been to a game. But I do know where the stadium is."

"What!" he yells, apparently more shocked by my lack of attendance than our close city proximity. "How long have you lived there?"

"Since college, so…seventeen years?"

I stare at Maddox, waiting for the realization to hit him that when I was moving here to go to college, he was probably on his way to junior high. I really want to ask him his age—or excuse myself to the bathroom to Google it—because I know it must be at least ten years.

So again…what the fuck am I doing here? This is an extremely handsome, much younger, football player. He can't actually be interested in a mid-thirty's divorcée, right?

"What made you come here for college instead of staying near home?" he asks.

That wasn't the follow-up I was expecting. But if he's going to ignore the glaring age difference, then fuck it, so will I. "It was the best school for both me and my ex."

"Let me guess… Nashville means Vanderbilt, which means doctor for at least one of you."

"Him," I admit. "I went into business. Wanted to have my own business one day."

"So you're beautiful and smart?"

I feel myself blushing at his words. "I don't know about that."

"Well I do," he says, moving in a little closer. His fingers delicately brush the exposed skin on my shoulder, sending shivers straight down my spine. "So, what kind of business?"

If he's only trying to get to know me to get me into bed tonight it's working. A man who listens? Who's interested in me? Who isn't making every conversation point about him? After spending nearly two decades with Justin, I didn't know this kind of man could exist.

And it's hot as hell.

"A bakery. Opened one last year with my brother over in the West End. It's called—"

"Holy shit, that's where I know you!" The player sitting next to Ainsley, who was introduced as her boyfriend, Linc, claps his hands in excitement. "I've been staring at you all night, trying to figure out why you looked familiar. You own Sugar and Sweets! Ainsley! This is the place I found with the brownies you like!"

"Seriously?" she exclaims, stopping her conversation with

Hannah to turn fully to me. "Linc discovered you a few months ago and we are *obsessed*. He brings me something every week. I don't know what you put into your brownies, but I'll pay you all the money in my purse right now for the secret."

I feel the blush coming over my cheeks at their praise. "Thank you. It's a small place, but it's mine."

"Oh no, we don't talk like that around here," Ainsley says. "We're proud of our accomplishments. And when you can make baked goods like that? You own that."

"Preach!" Shelby shouts out, holding her drink in the air. "Maybe she'll listen to you, because she sure as shit doesn't listen to me."

"In my defense, I'm trying," I say, knowing that me having confidence in my business, and doing it on my own, is something I'm still working on. "But thank you, Ainsley. I really do appreciate it."

"You're welcome," she says. "I know this isn't the best place to ask this, but I don't want to forget—do you do custom cakes and orders? I've been meaning to come in, but between my job and this guy's football schedule, I couldn't seem to get over there, and I have a few events that I'd love if I could order from you."

"Yes. Yes, I do," I say, a little shocked that the conversation has turned this way. My bakery isn't struggling per se, but I could definitely use the business. "Come in next week when you're settled. I'm there from open to close every day, so you really can't miss me."

"Amazing," Ainsley says with a smile before turning a stern glare and a pointed finger to Maddox. "Now, don't break her heart tonight. Because my sister deserves an amazing engagement cake that she doesn't know about yet."

Maddox puts his hands over his heart in a dramatic shock. "Ainsley, how dare you insinuate that I would treat this woman with anything but respect?" He adds to the drama by pulling me in tighter. "Plus, do you think that I would ever jeopardize the possibility of becoming a regular at a bakery where I know the owner? If you think that, then you don't know me at all."

"Your sweet tooth is going to save the day," Ainsley says.

"Damn straight it is," he says before turning back to me. "A day without a sweet treat is a day wasted."

I'm pretty sure he's talking about desserts, but the twinkle in his eye says he might be meaning a little more. I choose to ignore it, though, because I'm already very overwhelmed. "That's a good slogan. I'll have to remember that the next time I run an ad," I say as we both relax back into the couch we're sitting on. I also take notice that he doesn't make a point of releasing his hold on me. "So what's your poison?"

"I mean, what isn't?" His eyes light up at my question like he's a toddler about to tell Santa what he wants for Christmas. "I mean, any kind of cookie. Chocolate chip is my favorite, but they have to be soft. None of that crunchy shit. Also, people hate on oatmeal raisin, but if it's done right, it's fire. I don't always go for scones, but I could do one from time to time. Of course, there's pie. Pie is undefeated. Apple, specifically. I'll always have two or three slices of cake if there's cake to be had, and no, it doesn't matter the flavor or the kind of icing. I'll eat it."

I can't help but laugh. "So you really don't have a favorite?"

"Oh, I didn't say that," he says, the smile on his face right now accentuated because of the dimple in his cheek. "Because if you told me right now that I could only have one dessert for the rest of my life, I would have to say a bear claw. That is my favorite and my final answer."

I picked the wrong moment to take a sip of my champagne. I nearly choke on it because of his answer. "Really? A bear claw?"

"Hell, yeah," he says with confidence. "They're delicious. But why are you looking at me like that?"

Maddox is probably referring to the tilt of my head I'm doing now along with a raise eyebrow. "Because no man in his twenties—which I'm assuming you are, but also don't want to do the math of how much younger you are than me—has ever come into my bakery asking for a bear claw. You don't fit the age demographic of the normal bear claw consumer, who are collecting retirement checks."

"I'm wise beyond my years," he says.

"I'm sure you are."

The two of us share a smile and a quiet moment, even though the noise around us is deafening. The part of me that hates uncomfortable silence wants to try and quickly figure out something to say. But oddly enough, I don't feel like I need to. Which I can safely say hasn't happened in… well… maybe ever.

Luckily for me, one of his teammates breaks the silence for me.

"Maddox! We're going up to sing. You coming?"

He shakes his head and waves them off. "Nah. You guys go for it."

I think every set of eyes in the VIP area just turned to Maddox in a confused look. They're all speechless, and frankly, so am I?

"Really?" I ask. "The self-proclaimed karaoke connoisseur isn't going up to sing?"

"Not now," he says, turning more toward me. "I'd rather be here with you."

The way those words are delivered make my heart jump out of my chest.

Or my pussy.

Okay. Both.

"Are you always so direct?" I ask, still wondering what kind of man comes out and says things plainly.

"No sense in beating around the bush," he says. "Life is short. Why waste time with games and innuendos? I think everything in this world would be better if we said what we meant, went after the things we wanted, and lived every moment like it was our last."

His words hit me square in the heart. That kind of thinking, especially from a man, is so foreign to me. Justin was the king of games, lies, and innuendos. He'd talk out of both sides of his mouth and when he got caught, it would spin into a new lie. I can't even begin to list all the times he did it, especially when I started having an inkling he was cheating. Looking back, he'd been doing it for years, I just didn't notice. I was blinded by love and the promise I'd made to stay with him forever.

And then there's the last part of Maddox's statement about living every moment like it's our last. It's a mantra I've always wanted to live by, but never felt that I could. How could I live in the moment when I was married. Had bills. A mortgage. I thought then it was a luxury I didn't have. Now post divorce, I have my bakery and am rebuilding my life essentially from the ground up. It might sound good to live like you are dying, but reality always comes back to remind you about the world you live in and the responsibilities you have.

But maybe tonight it doesn't have to…

"Maddox?"

"Yeah?"

"What if I said that I wanted to sing a song? With you."

His eyes light up. "Any song you want. And I literally mean anything."

I can't wipe the smile off my face when I see Hannah jump up and start clapping. "Oh my God! She's going to sing! Shelby! She's really going to sing!"

"Fuck yeah," Shelby says. "I personally think you should go back to your show choir days."

"Show choir huh?" Maddox says as he stands up in front of me. "I should let you know, I'm quite the showman myself. As you could see from my performance earlier. And while I think my teammates are doing a hell of a job up there, I think a duet is exactly what this place needs."

My initial reaction is to change my mind when Maddox holds out his hand for me, even though I'm the one who suggested it. One moment of doubt is all I need to wonder if this is a good idea. I mean, after thirteen years of being married to a man who hated when I sang doesn't go away with the signature of a divorce paper.

Then I remember Maddox's words. Why I'm here this weekend. The dress I'm wearing. That Justin hated anytime I even hummed.

I smile up at Maddox, who's hand hasn't moved as he waits for me.

"I can really pick the song?"

Maddox's smile is at full wattage now. "Gorgeous, you can pick whatever song you like."

CHAPTER 5
MADDOX

I meant what I said that Gabi could pick whatever song she wanted. But I never would've guessed this one.

But you know what? Fuck it. I'm down to get my Danny Zuko on. Little does she know I played this role back in my high school musical days. All I'm missing is a fake leather jacket and some slicked-back hair.

I haven't sung this song in years and obviously never with her. But you wouldn't be able to tell that if you were in the crowd watching. She's playing off my moves and lyrics and I'm doing the same for her part. Though I have to remind myself that I need to keep up my end of the performance because it would be easy as hell to stare at her as she owns the stage. Between her voice and her moves, it's mesmerizing to watch her.

Then again, she could be pretending to be a mime and I'd still think it was hot as hell.

I don't know what it is about this woman, but somehow with every moment I spend with her, I'm more and more attracted to her. Yes, her face and body are fucking perfection, but it's more than that. So much more. It's her smile. The way she's the contradiction of confident but also a little timid in some ways. It's how this black dress is trying to kill me in front of hundreds of people.

I want to know about her. I want to know what makes her tick. I want to know what she's wearing—if anything—under that dress. Is she a satin or lace girl? Is it black to match her dress? Or did her boldness overtake earlier as well and it's nothing?

That last one might be a stretch of luck, but if I do get to experience it on the night I won my third championship, I'd consider this the greatest day of my life. I'm not getting my hopes up, though. She's fresh off a divorce and here with her girlfriends. Having a hookup with a guy she just met is probably not on her itinerary for this trip. And I respect that. Doesn't mean a guy still can't wish.

Or try.

So knowing that, I'm going to bask in these last few moments of the song, spin Gabi into my arms, and memorize her beautiful face as the song fades away.

"Ladies and gentlemen, our favorite duo, give it up one more time for Maddox and Gabi!" the emcee says into the mic as our song comes to an end. The crowd responds as everyone in the audience is standing and cheering as we take our bows. We each hand back our microphones as I put my hand on the small of her back to guide her down off the stage. Before we can take a step back toward our VIP section, Gabi twirls around toward me, simultaneously throwing her arms over my shoulders.

"That was… gah! That was so much fun!" she says, and it's in this moment I decide to buy her a karaoke bar just to see this smile multiple times over the course of my life. "Can I say thank you?"

"You can, but I don't know what you're thanking me for," I say, not missing the opportunity to place each of my hands carefully on her luscious, flawless, hips. "I sang a song with you. You'll never need to thank me for that. And if you ever want to do that again, all you have to do is give me the signal."

"I like that. But what's the signal?"

"It's your signal, I think you should come up with it."

Her eyes start shifting, like this is the hardest question she's ever been asked. "I think I'm going to need a few more drinks to come up with a perfect one."

"That I can also do," I say as I reluctantly move my hands from her hips but take one of her hands in mine. I also resist the urge to kiss her, which I think should be commended. "I believe there are bottles waiting for us."

We start weaving through the crowd and back to the VIP section. I receive some back slaps and high-fives along the way, though right now I don't know if it's because of my performance on the field tonight or the performance on stage. I hope both. They're equally impressive. Who else do you know can have a pick-six in the biggest game of their careers and then become an honorary T-Bird a few hours later?

It's why I'm one of a kind.

"That was amazing!" Ainsley exclaims as she jabs a finger to my chest. "That kind of song's not on your normal karaoke list back in Nashville."

"I didn't have a partner like Gabi then," I say, already thinking about how when we're back in Tennessee I can ask her out for one of the Fury's numerous karaoke outings. "Also, I didn't sing it back then because I was holding out hope that you and Linc would give it a try."

Ainsley narrows her eyes at me, like I knew she would. She's one of the good ones—one of the few women who can hang with the boys every night and not want to strangle us—and shockingly, most nights she does it sober. I've actually only seen her drunk once, which was also the only time I've ever seen her do karaoke. She swears she's never doing it again. That doesn't stop me from poking the bear.

"Nah, that one was meant for the two of you," Linc says as he grabs a shot glass. "But since we're all back here, I'd like to propose a toast."

"I like the sound of that." I reach down and grab two shot glasses filled with what looks like tequila, handing Gabi one. "What to?"

Linc smiles. "To being winners."

"To winning the big game!" Gabi says as she holds her glass up.

"To winning the divorce." I answer back, pulling her into me. "We're all fucking winners here!"

We laugh and hold up our shot glasses, throwing them back as the DJ puts on a song that elicits an "oh shit!" and a "hell yeah" from the group. Everyone in our area, and the entire bar, is now on their feet dancing.

Before I can reposition myself behind her, because holy hell do I want to dance with this woman, Gabi steps out of my hold. "Shelby! Hannah! Remember this song?"

"Heck yeah, I do!" Hannah screams as she stumbles over to Gabi. "Your twenty-second birthday!"

"Before you married the ass hat!"

The three start laughing as they chaotically jump and dance around to a song that I recreated the viral video with my bus—in middle school. The age gap should give me pause, but it doesn't. How could it, when all I can do is smile as I watch Gabi have the time of her life with her two best friends. Do I wish I was dancing with her? Of course. But I also know this is what Gabi needs. She needs to have fun. Be free. Not think about her divorce or the reason she's here. She needs to live. And honestly? It's a beautiful thing to get to watch.

"Uh-oh." The voice comes from Linc, who's now standing over my shoulder. "That's a different look."

I glance over to Linc, who's wearing nothing but a shit-eating grin. "What's that supposed to mean?"

He tilts his head toward Gabi. "I've seen the Maddox Gallagher's 'I'm going to take a girl home' look. The one-night look. That's not what's going on here, is it?"

I don't try and play it off. Linc has seen me in action too

many times to fall for any sort of excuse I could come up with. And honestly, I don't even want to deny it. This woman has had me in a chokehold since the moment she came up on stage and hasn't let go since.

"Do you believe in fate?" I ask.

"I didn't used to," he admits. "But now? Now I do think that everything is supposed to happen at specific times for specific reasons."

"That's all I keep thinking about," I say. "How long have you been going to her bakery? Months. Every time you bring it up, I say that I need to go with you sometime, but it never works out. I could've gone with you before. I could've met her before. But… something is screaming to me that tonight was the night I was supposed to meet her. That this is where our story starts. And that it's not just one night."

What would tonight be like if I would've tagged along with Linc at any point over the last few months? Would I have seen her? Met her? Flirted with her? I'd like to think all three, but it wouldn't have been like this.

Fate is always something I've debated about. I've never truly been able to land on a side of what I believe in. But I truly believe tonight was supposed to be like this. And that same gut feeling is telling me this night is far from over.

"Please be careful," Linc says. "She's not like your normal girls."

"No. She's different."

"In many ways."

Linc doesn't need to elaborate. The women I usually take home don't make me think about things like fate or destiny. They're the ones I take home because right now in my life, it's all about fun. No one expects anything more than one night, and I'm always up front about what this is. Nothing long term. I try to be careful about who that is—sure, a few wanna-be WAGs have snuck through, but I've been careful, and a little lucky.

Things never escalated. I'm always careful. Respectful. Giving. And so far in life, it's served me well.

And then Gabi sauntered on stage, and I have a feeling everything I've ever known is about to be thrown on its head.

I never believed in love at first sight. Never wondered about fate. But mark my words, I'm going to marry this woman.

"I know," I say as Gabi turns to me, heat in her eyes as she crooks her finger at me, beckoning me closer. "Excuse me now, Mr. Kincaid. I'm going to go see about a girl."

I feel Linc's hand slap my shoulder before I take the few steps needed. "Were you summoning me, Gabrielle?"

Her full name slips through my lips, but it feels right. Like so right.

"I was hoping you'd want to dance?"

I look behind her as Hannah and Shelby each give me winks and a thumbs up. "With you? Always."

There's a simultaneous smile on her lips and blush in her cheeks as she puts her arms around my neck. I pull her in closer, our chests now touching, which is only adding to the heat coming off us as our bodies start moving to a song that is in no way slow or soulful, but our movements are. I know when Linc warned me that she was different, he was talking about her age and stage of life. But what he didn't realize is that this feeling? The pull I have to this woman as our bodies feed off each other and the music? This, too, is different. I've been attracted to many women in my day, but never, and I mean never, have I been drawn to someone like this.

The beat of the song changes, the DJ mixing it to another slightly faster song, as Gabi turns in my arms, moving back so her ass is against my cock.

Cold water… my teammate's bare asses… blue cheese dressing…

Nope. It's no use. Even thinking about three things that should instantly make my dick limp are useless to the powers of Gabi, the way she's moving her hips, and this little black dress. My hands have a mind of their own, grazing down the sides of her body, through the curve of her waist before they grip the hips that I want nothing more than to leave fingerprints on.

"Are you trying to kill me?" I whisper into her ear as I wrap my arm around her stomach, bringing her back so tight into me that she has to feel my hardening cock.

I look on as she tilts her head to the side, her lips in a smirk that I'm dying to kiss away. "Not now. But the night's still young."

I can't even hide my physical reaction to her. And I know she can tell by the way her ass starts moving more against me. I swear, she's one body roll from me throwing her over my shoulder, finding a private spot in this club, and showing her how much she's fucking driving me crazy.

I let my head fall back, my body still moving as I watch Gabi dance in front of me, when I feel her suddenly still.

"Gabi?"

She doesn't answer, but doesn't move out of my hold, either. I look up to realize that she's staring at Hannah and Shelby, who each have a mixture of concern and anger on their faces.

"What?" she says, her voice the most serious I've heard it all night. "Whatever it is, tell me."

The two look at each other before granting Gabi's request. "Apparently your earlier performance has already found its way back to Nashville via the internet."

Gabi reaches out and grabs Hannah's phone from of her hands. I look over her shoulder, and yup, just as I thought. Our first performance of the night, when she came up on stage with me, has already started making the rounds on social media. The video itself is fine—it's me singing and Gabi dancing on stage, having the time of her life. We're interacting like I remembered, and honestly? I need to find a few people who have this video, because I want it as a souvenir of the night.

But I don't think the video is what's making Gabi's face turn eight shades of red right now. No, I have a feeling it's the caption that goes along with it:

Nice to know that while I'm here in Nashville, grieving the end of my marriage, my ex-wife is galivanting in Vegas, getting drunk, dancing on stage with dumb jocks and chasing five minutes of fame. Maybe this is why she wanted out so bad, so she could go live this kind of life. Sad.

Sometimes I hate being a man, because I have to be in the same category as this mediocre one. Also, how dare he.

"I'm not dumb!" I protest. "I graduated top of my class."

My joke misses the mark as I feel Gabi breaks from my hold and storms away from our roped-off area. I'm stunned for a second, not knowing what to do, until I see Shelby signal for me to go after her. I don't even hesitate, following Gabi into a hallway that's not private, but at least out of the way of the rest of my teammates.

"Where the actual fuck does he get off playing the victim card!" Gabi yells, and I'm not even sure she knows I'm here yet. "The asshole talks out of both sides of his mouth. He'll go on social media and fucking whine that I'm this horrible person who's galivanting around, which is rich considering he broke our marriage when he fucked her. I fucking *can't* with him!"

Gabi's paces become faster, and it's like watching a tennis match as she walks back and forth, random swear words coming out of her mouth that I didn't even know could be used together. And while I don't know the whole story, I already know I hate her ex-husband.

"Hey," I say, catching her mid stride.

"Maddox. Please…"

I shake my head because I have a feeling she thinks I'm going to tell her to calm down. Which I would never. "I'm all for you being pissed. I encourage pissed. But I want you to remember to breathe."

"Breathe?"

"Yeah, breathe," I say. "It can be angry breaths, but breathing is important."

It takes her a few seconds to hear my words, but eventually, her breaths go from short and huffy to more slow and even. There's still fire behind each of them, which I think is appropriate. Her ex sounds like a fucking jackass.

"How long did it go on?"

I watch as Gabi takes a big breath in, before slowly letting it out. "The divorce was about two years. That's not counting the year before it, when I knew it was over, after I found out he cheated and we tried to work it out. It's just… I felt like it was never going to end. Then he pulls this shit."

It takes a lot for me to hate someone. Normally I'm a pretty easygoing guy. But now that it's confirmed that he's not just an asshole, but a cheating asshole? Good to know for the future, if I ever meet him. Now I can punch him. I'm a lot of things, but I will never, and I mean never, cheat on someone. I've seen first-hand what cheating does to a person. I had to watch my mom grieve the loss of her marriage and also somehow still put on a smile while raising me and my sister. And if this guy is crying crocodile tears when he's the one who ruined things, then, disrespectfully, fuck him.

"I'm sorry," I say, clearly seeing how her demeanor has changed in a matter of seconds. "What can I do to help?"

Gabi shakes her head. "Nothing. It's…"

She trails off, but I watch as her eyes go from defeated, back to angry, before morphing into downright vengeful.

The transformation is fucking hot.

"Is the offer still standing?"

"What offer?" I ask, wanting to make sure I'm on the same page. "Don't get me wrong, the answer is yes. I just need to know what I'm doing."

Her smile is wicked, and it's making me fucking hard. Which is fucked up, but also doesn't surprise me. I love a woman with a little crazy in her. "He and his fucking girlfriend want to stalk me on social media? They want to talk about me? Then I'll give them something to fucking talk about."

Gabi takes my hand in hers and marches us back to our

group. When we return, Hannah, Shelby, Ainsley, and Linc are all waiting for us, eyes unblinking as Gabi and I walk back into the VIP area.

"You two ready to record another performance?"

Shelby grins and takes her phone out of her back pocket. "In high fucking definition."

Hannah already has hers out. "We'll get it from multiple angles."

"Oh! I can help!" Ainsley chimes in. "I come from a family who takes pleasure in revenge. I'm all in for this."

Gabi laughs as she turns back to me. "I know I didn't come up with a signal yet, but were you serious when you said that I never needed to ask you to sing?"

"As a fucking heart attack."

CHAPTER 6
GABI

"Ladies and gentlemen… welcome back to the stage… Gabi and Maddox!"

Maddox hands me my microphone and leans into my ear. "You ready, gorgeous?"

With a deep breath that doesn't do anything to ease my racing heart, I give him the most confident answer I can muster. "I am."

The music starts playing as we slowly start to walk on stage. I knew when I picked this song that Maddox started it off. I didn't pick it on purpose to give me a chance to settle in, but right now, I'm glad it does. My nerves are skyrocketing. I never used to be like this when I had a microphone in my hand. Give me a stage and a song—especially this song—and I'd be in my element.

That was before.

But that's why I'm up here. This weekend is about taking myself back. Regaining parts of myself that got lost or were taken during my marriage. And I have been. It started with a dare. Along the way I picked up a handsome football player. And me being up here and singing not just any song—but this song—is the final thing I'm going to reclaim.

My voice.

My song.

I'm taking it all back.

I watch Maddox as his verse comes to a close. The man is oozing confidence. I don't know what it is about him, but he should put it in a bottle and sell it. It's that charismatic. That electric. I don't know how a man can command a football field and a stage, but he is. And doing it damn well.

When I told Maddox the song I wanted to sing, I was worried he'd be intimidated by it, or rethink his words from earlier. I mean, this song is deep. Has layers. He seems like a smart guy, so he must have an idea that this isn't a random song.

But the man didn't hesitate. In fact, he got a little smile on his face. And now as he's singing it with a haunting tone to his voice, I can't stop staring at him. I'm sure the videos that Shelby, Hannah, and Ainsley are taking probably show me with my jaw dropped and my eyes unblinking. I have to right myself when his final note trails off and he slowly walks over to me, leans in, and gives me the lightest, but most meaningful, kiss on my cheek that I've ever received.

I was already fighting nerves. And now because of that I have to fight off butterflies as well.

"It's all you, Gabrielle. Wow'em."

I slowly pull away, letting those encouraging words take hold of me. His eyes are so focused on me. On the moment. If once in our marriage Justin had said anything like that to me, I don't know if I'd be in Vegas on my divorce trip. Yet, here's a man I just met, encouraging me with his actions, his words, his presence. It's something I've never had. And it's the reason the last bit of nerves leaves my body as I step up to the front of the stage.

I can hear that I'm hesitant at first. I mean, it's been a long time since I've sung this song, let alone in front of a crowd. Seven years to be exact. Sure, it's only a few hundred people, but that's a lot of eyes on you, especially after I've spent most of the night sharing the spotlight with my famous duet partner. When I hear a crack in my voice, I nearly stop. But like he knows I need an anchor, I see Maddox out of the corner of my eyes, who's looking straight at me. His gaze isn't wavering. His sole focus is on me. His soft smile hits me in the heart. His slight nod encourages me to go on.

So I do. I sing.

For all the years I didn't.

For the fact that I'm able to tonight.

I sing with every fucking breath I have.

And it's at the perfect time. I hit my stride as the chorus hits, and for the first time in seven years, I fucking belt out my favorite song.

It feels good. So fucking good. At some point in the song, my eyes are closed, and I'm becoming one with the lyrics. For all I know, no one else is in this bar. It's me and the microphone. And of course, Maddox. Because I wouldn't be up here without him.

I feel his presence coming closer to me before I open my eyes. He had to have seen the movie this song is from, because how else would he know the exact right time to come next to me, and will me to sing the riff of a lifetime?

Our eyes lock, and the encouragement I feel from his gaze is almost overwhelming. This shouldn't be the song I sing without practicing, let alone not singing for years. But somehow I'm doing it. And when I hit the final note of the run before dropping back into the chorus, I almost collapse from the energy leaving my body. But I don't, because like he's been all night, Maddox is next to me, physically holding me up as his hand takes mine, emotionally supporting me by being next to me, singing the last part of the song with me as our eyes never leave each other's.

If I tried to catch a glimpse of the audience right now, I'm pretty sure it would be nothing but a blur. How can I see anyone besides the man standing in front of me right now? Between the pull he has on me, the way my body has heated every time we've touched, and the gift he gave to me, for all I know, there's no one else here besides us.

As the final note trails off, everything starts coming back into focus as the roar of applause hits from the audience. My breathing is heavy and I have to remind myself that I just did that. That I sang that song. That the sound I'm now hearing is the applause for me.

I wasn't making a racket like Justin said. My singing wasn't screaming. It wasn't something to roll your eyes at.

I did that.

I took my voice back.

I took myself back.

The realization hits me like a freight train. The weight of everything crashes down on me, and if I don't get off the stage quickly, I'm going to pass out.

"You're not loud enough! Give it up for Gabi!"

Those are the last words I hear Maddox say as I try to give a wave before I disappear out of view. I can feel the tears already starting to hit my cheeks, but I don't want to cry here. I'm doing my best to keep them at bay, and I only have to make my way through one small group of people before I have a straight shot to the bathroom, where hopefully Shelby and Hannah will be waiting for me when they realize what's happened.

Except I don't. Because the second my feet hit the ground, the bubble I was in pops, and with that, I fall to the ground.

"Gabi!" I hear Maddox yell as my body loses all of its bone form as I melt to the ground. "What happened? Are you okay?"

I nod as I do a shitty job of trying to push aside the tears that are coming out in a tidal wave. I'm also pretty sure that my dress is riding up so high half of my ass is hanging out. "I'm fine, it's just… "

I don't have the words. I could. I do. But saying them right now? To Maddox, of all people? I just met the man. He doesn't need to hear my emotional damage on top of everything else I feel like I've dumped on him tonight. Plus, it's too embarrassing. Too shameful. Too… real. And I feel raw enough right now as it is.

"You don't have to say anything else." He comes down on

the floor with me—the floor that thankfully I'm too drunk to think about touching—and wraps me in his arms. "It's okay. I've got you."

I'm stiff for more than a few seconds, but it doesn't take long for me to sink into his touch. To let the strength of his hold protect me to let these tears out. To have a minute to gather myself where he won't let anyone near me.

"There we go," He whispers as he gently rubs my back. "No rush. Take as long as you need. We have no where we need to be."

I laugh through the tears. "Thanks for lying."

"Who said I was lying?"

I look up at him, which might not be my best move if I had any hopes about this night going further than this bar. I'm pretty sure I look like a drunk raccoon with mascara smearing down my cheeks. "You have to go back to celebrate with your team."

"No, I don't."

"Yes, you do."

"Maddox..." I say with a serious tone. I shouldn't be surprised when he answers right back.

"Gabrielle..."

We have a stare down for a beat. Is this man really trying to dig his heels in the ground about this? "Are you always this stubborn?"

"Some would say it's my middle name. Which is Jacob, by the way."

This man is infuriating. Hot. But infuriating.

"Maddox. I'm a stranger who invited herself into your night on a dare. I'm now crying on the floor of a bar. You just won the biggest game of your career. You're telling me you're willing to sit here and listen to me vent instead of having the night you rightfully earned?"

He doesn't say anything, and for a second I feel like I might've gotten through to him. But as soon as I think that, the man somehow gathers me into his arms, and stands up with me in them, before taking a few steps over to an abandoned chair.

This is something I can safely say has never happened to me before.

"Not only am I willing to listen, I *want* to listen," he says, his gaze holding mine where I couldn't possibly think about looking anywhere else. "You were meant to come up on that stage tonight with me. And I'm meant to be here with you right now. And if we spend the rest of this night in this chair, then so be it. But I promise you this, Gabrielle, there's no place else I'd rather be than here with you."

My vision might be blurred from the tears and the steady stream of alcohol tonight, but even with those impairments I can tell by the sincerity of his voice that this man is one-thousand-percent serious. My tears have started to subside, but now my body feels like it's crashed from the biggest adrenaline rush of my life, and the only thing holding me up is Maddox—physically and emotionally.

"I didn't think I was going to cry," I admit, my head falling to the crook of his shoulder. "It was just a song."

"A song is never just a song," he says. "Every song brings out some sort of emotion in us. And I have a feeling that song was a lot of emotions all wrapped up into one."

"You have no clue."

"I don't. I want to, but I don't have to know. You're right. We're basically strangers. But so you know, I can listen with the best of them."

I have a feeling he's not tooting his own horn with that one. The man seemingly is amazing at everything he does. And it's not that I don't trust him. It's that saying these words to anyone is hard. Hannah and Shelby are the only two who know, and even then I didn't tell them until after the divorce was underway. I was ashamed. Mad. Sad. The same emotions I'm feeling right now.

But I don't want to ever relive this again. I want this to be a full exorcism. And I have a feeling the only way to truly purge all of this is to say the words out loud. Even if it's to a man I just met.

"He never let me sing."

There. I said it. Not loud, but the words are out there. Though I'm not sure if Maddox heard me judging by the confused look on his face.

"Did I hear you right? I know it's loud in here, and someone is doing a horrible version of a horrible song, but did you say—"

I nod, actually wanting to say it again. "He didn't like it when I sang. So I stopped. Tonight was the first time I've sang in seven years."

His eyes go wide. "Seven years?"

I nod, then cringe at the way Justin's words could deflate me in an instant. Killing my confidence, and my joy. I knew Justin was never the biggest fan of my singing. He never came to any of my choir shows or musicals in high school. If it was karaoke night when we went out with friends, he'd always have some sort of remark when I said I wanted to sing. But that moment? When he walked in the door and said *"I just wanted to come home from the office and have some peace and quiet. Not have to listen to this fucking racket that's barely even words."* It was the worst thing he'd ever said about my voice. I knew then—and now—I'm not Nashville's next big star, but to hear my singing being called "a racket" doesn't exactly make a person feel good.

That was the last day I sang with even the possibility of anyone hearing me. I didn't want to sing in the house for fear that it would start a stupid fight, and at the time, I didn't think it was that big of a deal to give it up to preserve the peace. I wouldn't even sing in the shower. And then, as the years went on, I stopped all together.

In the grand scheme of the mental fuckery Justin put me through, me not singing is probably ranked around nine or ten on the list. But, it's a prime example of how he treated me and how so many things in our marriage got put on me to "fix" when I didn't break them. He had the formula nailed down: He didn't like something; he complained and picked fights about it; I swallowed it and sucked it up for the sake of squashing the fight.

Rinse. Repeat. Suffer.

But not anymore.

Seven years ago, I was listening to my favorite song. I was minding my business. Cleaning. Meal prepping. Doing my best to enjoy chores that I did as a wife.

Little did I know it was going to be my last day singing.

That is until tonight.

Tonight, I didn't just take my song back. I took back a part of myself that was long forgotten about.

"What… huh. " Maddox takes a few deep breaths, which I find pretty endearing. "Can I ask a follow-up question?"

His delivery makes me smile. "As many as you'd like."

"Okay, for starters, is your ex-husband a fucking tool?"

Laughing through the tears. Exactly what I needed. "Yes. He is. Though in my defense, he wasn't when I met him. Then again, we were sixteen so what did I know?"

"We're all tools at sixteen, myself included, but that's neither here nor there. But now, my second question is a series of questions."

How he's taking a pretty depressing statement and turning it into something that's making me smile is quite impressive. "Fire away."

"First of all, why? Follow ups to that are: had he heard you sing? Were you too good? Too powerful? Did he want to sing, couldn't, and was jealous of your talent? Did he have an ear worm where things that sounded good he thought sounded bad? Did he hate fun and joy?"

"Is that all?" I say with a smile.

"Probably not, but yes for now."

"Well, the answers that I know are, yes, many times, and he hated it. Called it a racket. Rolled his eyes whenever I did it. Don't know if he thought I was good or not. He couldn't carry a tune, so maybe. And no clue about the ear worm, but it's not a bad theory."

"I'm baffled," Maddox says, shaking his head before bringing his eyes back to mine. "If you were my wife, we'd be having concerts every day."

"You're sweet," I say as the tears finally come to a stop.

"Can I ask one more question that I think I know the answer to?"

"Of course."

"What we just sang? That was the song, wasn't it?"

"It was," I say with a nod, pushing back the last tear I refuse to shed.

"What a fucking asshole." Maddox says.

"He was," I say. "But even when he posts shitty things like he did tonight, I remind myself that we're no longer married and he's out of my life."

Maddox smiles. "He is. And as I see it, you got the last laugh. Because what you did up there? Now knowing the story about it? You gave a lyrical fuck you to him while simultaneously taking yourself, and your life back. And that's fucking badass."

"I don't know if badass was what I was going for, but I'll take it," I say. I'm done crying. My breathing is back to normal. But yet, I can't make myself leave the comfort of Maddox's lap. "Even with the unexpected emotional roller coaster I went on, I will admit, this was fun. Tonight. Singing. Being on stage. Hanging out with you and your teammates. You've made this night unforgettable. Thank you, Maddox."

"You're very welcome, Gabrielle."

A hush falls between us, and even though the bar is still loud as hell, somehow, in this little corner we've carved out for ourselves, it's silent. I feel every inch of him around me. His hands on my back. His thighs holding me up. His heart beating underneath my hand on his chest. I don't know if I ever had a moment with Justin that felt so connected. That in a room full of people, we're the only ones here, and I don't care if everyone or no one is looking at us.

I don't know what this feeling is. This pull. This connection. But I do know one thing: I want to kiss him. Or him to kiss me. Either way, I want to taste his lips and know what it feels like to have that kind of connection with someone. Maybe for the first time in my life.

I wanted this earlier, too. Before Justin's social media tantrum, I'd almost talked myself into it. Well, Shelby and Hannah did, but that's basically the same thing. In fact, Shelby tried to convince me to sleep with him tonight, but that's too much.

Right?

Would he even? Sure, the look he's sending me right now is that he wants to kiss me too. I think. I don't know. It's been years since someone has looked at me with any sort of desire or want, and the only person who has ever looked at me like that quit looking at me this way a long time ago. And even then, it wasn't like this. It didn't make my body heat. It didn't make me bite my lip because of the way his hand is slowly trailing up and down my spine. It's not making my body clench, because I'm pretty sure Maddox is hard.

For me. Maddox is hard for me. A thirty-five-year-old divorcée who has only ever had sex with one man in her life and almost forgets how to do it because of how long it's been.

Oh God, I've only had sex with one man…

I'm generally not the kind of person who thinks the worst of situations, but for some reason right now, it's all I can think of. What if my plane crashes on the way home tomorrow? There are so many things I haven't done.

I've never visited Paris. I haven't ice skated at Rockefeller Center or gotten the chance to watch my favorite musical on Broadway. And worst of all, I'd have died only ever having fucked Justin.

Fuck. No.

I refuse to hypothetically die and Justin's mediocre dick be the last thing I fucked. And Maddox, based on the way I saw numerous women look at him tonight, knows his way around a bedroom. He must be better than Justin, right? If what I'm feeling beneath me says anything, he's going to be bigger. And you know what, the rest will figure itself out.

Now I need him to say yes.

"Maddox?"

"Yeah?"

"Did you mean it when you said that you didn't have to go back and celebrate with your teammates?"

He nods, a boyish smirk forming on his face. "I don't. What did you have in mind?"

CHAPTER 7
GABI

When you get married at twenty-two to your high school sweetheart, there are a lot of things you assume you're never going to experience.

At the top of that list is a drunken one-night stand with a twenty-something football player.

But not only am I about to have that, I want it.

Holy shit, do I want it. I wanted it in the club the first time Maddox twirled me into his arms. I definitely wanted it when I was in his arms, dancing like no one was watching. Him holding me in his arms and letting me cry sealed the deal.

But I might die from sexual frustration from the little touches he's giving me right now in the backseat of this car. And if the man isn't inside me in less than twenty minutes, I will, in fact, combust.

That or two years, eleven months, and fourteen days is officially too long to go without sex. It's even been longer since I've had a proper orgasm. So yes, if he keeps this up, I will, in fact, perish in the backseat of a Lexus.

"Patience," Maddox whispers in my ear as he simultaneously starts drawing random circles ever so softly on my upper thigh. "We're almost there, Gabrielle."

The use of my full name sends chills through my body, like it's done every time he's used it tonight. I've never been a big nickname person. Justin called me babe for years. When we were young, I thought it was cute. By the time I realized I hated it, he'd been using it for so long I didn't have the heart to tell him I hated it. But I'm glad I didn't, because the first day he didn't call me that was the day I had my first real clue that he was cheating.

I was right.

Maddox saying "Gabrielle" feels… I don't know… intimate in some way. Like it's a name only for him. My mom only called me Gabrielle growing up when I didn't do my chores. I made sure at my graduation and on my wedding day that I was Gabi. For years I was Gabi Devereaux, then Gabi Landry, and now I'm back to Devereaux.

But right now, in this moment, I'm just Gabrielle. A new person. A daring person.

A woman about to get properly fucked.

"Hey," Maddox whispers in my ear. "I need you to know you're in charge tonight. Whatever you want to happen, happens. No pressure. No expectations. This is your night."

I know what he's doing, and it's sweet. I truly do appreciate where he's coming from. But this poor guy doesn't know that if he keeps breathing into my ear like he is right now, this driver's about to see how big his cock is when I whip it out and start stroking it.

"My night, huh?" I ask, turning so now it's my turn to whisper into his ear. "There's really only one thing I want."

Boldness is taking over my body as I let my hands start exploring up his thigh and… fucking hell, he's hard.

And big.

Exactly what I wanted.

"What's that?"

I turn my head even more, wanting to make sure our driver doesn't hear a thing. "It's been three years since I've had an orgasm that I didn't have to give myself. Think you can help me with that?"

I hear his breath hitch. "Three years?"

"Actually more. I rounded down."

"Fuck…" he groans as his lips turn ever so slightly into me, leaving a breath of a kiss at my temple. My breath hitches at the touch, but at the same time, the car comes to a stop. "Wait here."

He gives me one more kiss on my cheek before he opens his door and exits the car. I do as he says, my pulse thumping and my leg bouncing as I impatiently wait for Maddox to come around and open my door

"You didn't have to do that," I say as I take hold of his outstretched hand.

"And miss the chance to see you exit the car in that dress? Not a fucking chance."

He kisses my cheek one more time before keeping hold of my hand as we walk through the lobby of the hotel. My body is buzzing from the anticipation of whatever is about to come, and it's only heightened because it seems every few steps, we're being stopped. Fans wanting selfies. Hotel staff congratulating him. I can't help but smile and watch as Maddox interacts with everyone. He truly seems like a very happy, likable person. But what I can't get over is that during every one of those interactions, his hand was never not holding mine. He never broke contact. Not once.

And in this moment, I realize that yes, it's been a long time since I've had sex, but it's been even longer since I've been touched.

I might've missed that more.

I used to be a physical touch person. Holding hands, hugging, cuddling just because, it used to by my main love language. Of course, in high school, Justin was all about it. Who wouldn't want to hold hands—or always make out—with your homecoming queen girlfriend? He surely didn't complain about it once we started having sex.

But over the years, it dwindled, like so many other aspects of our marriage. There were no more slight touches. No more surprise kisses when he got home from work. Cuddling? Ha! Foreign concept.

Like my singing, the craving for physical touch went away. So feeling this… seeing that Maddox made a conscious effort to never lose contact with me, means more to me than he'll ever know.

"Sorry about that," he says as we step onto the elevator and he presses his key card to send us to one of the top floors. "I'd hoped…"

I don't let him get the words out of his mouth before my patience snaps and I'm backing him up against the elevator wall, initiating a kiss I didn't know I had in me.

Seriously, who the hell am I? Is Gabrielle my alternate personality, where I have an internal "fuck it" moment and kiss men in elevators? Hell, I might be. How would I know? I've been with the same man since I was sixteen years old. I'm a completely different person than I was back then. I don't know anything about myself. I don't know if I'm even doing this right.

But I know one thing—Gabrielle is in charge tonight. She's going to take what she wants. Do what she wants. And right now? She, and I, want Maddox.

And from every signal I'm getting from Maddox, he wants me too. His hands are around my waist, pulling me in so tight I can feel every inch of his hard cock pressing into me. His mouth is diving into mine, taking over control of the kiss, which I'm happy to relinquish. I've never been much of an initiator when it comes to things in the bedroom, but me kissing him out of nowhere might've opened a new door I didn't know I had a key to.

This kiss is… God… I don't have the words to describe it. It's intense and passionate. Spontaneous and exciting, but somehow also deliberate. With every swipe of his tongue and every brush of his lips, I feel myself falling more and more into the magic of this night.

I vaguely hear the bell of the elevator notifying us that we're on his floor, but I don't want to stop kissing this man, and apparently, he doesn't either. Instead, we keep our mouths connected as we stumble out of the elevator, running into the wall a few steps out.

That should've stopped us. It doesn't. Our hands are everywhere as our mouths and lips continue exploring and taking. I can taste the champagne on his tongue, but there's also a mint to it that's a little bit addicting. The way he tastes, and the way his mouth moves, is making me remember why I've always loved the simple act of kissing. And how much I've truly missed it.

But now I want more.

I don't know how we do it, but without ever losing our actual footing, or our lips ever coming unglued, we finally stumble down the hall to his room.

"Here," he whispers to me, his mouth now setting up camp in a place behind my ear that's about to kick start that orgasm I wanted so desperately earlier. "Take the card. Let us in."

I do as he asks, slowly turning around to face the door. In what should be an easy task is made ten times more difficult because now not only is Maddox doing his damnedest to give me a hickey, his fingers are toying with my legs at the edge of my dress.

"Come on, gorgeous… the quicker you let us in, the quicker I make you come with my tongue."

I want that more than anything, but how the hell am I supposed to concentrate on tapping key cards to doors when I feel my dress coming up my thighs and said tongue is doing something wicked at my pulse.

"Maddox."

"Inside, Gabrielle. Or else you're going to get that orgasm in this hallway. And I won't care who sees."

For a half a second, I consider that option, but then I come to my senses. Don't get me wrong, I want the orgasm. More than anything. But not in the hallway.

I'm feeling bold. But not *that* bold.

The second we step inside I don't have a second to think about anything before Maddox spins me around and presses me against the door. I'm in such deep concentration of his mouth, and kissing him even harder than I was in the hallway, that I don't feel his hands trailing down my body. Once I realize it, I don't have time to think, or even ask, what he's doing, before my question is answered.

His arms are hooking under my ass, picking me up, and pinning me against the door.

Oh… oh my.

I can feel the sequins of my dress scratching against my thighs as Maddox holds me up, but any discomfort is quickly pushed aside when I feel his mouth kissing down my neck, over the tops of my breasts that are exposed from the deep v-cut.

"So good," I breathe out, my hands clinging to his hair, burying his face into my tits even more.

How is this happening? I'm not a small girl. I have curves. I like to eat my sweets but remember to throw in a vegetable and protein in the mix. I know Justin was never happy that I'd lost my figure from back in the glory days. I used to not care—then I did care—then stopped caring again once I realized his view of me was tied into the entire way he felt about our marriage.

And he wanted to put me down to make himself feel better.

But the way Maddox is holding me up right now, the way he looked at me when we exited the car, and how he's been touching me since we've been alone, none of that matters. He doesn't care that I probably don't look like the typical woman who hooks up with football players. I don't think he'd give two shits about my jean size having two numbers. He wants it. He wants me. Which makes me only want him that much more.

"This dress is killing me," he says, pushing away the other

side of my dress, leaving my breasts exposed in the lace bra I'm wearing.

"Then you should do something about it."

I watch as Maddox's eyes glance down to my cleavage then back up to me. He's biting his lip and I might come from the look he's giving me alone.

"This dress. How attached to it are you?"

"I'm not. It was a twenty-dollar dress from a fast-fashion website."

"Perfect answer."

In a feat of strength I didn't know existed, Maddox, while still somehow balancing me against the door, rips the center of my dress nearly in half. I mean, it had a deep V, so it was on its way, but the man acted like the fabric did something offensive to him.

"Now that's better," he says, pushing the cups of my bra down, spilling my tits over top. "Exactly what I wanted."

"Fuck!" I yell as I throw my head back, hitting the door, as Maddox takes a nipple into his mouth. The combination of his mouth and tongue, along with his hand as he massages it, is about to send me into an orbit I didn't know existed. One I've never been to without penetration. And one I haven't been to in a very, and I mean very, long time.

Foreplay with Justin was… what's a further extent of nonexistent? Sure, many years ago he was all about it. I had a full chest in high school, and he was a teenage boy. But it never got better. He never paid attention to my breasts. Fingering me was so his dick could slide in. Oral? Ha! That's a joke.

And don't ask me if he played with the clit. I think that answer is very apparent.

To say that I'm out of my sexual element right now is the understatement of the year. But the way Maddox is downright worshipping my chest, feasting on my breasts like they're keeping him alive, is about to make me feel things I didn't know were possible outside of books and television shows.

"Maddox… how… please… more!"

My words are singular and don't make sense put together, but somehow he knows what I'm saying. Thank God one of us does.

"See, how I'm thinking," he trails off, licking around my nipple for good measure. "Is that if it's been years since you've had an orgasm, that means I need to catch you up to speed."

My breathing picks up as he starts grinding into my already wet center. "I… I've never had… multiple."

"I don't accept that answer," he says, crashing my lips for a hard kiss before quickly pulling away. "In fact, I'd like to prove to you how wrong that is."

Before I can say anything else, he slowly puts me back on the ground, but lowers himself to his knees immediately. I'm in a silent awe as I watch him slide my dress up, and then my silk panties down my legs.

"You're wet for me, aren't you, Gabrielle?"

If I wasn't already, I would be now with the use of my full name and the burning look we're sharing. "Yes."

He licks his lips. "Time to get you that souvenir."

I want to laugh at his joke, but this is no laughing matter. My ripped dress is pushed up to my hips. My panties are who knows where. And Maddox's tongue is fully inside me.

Ho-ly-fucking-shit…

I actually don't know what to do right now. My hands want to pull on his permed hair to push him further into me, but I don't know how much closer he can get. At the same time, I want to smack them against the door, hoping they can keep me grounded when the man eventually sends me into space by the way he's tongue fucking me. It's everything and perfect and I'm point-two seconds away from…

"Maddox!" I scream, my hands choosing to go for the hair, and I'm pretty sure I pull some out. If I did, he doesn't seem to care. No, the man is now doing his damndest to make sure to lick up every drop of my orgasm as he holds me to him, not letting me go as I start to come down.

"So fucking good," he says, my eyes slowly blinking. "There's one problem now."

That snaps me out of my haze. "Problem?"

His grin is devious as he stands back up. "Yes. Now the problem is I don't know how I'm going to make you come again."

Maddox swoops me up in his hold, my laughter filling the room as my arms having no choice but to circle around his neck. He makes quick work of the space, getting there in a few strides, before he lowers me to the bed. He doesn't take his eyes off me as he pulls the rest of my tattered dress over my head and removes my bra in quick fashion.

"It seems that we have another problem." I say, my champagne—and orgasms—confidence fully kicking in despite me sitting here now completely naked in front of this man.

"What's that?"

"You have on way too many clothes."

If I thought his smiles were devilish before, it's nothing to what he's giving me now. "Then we have to fix that now, don't we?"

I prop myself on my elbows, watching in awe as this man strips before me. Nothing over the top. Not like the male review show I went and saw last night with the girls. But it's without a doubt turning me on way more than anything I saw on that stage.

It's the eye contact. It's the way his brown eyes never leave mine as he unbuckles his belt, quickly snapping it off his waist before tossing it to the side. It's the way his arms flex when he reaches behind his neck and pulls his fitted T-shirt off his muscular chest in one deft move. And it's that damn smirk he gives me before unbuttoning his jeans, sliding them, and his boxer briefs, down with it.

"Jesus fucking Christ..." I didn't mean to say it out loud, and it was no more than a whisper, but I know he heard it.

"I could say the same about you," he says as he starts stroking his rock hard—and thick—cock. "Open your legs for me. Let me see that pretty pussy again."

Completely under a dick spell, I do as he says, watching in awe as he continues to work his cock. I mean, how can I not? It's big. He's hot as fuck. And he just ate my pussy like a starving man who recently ended a fast. How can I not be completely mesmerized by the show I'm watching?

To further prove that point, I let my hand travel across my stomach and down my pelvis, letting my fingers work my clit as our gaze never breaks from each other. I don't even think about it. It's like every part of my body has a mind of its own right now. Maddox's breath hitches and his strokes speed up as we pleasure ourselves in front of each other, our grasps on each other never breaking.

"Maddox," I purr, feeling orgasm number two coming quicker than I want. Or thought it was able to.

"What do you want, Gabrielle?" he asks, slowly bending over and grabbing his wallet out of his pants and taking out a condom. "Tell me."

I don't need to think too hard about that answer. "You."

One word. That's all Maddox needs to hear before he's on top of me, our mouths connecting like it's been days since he last did this, not just minutes. I'm thankful for his lips distracting me, otherwise I have to believe I'd be overthinking every single second of this interaction. Do I remember how to do this? Where do my legs go? Where should I put my hands? Should I keep my mouth shut and not say anything since that's how I'd been trained for years to act during sex? Or does he mind if I become a little vocal?

All of those questions, including any follow-ups, are quickly wiped away the second Maddox enters me. Including the one about me staying quiet.

"Fuck! Maddox!"

My back arches off the bed, an instant reaction to his cock fully inside me.

"My name has never sounded so good," he says as he slowly works in and out of me, allowing me to get used to his size. "That's it, Gabrielle. Feel all of me. Take every inch. Take everything you want."

How this man can combine words of affirmation and encouragement while making them sound dirty as hell is a skill that I didn't know someone could possess.

"That's it," he says, his pace starting to pick up. "You're taking me so good."

With every word coming out of Maddox's filthy mouth, combined with how his dick has somehow found a spot in me I didn't know existed, I could come right here right now. But I don't want to. I want this to last. If I'm going to do a divorce-party rebound fuck in Vegas, it's not lasting five minutes. Not if I have anything to say about it.

"Remember when you said this was my night," I say with a heavy breath, his speed picking up even more.

"I absolutely do."

I reach up, able to wrap my hands around his neck to pull him down to me. "Can I put in a request?"

My words elicit a low growl that vibrates through his body. "Anything you want. And I mean anything."

I don't know if we're going to go *there* yet, but I do like where his head's at. "I want to ride you."

He doesn't hesitate. In less than a second he has me scooped in his arms and rolls us over. "I'm yours, Gabrielle. Have your way with me."

My stomach flips at his words. Not the first part. At least, that's what I tell myself. I'm going to pretend it was because a young, hot, fit, and very, very, eager, man is telling me to have my way with him.

And I do. My hands are gripped to his defined chest as I start slowly, trying to remember how I used to like it. Over the years it went from being my favorite to the only way I could get an orgasm. Eventually, it stopped because Justin was over and done with too soon for me to have a turn.

But this? Those memories? They're going to cease to exist after tonight. All I'm going to remember is the way Maddox is looking at me right now—how he's making me feel like the most desired and wanted woman in the world—as his thick cock fills every inch of me.

"You look so fucking good riding me," he says, each of my tits in his hands. "I don't want to take my eyes off you."

"Then don't," I say as my confidence surges as I pick up my speed.

"Fuck fuck fuck… Gabrielle."

"You feel so good. I'm so full."

"Take what you want gorgeous. Take every last inch of me."

My speed picks up at Maddox's words. Before I know it, my back is arched, my hands are gripping onto his thighs, and I'm five seconds away from exploding on him.

"Maddox, I'm…"

"Me too gorgeous. Me too."

His fingers grip into my hips, guiding my hard movements that are just… about…

"Fuck!" I scream so loud the next room had to have heard me. Ask me if I care. The answer is no because I'm coming harder than I ever have in my life. The feeling is only amplified as Maddox immediately follows me, holding me down on him as he spills into the condom.

It takes more than a few seconds, but once the vibration stops buzzing through my body, I collapse onto Maddox, his arms wrapping around me so tight I almost can't breathe. We don't say anything—I don't know if I could if I wanted to—but I don't think words are needed.

Because this was perfect. Every single thing.

How he rolls me over, allowing him to get up from the bed to take care of the condom. How he brings me back into his arms when he comes back into bed. How he kisses my forehead and how his fingers gently rub up and down my arms, lulling me to sleep.

It's how he's still holding me when I wake up as the sun is starting to peek through the windows when I decide that I need to leave. Because this night was perfect. Everything I needed it to be.

And that's how I need to remember it.

CHAPTER 8
MADDOX

If there's one thing to know about me, it's that I love a parade. It could be a local Fourth of July one led by the town marching band or the big one on Thanksgiving Day in New York City. If it's a parade, I'm there. Sometimes with literal bells on if it's of the Christmas variety.

So one would think that the city parade honoring the Nashville Fury after winning the league championship would be a top-tier day in my book. Fans are lining the streets celebrating. All-day drinking is encouraged. Music is playing. The vibes are sky high.

Except for me. My vibes are crap. They have been all day and now that it's over, they're even worse. It's why instead of continuing the celebration at one of the many bars in Nashville with my teammates to commemorate our title, I'm sitting behind a makeshift stage, holding a beer I haven't touched, and wondering what is even life?

Sure I have another title. Brand deals that keep my pockets lined and my schedule tight. I'm about to sign a new contract that is going to keep me in Nashville, as well as very well payed. I have everything I could ever want.

Except her.

"Okay, I've had it, what the fuck is wrong with you?"

It takes me a second to realize that Linc is talking to me, and that's only because his words were accompanied by a smack upside the head by our fellow teammate and offensive lineman, Wyatt. "Ow! What the fuck was that for?"

"He's at least back to this planet," Wyatt says. "Seriously, are you okay? All day you've been acting like a damn zombie."

"Yeah, I'm fine," I play off, knowing damn well I'm not fine. "Just a little drunk."

"Try again," Linc says. "I saw how you pretended to take every shot given to you today. I'd guess you've had no more than four drinks since we reported eight hours ago, which makes you fine to not only drive a car, but to have the ability to not look like someone ran over the dog you don't have. So what gives?"

"Hey! Don't bring Sir Barkley into this," I say, naming the hypothetical shelter dog I plan on rescuing this offseason.

"And don't use humor to deflect," Wyatt scolds. "Talk."

I look around to see who's in listening range. All of our teammates seemingly cleared out to either head back home, or keep the party rolling at one of the nearby bars. There are bands playing on this stage for the rest of the day—when Nashville shuts down Broadway, the city makes the most of it—but for now, we're as alone as we can be.

"Fine," I say as I find a seat on a what I'm guessing will eventually house one of the speakers. "I'm in a funk. Nothing to worry about. I'm sure it'll pass."

Not exactly the truth, but not a lie either. Though judging by my teammates' glances, neither of them are buying it.

"You've been in this funk since we got back from Vegas," Linc says as he takes a seat next to me while Wyatt posts up in front of us, arms crossed like he's a bouncer at a club. Which he could be with this three-hundred-pound frame.

"I wouldn't say that," I lie.

"Quit fucking lying," Wyatt says. "When you got on the plane Monday morning I thought you were hungover. Then I saw you looking out of the plane window, headphones on, and I'm pretty sure you were mouthing the words to that song about being all by yourself."

"No I wasn't," I say, though I'm not about to tell him the song was actually about being her mistake. Because that's what I selfishly felt like—a mistake.

Which I know I wasn't. Or, I don't want to believe that to be true. But it's what I was feeling at the time because this is apparently what Maddox Gallagher feels like when he's the one who wakes up to an empty bed. Usually I'm the one leaving without saying goodbye.

"Wait!" Linc says. "Is this about the baker?"

I snap a look to him. "Her name is Gabi."

"Who's baker, Gabi?" Wyatt asks.

"This is what happens when you go off and have sex with your girlfriend instead of partying with us," Linc says. "We met her when we went to the karaoke bar. And Gallagher over here fell in love."

"No regrets," Wyatt says with a smile. "I'd much rather celebrate my way rather than hearing you assholes sing."

"Oh, but you missed quite the performance," Linc says. "Especially from our boy here and his new lady love."

"She's not my lady love," I say, though it comes out more like a tantrum. "She's…"

I don't have the words. I haven't had the words to describe her since the moment she stepped on that stage. Linc fills in Wyatt on what he missed, at least I think. I only hear about half of it. Because like I've done many times over the last five days, I let my mind travel back to that night and replay every moment.

Except the moment when I woke up to find her gone. I have a feeling that's about to come up once Linc gets Wyatt up to speed. So for now I'm going to remember the great parts of the night.

Seeing her come up on stage for the first time. Her sequin dress catching every one of the stage lights as her smile caught the rest.

The way we vibed on stage, like we'd been performing together our entire lives. How she felt against me when we danced. How she tasted of champagne when I kissed her. How even after one night and being in a sweaty Vegas bar, I could smell her sweet scent on the pillow when she wasn't there the next morning.

But more than anything, and what has been haunting my dreams every night this week, are her eyes. Those damn green eyes that I'm pretty sure I watched go through every emotion in one night. I saw them light up in excitement. I saw them darken in passion. I saw them vulnerable when she broke down. I saw them roll back into her head when I made her come apart.

That one was my favorite.

"So yeah, then Gallagher up and left us to go celebrate with some woman he met that night. Totally abandoned us."

"Hey!" I yell in my partial defense as I only heard the last part of what he said. "I said goodbye and she's not some woman."

My defensive reaction gets a big smile from my teammate.

"I know. And her name is Gabi and she was great. But it was clear you were in lala land and I needed to get your attention somehow."

"You could've just said 'Hey! Maddox!'"

"We did," Wyatt says. "Now talk. Because clearly, this woman has you all sorts of torn up."

I hang my head, not quite sure how to voice all of this out loud. Not because I'm not one to share—I probably tell these guys too much about my personal life—but never before have I felt a weight to it.

"Okay, fine. Yes. It's about her. She… I don't know. She got to me that night. I really did feel something more than a just a fun night in Vegas. And it was, believe me it was. Then, poof, she was gone."

"What do you mean she was gone?" Wyatt asks.

"I mean she was gone." I sit up enough to pull my wallet out of my back pocket, where the note she wrote me has been living since I found it. "When I woke up Monday, this was all that was left."

> *Maddox,*
> *I hope you don't mind, but I stole a T-shirt and sweatpants. My dress was... yeah.*
> *Thank you for a night I'll never forget.*
> *<3 Gabrielle*

When I woke up that morning and found the bed empty, I'd hoped she had just got up to use the bathroom. When she didn't come back, and I didn't hear anything except the air conditioner, I knew I was alone.

I don't know if the note made it better or worse. I appreciated that she left it, and that she told me she took some of my clothes. But I would have given her every piece of clothing I own and taken her to buy a whole new wardrobe for a few more minutes with her. Sure, I was looking forward to morning sex. It's my second favorite kind of sex. But what I wanted more than anything else was to see if what I felt was real, or if it was part of the magic of the night.

"Damn," Wyatt says. "She left?"

"Yup," I say, taking the note back from Linc. "I didn't even hear her go."

The two of them share a grin. "What are you two assholes smiling at? I'm going through it and you two are fucking smiling!"

"I'm just saying, karma is a fickle creature," Wyatt says. "Is this what Maddox Gallagher gets for all the times he's left before the sun came up?"

"All of those were different," I defend, not wanting to admit Gabi leaving me is some sort of cosmic payback. "Every one of those women knew what they were getting into before events occurred."

"Fair, but I still find it funny that the man who has made a name for himself around this town as the guy known for a good time but not a second time, is suddenly in his feels because a woman left and took a hoodie with her."

"Give him some slack," Linc says, and for a second, I think that this man is going to solidify himself as my best friend and defend me. "It was his favorite sweatshirt."

"One, it was a T-shirt, and two, you're both fucking assholes," I say as I pop up from my makeshift seat. "I liked her okay? I liked her for more than one night. I still do. I want to see her. But I can't and that's driving me absolutely fucking insane which is why I'm sober and sad on parade day."

"Damn," Wyatt says, taking a seat where I just was. "You're serious aren't you?"

"Of course I am," I say. "Did you think I wasn't?"

"Honestly? We didn't know," Linc says. "We call you The Enigma for a reason. We never know what you're doing or thinking and when we do, you go and do something that completely contradicts it. At least you have in the past. We didn't know she was *that* different."

They're not wrong about that. For my entire life, I've never fit into one specific box. I was the jock who also was in the school musicals. I was friends with the robotics team and the wrestling team. The two girlfriends I had in high school were a cheerleader and the captain of the math club.

Those glasses really did something to me…

Even as an adult, I've kept everyone guessing with who I really am. I'm the jock who has a foundation that promotes STEM programs for kids who don't have those kinds of opportunities at their schools. I make undercover children's hospital visits in the afternoon then later that night am being photographed at one of the Nashville bars with a swarm of women around me. The only thing that people know about me is that I'm a playboy. I'm not the kind of guy who's seen out with the same woman more than once.

At least I wasn't. Because there are pictures and videos out there of Gabi and I from Vegas. But if she showed up right now, I know for a fucking fact I'd make it my mission to be seen with her every day.

"She *is* different. There was something about her that got to me," I say as I start to pace in circles. "But there isn't going to be anymore. And I have to accept that."

"Not going to be anymore?" Linc says. "You do remember that she lives in town, right? Her bakery is three miles from here. We could go right now."

He starts to stand up, but I hold my hands up to stop him. "I appreciate you wanting to be my wingman right now, but it's more complicated than that. Believe me, I've wanted to go see her every day since I've gotten back. I've had to stop myself a few times. But then I remind myself that she left without leaving a number. Or the green light for me to contact her. That was on purpose. Take it from the guy—who as you pointed out—is a pro of the morning disappearance: there's always a reason why you do it."

It didn't take me too long—once I got over my initial sad boy feelings—to realize what Gabi's reason was. And it wasn't because it was a mistake, despite what my playlist was telling me. Our night together was a whirlwind, and from the little bits she told me, so is her life right now. She wanted it to be one night. To put an exclamation point on her weekend celebration. A true mark to the next chapter of her life. I get it. I respect it. But that doesn't change how I feel: that I wish I could have had that night, the next morning, and a lot of mornings and nights after.

But it's not what she wants, and if I'm a man of anything, it's of respect and consent. My mother, grandmother, and older sister, didn't raise a fucking bum. a.k.a., they made sure I turned out nothing like my father.

"I'm guessing her reason is because of the divorce?" Linc asks.

"I'd bet my season-ending bonuses on it," I say. "When my mom was divorcing my dad, dating was the last thing on her mind. She was trying to get back into the work force; making sure my sister and I were everywhere we needed to be; pretending everything was fine when it wasn't. From the little bits Gabi told me, this divorce is a complete restart for her. I've always prided myself on being able to read the room, or in this case the note. And with the clues I have, her life right now doesn't include dating the football player she met in Vegas."

"I still can't believe that asshole posted the video of the two of you on his social media," Linc says. "Like my man, get over it."

"She told me a few other things he did. He's a real piece of shit," I say, my blood starting to heat when I remember the look in her eyes when she told me about his feelings on her singing. "I'm going to guess that when she woke up, real life came back and smacked her in the face. And that leaving was easier than saying goodbye."

"That all makes sense, but that doesn't suck any less for you," Linc says "I know I was giving you shit earlier, but every one of us could tell that she was special. Even Ainsley was already talking about double dates and having a new WAG in the suite next year."

Oh God I never even thought of seeing her in my jersey. The thought makes me horny and sad all at the same time.

"I'm so sorry," Wyatt says, holding out his hand has he stands up, bringing me in for a back slapping hug. "But you need to know, you not pursuing her, that's an honorable thing you're doing."

"Look at me, Maddox Gallagher, the good guy," I joke.

"You are, and you know it," Linc says. "I know it sucks now. But believe me, you're doing the right thing. And who knows, maybe it's a case of right person, wrong time, but one day it will be?"

I laugh. "Really? When did you turn into one of those hopeless romantic types?"

I know the answer. It was the day he ran into Ainsley Banks. Literally.

"All I know is that there's timing to things in the world," Linc says. "If I had met Ainsley at any other point of my life, I don't know if it would've worked out for us. Someone, or some thing, was pulling the strings the night we came together."

"Are you saying that her being in Vegas at the same time as us was meant to be?"

Linc shrugs. "If I don't believe in that, then I don't believe in anything."

I nod and try to give a smile to my best friend, who really is trying to make me feel better. "Thanks man. Sorry again I wasn't in the celebrating mood today. I hope I didn't bring the team down."

"Nah," Wyatt says as we start walking back toward the crowds of people. "No one probably knew other than us."

"Good," I say, feeling a little better now that I've talked all of it out, but overall still sad. "Thanks for listening. I really appreciate you both."

"Anytime," Linc says. "Is there anything else we can do? Anything we can get you?"

"Besides the one thing I can't have?"

Linc laughs and shakes his head. "Okay what's the next thing to make you feel better?"

It doesn't take me long to think of what would make me feel better. And if Gabi is the one thing I can't have, this is probably number two.

"A bear claw."

CHAPTER 9
GABI

"Gabi, darling, can you grab us some cinnamon rolls to go? With the weather getting colder the next few days I don't know if we're going to make it in, and I don't know if I can go two days without a cinnamon roll."

I laugh at Phyllis, who along with her best friend, Kitty, have become somewhat regulars at my little bakery. "I'd be happy to. Anything for you Kitty?"

She thinks about it for a second. "Not a cinnamon roll, but I'd sure love a few bear claws. I'm so glad you're making them now!"

"I'm glad you like them," I say, quickly turning away so I can hide the redness that I'm sure is creeping up on my face. A reaction that is my own fault because I'm the genius who decided to add them to the menu this week after a certain football player told me he liked them.

Apparently this is what happens when you have orgasms—you do dumb things like panic in the morning, run from his hotel room, steal his clothes, and then put his favorite pastry on the menu in case he ever comes in even though you didn't leave your phone number or any indication that you would want to see him ever again and left without saying goodbye.

God I'm an idiot.

I know Maddox isn't coming in here. In my heart of hearts I know that. And I don't necessarily want him to. I think. Yes. I don't want him to come here. Because Vegas was a one-time thing. And as much as the words he said to me that night felt like more than that, I'm not naive enough to think this man is pining over me somewhere in his downtown condo. He's probably out and about, living his best life, which may or may not include meeting and hooking up with other women. And that's fine. It was an amazing night that will be remembered forever, but it's staying in Vegas. I'm fine with that really. I need to move on and live my life.

But you know, in case he does drop by, they're here for him.

No, not just for him. I mean, Kitty likes them so I have to keep making them. And I can't let her down.

"There she goes again," I hear Kitty whisper to Phyllis. "Staring off again."

"I bet she got laid in Vegas," Phyllis says, which fully snaps me out of my daydream. "Only a good man with a good tongue can snatch your soul like that."

"Excuse me!" I squeal. "I did not."

"Sure you didn't," Kitty says with a wink. "Go get our orders and try to come up with a better lie."

This is what I get for having regular customers. They know me too well. And have zero filter.

But they're right. And it's becoming a problem.

Since the day I got back from Vegas, I haven't been able to get this damn twenty-four-year old out of my head. Then I do something stupid like when I think I'm safe, I think back to when he ripped my dress because he couldn't keep his hands off me and literally made my legs shake from the orgasm.

Multiple orgasms.

With multiple ways of making it happen.

And he was twenty-four. I'm thirty-five.

I'm officially a cougar.

Yes, I looked up his age on the plane ride home from Vegas. And I maybe bought the internet package so I could read some articles about him. I didn't mean to read as many as I did, but the more I read, the more fascinating I found him in the most confusing way. One article talked about his foundation that he has for teenagers looking for STEM opportunities, while the other talked about a country singer he was dating last year. Another one showed him playing with sick kids at Nashville Children's Hospital, and the other was a slide show of every woman he was seen out with a few months ago.

Which makes sense. He's twenty-four, gorgeous, and has an infectious personality. It's why I told myself on the plane that I wasn't going to think about him when I got back to Nashville.

I made the bear claws thirteen hours later. And it's been downhill ever since. Because not only have I thought of him every day, I've been wearing his clothes a few too many times since I got home a week ago.

Damn you, Maddox Gallagher, and your love of bear claws, your comfortable sweatpants, your perfect penis, and your magic tongue…

I want to stop. I *need* to stop. Frankly, it's unhealthy. But between little things reminding me of him and our night together, my Spotify deciding that it wants to play that song every day now, the Fury's championship parade last week, and of course, my dreams each night, I can't help it.

It also doesn't help that everyday Hannah or Shelby asks in our group chat if he stopped by, or if I've contacted him. When I tell them "no" for the hundredth time while listing the long list of reasons that Maddox Gallagher is not good for my life right now, they decide to respond by sending some sort of picture of Maddox—mostly of the shirtless variety.

I might've hit download to all of them.

But downloading a few pictures and dating him are two completely different things. I'm fresh off a divorce. I'm still figuring out how to navigate life on my own. I have to stop myself from signing my married name on deliveries. There's a lot I need to do with my life before I even consider dating again. Especially dating a man who wasn't alive when we thought Y2K was going to make the computers blow up.

"Okay, no more thoughts," I whisper to myself as I lean into the glass, pulling out two bear claws, leaving one more for today. You know. Just in case. "You need to get over it. And him."

"Talking to yourself again Gab? I thought we came to the understanding that the imaginary friends in your head were, you know, imaginary."

I stand up away from the glass, ready to toss the tongs in my hand right at my big brother.

"You're not funny," I say, though I'm already softening by the smile Beau's giving me.

"I'm a fucking riot and you know it."

I shake my head as I close the glass case. "Give me a second to deliver these."

"Customer always comes first," he says, turning to watch as I head back to Phyllis and Kitty.

"We'd sure like to," Phyllis says as she stands up, not making it hidden that she's checking my brother out. Which... gross. I mean, I know what the world says about him. That's he's a cocky, six-foot-four, well built, bearded, professional golfer who is kind of an asshole but knows when to turn on the charm, making him a media favorite. To me he's the eight-year old boy who put frogs in my shoes knowing damn well the little fuckers freak me out.

He's also my knight in shining armor and the reason I'm standing in Sugar and Sweets.

But still... gross.

"Oh Phyllis, you make me blush every time I come in here," Beau says as he walks over to grab her coat off the rack by the door, stepping back next to her to help her put it on. "Here, let me help you into this."

"You're the only man I'm okay with getting me into clothes and not out of them," Phyllis says, which makes me immediately turn beet red, while also want to go hide in the kitchen. "You're a true gentleman Beau."

"Only sometimes, if you know what I mean," he says with a wink to my seventy-eight-year-old customer.

"Goodness gracious" I grumble. "Don't let him sweet talk you Phyllis. He's nothing but trouble."

"Don't tell her that, it'll only make her want him more," Kitty says as she puts on her coat and scarf. "Been friends with this woman for fifty years and to this day I have to remind her that we stay away from red flags, not run toward them like a goddamn bull."

"You know about red flags?"

"Oh sweetie. Red flags have been around since men..." she trails off, though I also think that she didn't need to finish that sentence. She's pretty much right. "Let's get you out of here before you get another restraining order against you. That other one expired."

"You shush!" Phyllis says, slapping her friend as Beau and I can't stop laughing. "It wasn't a restraining order. Howard asked the night orderly that I not be allowed to sit by him at bingo."

"Bye ladies!" I say with a wave as they exit the bakery. "Stay warm and out of jail please."

"No promises!" Phyllis calls out before she and Kitty exit the bakery. There have been a lot of great things that have happened since the bakery opened, and meeting those two has to be in the top three. When they're not harassing my brother or the other male clientele.

"Those two are a fucking hoot." Beau says as he grabs their cups of coffee off the table. "I think Phyllis pinched my ass."

"I wouldn't put it past her," I say. "Wait. Why are you cleaning up? You don't have to do that."

"Now, what kind of owner would I be if I didn't pull my weight around here?"

I tilt my head as I block his path to come behind the counter.

"The kind who comes in a few times a month to remind me that he's the owner."

"Gabi… you know that's not why I come in here."

"I know," I say, gesturing for him to sit at the counter. "It's just… my head is all over the place these days. And when you come strutting in, it's a reminder that it's another day that has passed that this place is yours and not mine."

"Soon," he says.

"I really hate that word…"

I feel like the word "soon" is a leading contender for my autobiography. When I was married, it was the word Justin used to put off something I wanted, but he had a convenient excuse for. Those include, but were not limited to, opening a bakery and starting a family.

During my divorce my lawyer would say "it should be over soon." I don't know what his definition of soon is, but two years to me isn't soon.

And now, soon I'll own Sugar and Sweets. I clearly trust my brother more than my ex, and even my divorce attorney, but I still fucking hate that word.

Except in this case, Beau is right. And this was the plan all along. I'm getting impatient and I know it. In my defense, this has been years in the making for me.

When Justin was heading to medical school, it obviously wasn't practical for me to work at, or try to start my own bakery. So I agreed to work a corporate accounting job until he finished and became established. Then it could be my turn.

The only problem was, that turn never came around. I think that was the first time I truly started hating the word "soon." Because that's what Justin would always say any time I brought up me quitting my job.

Soon… when we have a credit card paid off.

Soon… when the real estate market corrects itself.

Soon… it's not smart to open a new business in this economy.

After I found out he was cheating on me, I was devastated.

Not only did I spend years of my life loving that man, but I gave up everything for him. I felt hopeless. Defeated. Like my whole adult life up to that point was wasted. I hated my job. I hated living in the house where I knew Justin cheated. I hated everything.

Which is when my big brother stepped in to save the day. He might come off as a cocky asshole to the world, but the day he found me bawling on his couch, the man didn't hesitate. It helped that he always hated Justin, and he felt that him stepping in to help me was also a good middle finger to my ex.

Which is when he opened me a bakery.

It took him less than two weeks to find a location and buy it. This was a café before, so the bones were already here, but because he could, he made sure to outfit the place with the most up-to-date equipment, fixtures, and anything else I could need or want. He really was my hero because never in a million years would I have ever been able to afford half of the things he installed. And the man did his homework. By the end of this process, I'm pretty sure Beau knew more about baking equipment than I did.

From there, he told me to quit my job and that the two of us were going to open Sugar and Sweets with the agreement that one day I'd be the full owner and operator of the business, and he'd be the landlord of the building. He made sure to keep my name off every document, utility bill, and deed so that way Justin couldn't ask for one cent of the business during the divorce proceedings.

To the courts, I was Gabrielle (soon to be back to) Devereaux, employed by Sugar and Sweets. To Beau and I, I'm the future owner and operator of this business.

Soon. Please God let it be soon.

"All you need is a little time now to really get on your own feet," he says with encouragement. "Have a good year where you get some money in the bank and you feel like you're settled, and then we switch over the papers to your name."

"I know," I say. "I'm not ready yet. But one day. Soon."

It's the first time I've said that word with a smile.

"I haven't talked to you since you officially signed off on everything," he says. "I wish I could've been there to seen his swarmy face when he admitted defeat."

I laugh as I remember his look of complete depression. How he thought he wasn't getting off not paying spousal support is still hilarious."

"It was pretty funny. But I don't know if your presence would've done any good. Especially since I still think it was you who slashed Justin's tires when you found out he was cheating on me."

He holds up his hands in innocence. "I'll neither confirm or deny that action."

I raise an eyebrow, wondering if he'll ever tell me the truth about that. Or if it was him who also signed Justin up for an alien-believing cult's mailing list, which I only know about because he brought it up at a mediation thinking I did it. Though, that one has more of Shelby written on it.

"While I appreciate you wanting to be there, I was fine. Actually, Shelby came and scared the literal piss out of him. It was quite a sight to see."

"He's scared of Shelby?" Beau asks.

"Who isn't?"

"Me for one."

I roll my eyes. "Of course you're not. You're too busy hating her to be scared of her."

"I give back what I receive," he says. "And since she hates me, and I think she needs to take the pitching wedge out of her ass and lighten up every once in a while, to me that equals maybe not hate, but a strong dislike. And I'm definitely, I mean *definitely*, not scared of her."

I don't know why my best friend and brother hate each other, but they have our entire lives. On paper, they should be better friends than she and I are. They grew up playing golf together in

Louisiana. They're both now on their respective professional golf tours. They each know the pressures and work ethic it takes to make it professionally.

But the two can't stand each other. I don't think they've ever been civil to each other once in our lives, which includes my wedding when they were paired together. That was a mistake on my part. I thought I could make them like each other for one day. Instead they spent the entire time hitting each other or trying to make the other trip.

"You should've seen her in Vegas last weekend" I say. "She was fun and smiled. Danced and drank. She was talking to a football coach all night and seemed to really be enjoying herself. So, maybe it's just you who makes her scowl."

His face turns from annoyed to… anger? "I don't fucking make her scowl. That's her permanent look. I'm a fucking delight."

"Of course you are. The belle of the ball." I tease. "And I made up that I saw her smiling and laughing last week. A figment of my drunk imagination."

"Had to be," he says in a huff, which makes me laugh even more. "Speaking of Vegas. It looked like you had fun."

I feel my cheeks heat. Since he never messaged me about them, I'd hoped that any of the videos of me on stage hadn't made it to his feed. Judging by the shit-eating grin on his face, they did and he waited until now to bring them up.

"Yes, I had a very nice time," I say, quickly turning away to busy myself—and to hide by beet-red cheeks.

"Nice? You don't have a 'nice' time in Vegas. If you did, then you did Vegas wrong."

Oh big brother… if you only knew how right things were in Vegas…

"Do you really want to know how *much* of a *nice* time I had in Vegas or would you like to stop this conversation right here?"

He picks up on my specific emphasis of certain words and quickly shakes his head. That's what I thought. If there's anything to make brothers stop picking on their sisters, it's tears and the threat of sex talk.

"Yes please," he says. "Stopping is good. Especially because I have a feeling your nice time was with Maddox Gallagher. Stopping is *very* good."

"That's what I thought," I say as I lean down to pick something off the floor. As soon as I do, I hear the bells above my door ringing, alerting me that someone is here.

"Welcome in!" I yell from my awkward stance, but as I slowly stand up and look through the display glass to the door, I immediately go back down, wanting to hide from whoever walked in.

Because that whoever is wearing Nashville Fury gear. And not just any gear—a gray warm-up set that I learned in my post-Vegas, airplane, social media, stalking is one only players wear.

"Gab? You good down there?"

"Yup! Fine!" I call out to Beau. "Dropped something."

My heart. That's what dropped. Which is funny considering I'm pretty sure my blood pressure is spiking at this moment. I don't even know if it's Maddox—it looks to be a player about his height and a similar-ish build—but the presence of the orange, fire logo is enough to make my brain go a million miles a minute while my heart tries to beat out of my chest.

Is it him? After a full week of nothing, is he coming in here? Every day, every time the bell rang, a little bit of me hoped it was him. When it wasn't, I felt relief and slight disappointment.

It's fucking confusing.

I mean, if I do see him, am I happy about it? I wouldn't be mad. I'm sure it would be nice to see him. He's a nice guy who made my divorce trip memorable. In so many ways.

Which is also why I don't want to see him. What we had in Vegas was perfect. A true vacation hookup that was magical in so many ways. If I see him again, that memory might become skewed, and I don't want to ever forget that night for exactly what it was.

Then again, if he came in here and asked me for a repeat performance, I don't know if I could say no. I mean, I can still feel his tongue between my thighs. No way I have the willpower to say no to that.

Except I'd need to. I'm not in a position for anything, even another fun hookup. Definitely not a relationship. Though I don't think Maddox is the relationship kind of guy from the things I've read about him online. Also, bold of me to assume he'd want that with me. Then again, I haven't seen pictures of him out and about in the past week, let alone pictures with him and another woman. Not that I've been looking. I haven't. Much.

God this is confusing. And I've officially graduated from hot mess to dumpster fire.

"Linc Kincaid?"

"Beau! What the hell are you doing here?"

I let out a huge breath—relief with a side of disappointment —as I stand up to see my brother and Linc sharing a bro hug.

"You two know each other?"

"Gabi! You didn't tell me that Beau was your brother."

"Apologies," I say. "I didn't realize there was a secret Nashville athlete club that introduced all of you together."

"Same agent," Beau says as Linc takes a seat next to him. "Which means we've been at more than a few parties and events together."

"What a small world," I say, trying to keep my face even. And also trying not to look over Linc's shoulder to see if anyone else in a Fury warm-up is about to walk in. "Can I get you something Linc?"

"Please," he says, eyeing the glass case next to him. "Two brownies for Ainsley—who sends her love by the way. And I'll take, let's see… I'm not sure what I'm in the mood for."

"I'm partial to the carrot cake bars," Beau says. "I know it's not the sexiest option. But they do the trick. Can't go wrong with a cinnamon roll. And she recently added bear claws to the menu."

Please don't know those are Maddox's favorite... please don't know those are Maddox's favorite...

Linc's eyebrows go up. "Bear claws you say? I've heard a thing or two about those."

Fuck. He knows.

"Yeah, I try to keep the menu fresh. Bear claws felt right." I say, quickly going to grab brownies for Ainsley and everything that Beau listed for Linc.

"You haven't made those in forever," Beau says, completely clueless on why bear claws have become an important part of conversation. He starts to say something when his cell phone rings. "Excuse me. I need to take this."

I finish bagging up Linc's order as Beau steps into the kitchen for privacy.

"Have you recovered from the parade?" I ask, desperate to make small talk.

"I have," Linc says. "Now back to my normal offseason routine. Which means Monday nights I bring Ainsley dinner and dessert at work."

"Seriously? That's adorable." I say, heading back to the counter to grab an extra brownie.

"It's our thing," he says. "But, she did instruct me since I was coming in here to see if I could get your contact information so she could message you about a cake order? Her schedule is all over the place so she didn't want to miss you and get the order in too late."

"Oh yeah. Sure," I say, reciting my personal number for Linc as he punches it in his phone. "She can text or call me whenever."

"Thanks, I'll let her know," he says, taking his card out of his wallet. "How much do I owe you?"

I shake my head. "On the house."

"Absolutely not," he says. "I'm all about supporting local businesses. How am I supposed to do that if I get free things?"

"You can pay next time," I say. "This is the least I can do to thank you."

"Thank me? For what?"

"How nice you and Ainsley were in Vegas," I say. "To me and my friends. It was an unexpected night, but you guys were very welcoming. I appreciate that."

He slips his card back into his wallet, but then pulls out a twenty and stuffs it in the tip jar. "No thanks needed. You were a part of the celebration. I can't imagine the night without you there."

Linc seems like a genuinely sweet guy. When I was doing my light reading on the plane ride back, articles popped up about him, so I read a few. The guy had a hell of a year—both good and bad—both on and off the field. I'm glad he seems to be in a good spot, and he's got a girl like Ainsley next to him.

"Well thanks again. Tell Ainsley I said hi and to seriously text me whenever she wants."

"I will," he says, picking up the bag and standing up. "And, for curiosity's sake, if a certain teammate of mine wanted to get a hold of you, and since I have your number, do I have permission to give it to him as well?"

Oh that was smooth Linc Kincaid. Very smooth…

"I—" I start to say something when I realize I have no idea what I should say. I know what I should say, and that's the word no. One syllable. Easy off the tongue. Or, maybe something nicer like "that's sweet but I don't think it's a good idea."

Because it's not. Either of those replies are what a smart person should say.

But I'm not a smart person. Not right now. Because clearly my head is taking the day off. My heart hasn't worked in eons. Which leaves my vagina to make the decisions. She's been begging to be in charge for years. Especially after coming out of retirement in Vegas. Which is the only reason I can fathom that I say the one word I shouldn't.

"Yes."

CHAPTER 10
MADDOX

MADDOX

Hello.

T oo boring. Let's try again.

What's up?

Who am I, a fuck boy? I mean I am. I was. I might be. Am I reformed?

Hey, Gabi, this is Maddox.

The only way I'm sending this is if my next message is going to ask about her car's extended warranty.

I haven't been able to stop thinking about you…

Well that's creepy. True. But creepy.

I throw my phone down on the couch, pinching the bridge of

my nose because for the life of me I can't figure out what to text Gabi.

Because it has to be perfect.

When Linc sent me the text with her contact, I thought he was playing some sort of fucked-up joke on me. Which would've been cruel. I asked him twenty times if it was for real or not—and texted Ainsley because the woman would never lie. I only believed him after I confirmed with her.

But that has only led me to staring at my phone for the past hour trying to figure out what to say to the woman who's been keeping me up at night. Which is very much not like me. I've been with women. Plenty of them. I've had hot nights. I've had crazy ones where the location of the exploits might not have been the most private. I've been with women that some men would give an appendage to be with. Yet, one night with Gabi has put me under some sort of a spell. It's like I've been reverse dickmatized.

Yes, that has to be why I'm picking my phone back up, but staring at it like it's a foreign object. Never in my twenty-four years have I ever been nervous to approach a woman. I asked out my first girlfriend when I was six years old. She was in third grade and road my bus. She always had the prettiest bows in her hair, so I told her that. Next thing I knew we were holding hands every day and I was carrying her books to class.

Wait! Is that where my love for older women started? I should talk to the team therapist about that...

Needless to say from that first relationship with Bella Summers until this very moment, I've always been the guy to step up and ask a woman out. Or for her number or socials. Send the first message without that bullshit three-day rule. Rejection? Rejection is scared of me.

Until now.

"What is wrong with me?" I say out loud as I grip my phone tight in my hand. "At the end of the day, she's just a woman. But she's not. She's... fuck! I've never not had words. Am I in a trance? Is this a pussy trance? No. It can't be because I was hypnotized when she walked on stage. Why am I a bumbling idiot right now?"

I let out a deep breath, doing my best to collect myself. "I'm just a guy. She's just a girl. I'm going to send her a message to see if she'd maybe want to go to get coffee. Or marry me."

Am I being overdramatic? Possibly. Because yes, I know it's one text message. It's not the actual make or break for whatever we're going to be, but it's important. This moment right here is chapter two in our story. And considering I didn't think there was going to be a second, I'm not going to take the chance of sending some dumbass text with a dumbass opening line. No. When she opens my text from an unknown number, I want her belly to flip. I want her heart to flutter. I want her to instantly be transported back to that night in Vegas.

"That's it!" I scream, sitting up on my couch ready to type out what came to my mind. Except that when I look at my screen, things are not what they should be.

There should be no messages sent. And yet, there is one.

And it's not a text.

It's a voice memo.

And it says delivered.

"Fuck fuck fuck..." I murmur, jumping up from the couch and starting to pace around my living room. "What the fuck did I say?"

Except I know what I said. I was talking to myself about how I'm already basically in love and would marry a woman I've spent one night with. I used the words "pussy trance" which I don't even think is a real phrase.

"Fuck!" I yell again, my fingers flying over the phone, wondering if I can unsend a voice memo.

Can you? I honestly have no fucking clue, but that doesn't stop me from quickly trying to Google "I'm a dumbass and sent a voice memo to a woman. Help me undo it." Unfortunately, that's not giving me the best search results.

Just when I think I've found a helpful article, my stomach drops when I see a return message.

One from a contact labeled "Future Wife."

Because yes, I'm already down bad for this woman.

> FUTURE WIFE
>
> Pussy trance? I didn't even know that was a thing, let alone that I was capable of it. Wait, is this one of those things you youngins say these days?

My first thought is to be absolutely mortified. She heard it. She heard it all. My entire rant about wanting to marry her after one night—which I'm only really half serious about—and being in a pussy trance.

My second is that out of everything I said, that's what she came back with. Slightly busting my balls about my words and poking a little fun out of the awkward situation.

Yup. I'm pretty much in love with her.

> Not all youngins. Just me.

> You should send the word to the dictionary people. Or get a trademark. You don't want anyone stealing your intellectual property.

> Or we could keep it between us and also maybe forget that I sent you that voice memo?

> Not a chance in the world 😉

I lay back down on my couch, smiling at my phone like a goof as I read Gabi's words.

> Okay, but can you at least give me a do over? Send you the text that I wanted to send?

> Sure. But just so you know I downloaded that and am saving it forever.

Forever? A woman after my own heart.

I take in a breath, and I don't know why I was stressing too hard about it. Because as I type this, it's the easiest two words I've ever strung together.

Hey Gabrielle.

Hey, Maddox. How have you been? I'm so surprised you texted me! I didn't know if you even remembered my name or not!

Smart ass.

Had to throw in one crack. But seriously, how are you?

Better now that the mortification has slightly worn off.

Okay, well then I'm going to get this out of the way now. While I'm flattered that you proposed marriage, I'm going to have to say no at this time. Being that the ink isn't dry on my divorce, there's probably a waiting period in the state of Tennessee. So at this time, I'm going to have to say no.

Does that mean at another time you'd say yes?

You really are something else, aren't you?

So I've been told.

For the next fifteen minutes we fall into easy conversation. She asks me about the parade and the media blitz since I've been home. Which makes me smile because that means she's been paying attention. I ask her about the bakery and what she's been up to since getting back from Vegas. While the conversation is effortless, I probably need to address the mini elephant in the room.

> I hope you don't mind that I texted you. Or I should say voice messaged you badly.

I don't at all. The voice memo, which will forever be saved, brightened my day.

> Glad to help.

I was actually wondering if you were going to text me or not…

> I wasn't going to contact you after Vegas. But when Linc said he ran into you…

I trail off the text, not quite sure what to say. Luckily, Gabi does.

I've been wondering what was the best way to get your clothes back to you.

Well I'm glad you did. I've been wondering what was the best way to get your clothes back to you.

My clothes. I almost forgot she took a T-shirt and sweatpants from my luggage. I smile, thinking about what she had to look like leaving my room that morning. Hair a mess. Makeup for sure ruined. Clothes too big for her, but better than a tattered dress.

What I would've given to see her. Or better, what I'd give to see her in them now. I shut my eyes for a second, easily envisioning what Gabi would look like in my T-shirt, and nothing else. Her walking around my apartment in just that—maybe nothing on underneath—after having her in my bed. Or maybe we're fresh from the shower and those are the clothes she put on with her wet hair and no makeup. The white T-shirt clinging to her chest. God what I'd give to have that.

What I'd give to have any of her.

> You're not returning them. You're keeping them.

Maddox, I'm not keeping them.

Yes you are. They are now the property of Gabi... shit... I still don't know your last name.

They're your clothes. I feel bad that I took them without permission.

And I have plenty. Plus, if you want more just ask. I will send you as much team apparel as you want. I happen to be very good friends with the head of our apparel and equipment departments.

But I stole them. They're your clothes.

You confessed at the scene of the crime. To me that's informed borrowing.

Are you sure? Because now I feel bad.

Don't. I'm glad I had something for you to wear.

You're one-thousand-percent sure you're not mad?

Gabi, the only thing I'm mad about is that I didn't get to see you in the morning and kiss you when I woke up.

Shit. I didn't mean for it to come out like that. I'm not mad. I understand why she did it. It's just... fuck I need to make this right.

Gabi, I'm sorry. I didn't mean that I was mad. I... just wish I had seen you.

No, you're right. I should've woken you. And, I'm really sorry I left. I just... I had an early flight and I needed to get back to Shelby's.

I know. You don't need to explain anything.

I feel like I do.

You don't. I wasn't really mad. Sad is a better word.

I'm sorry I made you sad.

Don't be. But what would make me even sadder is if you returned my clothes.

You don't play fair.

I never said I did. Now, tell me about what kind of bake goods you offer. I feel like I need a sweet treat soon.

What's your favorite color?

Why would you need to know that?

Humor me.

Blue. I lean more toward baby blue, but really, any blue. Why?

No reason.

Maddox...

Gabrielle...

Are you just making conversation? Or are you asking for a specific reason?

It's a surprise.

See that's the problem. I'm not a fan of
surprises. Surprises in my history have never
been good.

Surprises can be fun!

No, they're horrible.

Not my surprises. Trust me.

Famous last words…

Maddox Gallagher…

Gabrielle I-Still-Don't-Know-Your-Last-Name…

Why am I receiving a gift with a various amount
of things that are all blue.

Yay! You got my Blue Basket!

The what?

Blue Basket! The name was easy to come up
with once you told me your favorite color. It's
like a Boo Basket, only blue.

What's a Boo Basket?

It's a Halloween basket I saw some of the guys
get their girlfriends this year.

You know I'm not your girlfriend, right?

Minor details...

Maddox...

Gabrielle...

What am I going to do with you?

I have some ideas 😈

I left myself open for that one...

Can I ask a silly question?

You can ask me any question you want at whatever time about whatever topic. Also, the sillier the better.

Bold statement.

But true.

Okay, I'm going to come out and say it.

I like a woman who takes charge. 😊

Okay. That!

That what?

You're flirting with me.

Phew. I'm glad you realized it. Between the voice memo, the clothing conversation, my present, and that I admitted in the first message that I have plans to one day marry you, I was wondering if you were picking up the vibes that I do in fact like you and that I am, in fact, flirting with you.

But why?

Why what?

Why are you flirting with me? And buying me presents? And telling me to keep your clothes?

And don't forget professing my want to give you my last name in the first message I sent to you.

Was that serious?

If you want it to be.

Maddox. What are you doing?

Is this the silly question?

It's a prelude to the question.

Okay, well then the answer is yes I'm flirting with you. And it's because I like you and I want to see you again.

You can't say things like that.

I can't say the truth?

Maddox...

Gabrielle...

I'm not ready to date. Or anything for that matter.

I understand.

I do feel bad though. Because you're sweet. And I did have… that night was everything to me. And I've loved talking to you these past few days.

Ditto to everything.

It's just… I don't have the capacity right now for anything serious. Or semi-serious. Or even casual.

I understand. I'm a child of divorce. I remember my mom those first few years. It was starting your life over again.

Exactly. Which is why I have to be honest and up front with you. I don't want you to think that there could be anything more in our future when I don't even know what tomorrow holds.

I knew a conversation like this could happen, and that this would be the outcome, but that doesn't lessen the blow any. Yet, I can't let this be the last time that I talk to her. There's something between us. She was meant to come into my life. Our story doesn't end here. I know it.

So, I'm going to take what I can get. Even if that means the one "f" word I hate most in life.

I appreciate your honesty. But can I ask you a question now?

Sure.

I know you aren't interested in anything, but can we be friends?

Friends? You want to be friends with me?

I want to be in your life any way I can. And if it's only friends, then get prepared to call me your bestie.

One, you typing bestie feels very odd. Second, Shelby and Hannah might not take too well when they find out you're invading their turf.

Tell them to bring it on. Because I'm about to be the best fucking friend you've ever had.

CHAPTER 11
MADDOX

I take pleasure in the small things in life.

A beautiful woman. These days, ones named Gabi.

A juicy steak served medium rare.

Your music app always playing the right song when set to shuffle.

An opposing quarterback throwing the ball thinking he has his target, only for me to jump in front out of nowhere, picking it off and running it to my end zone.

But more than any of those things, what to me is the simplest and most perfect thing in this life, is a sweet treat.

Specifically a bear claw. But I'm not picky.

And if that treat happens to come from my new favorite bakery that I haven't tried yet, but am standing outside of, then so be it.

It took all I had to not be her first customer of the day. I could've. I was awake. My body always has a hard time adjusting from the in-season schedule to my offseason one. During the football season, my days are so regimented—which for me includes when I wake up—that when it's suddenly over, I usually need a few weeks to adjust.

Today wasn't a case of me waking up at my normal six in the

morning. No, this came from me not being able to sleep a wink last night.

I couldn't stop thinking about her or our conversation. Even though it was all over text, I swear I could hear her voice. The playfulness in some parts. The vulnerability in others. Her sass and wit. The seriousness when she told me that we couldn't ever be more than friends.

Which is when my inner voice chimed in trying to come up with a plan to be what she needs, while also holding out hope that one day she'll change her mind.

I was up two hours earlier than normal—and that was after me talking myself out of going to the bakery and bringing her coffee. However, that meant that my morning routine of working out, eating breakfast, answering emails, and a meeting with my agent, were all done well before noon.

After realizing being there when her doors opened was a bit much, I decided that maybe I'd go around lunch and bring her something to eat. That felt more nonchalant. Except I don't know what she likes to eat, and I wanted it to be a surprise, so I retreated from that thought.

I was scrambling. I cleaned my condo to keep busy, hoping that the movement would spark an idea. I tried to play a video game, but got bored with that in three seconds.

Then it hit me: I need a hobby. And not just any hobby. Baking.

I mean, it's perfect. I've wanted something to do to keep my hands and mind busy this off season. What if I learn to bake? And not fumble around on YouTube or study every second of a baking television show, but I get my favorite baker to teach me the ways. If she happens to fall in love with me during this process? So be it.

I'm a fucking genius.

I look up to the baby blue and white sign that reads "Sugar and Sweets" before looking through the huge front window. It's not a big building, but I can tell from the outside it's the perfect size to have a quaint bakery that seats plenty. I can see there are a few college students packing up their things to leave, and two elderly women sitting at a table. It's not long before Gabi approaches the two women, setting down two plates, before taking a step back. I don't know what they said to Gabi, but she's holding her stomach as she laughs.

I'm glad I didn't go in right away. I needed a second to get my wits about me. If I hadn't, there was a very good chance I was going to walk in, see her, forget our conversation last night, and kiss the hell out of her. Which I know I can't do. I won't do. So I'm going to stand out here for another minute and figure out how the hell I'm going to be friends with a woman I'm fucking crazy about.

"You can do this Gallagher," I whisper to myself. "Don't come on too strong. Be her friend. Ask her to be your baking teacher. Get a bear claw. That's all you're here to do."

With those parting words and one more breath I crack my neck for good luck and slowly make my way inside the bakery.

"My oh my, who do we have here?"

"A hot piece of ass, that's who."

Excuse me… what did they just say?

I stop in my tracks, barely two steps inside the door, because I'm all sorts of flustered. This is not how I expected my grand entrance to be. I try to scramble to figure out what to say, or how to react, to the two older women who are clearly staring at my dick right now, when one word snaps me out of my stupor.

"Maddox?"

My name is barely a whisper on Gabi's lips. Lips I want to kiss. Lips I still remember tasting like champagne and perfection. But they're loud enough to bring me back to the present, and really take a look at my girl.

My friend. Shit, yes, my friend.

"Hi, Gabrielle."

Neither of us move as we take each other in. I needed those few minutes outside to prepare myself, but I still wasn't ready to see her. Her hair is pulled up in a crazy type of pony tail. She has on barely any makeup and is wearing an adorable blue and white apron that matches the sign out front. Her smile is small but beautiful, and I hope a little bit it's because she's happy to see me.

Just friends. You're going to be friends. So don't stare at her chest in the v-neck T-shirt.

"Oh I know what's going on here," one of the older women says. "They've banged."

Like glass shattering, those two words snap me out of my daze. "Um… we… "

"Oh they for sure have," the other woman says, standing up and walking next to me. "You're a cute little young thing aren't you? Good job Gabi. I like 'em younger too."

What the hell is happening?

"Phyllis, please," Gabi says, snapping into action and coming to pull me away from the woman apparently named Phyllis. "This is Maddox. He's my friend."

"Naked friend," the other says, outstretching her hand. "I'm Kitty. Nice to meet you Maddox."

I return the gesture as I try to get my wits back, because these two are throwing me for a loop. "Nice to meet you Kitty. And yes, I'm a friend of Gabi's."

"Sure you are," she says, adding in a wink for good measure. "If you're her friend, then why have we never seen you here before?"

"We're here every day," Phyllis says as she sits back down. "And yet, this is your first time here?"

When I decided to come in to surprise Gabi, I ran through a few different scenarios of how this was going to go. None of them were me facing off against a blue-hair interrogation. But I'm Maddox Gallagher. I go up against some of the best athletes in the world. I can handle these two.

Maybe. Probably. Except Phyllis keeps winking at me and I'm pretty sure Kitty's hand is on my arm.

"It is," I say, doing my best to turn on the charm. "Gabi and I recently met. But I've heard her baking is top notch."

"It is," Phyllis says.

"Well then I need some recommendations. What's good?"

"She's a fan of the cinnamon rolls," Kitty says. "As for me? I'm partial to the bear claws."

"A woman after my own heart," I say, adding in my own wink. If they're going to flirt with me, then I'm going to flirt and charm them right back. Especially because I have a feeling that if I can win them over, that's only going to help my cause. "They're my favorite. You didn't eat them all, did you?"

"Oh I couldn't if I tried," she says. "Wait! You say you two just met?"

I look up to Gabi and her suddenly very red cheeks and unblinking eyes.

"We did. About two weeks ago now?"

"Well isn't that funny," Kitty says. "That's about the time she put bear claws on the menu..."

I look to my "friend," whose eyes are about to pop out of her head. As for me? I'm smiling ear to ear. "Is that so, Gabrielle?"

"It is," Phyllis answers for her. "Says she was inspired."

"You call her Gabrielle? That's beautiful," Kitty says.

"Beautiful name for a beautiful woman," I say to my two new best friends. "Now, how about that bear claw?"

My face is in full smirk mode when Gabi grabs me by my T-shirt.

"We'll be back. Please don't burn the place down," she says, literally dragging me by my shirt through a swinging door and into the kitchen. "What was that!"

"What?" I ask, playing innocent. "I was making friends with your customers. Who seem like a fucking hoot. I think Kitty was trying to feel me up."

"She probably was," she says, clearly flustered. "What are you doing here?"

"I wanted a bear claw."

She puts her hands on her hips, her eyes turning serious. "Maddox…"

"Gabrielle…"

Oh… is this now our thing? A stubborn standoff? It happened in Vegas. And over text. I like it. It's hot. Especially because I want to kiss the stubborn look off her face.

I can't. But I want to.

"Maddox, I know you said you wanted to be my friend."

"I do."

"But that doesn't mean you have to come into my bakery."

"Why wouldn't I?" I ask. "For one, I'm a big proponent of supporting local businesses. Also, Linc and Ainsley weren't lying that I have the biggest sweet tooth on the team. And I was out running errands today, and I thought a bear claw sounded delicious. So here I am. Now, where is that almond goodness?"

I pretend to start looking around after slightly fibbing my reasons for being here, when I feel Gabi's hand on my arm. "You're really okay with being friends? This isn't some sort of ploy to get me to go out with you?"

I shake my head, turning to fully face her. "Would I be lying if I said I didn't like you anymore? Yes. If I said I shut off the feelings immediately, I think everyone would know I was full of shit. And if you told me right now you changed your mind, I'd be walking out to that dining room, kicking Phyllis and Kitty out on their behinds, and kissing you until you couldn't breathe."

Her cheeks are flushing again at my words, but I ignore the urge to cup her face. Instead I take a breath of my own, wanting her to know how serious I am. "I have a feeling that you need a friend. I know Shelby and Hannah don't live here, and going through what you're going through, I'm sure it can get a little lonely. And if I can help you with that, for whatever you need, I'm here to help you. A shoulder to cry on; someone to vent to; someone to get you drunk because you've had it; someone to run errands with because you don't want to be alone; I'm your guy. I'll be whatever you want me to be."

Gabi doesn't say anything for a second, truly assessing if I'm serious or not.

"And what do you get in return?" she asks. "I'm pretty sure you're not hurting in the friend department."

"You're right, I do have a lot of friends," I say. "But I had a feeling you'd want to offer me something in return, so I have an idea."

This makes her eyebrow raise. "And what's that?"

"I need a hobby."

"A hobby?"

"Yes. A hobby. The offseason can get boring and mundane. So, I was thinking, maybe I could learn to bake? And that you could teach me."

By the way her eyes bug out of her head, I don't think she ever thought that's what I was going to say. "You want me to teach you how to bake?"

"Exactly," I say. "Nothing fancy. Cookies, cupcakes. Oh! I've always wanted to know how to make a tarte."

"A tarte?"

"Yes. Specifically apple. I love all things apple."

Her eyes are rapidly blinking now. "You're serious aren't you?"

"About sweet treats? Always. So, when do we start, Teach?"

CHAPTER 12
GABI

"Don't dump all the flour in at once," I direct Maddox as I crack open a Coke Zero. I've lost count of how many I've drank today. But's it's not a problem. It's only a problem if I admit it. "Do a little bit at a time or it's gonna go flying everywhere."

"Got it," he says, his nose scrunched as he concentrates on perfectly dumping the dry ingredients into the standing mixer bowl. "Just a little bit at a time…"

I lean against one of my prep tables, a huge smile on my face, as I take a sip of a crisp soft drink and watch Maddox in full concentration mode as he makes his first batch of chocolate chip cookies. In this moment he doesn't look like some big, bad, football player. Or even the charismatic man who swept me off my feet in Vegas. No, in this moment, he's a guy trying to learn a new task. A hot guy who's wearing an apron that shouldn't make him better looking than he already is.

It's honestly not fair.

"I'm glad we were finally able to do this," I say, taking my eye off him so I can start prepping ingredients I need to open the bakery tomorrow morning. "I'm sorry it took me so long."

"No apologies needed," he says, not taking his eyes off the mixer. "You're a busy woman and I'm a bored football player. But now I'm about to be a bored football player who knows how to make cookies."

We were supposed to start last week, but life got in the way for both of us. He had to suddenly go out of town for an endorsement photoshoot and when he got back, I wasn't feeling great. I think I caught a stomach bug.

So now here we are, and honestly, I can't believe he actually wants to do this. This being the baking lessons *and* being just friends. I believe him, but I don't at the same time. I mean, he's a good looking, single, professional football player in a town packed with beautiful women. Fun women. Women who don't spend their weekends looking up recipes while watching the same show on repeat because she can't decide on a new one. In no way, shape, or form, should Maddox Gallagher be spending his Friday night in a closed bakery learning to bake chocolate chip cookies.

But here he is. He brought dinner and refused to let me pay for my meal, hasn't tried to make a move on me once, and is now watching the standing mixer like it might run away.

He's too cute for his own good.

And mine.

Because I know in my heart of hearts, and the brain that is firmly rooted in my head, that I'm not ready for any kind of emotional or physical relationship. Not with Maddox, not with a more age-appropriate man, nor with the guy back in Louisiana that my mom reminded me is available once I told her I was getting divorced.

I've told her numerous times he's gay. She doesn't care.

But Maddox was right about one thing, I do need a friend. Sure, I have Shelby and Hannah, but with them not living in Nashville, and having their own lives, it's not the same as having someone that's a cup of coffee away. I used to have some around town, but over the years, they've fizzled out. College friends. Coworkers I grew more distant from because Justin didn't like me hanging out with them after work hours. That's what happens when your life revolves around your marriage and you let a certain part of you go. Sure, I have Beau, but he only lives here part-time. And now with golf season basically here, he's off training and getting ready for his first tournament on the West Coast.

Which leaves Maddox, my unexpected friend, the man I didn't see coming, who I wish I could give more but I'm glad is in my life nonetheless. The man who sends me a good morning text each day, who sent me a Blue Basket just because, and is looking unfortunately adorable as he bites his lip as he makes his very first batter.

"This is easy," he says. But the words come out too soon as I watch him dump way too much flour into the running stand mixer, making it puff out nearly all the flour straight onto his face. "Shit!"

I can't help but laugh as I walk to the sink and grab a paper towel, wetting it down, as Maddox tries to comb the flour out of his eyes. "I told you a little bit at a time."

"I was but it was taking too long," he says.

"It's a process," I say as I step into him so I can wipe the flour off his face. "It's all about patience. But it's good to know now that if you aren't a patient man, then maybe baking isn't for you."

I'm in the middle of wiping off the flour from his cheek when I feel his fingers wrap around my wrist, stopping my movement. I look up to see his eyes on me, his brown eyes only focused on me.

"Believe me, Gabrielle, I'm very patient. And I'm getting better at it every day."

I swallow the sudden lump in my throat as I'm unable to look away from his heated gaze. I also don't miss the double meaning of his words. I know he wants more. He's been more than clear about that. Sure, he said he could be friends, and I *do* want that, but the connection between us isn't going to go away—as much as I want it to.

And as much as I want to pull away, I can't. And as much as I want to say I don't want it, if he leaned in right now, I'd let him kiss me.

I want to let him. I want to feel the way I felt in Vegas. I want to know if the magic we created was regulated to that specific bubble in that specific time.

I can't. I want to. But I know I can't open that box back up.

"It's a good quality to have," I say, desperately needing to fill the empty silence.

"So I've heard." Neither of us move. His fingers are still wrapped around my wrist. Our eyes are still unwavering. The only thing that has changed is that I'm pretty sure I feel his dick getting hard and I know something is happening to me just from a look and the moment. "Want to know what another good one is?"

"What's that?"

"Understanding."

His head drops slightly, bringing our foreheads together. "I'll always try. Always."

God, he's a good one. Sure, he's young and a little bit of a puppy with his energy. But at the same time, he has this old soul that makes me sometimes forget that I could've babysat him in another life. And when his brown eyes take me in? When he flashes that dimple? When he touches me in any sort of way? I forget everything. My name. Our ages. That I'm freshly divorced. All of it.

I hate all of this.

I'm a second from saying "fuck it" and kissing him like I want, but it's at that moment I'm scared shitless by a bag of flour falling from a shelf and landing with a loud "thud."

"There. All cleaned up," I say, quickly dabbing off the last little bit of flour on his cheek before I step away and hustle over to the rogue flour. I need out of the Maddox bubble before I do something dumb like I was about to do. "You probably didn't lose that much flour. I can add in a little more so we don't let the batch go to waste."

"Sounds good," he says, noticeably clearing his throat before walking toward the table where we ate dinner earlier. "Mind if I turn on some music?"

"Not at all," I say as I do my best to eyeball how much flour I need to replace from what exploded into his face. "Pick whatever you'd like."

I'm not quite sure of Maddox's taste in music. I expect a rap song that I have no clue what they're saying. But to my surprise, it's a country song that takes me back to the very first day Sugar and Sweets opened.

I don't think I slept a wink the night before we opened. I should've. I was exhausted. I, along with Beau and the construction crew he hired, had been working extremely long hours to get the place running.

When I walked through these doors at four in the morning, ready to bake for the first official day, I remember the feeling of freedom. I stood in the kitchen, surrounded by ovens and mixers, and closed my eyes and let the feeling warm over me. I let myself memorize the moment when I was becoming the person I wanted to be. To have the chance at the dream I'd always dreamed of.

And then I turned on the music. It was this song playing. A song about starting over. It felt like fate. I didn't sing along with it. Sure, I wanted to, but at that moment, I needed to take it in. And I'm glad I did. It let me live in the moment. The moment where I knew that I was now living my dream the way I wanted to.

But more importantly, I smiled.

In that singular moment of happiness, I knew that all the hardships of the divorce and leaving Justin were one-hundred-percent worth it.

"That one's my favorite."

Maddox's words snap me out of my daydream. "Your favorite what?"

"Smile," he says, his own shy smile making an appearance. "The one where you don't realize anyone's watching you."

I really need this man to stop saying things like that or else this friend thing is going to go out the window.

I don't respond, because what do I say to that? Instead, I go back to working on the batter. I feel my heart rate starting to come down a little, but that's when I see in my periphery, Maddox doing some sort of dance.

"You can line dance?"

His moves become even more exaggerated. "When you grow up in the cornfields of Iowa, you can't help but get a little country in your blood. Between that and moving to Nashville as an adult, might as well throw a cowboy hat on me and get me some boots. Yee-haw, motherfuckers."

I laugh at his now ridiculous line dancing, while doing my best to not picture him in a cowboy hat, fitted jeans, and boots, because that visual should be illegal.

Or worse. Me riding him in said cowboy hat.

"Are you a country fan?" he asks.

"Of course," I say, probably too quickly since I'm trying to finish mixing the batter and getting X-rated thoughts out of my head. "I'm a girl from Louisiana. It's that and southern rap. Those are the options."

"I've always wanted to go to Mardi Gras," Maddox says.

"I'm sure you have," I say teasingly. "I was born closer to Baton Rouge, but Mardi Gras is something that every Louisianan has experienced."

"Is it one of those things that as you grow older, you get more tired of it because you've known it your whole life?"

"Kind of," I say. "When we were kids, the daytime parades were always fun and a little bit more family friendly. But as we got older and we started learning about the real parties, we all couldn't wait for that first time we could end up on Bourbon Street."

"I would've totally snuck down there."

"Oh I did. I was seventeen. By far the most rebellious thing I've ever done."

God it was fun. It was my group of friends from high school, including Shelby and Hannah. Actually, Shelby orchestrated it. Hannah panicked the whole time that we were going to get caught. The guys we went with, including Justin, were drunk from the moment we pulled out of the gas station parking lot we met at. We were young and wild and free. We didn't know about true hardships. Or loss. Or that the boy you were holding hands and dancing with on Bourbon Street would one day devastate you in ways you didn't think imaginable.

"Did you get caught?" Maddox asks.

"Yes and no. Our parents knew, but we didn't get in trouble. Sneaking out for Mardi Gras is a rite of passage. They knew they couldn't say a thing to us because they did the same thing when they were our age."

"Do you go back often for it?"

"Not really. I did in college—you know, when we were legally old enough to drink. But after a while, like you said, it kind of lost its luster."

"When was the last time you went back?"

"Jeez… maybe eight, nine years ago? Justin and I…"

I trail off as I think about that night. We went to visit family and friends. A group of guys we went to high school with were going down for the night, so we tagged along. I ended up getting sick and passing out before nine o'clock. He stumbled in around four in the morning smelling like a perfume that wasn't mine.

I chalked it up to old friends, crowded bars, and the party that is Mardi Gras.

He'll never admit it, but I'm convinced that was the first time he cheated.

"Can I ask you a question?" Maddox asks, walking back toward me as I turn off the stand mixer.

"Sure."

"Why did you stay here?"

"Why did I stay where?"

"Nashville. Your family is in Louisiana. Hannah is there, right? Why did you stay in a city that you lived in because of him?"

I stop what I'm doing and wipe my hands on a towel, assuming the same position as him with my backside against the table. "I know that's what it seems like on the outside, but that's only because he had the career first. He was always going to make more money than me once his schooling was over. That doesn't mean he has more of a claim to us being here."

We start rolling our cookies, working side by side. I don't mind sharing this story with him, but not having to look him in the eye will make it so much easier.

"Vanderbilt was actually my idea, Justin came along for the ride." I scoff as I realize that was the last time he went along with one of my ideas. "I'm sure when I started looking at colleges, I convinced myself coming here was because of the school. That it was the right college to attend for a would-be business woman and a doctor. But in reality, I'd always had a love for Nashville.

"Being a music fan, I adored the idea that any night of the week I could be out and hear someone singing who could one day be accepting a Grammy. I loved that when you got off the plane at the airport there was live music."

"The guy out front of Tootsies in the airport is really good," he adds. "Heard him sing Tennessee Whiskey once and I swore it was actually the real singer."

"Exactly. My parents brought me here when I was eight and I'd been enamored with it ever since."

I turn to look at Maddox, and to my surprise, he's also looking at me. Hanging on to every word I say.

"I was going to make this work no matter what. Because in reality, I'm the reason he's here in the first place. And like hell if I'm going to leave."

"Fuck yeah," he says. "Good for you standing your ground."

"Thanks," I say as I turn my attention back to the cookies. "Okay, into the oven for nine minutes."

"Nine minutes?" he asks as he puts the trays in the oven. "Why not ten?"

"Because eight isn't enough and ten's too many."

"Yes ma'am," he says with a mock salute as we walk back over to the table where our things are. I grab the Coke Zero and take a sip while Maddox sits across from me.

"So since you've been in Nashville a lot longer than me, what are your favorite things to do here?"

I think about his question for a second, and immediately feel a sense of gloom. "Is it sad that I don't know?"

"Depends on why you don't know."

I take another sip before setting it down as I gather my thoughts. "Because I've never gotten to experience this city like I wanted to."

Maddox leans forward on his elbows. "Why not?"

"In college I was working two jobs and going to school. The option for night life wasn't in the budget for me."

"I'm guessing it was for douche bag?"

That makes me smile. "Of course it was. He always found a way to head out with his friends—especially during undergrad. After graduation, if we went out, it was mostly whatever he wanted to do. And it was never things I wanted to do. I've never been to the Opry or to the Ryman. I've never been to a Fury game or any sporting event for that matter. Heck, I've only been on the rooftop at Tootsies once. What kind of Nashville-ite am I with that kind of resume?"

"The roof is crowded, you aren't missing a lot," Maddox says with a wink. "But the Fury game? That's unforgivable."

"I know, I hear they're pretty good," I tease.

"Are you going to go do those things?"

I shrug. "I want to. Maybe. Eventually. When things settle down."

"Or you could start now," he says. "No better time than the present."

"I know, but I don't have anyone to go with. And I know I should feel empowered enough to take myself to a concert, but it's… I don't know… unsettling."

"Ahem," he coughs, making overdramatic gestures to himself. "I'm right here."

"You'd go with me?" I ask, raising an eyebrow.

"Of course. What else are best friends for?"

How could I forget? "Really? Because one of the things I want to do next Christmas is walk through the lights at Opryland. You'd do that?"

"Are you kidding me? I fucking love Christmas. I'll drive the damn sleigh." As the words leave his mouth, I watch a lightbulb go off above his head. Not really, but the way his brown eyes light up it might as well have. "Oh! Let's make a list!"

Like a whirlwind, Maddox reaches over for the book bag he brought and pulls out a… notebook?

"Do you always carry around a random notebook?"

"In season, yes. For plays and to take notes in meetings. I know everything is on tablets these days, but I like making hand-written notes. Helps me remember."

"You really are a forty-year-old in a twenty-four-year-old body."

"Guilty as charged," he says as he opens up a page. "I brought this today so I could write down the recipes and any notes. Which I need to jot down the thing about not too much flour at a time and the nine minutes. But! We can take a page and start making date night ideas."

I raise an eyebrow. "Maddox..."

He looks back at me with an equally challenging look. "Gabrielle."

The fact that he always comes back with my full name when I say his like he's in trouble, is both endearing and frustrating all at the same time. Endearing because it's him. Frustrating because I know he's about to charm me into something.

"I told you. No dates. I can't date you."

"Dates? Did I say dates? That must've been someone else." He waves me off like I was hearing things. "I meant friend dates. I forgot a word. Silly me. Old hypothetical age and all. Makes me forget things."

I laugh under my breath. "Listen, this is sweet but—"

"But nothing," he says. "Call them friend dates. Call them hangouts. Make up a word, for all I care. What I want you to do is write down nine things you want to do from now until the end of the year. I'll add on any ideas I have. And this is going to be our Best Friend Activities Book."

I look down at the notebook then back up to Maddox. God, this man... his smile is big and there's a twinkle in his eyes. I know I questioned whether or not I could be friends with a man who I've one: slept with; two: who has feelings for me; and three: smells really good which doesn't help the fact that I'm apparently now a horny woman. But the genuine smile he's giving me right now... I don't know how I can say no.

"Nine things?" I ask.

"Yup. Because eight isn't enough, and ten is too many."

As if on cue, my phone alarm goes off, alerting me that the cookies are done.

"Oh! Let me get them!" Maddox says, jumping up with all the energy of a golden retriever.

"Don't forget the oven mitts!" I call out.

He comes to a screeching stop, grabbing the mitts that I leave next to the oven, as he opens it and pulls out two trays of over-sized chocolate chip cookies.

"Holy shit! I did it!" he exclaims. "I mean, you helped. But I made cookies!"

I laugh as I watch his excitement, before looking down again at his notebook.

I need to say no. Tell him thanks, and that his heart is in the right place, but that this is a little much.

Except I know damn well I'm not going to.

CHAPTER 13
MADDOX

"Phyllis! Kitty! Two of my favorite girls. How are we doing on this beautiful March day, besides looking as gorgeous as ever?"

My words make the two older women blush, but Gabi rolls her eyes as she takes their plates away. I'll admit, that first day these two had me off my game. But since then? I've been able to charm them a little more each time.

And I'm ready each time Phyllis pinches my ass. She's got strong fingers.

"How's our favorite hotty doing today?" Phyllis asks, patting the seat next to her for me to sit down. "We haven't seen you in a while."

"I know, and I'm sorry," I say. It's been over a week since I've been here, which was the same day as my baking lesson. I feel guilty as hell about that. "I'm trying to negotiate a new contract so I can buy you two all the baked goods you could ever want. Those kinds of talks take time."

"Oh you," Kitty says, giving my arm a slap. "Nonetheless, it's good to see you."

"Good to see you, too."

The last week has been an odd chaos of random things that

have kept me busier than I'd like to be in the offseason. There were a good amount of contract negotiation meetings, but my agent and the team lawyers are finalizing my new four-year deal as we speak. I'm not the highest paid safety in the league, but if I keep going the way I have been my first four years, come time for the next contract, I could be.

On top of that, every single offseason commitment I had seemed to be scheduled over the past week. A few days with my charity; meetings with some of the companies that I have endorsements with; shooting a commercial for one of those. Sure, all of those are good for my bank account, but they're bad when it comes to seeing the one person I want to see every day.

Actually, maybe it's good that I've been away. Not because I don't like spending time with her, but because I like spending time with her too much. And the more time I spend with her, the more I want to kiss her.

And I can't do that. That's not what friends do.

So, yeah, maybe time away was for the best.

Oh, who am I kidding? I'm a smiling fool right now as I watch her come out of the kitchen, carrying a tray of brownies. Her apron is tied around her waist, there's floury patches scattered randomly on her body, and the shirt she's wearing isn't supposed to be sexy, but it's giving a peek at her cleavage, and I swear I might cry they look so good.

"Jaw up, Maddox," Kitty says with a slap on my leg. "They're just boobs."

Damn. This is what I'm reduced to. Staring at her tits like I'm a horny teenager. Also, are they bigger?

"Sorry," I say, turning away from Gabi and all thoughts of her lips and her boobs. "So what's new with you two?"

Both of them simultaneously raised eyebrows. "Small talk, Maddox? You're better than that."

I shrug at Kitty's words. "It was worth a try."

"Let's try again," Phyllis says. "Be real with us. Is this a physical thing? No judgment if it is. We just need to know what direction you want to take this so we can make sure to push her the right way."

God I love these women. I'm going to need to find out when their birthdays are. I have a feeling they'd love it if some of the Fury players dropped by for their parties.

"It was. But it's not now," I admit. "It's just… she…"

I've never been one to stutter over my words. Every team I've ever been on has loved me because of how easy I am with the media—giving the right answer while also not giving away too much. But in this moment, I can't articulate out loud what Gabi is to me.

Sure, I'm very attracted to her physically. That's obvious to anyone with eyes. But it's more than that. It's her smile. Her laugh. The way she interacts with customers. The way she can be so vulnerable at times, but I also know she's also the woman who randomly jumped on stage to dance to a song with a complete stranger. The way her voice and stage presence captivated an audience. She's the woman who I want to get to know better, whatever way she'll let me.

"We get it," Kitty says, gently patting my arm. "And so you know, she's happy when you're here."

I turn to where Gabi's standing at the glass case, grabbing the bear claw I didn't ask for yet. "You think?"

"Oh yes," Phyllis says. "Every time someone walks in, her face is a little hopeful when she turns to see who it is, and it's always a little sad when it's not you."

"But today? Today it was a smile that she tried to hide. But we saw it," Kitty adds. "Because we see everything."

"Well I appreciate the kind words," I say, needing to not let my brain, or my heart, get excited over a smile. "But unfortunately, we're just friends."

"Horse shit," Kitty grumbles. "You can't be friends with someone you've seen naked. It's not right."

"I bet that's why she smiles," Phyllis adds. "If I saw this guy naked I'd be smiling every day."

Yes, I can handle these two better than I could day one, but then they go and say shit like this and I feel my cheeks flush in point-two seconds.

"I've also seen her ex," Phyllis says. "And I'm not one to judge a person's taste—different strokes for different folks and all that—but he's not you. Definitely doesn't have your ass."

If I had water, I'd be choking on it right now. "Phyllis!"

"What! It's true. He's a scrawny little man. I bet he has a little—"

"Okay that's enough," I say, needing this conversation to stop because I don't know where it's going, and though I love knocking the fuckhead, I feel like it's a train about to go off track.

Kitty leans over and puts her hands on my elbow. "What my uncouth friend is trying to say is that our girl has been through it. We're pretty good at overhearing things, and we overhead a lot during the divorce. That ex? He's a real piece of work. He screwed her up good."

"She's told me a little," I say. "For the record, I'm not a fan of him either."

"Oh you could take him," Phyllis says with a wink. "Please be good to her. That's all we ask for. That and to see a few more butts in these seats. But we'll take you making her smile."

"And that's all I want to do," I say. "I want to make her smile every day."

"Well shit," Kitty says. "That's so sweet I'm going to cry."

"Oh no, there's no crying around baked goods," I say, trying to change the mood. "Unless they're that good."

"Is that my new slogan?" Gabi asks as she sets down my bear claw and a bottle of water. "What are you three yapping about?"

"Oh nothing," Phyllis says as she scoots back her chair. "Thank you again Gabi for a lovely afternoon. We need to get going to make it back in time for bingo."

"We don't have bingo today," Kitty says. "It's Friday. We don't do bingo on—"

Phyllis slaps Kitty's arm. "Yes Kathleen, we do. Don't you remember they moved it?"

Phyllis stares down Kitty in a way that's not discreet in the least of what she's trying to pull here, especially when she adds the obvious looks from me, to Gabi, back to me.

"Oh that's right!" Kitty says. "You two have fun. Time for bingo! Now, don't do anything we wouldn't do."

I stand to help her up and get both of their coats on. "Why do I have a feeling that's not a very long list?"

"Because it's not," Phyllis says. "See you tomorrow, Gabi. Maddox, hope to see you too."

In true Phyllis fashion, she gives my butt a squeeze before she and her sidekick make their way out of the bakery.

"I don't know whether to laugh or press charges," I say as I sit back down.

"I love them, and they're pretty much keeping my business open right now, but one day they're going to flirt with the wrong guy and it's going to be very, very bad."

"I mean, some men like older women," I say with an exaggerated eyebrow wag. "I would know."

My shameless flirting only earns me an eye roll. "So what brings you here today?"

Not a shut down. Not encouragement. I'll take it. "Just wanted to see you. I had the day free, which hasn't happened a lot lately, so I thought I'd stop in and say hi. I hope I'm not interrupting your day."

"Well, hi," she says, a relaxed smile coming across her face. "And no interruptions. It's been pretty slow, which means I'm all caught up."

I think back to the comment that Phyllis said about wanting to see more people in here. I've never come in during the morning hours, but each time I'm here in the afternoon, it's always slow. I've chalked it up to the time of day. But is it more?

"Can I ask you a personal-ish question?"

"You can. I might not answer."

I lean down closer, wanting to whisper even though we're the only two in here. "Are you… is the bakery… doing okay?"

I hate to ask her this, but I like fixing things. Give me a task to do and I'm your guy. On the football field, it's to either take away the ball or make sure the opponent doesn't score. I'm not sure exactly what I can do yet, but if she needs it, well… I have an offseason of free time to do it. And I'm very good when I have a task. Keeps the squirrel brain calm.

"It's… fine," she says, but by the way the word comes out a little defeated—and growing up with a sister—I know that doesn't mean fine. "Could it be busier? Sure. We usually get a decent crowd in the morning. By lunch, it's pretty much fizzled. It's not doing bad enough yet that my brother is threatening to shut it down, but I don't know how much profit he's making."

"Would he shut you down?" I ask. "Wait. You have a brother? Who owns the bakery?"

A soft smile comes across her face at the mention of her brother. "He'd never. He knows this is my dream. He's living his, and he wants me to have mine."

"And this was it?"

She nods with a smile. "I was always baking with my mom and meemaw. I loved coming up with new recipes, or adding different flavors and putting spins on things."

"Sounds like this was your calling."

"I wanted it to be. But sometimes you don't have the luxury to chase dreams. And for many years, I thought I didn't."

I feel my fists clenching as Gabi talks about her ex and how much she hated her job. How much he dicked her around for years about opening the bakery.

One punch. That's all I'd need…

"So that's when Beau stepped in," she says. "In a matter of weeks he was buying a building, he was telling me a name to put on the business license, and Sugar and Sweets was born."

"Sounds like a pretty good guy."

"The best," she says with a smile. "Protective over me, my mom, and anyone he loves. Competitive to high heaven. But most of all? He's smart and a little calculated. But maybe more than all of those? Is that he hated my ex-husband. Getting to open this bakery not only gave me my dream, but it was a good middle finger to him. Hell, he might've done it for that reason alone."

"I love that. Sometimes we're not petty enough."

That makes Gabi laugh. "Petty and spite. Maybe that should've been the name of the bakery instead of Sugar and Sweets."

I laugh but shake my head. "Nah. I think you hit the nail on the head with this place. You should be proud Gabi. It's amazing."

"Thanks," she says, a blush coming across her face like it does any time I give her a compliment. "Though I don't know if you should keep eating here. "

"Why is that?"

She signals down to my bear claw. "Keep eating those, and anything else you get me to teach you to bake, and you're going to be out of shape for next season."

I wave her way. "My dietitians know about my sweet tooth. Plus, it's the off season. I'm allowed to indulge."

"But what about when the season starts? Are you still going to be averaging three bear claws a week?"

"Oh, it'll go up to five," I say with a wink. "Especially if I start the season with an interception every game."

"I can see it now," Gabi says, her hands pretending to unveil a billboard. "My new advertising slogan: Come to Sugar and Sweets. Get a bear claw. Play like Maddox Gallagher."

Holy shit… my future wife and current friend is not only gorgeous, but she's a genius too.

"That's it!" I shout, grabbing my phone out of my back pocket and handing it to Gabi. "Will you take a picture of me please?"

"What are you doing?" she asks, very confused, as I hold up the bear claw to my face as I prepare to take a massive bite.

"Take my picture!" I say with the pastry half in my mouth. "Mmmm, so fucking good."

"I have no clue what the hell is going on."

I don't reply to her, instead throwing on a filter that I'm known to use, and type a few words out, but I can feel her eyes on me.

"There we go. Perfect!"

"Maddox…"

Yup. The stern way she says my name. I fucking love it.

"Gabrielle…"

She's giving me a look like a few of my teachers did when I was in school. Like I've been very bad and she wants to make sure I know it, but I'm still not going to get punished

It's a little hot. If she would be wearing her glasses right now I'd be saying fuck this friends bullshit and I'd be eating her out under this table.

"Maddox, I asked you what you're doing?"

I finish typing my caption, and hit post, before looking at a very concerned Gabi. "Testing out the new ad campaign."

Smiles.

All smiles.

Because Gabi has a line out the door.

Fuck yes.

I should've known something was happening when I had to

park three blocks away from the bakery. Then I turned the corner and the line.

I fucking love this for her. I love that I was able to make it happen with one social media post. But mostly? I love that I know for a fact these people are going to be returning customers because no way they're going to have one of her baked goods and not want more.

When I make it to the sidewalk, I hear people whispering, wondering if it's me walking next to them. Any question of my identity is thrown out the window when one woman yells "Holy shit! Maddox Gallagher! He really does eat here!"

"I do," I say to her as I pose for a selfie. "The bear claws are awesome, but really you can't go wrong with anything. I hope you all enjoy!"

I squeeze through the door, which no one bats an eye about, as I stand against the back wall and look on at the craziness. Every time I've been in, it's usually only Phyllis, Kitty, and a few random other customers. But now if the two elderly women tried to come in they wouldn't be able to find a place to sit. Every table is being used and there's a host of people standing to the side waiting for their orders. Two college-aged girls are working behind the counter who I've never seen before.

Then there's Gabi, who's looking as frazzled and beautiful as ever. Her hair's more of a mess than normal. She normally has traces of flour on her, but it looks like she just walked out of the bag. But that's not stopping her from taking the time to talk to each customer, thanking them for coming in today and apologizing for things she was out of. Her smile is ear to ear, and I don't know if I've ever seen anything, or anyone, more beautiful.

Fuck I have it bad…

Gabi catches me staring across the room and I give her a small wave. I purposely don't walk over, not wanting to get anyone in a tizzy if I cut the line. But when she gives me a nod, signaling me to meet her at the end of the counter, I push off the wall and make quick work of the space between us.

"Seems as if the new advertising campaign worked," she says with a smile that's as big as I've ever seen it. "It's been like this all day. I'm going to run out of everything in an hour if it keeps up like this and it's barely noon."

"That's a good problem to have, right?"

Though by the worried look in her eye, I'm not sure it is.

"I mean it is," she says. "And don't get me wrong, it's a problem I never thought I'd have. But at the same time, I hate feeling like I let people down."

"I get that," I say, suddenly getting an idea. "Are there things you could bake quickly so you could at least have something to sell?"

My suggestion takes her by surprise. "I mean sure. I could do some basic cookies and cupcakes. Brownies and easy recipes. But I'm needed out here to help the girls."

"No you aren't," I declare, clapping my hands together. "I'll help."

Her eyebrows shoot up. "You'll help?"

"Yeah," I say as I walk around the counter, grabbing a blue and white apron that's part of the uniform for Sugar and Sweets. "You go back and bake the treats. I'll help…"

"Lexi and Jada."

"I'll help Lexi and Jada with whatever they need. Or if you need me in the back, I'll be your helper."

Gabi looks at me for a second, assessing if I'm serious or not. "Are you sure?"

I nod and take her by the shoulders, turning her around toward the kitchen. "You go do what you do best. And I'll do the same."

She looks back over her shoulder. "And what's that?"

As I'm about to say something, I hear people yelling "Maddox!" with cameras coming out to take pictures of me in an apron.

"Giving the people what they want. And today, they want sweet treats served by Maddox Gallagher."

CHAPTER 14
MADDOX

I once played a college football game that went into six overtimes.

In high school I was a three-way player and most Friday nights I was on the field for every play of the game.

I'm a professional athlete who has his body slammed every Sunday by guys who don't fuck around in a weight room.

So tell me why I've never been so tired as I am right now after working at a bakery for six hours.

"Here Gallagher, you earned it."

I look over my shoulder to see Gabi—who looks tired, but not as tired as me—setting down a bottle of water and a bear claw. "I thought we sold out?"

"We did," she says as she sits across the table from me with her own treat. I notice she went with a jumbo brownie and her standard Coke Zero. "I might've put one aside for you earlier when I realized that suddenly the bear claw was going to be making a comeback among the Gen Z and millennial clientele."

"You did?" I say, trying to keep it cool, even though inside I'm doing cartwheels. "Being your favorite customer is starting to pay off."

She smiles as she uses a fork to cut off a piece of brownie. "I don't know if you're my favorite. Phyllis and Kitty are much more entertaining."

Those are the words that came out of her heart-shaped lips, but the smile on her face is saying that I'm in fact her favorite. I'm claiming it as another win. "Have you ever had a day like this?"

She shakes her head and sits back in her chair. "Never. Not even the grand opening. And I thought that day was insane."

Insane is an understatement. Normally, Gabi closes at five, and according to her, it's usually so slow that she's cleaned up and out of the door by five fifteen. Tonight we had to stay open until six to serve all the customers in line, and that was after cutting off new guests at four-forty-five. And even by that point, she was down to cupcakes, brownies, and a few cookies that made it through the day.

It was a sight to see. And I'm so damn happy for her.

"Well let me propose a toast." I hold up my bottle of water, and she does the same with her can of Coke Zero. "To the first of many successful days at Sugar and Sweets."

"Your mouth to God's ears," she says. "Thank you again. This… I don't have words."

"You're welcome, but you never have to thank me," I say. "I like to see good people—especially my friends—succeed. And if I can do anything to help make that happen, I make sure I do."

"As easy as that?" she asks.

"Yeah. Easy as that," I say. "There's too much shit in the world and too many people bringing others down. So when I can lift something or someone up, or help someone out, I do it."

She sits back, giving her head a little shake. "You're something else."

"In what way?"

"Oh let me count the ways," she says as she sits back in her chair. "You're a twenty-four-year-old professional football player who eats bear claws. You run a STEM program for kids and also take your free afternoons during a time when most football players are probably hibernating to work unpaid at a bakery."

"Whoa! I'm not getting paid!" I tease.

"Sorry. Should've told you that up front."

"Can I work for baked goods?"

"Obviously."

"Well then we're just fine."

We share a smile before she continues on.

"Then there's your personal life. You're insistent on being my friend even though I know you want more. On the other hand you've been called the playboy of the Fury, have multiple videos of you singing karaoke on the internet, and were rumored to be dating a country star last year. I've run the numbers and frankly, that math doesn't math."

"Someone Googled me..." I add in a wink to go with my little tease. Also I don't miss that she made mention about my feelings. I don't know if it's good or bad, but I'm going to go with the vibes that it was a good thing.

"It was a long plane ride home from Vegas," she says, before a shocked look comes over her face. Oh I have a feeling she wasn't supposed to say that quiet part out loud.

"Vegas?" I ask, suddenly very giddy about this new information. "You were reading about me on the way home from Vegas?"

Her face flushes into a color that rivals a cherry tomato. It's cute as hell. "I might've... I was a little curious as to who you were."

"Sure..." I tease as I lean in closer. "But the most important question, is were you wearing my clothes while you did it?"

My question was to push her a little more, or if anything she could give me one of her eye rolls that I secretly love. I wasn't expecting her to bite her bottom lip. Or for her face to flush.

"Gabrielle..." I think it's the first time in our short history that I've said her name first. It's also the first time since we've been in Nashville that I feel the sexual tension this thick between us. And it's been thick. "Did you keep my clothes on when you flew back?"

She slowly nods. "I couldn't take them off."

"Do you still wear them?"

She nods, the blush coming back across her cheeks. "The T-shirt. To bed."

I don't mean to let out a groan, but I can't keep it in. The thought of Gabi wearing my T-shirt then—and now—has me fucking hard in an instant. I know I told her to keep the clothes, but I figured because she was so adamant about giving them back that they were sitting in a drawer. Never in my wildest dreams did I think she was wearing them regularly.

Great. Now I'm jealous of a piece of fabric.

"Maddox…"

"Gabrielle…"

Normally our little standoff comes when Gabi is trying to make a point. But this is different.

My name on her lips was breathy. A plea. She's telling me to kiss her. Or to back away. I don't know which. I don't think she does either.

Fuck I want to. I want to take those lips and fuse them with mine. I want to taste her sweet mouth. I want to hold her face in my hands and kiss her until neither of us can breathe. I want to take her back to her place and have her put my T-shirt on only so I can take it back off—but not before I lick that sweet pussy while she wears it.

But I can't. I won't. She might want it, I for sure want it, but I want something more than that—I don't want her to regret it when it's over. She's been adamant about being not ready to move on, and I need to respect that.

Which is why I'm going to pull away. I'm going to swallow my want—and tell my cock to calm the fuck down—and walk away.

And I'm going to hate every second of it.

I tap my forehead to hers and hold it there for the longest second of my life before I slowly pull away.

"I need to go grab my phone." My voice cracks at my clear lie. "I left it in the back."

She knows it's a weak excuse, but she doesn't call me on it. "Okay."

That one word is barely a sad whisper as I start to walk away, my head hanging, before I hear Gabi call my name.

"Maddox?"

I turn back around before I push through the door to the kitchen. "Yeah?"

"Thank you."

I slowly nod in acknowledgment, glad I made the right decision, but don't say anything else as I walk back into the kitchen and immediately press my hands into one of the prep tables.

Fuck!

I want to scream it out but I don't. I don't want to freak her out more than she probably already is, and really, that shout would be at myself, not her.

Because what in the actual fuck was I thinking when I said that I could be friends with this woman? What? Did I think because I was admitting that I still had feelings that I was beating the psychology of all of this? I mean for fuck's sake… the first thing I ever thought about her when she walked up on stage with me was that I loved her. She's still in my phone as "future wife."

All I know is that I need to get a hold of myself. Figure out how to either bide my time until she's ready for the next step or navigate how to be around Gabi while respecting that we can only be friends. All of this while also not dying from a combination of confusion, stupidity, heartbreak, and blue balls.

My head is down as I take a few deep breaths to try and calm myself down, when I hear the back door of the bakery open.

"Hello? Who's here? Why are the fucking lights on?"

My guard immediately goes up when the sound of a

booming male voice echoes off the walls. As soon as he's done screaming, I hear the back door slam shut. I don't say anything—you don't tell the murderer where you're at for him to come and get you—but my eyes are wide and my breathing picks up. I want to warn Gabi that someone's here, but I also don't want to lead the would-be burglar and/or murderer straight to her. So I do the next best thing I can think of—I look for a weapon to protect myself and the woman I'm mildly obsessed with.

I'm scrambling as the stranger keeps yelling out warnings for me to come out and show myself. Does he think I'm the intruder? He's the one breaking in after hours, likely to either rob or murder me. Which is why I need something to protect myself with.

Yes. There it is. The biggest wooden dough roller I've ever seen in my life. I joked with Gabi earlier that she could knock someone out with this when she asked me to hand it to her. Little did I know I was foreshadowing the future.

I use both hands to pick it up by one of the ends, positioning it above my head so I'm ready to strike down whoever's about to come around the corner. I'm in a baseball stance, staring at the hallway when I see the figure slowly walking toward me.

"Maddox Gallagher? What the fuck are you doing here?"

It takes me a second to register who's looking at me. Because what the hell is one of the best golfers in the world doing walking into Gabi's bakery?

"Beau Devereaux?"

I blink a few times, even though I know my eyes aren't playing tricks on me. Because seriously, what the fuck is Beau doing at Gabi's bakery?

Beau… Gabi's brother is named Beau… what are the fucking odds…

I've met Beau a handful of times at various events around the city. He and I, along with Linc and a lot of other athletes in Nashville, share an agent, so many times we're found at the same charity functions or press events. We also both have endorsements from one of the top shoe companies in the world, so seeing Beau isn't uncommon.

But seeing him at a bakery is.

"What the hell are you doing here after hours?" I ask in confusion as I finally get my wits about me. I mean, it is his bakery, but the timing still strikes me as odd.

"The better question is what the fuck are you doing here? And why are you wearing a fucking apron?"

Damn. I know we're both confused about the situation but his tone is so aggressive. Then again I'm still holding the rolling pin. Which is my only line of defense against the six-foot-three golfer who never misses arm day, can drive the ball three-hundred-and-fifty-yards routinely, and is looking at me right now like he could take me out with one punch.

And I might be a professional football player, but even I know in this instance, I don't stand a chance. You don't fuck with a brother who is looking at you like he knows you fucked his sister. Even with the rolling pin.

"I was helping Gabi out today. She was busy. Is that why you're here?"

Beau doesn't answer, instead starts slowly pacing in a circle around me like I'm his prey.

Am I prey? I've never been prey. I've never even been in a fight. I'm a lover, not a fighter.

"You know I didn't think of it when I saw the videos of you and my sister after Vegas," he says slowly. "I was just glad my sister had a nice time with her friends."

"They were great," I say, trying to ease the tension. "Hannah. Shelby—"

The way his head snaps toward me is enough to make me jump back. "I wasn't done."

"Apologies." I sit down on the stool like I'm getting yelled at in the principal's office. I mean, it's not a far stretch considering Beau has about thirteen years on me.

"As I was saying, I'm glad she had fun. She deserves it. And if that included partying with some football guys, then so be it. I knew most of you. We're all Nashville athletes. And for the most part, y'all are pretty good guys."

"Thanks?" I say, though I don't know if he's referring to me in this instance based on his tone and glare.

"Then I saw the videos of you and her," he continues, which is when I know I'm not in the good guy category. "Seeing my sister sing like that, it was a sight to see. Her fucking asshole ex was a piece of work and I hadn't seen her that happy in a while."

"For the record, I hate him too and I don't know him," I quickly say, feeling like I need as many brownie points as possible.

"Noted. But that doesn't change the fact that I couldn't help but notice how you were flirtin' with her. How she was smilin' at you. How you were lookin' at her. You'd have to be blind to miss that."

He's not wrong. I have the videos and photos. One might be my screen background.

"And now… here you are in her kitchen. In my kitchen! Wearing an apron. And I know we don't know each other well Gallagher, but I know that a man doesn't come down and work at a bakery because he's bored. Especially a guy with your kind of reputation."

I hold up my hands in defense. "I get where you're coming from. Or what you're probably thinking. But Beau, I promise you, I have nothing but good—"

"What in the hell is going on back here!"

Gabi comes storming through the kitchen, eyes big and purely focused on Beau. I've said from the first moment that I love this woman. But with her timing at this moment, I fucking *love* her.

"Beau? What are you doing here?"

I let out a breath, happy that I don't think he's going to kill me in front of his sister, and that I'm not the only one weirded out about why he's here more than an hour after closing time without any notice.

"Me… I…" Beau is stumbling over the question, which probably has something to do with the daggers Gabi is staring into him. "I came in to get a few invoices. Why are you both here and why is Maddox my newest employee?"

"Maddox saved my day today," she says with authority and I can't help but puff out my chest a little bit at her words. "We were slammed all day today. If it wasn't for him I don't know how we would've made it."

"Really?" He looks back and forth between the two of us. "I mean, that's great. I'm thrilled for you. But why was it so busy?"

I look out of the corner of my eye to Gabi, who's giving me the same look.

"It's also because of Maddox," she says with a smile that hits me straight in the heart.

"Maddox?" Beau says, clearly a little confused.

"He made a post about the bakery yesterday on his Instagram. When I went to open the doors this morning, I already had a line. It didn't stop at all during the day. It took us more than an hour after normal closing to get everyone through. It was… the most amazing day."

My heart doubles in size looking at the smile on Gabi's face. Yes, I've always made sure to help others when I can. It's one of those things my mom drilled into me early as a child. But what I did today with one picture, seeing how Gabi is lighting up talking about her business and the success, I don't know if a feeling will ever top this.

"So you let him post on Instagram for you?" Beau shouts, giving Gabi and I both a jump scare. "He can post about this place but when I offer you tell me you don't want to use my name for clout?"

"That's different," Gabi snaps back, stepping up to her brother who has more than a foot on her in height, but that isn't deterring her.

"How?"

"Because I didn't tell her what I was doing," I say, needing to defend myself, and Gabi. "I took a picture and posted it. You think I don't know how stubborn she is? How she'd never let me do it if I told her? So I asked for forgiveness instead of permission. Do you have a problem with that?"

Beau and I eye each other, and he may have a few inches on me—and also by the looks of it has a better arm workout than I do—but I'm not backing down. He seems to realize this as I watch him rub the back of his neck as his breathing calms down.

"I'm not sorry I did it," I go on. "Gabi deserves to have that kind of line every day and if I can make it happen from one post, then I'm going to do it."

"Well that we can agree on," Beau says before turning back to Gabi. "I'm sorry I blew up. I'm so fucking happy for you. You know I want you to have every bit of success in the world, right?"

"I know," she says, stepping into her brother's embrace. "I think we're all a little surprised by seeing each other and this got out of hand very fast. Can we start this all over?"

"Sure," he says as he gives her one more squeeze before letting go and turning to me and extending his hand. "I'm sorry Gallagher, but thank you. I know she's thankful for it and I am too."

I return his handshake. "I appreciate it."

We share a firm handshake before stepping back. When we do, Beau starts pointing back and forth between Gabi and I, his finger following his eyes. "So… are you two?"

I turn to Gabi, because no way in hell am I answering that to her brother who five seconds ago wanted to murder me.

"Maddox and I are friends," she says as she turns to look at me. "He's been a really, really, good friend."

I knew what she was going to say. I could've predicted it word for word. Doesn't make the sting any less potent.

The silence is interrupted by the ringing of the bakery phone.

"Can you two behave while I get that? I have no idea who is calling this late, so it might be a minute."

"Yes," we both say a little sheepishly. Neither of us say another word until the kitchen doors swing shut and the phone stops ringing.

"I need to apologize too," I say. "I didn't know who was coming in. I knew she had a brother and that he owned the bakery, but she never told me her last name. I didn't put two and two together."

"No worries," he says as we both take a seat at one of the prep stations. "Gabi doesn't want to use me or Shelby's name or notoriety for a leg up. Even though we'd both give it to her without a second thought. But that's Gabi, stubborn to do things her own way."

I chuckle. "I've picked up on that."

That makes Beau smile. "That's what I think set me off about her allowing you to do this. When we first opened, I told her I wanted to make calls to promote the bakery. Local media, some bloggers, that sort of thing. I was going to pitch it that I was opening a new bakery with my sister as the head pastry chef. Really sell that it was a family business. She refused. She wanted to build this business from the ground up with me being as silent of a partner as possible. And then here you come swooping in…"

"In my defense, I really didn't give her a choice. I took a picture and posted it before she even knew what I was doing."

"I'll keep that in mind the next time someone figures out I own this place and wants to do a story."

"Is she always this stubborn?" I ask. "Like I'm stubborn, but she's giving me a run for my money."

That makes him smile. "Since we were kids. And since the divorce started? It escalated times a thousand."

"Good to know," I say. "I brought her dinner the other night and I had to pretend that I let her pay me back."

This makes Beau laugh. "What'd you do with the money?"

"Slipped it back in the register. I'm sure at some point she noticed that she was twenty bucks over. But she at least didn't say anything."

Beau softens at my gesture. And for the first time since he came barreling in, I feel like he's not three seconds away from punching me.

This is the most I've ever talked to Beau in the years that I've casually known him. If we do ever talk, it's chit chat about our respective sports, mutual business acquaintances, that kind of thing. But even though I don't know the man well, I know for a damn fact that both of us care for Gabi, and right now that's all that matters.

"I'm gonna ask you a question, and I'm gonna really need you to be honest with me," Beau says.

"Shoot." Even though I have a feeling what's coming.

He clasps his hands together and leans his elbows on the table. "I know she said you're friends. I know you agreed. But I saw the Vegas videos. I also have eyes. I hate to put it in these terms, but I have to know… what are your intentions with my sister?"

If he had asked me this question when he first walked in, I would've probably lied, fumbled, and said anything to make sure that he wasn't going to murder me. And while I don't know if I can tell him the whole truth right now, I know I don't have to lie.

"I care about her," I begin. "I care about her a whole hell of a lot. But on that same note, I know she's not ready for anything."

"She told you about the divorce?"

I nod. "Enough for me to know that if he walked in here right now he'd be a bloody mess on the ground."

"Another thing we can agree on," he says with a smile. "So, you're really willing just to be her friend?

"I want her to be happy," I say. "I want her to smile every day, and if I can be a reason she does that, then that's good enough."

Beau gives me a knowing smile. "Can I give you a piece of advice?"

"Absolutely."

"Don't push her," he says. "Gabi was always so independent but lost that part of herself during her marriage. She's getting it back. She wants it back. If anything between you two ever happens, it's going to be because she says so. On her terms."

I smile, because for the first time in weeks, I strangely feel good about things. Because Beau isn't telling me to back off. Or to get the hell away from her. He might not have come out and given us his blessing, but he's not scaring me away either. "That I can do."

He laughs. "You're really willing to wait for her?"

All I can do is smile. "I'll wait forever."

CHAPTER 15
GABI

If there's one thing for certain when you're a resident of Nashville, it's that traffic is never going to cooperate with you. Need to be somewhere quickly? Don't worry: route 40 is going to make sure you're twenty minutes late.

Ugh! Just once I needed traffic to be smooth. I'm already a half hour late delivering cookies and cupcakes to Maddox's foundation. Then again, me running behind has been the story of my life for the past week.

Ever since Maddox's Instagram post last week, the bakery has been nonstop. Not as bad as it was that first day, but it's consistently steady, which has meant I needed to make changes, and fast. Jada and Lexi have gone from working a few days in the week, but just in the mornings, to splitting each morning and afternoon. I've even hired a few of their friends for some random hours here and there. I'm putting off hiring a second baker, but that's probably going to have to happen soon. Sure that means I'm barely sleeping, but it's fine. I enjoy the work. This is my dream. I refuse to complain about success, because who knows how long it's going to last.

What I will complain about is how fucking tired I am. Like so tired. Today was the worst, which is why I'm running late. I couldn't make myself get out of bed. I got to the bakery an hour late and an IV drip of Coke Zero wasn't going to help me today.

I inch the car forward, welcoming any movement in traffic, when my bluetooth signals a phone call from Shelby.

"Perfect timing," I say. "I'm sitting in traffic."

"Sounds like fun," she says in her deadpan way. "Wait. Why are you driving in the middle of the day? Shouldn't you still be at the bakery?"

"Yes I should be. But I need to make a delivery."

Please don't ask to who... please don't ask to who...

"Delivery? Who are you delivering to?"

Damnit. I shouldn't have said that. But I know even over the phone, she'll call me out if I try to lie.

"Maddox."

There's silence, but somehow I can hear her smile. "You don't say..."

"It's not like that."

"I never said it was."

"He's having a party for the kids at his foundation today and he ordered cookies and cupcakes. I was behind because of how busy I've been and I'm overly exhausted from this past week. So since they weren't done in time for him to pick them up, I offered to deliver them. That's it."

"Doth protest quite loudly," Shelby says. "Funny that I didn't ask anything and yet you felt the need to information dump."

"I was getting ahead of your follow-up question."

"Bold of you to assume I was going to have one," she says. "But since we're on the topic of Maddox, how is your boyfriend?"

"He's not my boyfriend," I say with a little too much fight.

"Ah... doth protesting again..."

"Why are you saying 'doth' so much?"

"It's a fun word. Try it sometime," she says. "Now, back to the good stuff. Has the youngin' asked you out again?"

I let my head fall into the window. "He hasn't."

"Are you disappointed in that?"

"What? No. Why would you ask that?"

"I don't know, maybe because you let out a sigh before you answered?"

"I did not sigh."

"Fine. I must be hearing things. No one sighed and he's not your boyfriend. Got it. All the words you're saying are one hundred percent the truth"

I might've sighed, but I'm not going to admit it. Because Maddox is the kind of guy who makes you sigh. I never would've thought to describe someone like that, but for Maddox, it fits.

I mean, what's there *not* to sigh about? Between his good looks, his demeanor, and the fact that he's a good person, the man is a real life heartthrob. And that's not even tapping into the memory of our night together. How safe I felt in his arms after pouring my heart out through a song. How I can still taste the tequila that lingered on his tongue. I can feel his hands holding onto me as he pinned me against the door. How my body came alive when he entered me for the first time.

And yes, I might've sighed a little because he hasn't asked me out again. I'm not even sure I can say yes. I mean, I can't. I know this. But does he even want to? Sure, there have been moments where I thought he wanted to kiss me. Little things he said. Is he really respecting my boundaries or did I push him too hard in the friend zone and now the opportunity might never come when I'm ready for it? If I'm ever ready for it?

So yeah… sigh.

"You know," Shelby says, breaking through my thoughts that were about to head into PG-13 territory. "You *could* date him if you wanted to."

That gets a laugh out of me. "You know I can't," I say, wondering why we're having this conversation again. We have it weekly during our calls with Hannah when she always tries to convince me to give Maddox a chance. "I've told both you and Hannah a dozen times I can't."

"Not really."

"What's that supposed to mean?"

"It means that you've said why you shouldn't. You've never told me why you *actually* can't."

"Because," I say, wondering what she needs me to repeat. "He's twenty-four."

"That's not a can't. He's a legal adult. Try again."

"Shelby, I could've babysat him."

"But did you?" she asks. "Because unless Iowa is somehow now a parish in Louisiana, you didn't."

"I'm talking in theory," I say, getting more flustered as traffic finally starts to inch forward. "But it's not just that. Do you not remember that I'm recently divorced?"

"I do. Thank fucking lord."

"So yeah."

She doesn't say anything for a moment. "So yeah what?"

"So yeah I can't date yet."

"Says who? Was there a clause in the divorce agreement that says you're banned from dating for a year? Because if so, that's some bullshit considering fuck face started dating other women while you two were still married."

"There's no clause. It's just…" I trail off because I don't know what I want to say. Because those are my reasons. They should matter. They do matter.

At least, I thought they did.

I shouldn't be ready to date, should I? Sure, the divorce was just finalized but we've been separated for more than two years. If it was anyone else telling me this timeline, I'd tell them to do what makes them happy.

Or *who* makes them happy.

"It's what?" Shelby asks.

"It's… am I ready?"

It's the first time I've said anything like that out loud, but it feels good to acknowledge the fear.

"Now that is a reason why you maybe, or maybe not, use the word can't," Shelby says. "How about this… let's break everything down."

"Always my analytical friend," I say with a half smile.

"Data never lies."

If there's one thing to know about Shelby, is that she looks at things from every angle, and usually has facts and examples to back things up. It helps her in the game of golf—what's the yardage? The angle of her shot? What club should she use for maximum outcome? What did she use the last time she was in a similar situation? She takes that approach to life too, which is nice to have when you're the friend that feels like she's slowly going out of control.

"Let's start off with basic questions, do you like him? And don't give me any qualifying reasons. It's a simple yes or no. Do you enjoy him as a person?"

I couldn't lie if I wanted to. "Yes."

"Do you like it when you spend time with him?"

"Yes."

"Do you want to fuck him again?"

"Shelby!"

"What? It's important for the data."

"I hate you," I say. "But the answer is yes."

"Don't hate me. Hate the facts," she says. "Okay, so based on our early data, results say you should give the guy a chance, or at least see if there's something there."

"Shocker. Your data is telling me something you wanted it to."

"You know that's not the case so quit being hard headed." I'm a proponent that you need different kinds of friends in your life. Ones who will hold your hand while you cry. Ones that will commit a felony with you. Ones that will tell you when the jeans make your butt look fat. Luckily for me, Shelby is all of those wrapped into one. "In all seriousness, I think you should give the guy a chance. Sure, the age thing might be a little weird, but only if you make it that way. Is there anything that he's done that's like 'whoa. You're too young. I can't fuck you again?'"

"Besides his hair cut?" I say, though my voice is light when I do. "I don't. He's… he's a good guy Shelby. He makes me smile. He supports the bakery. He makes me laugh. He brought me Coke Zero the other day because I was out. He has this ridiculous notebook of Best Friend Activity outings for us to do because he knows I'm not ready to date. He's…"

There's the sigh. I heard it that time.

"If you already didn't know the answer before, I think you do now."

She's right. I know she is.

"But am I ready for something? You're right, at the end of the day, I do like him. It's just… it's fucking scary Shelby."

"Of course it is," she says. "No one is saying it's not. Any relationship is scary. You'd be scared if he was three years older than you."

"That's true."

"Also, you know you don't have to marry every relationship you're in, right?"

I laugh. "In theory I do."

"In fact, I recommend you don't. Date. Have fun. Have some orgasms. It doesn't have to be serious."

"Says the woman who doesn't know what a serious relationship looks like."

"You got me on that one."

Shelby has never been one to settle down. In fact, I don't know if she's ever seriously dated anyone. If she has, she hasn't told me.

"I'm not sure what Maddox wants, or even what I want," I say, choosing my next words carefully. "But you're right. I do like him. I do want to try. And maybe… we take it slow."

Yes. Maybe. Okay. That sounds good. Would I love to be

brave like the woman I was in Vegas? Sure. She was fueled by champagne, spite, and a sequin dress. I'm sure she's still in me somewhere, but for now, we're going to channel a little of her courage and start things slow.

And for the first time in weeks, I feel a little lighter. A little happier.

"I think that's an amazing idea," Shelby says. "But maybe not slow on everything. Definitely sleep with him on the first date."

"I thought you weren't supposed to do that?"

"You don't count because you've already slept with him."

"I'm doing this all backward, aren't I?"

"Nah. Everyone does things different," she says. "Just make sure you tell Hannah before the date. Otherwise she'll cry that she didn't know."

"Sounds good," I say with a smile, and that's not because traffic is finally going the normal speed limit. "Okay, enough about me and my love life and my deliveries. What did I do to deserve a coveted phone call from Shelby LeBlanc?"

Shelby is more of a texting friend. The only reason she's good with our weekly phone calls is because Hannah guilted her into it. She might come off as hardened and standoff-ish—the word bitch is also often thrown around, then again, I'm pretty sure she told people to call her that—but at the end of the day, Shelby is the friend you want in your corner. She's fierce. Loyal. If she loves you, she does it with her entire chest. So yeah, some might call her a bad name or two, but I call her my soul sister.

"I was seeing what your schedule was next week?"

"Nothing out of the ordinary. Why?"

"I'm coming to Nashville."

Out of all the things I expected out of her mouth, that was the last one. "You? Coming to Nashville? On purpose?"

I've lived in Nashville since I was eighteen and Shelby has come here a total of three times. I don't know what she has against the city, but she's made it an active point to avoid it.

"I know, I'm as shocked as you are," she says. "But desperate times call for desperate measures."

"Can I know what those desperate measures are?"

Now it's her turn to let out a sigh, but it's not the dreamy kind. "Not yet. I don't want to admit out loud what I might have to do until I do it."

"Well that's ominous."

"Believe me, it's worse than that."

The one thing that has gone my way today is that there's a parking spot right by the door, which is good considering I have at least three trips worth of cookies and cupcakes to bring in.

I open the hatch of my SUV to take out what I can grab on the first trip. I don't know how many people are here and if they're really going to eat ten dozen cupcakes and another ten dozen cookies, but that's what Maddox ordered and paid for. Actually, he paid more than he needed after I offered to give him a discount. We settled on my standard rate. Of course, that was after we gave each other our now standard "Maddox" and "Gabrielle" looks, wondering who was going to crack first. The normal rate was the best compromise either of us were going to get.

I smile as I think about the interaction as I walk my way through the door. The only reason I know I'm in the right spot is because of the big logo on the door that says "LaunchPoint Labs." If you were to drive by and not know what this place was, you'd assume it was a semi-truck garage or something to that capacity. But as I walk in, I quickly realize this place is nothing of the sort.

The ceilings are high and the space is wide open and I don't know what a robotics team fantasy land looks like, but it has to rival what I'm seeing here. Everywhere you look there's some sort of project in the works. A car on a lift. At least four robots on tables and one standing in the corner, greeting me as I walk in. I look up, half expecting to see a drone flying over.

But there aren't any students working on any of these projects. In fact, there's barely a whisper to be heard. And that's because every eye and ear in attendance is fully trained on Maddox.

"You guys have no idea how much you impress me every single day." Maddox says. "Does anyone know why I started LaunchPoint?"

Only a few kids raise their hands, and I hope that means he's going to tell the story. I've never heard it, but knowing the mysterious ways Maddox works, I can't wait to hear the origin.

"Sports have been part of my life since I first put on a pair of cleats," Maddox says with a smile. "But with that, my mom always made sure to tell me that my grades came first. Do any of your parents tell you that?"

Nearly every hand raises in enthusiasm, and I take a second to put down the box of cookies on a table so I can lean back against the wall and listen.

And sigh.

"See. Moms are smart. But I didn't always think that. One year, I think I was in eighth grade, I tried to test that theory. I got my first D in math. The coaches were going to let it slide and let me play, but my mom? Guess where I was during basketball season?"

"Not ballin'."

"At home."

"Gettin' a butt whoopin'"

Everyone laughs at the answers that are shouted out from various kids, and each answer only makes Maddox smile bigger.

God that smile… it's literally lighting up the room. I don't know if I've met a man who smiles as much as he does. He's always finding joy in things. Trying to make people happy. Laugh. I know I for sure have smiled more than I have in years, and a lot of that has to do with Maddox.

Okay most. Nearly all.

Fuck I'm screwed…

"That one time of getting my butt whooped was all I needed to get me in gear," Maddox continues. "From there on out, I used my brain. Got good grades, which meant I was put in the honors classes. And sure, there were a lot of my teammates in class with me, but I was also getting to meet with kids I had never really talked to. Classmates who liked robotics, and math—"

"And science."

Maddox smiles and nods at the interjection. "And science."

I can't take my eyes off him. Which is when I see the second he notices I'm here. Our eyes lock, and I swear for a second, every student and adult volunteer in the room disappears. And all from a little wink he gives me.

Yup… I'm definitely screwed.

"My high school was all about sports," Maddox says. "We were always one of the best football teams in the state. Our wrestling program produced state champions regularly. I graduated with athletes going to college in nearly every sport, girls and boys. So of course, that's where the money went. Turf field. Weight rooms that rivaled professional football facilities. But I knew as well as anyone that not every kid at our school was a star athlete. I became friends with those kids, and they were geniuses. So freaking smart. But they didn't have anywhere besides the classroom to show it off. No robotics team. Or STEM programs. And I always hated that for them. Because if there had been a robotics team, my school would've been more dominant than we were in football, and that's saying something."

"Is that why you started LaunchPoint?"

His smile softens as he nods to one of the young girls sitting in the front row. "That's exactly why I started it. Don't get me wrong, I love sports. Clearly, it has made me the man I am today. But sports aren't the be-all, end-all. And I think you, every other LaunchPoint member here, have opportunities to chase their dreams and expand their minds."

Maddox looks up to me again, and I think for the first time since I met him, he blushes.

"Every time I come in here, I'm more in awe of each and every one of you. I know some of you may look up to me, or maybe to my teammates on the football field, and think we're your heroes. And that's great. Everyone needs to have someone to look up to. But let me tell you this, you're mine. The things you're building here? The innovations I see? I'm in awe of all of you. And I want you to know that from the bottom of my heart."

A few of the adults clap. I'm one of them.

"Now why do I bring up role models?" Maddox asks. "It's the reason I asked everyone to come here today. I'm proud to announce that we're going to be starting the LaunchPoint Mentorship Program. And you guys are going to be the ones leading the way. You're going to be the ones helping elementary students with their first builds and ideas. You're the ones they're going to look up to. They're going to see the drone you built. Or the car that you completely revamped and made into a smart vehicle. And maybe they have dreams of playing a professional sport. That's fine. But maybe they're also going to have dreams of building robots and making scientific discoveries that'll change the world. And they're going to see what you're doing here, and they're going to want to be exactly like each and every one of you. In fact, I know they are."

Well shit now I'm crying...and sighing more than ever...

I mean, how am I not supposed to sigh with hearts in my eyes? This man is... he's so many things. He's good and pure and has good intentions in everything he does. He's honest and funny. He's handsome and charming. He's smart without showing off about it. He's a showman while also somehow reserved and private.

And I think I'm about to ask him on a date.

That last hit of realization should be scaring me. But Shelby is right. Why can't I? The man makes me happy. He makes me smile. Unless Vegas was a drunken fluke, he makes me feel good. Why wouldn't I want more of that in my life? The answer is I do. And I'm going to get it. So I'm going to channel every ounce of courage and confidence I had in Vegas, and somehow without alcohol or a sequin dress, I'm going to ask a man out on a date for the first time in my life.

Maddox quiets down the crowd as I pick up the box I'd set down. "In honor of kicking off the mentorship program, I thought what better way to celebrate than with some desserts. And luckily for me, I happen to know the best baker in Nashville."

Maddox pauses to nod back to me, a smile from ear to ear glowing on his face. "Everyone say hi to Miss Gabi."

The kids do as asked, and I give a small wave with my half-free hand. "Hi everyone. I promise there are more, I just didn't have enough hands. I'll put these down and go get the rest."

Maddox shakes his head. "Do I have any volunteers who will go to Miss Gabi's car and bring in the rest of the desserts?"

Hands don't even need to be raised because at his request, six boys and girls jump from the floor and sprint to help. I start to walk over to the table where all the food is displayed, but before I can make it three steps, Maddox is somehow in front of me, taking the box out of my hands.

"I got it," he says, and for a second, I think he's about to kiss my cheek, but he steps away. "Thank you again for bringing these."

"It was the least I could do," I say as he puts them down. "Plus, now I'm glad I did."

He doesn't know the double meaning of my words as he

turns back around to face me. "So, my staff is going to get the kids all fed. Do you want a tour? Or are you hungry? I can get you some pizza."

I shake my head and give myself one more deep breath for courage—even though I half wish it was a shot of tequila. "Actually, can I talk to you for a second in private?"

Concern comes over his face. "Sure. Is everything okay?"

"Yes," I say confidently, not wanting him to worry as he takes me into an office and shuts the door. But as I quickly look around, I realize this has to be his office. Pictures are carefully placed on shelves and the desk—all of him with different students who I'm assuming are LaunchPoint attendees. There's of course a Nashville Fury football, a few trophies, but what pulls me in the most are things that have nothing to do with football. Schematics on the wall of different projects. Pictures that you can tell kids colored for him. But what pulls at my heartstrings the most is a huge certificate that looks like it was drawn by elementary students that says "Person of the Year."

Sigh...

"That speech... it was amazing. All of this? I've only seen a little of it, but you should be really proud of what you're doing here."

I see him blush at my praise as he goes to stand against his desk, his biceps inadvertently flexing as he balances himself against the edge. I don't know how a man can look this sexy while I'm also reminded everywhere I look of how good of a guy he is. But no matter the how, it's what I needed to assure myself that what I'm about to do is the absolutely right decision.

"Thank you. It's always fun seeing the kids' reaction when they hear it."

"I can tell." I shuffle my feet back and forth, realizing I have no idea how to shift this conversation from his charity to what I want to ask him. Are my next words "want to go out tonight as not best friends?"

"Are you okay?" he asks, taking a step away from the desk

and cutting the distance between us. "Your eyes only bounce around like that when you're thinking really hard, and they're currently going a mile a minute."

I look up at him, in more awe of him than I was before. "You notice things like that?"

"I notice everything about you Gabrielle."

He takes two more steps closer, his eyes not letting my gaze go for even a second. He's so close his cologne is overtaking my senses. He's close enough that my heart rate is picking up, though I don't know if it's from him and the words he said or the question I want to ask.

Who am I kidding? It's both.

"Everything?"

He slightly nods while simultaneously gently pushing a stray piece of hair behind my ear. "There's not a single thing about you I don't memorize."

And with those few, but ever so meaningful, words, Maddox Gallagher officially breaks down my final wall.

"Do you have plans tonight?"

My questions takes him slightly off guard. "I... I didn't have any plans. Why?"

Now or never Gabi. Put on the sequin dress.

"I was wondering... because you're free... and I'm free... that maybe we could do one of those Best Friend Activity ideas... but maybe not... as best friends?"

It's not as confident as I wanted it to be. If I'd have timed it, there were at least three seconds of pause between every word... but I did it.

But Maddox is silent. I actually want to put my finger under his nose to see if he's even breathing. I'm about to when his next words are barely above a whisper.

"Are you saying that you want to go on a date with me?"

The cautious hope in his voice is enough to make me melt. And if I wasn't confident before about this decision, I am one-hundred-percent now.

"I am. I was thinking that maybe we could get dinner. Then maybe—"

Whatever I was going to offer as an option doesn't get vocalized because before I know it, Maddox has pulled me in, dipped me low, and is kissing me with everything he has in him.

"Maddox!" I say, a giggle escaping me. "What are you doing?"

"Doing what I've been dreaming of doing for the past month."

Maddox's lips come to mine again, and now that the shock has worn off, I can take in the moment. I didn't know how much I truly remembered from our night together, or if over the last month it's only become some sort of distorted fantasy wrapped in a memory. But his kiss feels familiar. His hold feels comfortable. And if I had any doubt if I was making up how my body felt against his, I can tell myself that I wasn't imagining anything.

"So is that a yes?" I ask as we pull away, our foreheads still touching.

He laughs and leans back in for one more small peck. "Oh, Gabrielle… that's the easiest yes I've said in my entire life."

CHAPTER 16
GABI

When I asked Maddox to do something tonight, I didn't expect much. I mean, it was already three in the afternoon when I left LaunchPoint and I still had to go back to the bakery to help the girls close. When I told him the earliest I could be ready was six thirty, he didn't bat an eyelash that it would be a problem. He simply told me to wear something that was casual but I felt good in, to be ready at seven, and that he'd take care of the rest.

That might've been the sexiest thing he's ever said.

I really hope sooner rather than later I quit comparing everything Maddox does to what Justin did. But how can I not when Maddox is the anti-Justin? Justin's plan for our first date was going to the movies with his friends. We were in high school, so I never thought anything of it. And yes, he asked me to prom, but I picked out his suit and the flowers. I picked out my own engagement ring and he did a horrible job at not giving away when he was going to propose. And of course, by the time we were married, there wasn't a lick of initiative when it came to nurturing our marriage and keeping the spark alive.

Yet here's Maddox, planning dates, texting me when he was on his way, coming to my apartment door to walk me to his car, opening the door for me. I know in the grand scheme of chivalry, all of these aren't groundbreaking efforts, but to me, they're everything.

"So what are we doing?" I ask as he pulls off the exit. "Wait, are we doing something downtown?"

"We are, but I'm not telling you what," he says with a boyish grin. "I like surprising people."

"I told you I don't like surprises, right?"

"You did," he says as he slowly makes a left turn onto the top of Broadway. "But I'm going to see if that's because you've never had a surprise from me."

"You think you can change my mind on surprises?"

He shrugs. "I got you to change your mind on this, didn't I?"

Touché, Maddox Gallagher… touché.

"I'll be willing to try to be more open to surprises," I say. "But in return, you need to do something for me."

He glances my way while also taking my hand in his. "Name it."

"Next time we go on a date, and you have something planned downtown, please let me drive to you."

He shakes his head no. "Sorry. Can't do that."

"Maddox…"

"Gabrielle…"

Our stubborn is facing off again, only this time, I'm not letting him win. At the end of the day, something has to be practical about whatever this dating/relationship/friendship is. Me driving to him can be one of them.

"Maddox, all I'm saying is that it makes zero sense for you to drive across town to pick me up, only to go back to where you live. I can drive and I don't mind doing it."

We're at a standstill, giving Maddox the opportunity to put the car in park so he can fully turn to me. Our hands are still joined, so he uses the connection to pull me in closer to him. If the console wasn't between us, I'd nearly be on his lap. Not that that's necessarily a bad thing.

"But I do mind," he says, his words with a firmness I haven't heard from him. Not in a scary way, but in a he-means-business way. I like it. "I really don't want to think about your ex right now and how I can only assume he treated you, but I need you to know how this is going to go. I'm going to pick you up. I'm going to plan dates. I'm going to open your car door when you get out tonight. I'm going to hold your hand and make sure I walk closest to the street. And never, I mean never, will I make you drive anywhere again. Not because I don't think you can. But because how I see it? I'm the luckiest guy in the world that I get to be with you. Which means I'm going to do everything in my power to make sure that you're treated exactly the way you deserve. Which is like the queen you are."

Not one word that came out of his mouth was sexual. But I can safely say that I've never been more turned on in my entire life.

When I don't say anything, Maddox takes the opportunity to lean in and gently kiss the corner of my mouth. "Is that okay, Gabrielle?"

God... the way he says my whole name makes me want to suggest skipping the actual date and going straight to his condo. "Yeah... that's okay."

"Good," he says, kissing my hand as traffic starts to move. "Now let's get you that surprise."

"I still can't believe you brought me to a hockey game!" I haven't stopped smiling since we got to our box seats at the Music City Rockers' game, but how can I not? Not only is this my first hockey game, but it's my first professional sporting event ever.

More importantly than that, it's something off our list. Something I said I wanted to do. And he made it happen in hours.

"So I gave you a good surprise?"

I turn to Maddox, who seems genuinely nervous. "The best."

I punctuate my words by leaning over the small arm rest to give Maddox a kiss. Nothing big. A little more than a peck. But I hope he realizes how much more it means to me.

And judging by the smile on his face when I turn away, he absolutely does.

This night has been perfect. Apparently, Maddox made a few calls and was able to get us seats in the box owned by the Nashville Fury. Luckily for us, no one else was using tickets so we had the entire box, and the seats outside it, just for us. We ordered dinner from the menu that I'm sure is not available to regular patrons of the game, and I'm so full I couldn't eat another bite. We've had as many drinks as we could want, but the smell of beer for some reason made me slightly nauseous. So I stayed with my Coke Zero to make sure that nothing was going to get in my way of what I think is, so far, a perfect first date.

"Are you a hockey fan?" I ask as the teams take the ice for the third period.

"It's actually the one sport growing up I didn't play," he says. "I had friends who did, but I never took an interest in it. Then again, my dad made sure I had a football in my hands from the moment I was born, so I don't know if I had any other choice."

"I bet he's glad he gave you that football."

Maddox doesn't say anything, but I immediately know that I said something I shouldn't have. "Oh Maddox. I'm sorry. I didn't mean to bring up—."

"It's fine..." He pauses for more than a few seconds, his eyes turning sad. I reach across to take his free hand in both of mine, hating that I inadvertently brought up a sore subject. We've talked a few times in the month we've known each other about our personal lives—families, upbringings, those kinds of things. He'll go on and on about his mom, sister, and niece. But it's now dawning on me that he's never brought up his father. "My dad left before I even got into kindergarten. One day he was there, the next day he was gone. No note. No goodbye. Literally pulled the 'I'm going to get milk' and never came back."

"Oh Maddox…" I suddenly hate that there's this arm rest between us because I want to crawl onto his lap and hold him.

"No, it's okay. It's just… I'm actually not mad at him. At least, not anymore."

"Really?" I can't imagine ever being able to get to that spot in my life. Then again, I was blessed that I never had to think about it. My parents have been married for forty years and are currently planning a summer cross country RV trip. "I'd be fuming and my therapist would be able to buy a new car with how many sessions I'd need."

My joke makes him half smile. "Oh don't worry, my therapist is very well compensated."

A man in therapy? Add this to the things Maddox Gallagher does that aren't supposed to be sexy but absolutely are. Actually, this might take the top spot on my list, which overtakes him wearing an apron and a backward hat.

"She's helped me realize that I'm who I am because of what I've been through," he continues. "Yeah, it sucks that I grew up without a dad. One day I hope I can be the dad I never got to have. But at the end of the day, I like the person I am. I hate thinking that I could be another version of myself. Sure, I'm not perfect. There are some things I've done I won't do again, but at the end of the day, I'm proud of what I've accomplished and that I'm not a horrible guy."

"Not horrible in the least." We share a smile as a tiny blush comes across his cheekbones. "Do you think about that what-if? What your life might be like if he stayed?"

"Not really. Honestly, the one I think about the most is wondering if he's watching me. If he sees the man I've become despite him. Did he see me win my rings? Did he watch my workouts at the draft combine? Does he tell people I'm his son? Or does he even care?"

Maddox is trying to be so strong right now, but I hear the slight crack in his voice.

"I bet he does, and he's probably kicking himself for giving up the chance to be in your life," I say. "And if he doesn't care, or hates to see you successful, then fuck him and keep doing you. To me there's no better revenge than thriving knowing people hate you for it."

"The same can be said for you," he says. "You thriving after your divorce? Your ex having to acknowledge it? Now that's what I call sweet revenge."

Fuck this arm rest.

I stand up and take the half step I need in order to situate myself on Maddox's lap. Before he can ask what I'm doing, my lips are on his, kissing him with all the compassion and pride I can feel after that admission—and how he simultaneously made me realize something that I hadn't even realized I was doing for myself.

If Maddox cares that we're having a very PDA moment right now, he doesn't show it. In fact, his arms are around my waist, holding me tight, as our kiss deepens into one that's about to become not family friendly. I'm about to run my hands through his curly hair when I hear the tell-tale sound of one of the most iconic Prince songs of all time. And I can't help but wonder if they're playing this song because the name of it is exactly what we're doing right now.

"Ladies and gentlemen! Looks like the Nashville Fury's Maddox Gallagher is going to start off our Kiss Cam for this evening!"

We pull away and I immediately bury my face into Maddox's neck. But him? He's not shying away from it. I catch him out of the corner of his eye waving for all to see, a smile on his face from ear to ear. I turn my eyes a little more, which gives me a view of the Jumbotron directly above the ice. I see the two of us enclosed in a pink glitter heart as the song continues to blast through the arena.

"What do you say, Gabrielle? One more for the fans?"

I slowly pick my embarrassed face up from the hole I was trying to dig into his shoulder. "How do you do it?"

"Do what?"

"Make me do things I didn't think I'd never ever do."

He puts his hand on the back of my head. "I guess I'm a bad influence."

Maddox pulls me in for another kiss, which gets a huge round of applause from the fans. When it quiets down, I have a feeling the camera has panned off us, but that isn't stopping us. It should. We're in an arena with seventeen-thousand people. I'm sure there are videos being taken of us that will be all over social media before we leave tonight. But like I told Maddox, the best revenge is thriving. Being happy.

And that's what I am. For the first time in a very long time, I'm happy. And that's because of this man right here.

"I think we have a habit of creating public spectacles," I say as I pull away enough to catch my breath.

"I think there's worse things we could be known for."

Maddox gives me one more kiss before I reluctantly move from his lap and go back to sitting in my actual seat. I don't know what I expected from the game—I've watched less than five minutes of hockey in my entire life—but I'm enjoying it. It's fast paced. A little violent. Blink and you could miss something.

"I don't know how they do it," I say as a shot goes flying toward the goalie.

"How do who do what?"

I point to the goalie. "The goalies. The pucks are coming so fast. And they're wearing so many pads. How do they move their bodies like that?"

My observation makes Maddox smile. "I'm not sure. I never thought about it. But I can ask Finn for you."

"You know the goalie?"

"Yeah, he's a good guy. Solid karaoke singer. A little crazy, but from what I've heard that's the standard trait of goalies. It's why they're the ones who signed up for getting pucks blasted at them."

It's like he could hear us talking about him, because at that moment, Finn makes another crazy save. I don't know how he did it, but he went from a near split to all but leaping to his opposite side to make a save with his glove.

"Is he also part of the Nashville Professional Athletes Club?" I tease.

"If that's what we're called, being signed to West Athletes, then yes," Maddox says. "Let's see… there's him… oh, and Asher Reed. Number 18. He's there on the right. Good guy. Pretty grumpy so I don't talk to him much. He's got a kid, so he doesn't come to a lot of the functions that the other athletes signed with West have to, but he gets a pass."

"A kid pass?"

Maddox shakes his head. "He's a widow. Lost his wife a few years ago in a car accident. Was fucking tragic."

"Oh dear," I say as I look back onto the ice to find number eighteen. He's expertly skating backward, tracking the puck and the player coming toward him. I don't know how he does it, but somehow out of nowhere Asher stops on a dime, intercepts the pass, and somehow shoots it ahead for his teammates. It's quite impressive.

"I can't skate for anything," I say as Asher slams another player into the boards. And not just slam. The guy crumbles to the ground. "Oh my God! He just…"

Play on the ice stops, but that's because the guy that Asher hit into the wall isn't getting up. Before I can tell what's going on, referees are blowing whistles and I think everyone on the ice is fighting someone.

"My first hockey fight!" I squeal, clapping my hands. I'm locked in. Not blinking. Punches are being thrown. Refs are trying to break it up. Gloves are flying. Sticks are scattered on the ice. Fans are shouting "let them fight!" while I'm watching in awe.

"Are you okay?" Maddox asks.

His question takes me by surprise. "Yeah? Why?"

"You yawned like this is the most boring thing you've ever witnessed."

I did? "Oh, no. I love this. I really yawned?"

"A big one. Are you tired? Do you want to go home?"

"Yeah, I guess I'm tired, but no I don't want to leave," I say as I fight off another. "I guess this is the price to pay for a busy business."

"But you have tomorrow off, right?"

"I do," I say as I lean into him, his arm around my shoulders as the fight starts to calm down. "My big plans for the day are to not leave the couch and have every meal delivered to me."

"My perfect Sunday Funday," Maddox says. "Maybe you'll want some company?"

I wonder if that company is because our date is still going, or it's going to be part two. Either way, I'm a fan. "Only if that company includes a binge watch of that fantasy show you were appalled I'd never seen an episode of?"

"Another check off the Best Friend Activity to-do list?"

"Technically yes. But I think the list needs a new name."

Maddox couldn't hide his smile if he tried. "Yeah? Have any suggestions?"

I lean in, just far enough away that our lips aren't touching, but so close I feel as if I can taste him. "Maybe something like Date Night Ideas?"

"Girlfriend-Boyfriend Activities?"

Now it's my turn to smile. "I didn't realize I was your girlfriend."

"You're not. Yet," Maddox says before leaning in, brushing his lips against mine ever so slightly. "But I hope that changes very, very soon."

We lean back in, our lips seemingly unable to stay away from the others. This time there's no song to interrupt our moment. No crowd cheering us on. Just two people who can't wait anymore.

"Maddox?"

He pulls away, but leaves his forehead tapped to mine. "Yes , Gabrielle?"

"I'm ready to leave."

CHAPTER 17
MADDOX

There are many athletes who don't bring women back to their homes for various reasons. Mostly privacy. Some are just assholes. I was never one of those guys.

Sure, there were a few crazies that I hooked up with since moving to Nashville that looking back, I'd rather them not know where I live, but at the end of the day, I didn't mind having a woman in my space. I knew she wasn't staying long, or coming over again, so I felt like it didn't matter.

But as I stand with Gabi in my elevator, hand in hand as we make our way to my top-floor condo, the moment isn't lost on me that she's coming into my home. And unlike the others, Gabi isn't a one-time thing. I don't want her to be. I want her to stay as long as she wants. I want her to have a toothbrush on my counter and a drawer in my dresser. I want my pillows to smell like her and Coke Zero to be always stocked in my refrigerator. I want to see her walking around my house in that T-shirt she took from me that first night with nothing on underneath. I want us to fall asleep on the couch together because we put on a movie that we both promised each other we'd stay up for.

I want it all.

"Oh my," Gabi says with wide eyes as we walk through my front door. "It's gorgeous Maddox."

"Thank you," I say as I slip off my shoes. "I'd take credit for the design choices, but then I'd be acting like I have any idea what the designer did besides give me a space that doesn't scream 'I'm a douche.' Which was my only requirement."

That makes her laugh. "You hired a designer?"

"I did when I bought this two years ago," I said. "She's local. Specializes in creating spaces for men. She's Ainsley's sister and Linc recommended her. Since I have no clue what's an appropriate amount of pillows, I paid her whatever she wanted. The most Type A woman I've ever met but man she hit every nail on the head."

"Sounds like my kind of gal," Gabi says as she walks over to the floor to ceiling windows that give a perfect view of the Nashville skyline. A few lights are on in the living room, but they're soft, allowing the natural light of the view to frame Gabi in the space. I swear as I take her in, she has a glow around her. It's one I could stare at all night. But I'm not. Because more than needing to look at her, I need to feel her in my arms.

She doesn't even jump a little as I step behind her, wrapping my arms around her waist and pulling her back into me. Her head falls back against my chest and she immediately relaxes in my hold.

"Are you still tired?"

She shakes her head as she turns around to face me. "Not at all."

Neither of us need to say anything else as our lips find each other's. I pull her closer to me, wanting to feel every part of this first kiss.

Sure, I know it's not our *actual* first kiss. It's not even our first kiss today. But it's the first one that doesn't feel like it has some sort of rush to it. Or has outside factors or excitement. It's only me and Gabi, alone, no timer or audience, just finding each other.

And it's as perfect as I thought it would be.

Wanting more of her, I reach down beneath her thighs, lifting her up so she has no choice but to wrap her legs around my waist as I walk her to my bedroom. Sure, I could've gone to the couch. It would've been less presumptuous.

But I know my girl. And I feel the way she's grinding into me. There's no doubting what she wants.

Our kiss becomes more desperate as she pulls me in tighter. Thankfully, I didn't shut the door earlier so I don't even have to kick it open before taking four long strides to my bed where I lay her down.

I didn't mean to go down with her, but her arms are glued around my neck, I had no choice but to. Though, there are worse places to be than in my bed, wrapped up in Gabi, and kissing her like all we want in the world is each other.

There are many things I had wished happened between us in Vegas. Some were ones I thought of that night but had to prioritize. Others I fantasized about after. According to my therapist, there are likely some things I romanticized. I get that. In theory. But the night was so crazy and amazing and magical and insane how could someone not?

But now that I'm laying here with her, feeling her hands go underneath my shirt, slowly working their way up my chest, the way our mouths are moving in sync like they're meant to be together… I think I didn't romanticize anything. If anything, I undersold this.

This is perfection in its purest form.

I lift her from the bed and set her on my lap, wanting nothing more than her shirt to be gone so my lips can travel exactly where they want. When I break our kiss, she lifts her arms for me. But it's her bouncing eyes that have me concerned.

"Gabi? Talk to me gorgeous."

It's dark in my room, but I can still see her blush because she knows she's been busted. "I'm just in my head. Don't worry about me."

"Not worry about you? Ha! Let's try that again," I say as I pull her black off-the-shoulder sweater over her head and toss it to the side. And as much as I want to devour her tits right now —which are perfectly waiting for me in a black lace strapless bra and I swear to God they're bigger than I remember—I have one thing to do first. "Talk to me. Don't hold back. I want to know every good, bad, or ugly thought that's bouncing around in that beautiful head of yours. Because the good ones I want to make sure happen, and the bad ones I want to fuck right out of you."

My words give her a hint of a smile. "Before… in Vegas… we were drunk. There was the heat of the moment and I had liquid courage and adrenaline racing through my veins. But tonight…"

"Tonight's different," I assure her that I'm on the same page. Because she's right. It is. "We're different. We're not strangers anymore. We're not two people who were at the right place at the right time. But know this. The words I told you that first night? Those don't change. This is your show, Gabrielle. Always. You're in control, unless you don't want to be."

That seems to take her aback. "If I don't want to be?"

I had a feeling that her fucking asshole ex was a hit it and quit it kind of guy. From what she's told me about him, and how she reacted to my touch in Vegas, he fits the stereotype. Those guys are dickheads who never deserve a cool pillow. It's baffling to me that you can be with someone like Gabi—warm and sweet and caring and strong—and not want to give her the world inside the bedroom and out.

Oh well. He wants to fuck up and fuck around? I'll gladly take what he gave up.

"I'm all about making sure that you get everything you want," I say, my hand trailing down the side of her face. "If you want it? Ask for it. Whatever you want to do, tell me. Or, if you don't want to think, don't know what you want, or in a case like tonight, are tired and want to turn your brain off and feel, then that's what will happen. Let me take care of you."

Her eyes somehow get a shade darker at my suggestion of option three. "You'll... take care of me?"

You have no idea how I can take care of you...

I kneel down in front of her, making us more at eye level. "Have you ever had a night where it's all about you? Where you just feel? Where you don't have to think or ask or maneuver your way into a position for a hint of pleasure?"

She shakes her head. "Never. Besides... with you."

I take her chin in my fingers, bringing her in a breath away from my lips. "And that's how it's always going to be."

I lean in to kiss her one more time before standing us both up from the bed. She looks a little confused when I pull away, but doesn't take her eyes off me as I kneel before her.

"First off, you have on way too many clothes," I say as I unbutton her jeans before sliding them down her legs. I trail kisses on her stomach, and each of her thighs, as I take them down, purposefully ignoring the place I want to be so badly.

"That's it. Step out of them. These too," I direct, bringing down her lace panties next. I don't know who invented lace, but I'm pretty sure it was created as a way to break down a man. "So fucking pretty."

I stand up, kissing her perfect, luscious, body as I do. I squeeze her thighs, loving the thickness of them. I place open mouth kisses from her hips, across her stomach, to the other side, loving the sweet taste of her soft skin. I run my tongue around her naval, making her grab onto my shoulders as I feel the shiver go through her body. She lets those hands trail down my chest as I stand up to reach behind her, unsnapping her bra with one flick of my fingers.

"You're good at that," she teases.

"Oh Gabrielle... you have no idea."

I take her hand in mine as I walk us back to the bed, but not before opening up a bedside drawer. Gabi starts to say something but quickly swallows her words when I pull out a vibrator and not the condoms I think she thought I was getting.

I will. Later.

I adjust the pillows against the headboard, giving me something to rest against as I spread my legs, giving Gabi a perfect nest to sit in. "Come here gorgeous."

She does as I say, but I see her eyes bouncing back and forth between the wand in my hand and my unwavering eyes.

"Have you ever used one of these?"

She nods and I look down to see her eyes double in size as I turn the vibrator on. "Yes. But not… with someone."

I growl into her ear as I pull her into me. "I love giving you firsts."

I've barely tapped her skin with the device and she's already squirming in my hold. "I know this is out of your comfort zone. Something new. But lean into me. Feel everything. Try to turn your brain off. Forget about the bakery and orders and recipes. Forget about the last two years. Just think about here and now. Me and you."

"Okay…"

Her whispered word in combination with her body's reaction as she starts to feel the vibrator is making me regret not taking my jeans off before I climbed into bed. Then again, this is giving me an extra layer of protection to not abandon my plan and fuck her until she screams.

Again, I will. Just not yet.

"Like that?" I say as I slowly start letting it travel down her chest. I drag it across her chest before letting it roll over a nipple, making her body convulse under me. Her head is thrown back against my shoulder as I hit every place that I did minutes before with my lips. Her hips… across her navel… other hip… back to the navel before going down to the place I can tell she's silently begging for.

"Or maybe like that?" The second the vibrations hit her clit, she nearly jumps out of my hold. "You like that gorgeous?"

She nods, her body squirming as much as it can as she's encaged by my body. "Yes… yes… "

"That's my girl."

I doubt that in a million guesses and in a million years, Gabi would've never thought coming back to my place would also include me using a vibrator to give her the first of many orgasms she's going to have tonight. Many women don't. Apparently, according to previous women who have gotten to dig into the drawer of fun times, men think using toys is a crutch. Or that they're so good they don't need them. But me? I'd never be naive enough to say I'm God's gift to sex and that using toys makes me bad in bed. I subscribe to the motto of "double the pleasure, double the fun." Plus, if there's something that I can use on Gabi right now to not only get her out of her head, but make sure she has the hardest orgasm she's ever had in her life? Then I'm going to use it until she begs me to stop.

Gabi's body is squirming, her face is flushed, and her breathing is picking up. It's the sexiest thing to watch. And looking at her is the only reason I hear the words come out of her mouth.

"Maddox," she whimpers. "I—"

I know I said I was going to take the reins tonight, but when my girl wants something, my girl gets it. Full stop. "I what? What do you need? Use your words."

"Mo—More…"

"My gorgeous girl wants more?" I say, turning up the vibrator one more tick. "Like that?"

She nods furiously, her hair scratching my chest. "Yes… but… I want… your…"

"That's it. Tell me what you want."

"Your… fingers…" Her words are all moans and I've never been more turned on in my whole life. "Fuck me with your fingers, Maddox."

"Fuck yes…"

My words come out in almost a growl as I adjust my hold on her, giving me the best angle possible to keep her against my body, while also letting my fingers go to the place we both want them to be.

"Holy fuck you're dripping," I say as I easily insert two digits. "Is this all for me?"

"All for you," she repeats, her eyes closed as her head presses against my shoulder.

I slowly work my fingers because I can't take my eyes off her right now. She's so relaxed. Truly letting herself feel everything. Her eyes aren't bouncing. The hamster wheel in her brain isn't moving at a hundred miles an hour. She's here. Feeling every sensation. And we've barely begun.

"Let's go a little more," I say, flicking the wand up a notch while I speed up my fingers. "How does that feel?"

"It… feels…" The words die on her lips, but she doesn't need to tell me. I can feel it. Her hips are jutting up from the bed. Her hands are reaching for anything to brace herself before landing on my thighs. Her back is arched as I fuck her with my fingers at a rapid speed now, her pussy gripping me so hard that I can feel the second she—

"Ah!" she screams—as she should. Because my girl just squirted all over my bed.

And it was fucking hot as hell.

I slowly turn down the vibrator in tandem with slowing my fingers down, doing my best to bring her back to earth, because I'm pretty sure she went into orbit.

"That's my girl," I say as her breathing calms down. I for some reason figured that she'd need a second to recover, but it's the opposite. The second I remove my fingers from her center, Gabi flips to her knees, eyeing me like I'm her prey.

It's hot as fuck.

"Pants off," she commands, doing the action for me because the switch in her has officially flipped.

"Yes, ma'am," I say, loving this side of her. I didn't think it was a one-night in Vegas thing. And if a good orgasm does that, then I'd be happy to help her with that every day of the week and twice on Tuesdays.

I know the saying is Sundays, but I have games on Sundays. Tuesdays, I'm always home.

Her eyes haven't left mine as she finishes pulling down my pants and boxer briefs before she crawls back up my body. Her tits are dragging against my legs and as much as I want them in my hands—and in my mouth—I can't think about it. All I can think about is this goddess that's about to climb onto my dick.

"Whatever I want, right?" she asks, and all I can do is nod. "So I can ride your cock until you make me come again?"

Note to self: Tomorrow, while she's resting in this bed, because she's not leaving it, go out and buy a wedding ring.

"Abso-fucking-lutely."

Her smile is wicked as she takes my cock in her hands, giving it a few strokes before lining it up to her center. "Good boy." Gabi sinks down into me, and I didn't realize that I liked being called that, but holy fuck, I do. "Now fuck me until I come again."

"With pleasure."

It's the final words out of my mouth as I grab onto her hips, pistoning up into her with everything I have in me. She's still soaked from her orgasm and—

Shit. We're not using a condom. But I can't stop. I don't want to stop. By the looks of her head thrown back, her nails digging into my chest, and her back slightly arched, Gabi doesn't want to, either. And frankly, you couldn't pay me a million dollars right now to stop. I know the pull-out method is something sixteen-year-old Maddox would think is okay, but it's going to have to work for twenty-four-year-old Maddox, too, because wild horses couldn't take me away.

I let my hands travel up her body, each of them cupping her tits as she continues riding me. It's a beautiful sight to see, between how wet she is, how fucking hot she looks, and how

I've been hard all night for this woman, I fear this is going to end sooner than I want it to.

"Fuck… Gabi…" I grit out, letting my hands grip her hips again. "I'm going to—"

"Yes… me too…" she agrees, her hands now moving back to grip my thighs. "Make me come, Maddox. Please."

The desperate plea on her lips and the feeling of her body tightening on me sends me into a blackout. I feel her orgasm on my cock. I feel her tightening around me. And before I know it, I'm spilling into her as she screams my name for all of Nashville to hear.

I don't pull out. I don't even try. Because this is the closest thing to heaven I've ever experienced, and I'll ask for forgiveness later.

CHAPTER 18
GABI

I'm not quite sure what's happening right now, but either my vibrator has found its way to my coffee table and has somehow turned itself on, or there's an earthquake that's only shaking my living room furniture.

I pop one eye open, not wanting to fully wake up from the much-needed nap that I took after work, to see my cell phone traveling across the table because it's vibrating so much.

That makes much more sense than a traveling, self-powering, vibrator.

I pick it up—still groggy from the kind of nap that makes you think you've missed the school bus—to see a host of missed texts and calls.

MADDOX

I'm here.

Gabi, everything okay? I'm here with the pizza.

Gabrielle. Answer your phone.

I'm calling. Pick up.

> I see your car. Are you okay? Have you been kidnapped? Also, if this is the kidnappers, where have you taken my Gabrielle?

> Gabi seriously, you have three seconds to answer your phone or I'm calling for a wellness check.

As he said he would, my phone starts buzzing in my hand with an incoming call from Maddox.

"Hey, sorry. I—"

"Oh my God you're alive!" he screams out, and even though I'm in a second-floor apartment, I'm pretty sure I heard him in the parking lot. "Okay, come and let me in. I need to make sure you're okay."

"I'm fine. Come on up," I say as I toss the throw blanket off me and slowly stand up from the couch, but almost fall back over because my body is so tired.

Shit, I thought the nap would help. I never sleep when I come home from the bakery. There's only a few hours of awake time for me that I can get things done around my apartment. But today I was exhausted. I actually don't remember the last time I *wasn't* tired. And I didn't want to be tired for Maddox's and my date tonight that's consisting of pizza, puzzles, and another few episodes of the dragon show we started binging when I stayed at his house last weekend.

But judging by the way I'm wobbly when I walk, the fog that refuses to leave my brain, and feeling completely off kilter, date night might need to be rescheduled in favor of me getting a full ten hours of sleep.

Busy is the new normal of the bakery. I used to wake up at four in the morning, but now that's my arrival time. I've been staying later than normal to be able to prep everything I possibly can for the next day so I don't have to come in at three. I really need to hire a second baker, but for some reason, my belief that I can do it all myself is stopping me. Which is why I'm running myself into the ground. Between my now-booming business and starting whatever this is with Maddox, I don't feel like I've stopped in days. Apparently today is the day my body said "enough" and is forcing me to sleep.

When I open the door, I smile as my sleepy eyes take in Maddox. He's holding a pizza and a Lego set in one hand and a twelve-pack of Coke Zero in the other.

"Thank God you're alive."

"You're dramatic, you know that right?" I say as I take the pizza and Legos from him, moving in to kiss his cheek. "Come in. Sorry I didn't pick up. I was taking a n—"

I've barely had the pizza in my hand for five seconds, but as soon as the aroma hits me, I nearly drop it.

"Gabi? Are you—"

I quickly nod, toss the pizza and Legos on the kitchen counter, before sprinting to the bathroom.

What the hell is wrong with me?

I kneel over the toilet, my stomach doing actual backflips, as I throw up... nothing. Some water, but that's it. This is the grossest feeling in the world, but I don't think there's anything in my body for me to throw up. I had a bagel for breakfast at five this morning. A salad with some chicken for lunch. But both of those meals were cut short due to baked goods needing finished or customers needing served.

Maybe it was bad chicken? Though, I feel like if it was, it wouldn't have taken me this long to relieve it from my body. Or it would've come up now.

"Gabrielle? You okay?"

I shake my head as it rests on my elbow against the toilet. "I don't think so."

Normally I'd put on a "I'm fine" front—it was my default mode for so many years—but I don't have the energy.

Maddox doesn't say anything, but I do hear water running from the sink. My stomach starts to rumble again, but as I try to squirm to try and make myself comfortable, I feel something cold on the back of my neck.

"There we go," Maddox whispers as he gathers my hair away. Wait… is he putting it into a ponytail? "It's okay. I've got you."

I let out a sound that probably rivals a sex moan with how good the coolness feels against my skin combined with Maddox's gentle touch as his fingers stroke up and down my back. And for the first time since I came flying in here, my body starts to settle down.

"Thank you." I mumble, slowly turning my head so I can see him as he sits on top of my bathtub. "You don't have to stay. I'm sorry my stomach ruined date night."

He gives me the kindest, softest smile. "Absolutely not. I have nowhere to be other than right here."

His words send me back to our fateful night in Vegas. It's not the exact thing he said, but the feeling of comfort is. Maybe even more so now that we're more than friends. Because if there's one thing I've learned about this man, is that he's going to show you in every way he can that he's there for you in any situation.

Take what he's been doing at the bakery. At this point I actually do need to put him on the payroll. He's been there almost every day since his post went viral, checking to see if he can help. Last week he learned how to ring customers out. The day before that he put his muscles to work and put away the delivery shipment of dry goods I got.

That was a view I didn't mind looking at.

Then there was yesterday when I walked into the kitchen to see him washing dishes—and not because I asked him to. I told him I didn't need any help, but he saw the stack of dishes in the sink and did them. I told him I could handle it, which led to him pulling me in, kissing me senseless, before smacking my ass to get me out of the kitchen.

I liked that a whole lot, too.

That wasn't even the best part. When I went back to check on him an hour later, he had his ear buds in, singing a song at the top of his lungs that was popular when I was in college but he was in middle school. His hips were moving to the beat as he sang the song as loud as possible. It was adorable.

He's too adorable.

And I'm royally fucked if I think for one second that I'm not falling hard for him.

I mean, he checks in every morning to see if I need breakfast. Before we got together, he would always text me goodnight. Now my goodnights are soft kisses on my forehead before he pulls me into him because even though my alarm goes off at an ungodly time, he insists on staying over every night.

And now here he is, taking care of me when I'm sick. Which he doesn't have to do. Most men would've heard my gags and hurling and made a beeline out the front door. I know the man I used to be married to would have—and did one time. I believe once when I was sick his line was "I'm around sick people all day. I don't need to come home to it."

Yet here Maddox is, rubbing my back to make sure I'm okay. Applying another cold compress on my skin. He thought enough to put my hair in a ponytail so it didn't get in my face.

It's at this moment that any qualms I had about his age, or if I was ready to do this, are out of my mind. Because I don't care if he's twenty-four or eighty-four, he's treating me better than I ever thought possible. And that means more to me than any number.

"What can I get you?" he asks. "Water? Ginger ale? Crackers?"

"Those sound great and horrible at the same time," I say, finally able to sit up and move myself against the wall because I might be upright, but I don't know if I can balance by myself. "I don't know what's wrong with me but I feel like absolute death."

"Did you eat something weird?" he asks. "Running a fever? The flu?"

I shrug. "I didn't eat much today and I feel like if it was that, it would've hit me earlier. I don't have a fever or have any other flu-y symptoms. I'm so tired and also I feel like if I move one inch the nausea is just gonna come rushing back."

I let my head hit the wall behind me, which is the first time I take in Maddox. He looks so concerned for me. But in a matter of ten seconds his face goes from worried, to me thinking that I'm so far gone that an actual light bulb went off next to his head.

"What is it?" I ask.

He swallows a lump in his throat like he's nervous. "I know this is a very personal question, and you don't have to answer it, but hear me out. When did you last have your period?"

Oh he's got to be kidding…

"Maddox. I know we forgot to use one the other night. But it doesn't happen that quickly."

"I know that," he says, though by his tone of voice, I'm honestly not sure. "I'm just saying that we've had sex more than once."

Okay, now he's truly ridiculous. "Maddox…"

"Gabrielle…"

Shit. He's not joking. There's no dimple with his smile. There's no twinkle in his eyes. He *actually* thinks I'm pregnant.

"I know it's crazy," he continues. "All I'm saying is that it's been a little over a month since Vegas. And the symptoms you're having heavily rival what my sister looked and went through when she found out she was pregnant."

"How do you know that?"

"She found out when I was home from college," he says. "And what you're feeling like, that was her. For weeks. Random nausea. Extremely exhausted. Then boom. Eight-ish months later, I became Uncle Maddox."

While I'm sure the sight of Uncle Maddox playing with his niece is cute as hell, I can't let my mind go there, because I have to quash this idea he's having. Because the man is out of his mind.

I'm not pregnant. I can't be.

"While I can see why you'd think that, I'm not pregnant," I say definitively. "We used a condom."

"I know, but it says on the package that they aren't a hundred-percent effective. Didn't you see that on that one show? Plus, if anybody's sperm could break free it would be mine."

I fully roll my eyes, because everything out of his mouth right now is utter insanity.

"Super sperm? You're telling me you think your sperm can beat the odds?"

"I've been beating the odds my entire life. Wouldn't shock me."

I can't with this man. Or this conversation. "Maddox, thank you for the WebMD suggestion, but you don't have super sperm and I am *not* pregnant. My period…"

I trail off, because I have to think back from the last time I had it.

Shit. It was before Vegas. I remember being excited that I didn't have to pack tampons.

Oh fuck… I missed my period.

I. Missed. My. Fucking. Period.

My eyes double in size and I'm pretty sure I don't blink for the next five minutes. Am I breathing? Not sure. How did I not realize it? I mean, I guess it makes sense with the insanity of the bakery and my newfound relationship with Maddox. I've been exhausted, but I've been putting in crazy hours. Never would I have thought for a second it was anything else. Except…

"You're late, aren't you?"

"I am," I whisper, not wanting to truly say it out loud. I do manage to push myself up from the wall, but I'm a little off-kilter from my episode. I start to stumble, but Maddox is immediately next to me to catch me, his hands really the only thing holding me up at this point.

"I got you," he says. "And I'm going to be here. For everything."

I shake my head, because he needs to take about forty-two

steps back. "Maddox, you're sweet, and I understand where you could think this, and why the evidence is pointing that way, but I'm not pregnant. It's just… well it can't be."

He gives me a look that we both know that "can't" might not be the best word right now.

"Can I suggest something that I think will make most of us feel better?"

"And that would be?"

"Take a pregnancy test," he says.

"Seriously?"

"Seriously," he says, taking each of my hands in his. "Think of it as you doing it to prove me wrong. I know you love doing that."

Only Maddox Gallagher could make me laugh in this truly terrifying moment. Because how the hell is it even a remote possibility that I could be pregnant.

We used protection. Sure, the sex was intense, but I think I would've noticed if it fell off or was busted in some way. Right? No way Maddox has fucking turbo sperm.

Also, how in the actual hell could it happen that the one time —*the one time*—I'm a little reckless and try to do something to make me feel good, that something like this could happen.

But damn it did feel good. Up until this moment, I've had zero regrets about my night with Maddox. It's led me here, and I'm truly happy. Except now that I'm wondering if I brought home a souvenir I didn't know I purchased, was being reckless worth it?

"Hey," he says. "Talk to me."

I shake my head, because I don't even know the first thing to say, so I quickly revert back to our prior conversation. "You're right. I won't be able to sleep if I don't know."

And then when I do know—and if it's positive—my brain is going to be going in a million different directions.

Like how I always wanted a family, but that was before. How having a baby wasn't even on my radar. How the life I just got back is about to be upended. How Maddox and I are so new, what is going to happen to us if we're now about to be parents.

"Okay. I'll be right back."

Maddox's sudden movements snap me back to reality.

"Where are you going?"

"To get you a pregnancy test," he says. "I already had plans to go get you ginger ale and crackers and anything else that you personally want to help your stomach, so now while I'm out, I'll pick up a pregnancy test."

Is this man for real? Also, how the hell is he not freaking out by this?

"Seriously? You're going to go and buy a pregnancy test?"

"Of course. You go lay down. I'll be back before you know it. Don't worry about a thing. I have everything under control."

CHAPTER 19
MADDOX

'm freaking the fuck out.

Like. Freaking. The fuck. All the way out.

Pregnant? She's pregnant? I mean we don't know she's pregnant yet, but I'd bet my newly inked fifteen-million-dollar-a-year contract that she is.

Shit. Money. I need to start the baby a college fund. And a trust. I'm going to forget. While I'm here, I need to swing through the notebook aisle and grab one for all the baby to dos.

I get those first before making my way over to the ginger ale and crackers area. I want to drag this out, because the gravity of this entire situation is finally hitting me, but the store isn't that big, and the crackers and the ginger ale are only an aisle apart.

Lovely.

I slowly walk from the grocery part of the store over to the pharmacy side. I stop to browse some contact solution—I don't wear contacts—before meandering past the cough medicine. My detour is proving me well because I see some anti-nausea medicine. I should definitely pick some of that up for her.

Wait. Can she take this? I don't know how any of this works. I turn over the box, quickly reading it, only to see she can't. Phew. Good thing I read it. I'd be the worst expectant father in

America if I poisoned my baby the first day I knew about it. And that says something considering I grew up with the worst father in America.

No Maddox. Don't go down that path. Focus on the now. Focus on Gabi. You can have a panic attack about that later.

That might be the pep talk I'm giving myself, but it's been hard as hell to keep those thoughts at bay. When I had the first thought that she was pregnant, I was happy as hell. Then I saw her face. Her concern. How she was nothing but terrified at the possibility. I'm not sure where she stands on what the next steps would be, but that's a problem for the future. Nothing can happen until we know.

And until then, I'm going to do what I can for her. Before it was someone to hold her. Now it's someone to get her a pregnancy test. I can freak out about my thoughts at a later time.

"Holy fuck," I whisper, standing in front of what is no less then ten-thousand pregnancy tests. I look up and down the shelves, wondering where I even begin because I'm so far out of my depth it isn't even funny.

Do I call someone for help? No. I can't tell anyone about this yet. Honestly, Ainsley would be my first call since she's a labor and delivery nurse, but that means she'd tell Linc, who'd tell Wyatt, and next thing I know the team is planning a gender reveal. I can't call my mom or sister because they'll freak out more than I am.

I pick one off the shelf and read it, this one saying that it's for pre-detection. Which makes no sense. If it can detect it, doesn't that push it past the "pre" phase?

But we could be in that territory, so I put it in the basket.

As I go down the line of tests, I realize that they're all kind of the same, but all a little different. Why are there so many? There shouldn't be this many. Some tell you that they're detecting two weeks earlier than others. Some have lines. Some have words. There's a thing called an ovulation test. What is that? Do I need to get that?

Fuck it. They're all going in the basket.

What am I doing? I have no clue. A fact I'm sure is evident to any stranger walking by as they see my basket overflowing with tests. Or… is this smart of me? You can't fuck it up if you buy them all.

I'm a fucking freaked out genius.

I do one last glance over the shelves, grabbing one more just in case, when I feel a slight tap on my leg. When I look down, because it basically feels like a little stick poking me in my thigh, I see the biggest blue eyes I've ever seen in my life.

"Candy?"

I look around to see if there's an adult anywhere in the vicinity, but nope, I'm alone in the "oh shit I'm about to be a parent" aisle.

"No sweetie, there's no candy here," I say, crouching down to her eye level. "Is your mommy or daddy here? Maybe they're shopping for candy?"

She seems to think about it for a second when I hear a booming voice from an aisle over.

"Adalyn Marie! I'm not playing! Quit hiding!"

I smile, because this girl's face morphed into the most mischievous thing I've ever seen. Little giggle and all. "Is your name Adalyn?"

She nods but puts her finger up to her lip like I need to keep the secret.

"I don't think I can do that kiddo," I say. "Sounds like your dad is pretty—"

"Adalyn! Thank fuck! You can't run off like that."

I stand up to step out of the way as he scoops Adalyn in his arms.

"Bad word!" she says, her lips going into a pout that I think is supposed to be her mean face. To me though it's adorable and I want to still get her the candy she asked for.

"Fine. I'll put money in the jar when I get home, but you

need to put a quarter in it too," he says. "What did I tell you about running off?"

I lean back down to pick up my overflowing basket when the dad turns to me. "Thanks for… wait, Maddox?"

I didn't see the dad's face until now because of our angles and the ballcap he's wearing, which is how I didn't realize that this little girl belongs to Music City Rockers' defenseman Asher Reed.

"Hey Asher," I say, trying to subtly hold the basket behind my legs. You know, like he's not going to realize what aisle we're in. "How've you been?"

"Good now that I'm done having my heart attack because of this one," he says, giving her a little boost in his hold. "Thanks for finding her."

"She found me," I say, giving my new little bestie a smile. "She was looking for candy."

He laughs and half rolls his eyes. "Sounds about right. I swear I took my eye off her for a second."

"I get it," I say, even though I don't, but it feels like the right thing to say. I also feel like I need to change the topic of conversation away from kids, which might deflect from my basket. "I was at your game the other night. Amazing fucking game man."

Before he can respond, I have a tiny finger pointing at me. "Bad word!" Adalyn narrows her eyes at me, making it known she's not messing around. "Jar."

I know she's trying to run a tight ship here—swear jars aren't to be messed with—but her little face makes me want to laugh and still buy her all the candy. "My apologies Adalyn. What's the fee?"

She thinks about it for a second, and I don't know how Asher doesn't give this sweet child anything she wants in life. Or how I'm ever going to say no to my future child. "Five dollars."

"Fair price," I say, putting down the basket to fish my wallet out of my pocket. I don't think anything of the action, that is until I hand Adalyn the money, and I see the look of recognition in Asher's eye.

"Everything okay Gallagher?"

I don't know Asher well. He's also signed to West Athletes, but so are a lot of other players around the city. We've made small talk at events we've had to attend together, but that's the extent of it. He was never the friendliest guy to begin with, but then after his wife passed, he became even more closed off. Which I surely can't blame him for. I can't imagine being a widow at thirty.

But at this moment, I feel like he's the only guy I can talk to.

"I'm… not sure," I say honestly. "It's… we think she might… we don't know…"

He nods his head and switches Adalyn to his other hip. "Can I give you a piece of advice?"

I let out a huge breath. "Please. I… this has all happened in the last two hours and I feel like I'm drowning right now. As you can tell."

Asher laughs as I hold up the basket, which causes two tests to drop to the floor.

"First off, you don't need all of those," he says. "But if it makes you feel better, get five different ones. But forty is a bit excessive."

"I figured it was better to be safe than sorry."

"Normal response. And so is feeling overwhelmed." He pauses for a second and gives the slightest glance over to Adalyn, who's trying to squirm out of his hold. In what I'd deem a pro dad move, he slides his cell phone out of pocket and hands it to her, which settles her immediately. "Even when you're trying to get pregnant, the moment you think it could be happening, you're freaked out. Everything suddenly becomes very real and really fucking scary."

"Bad word!" Apparently Adalyn is listening.

"Bill me," he says without missing a beat. "What I'm getting at is, it's okay to be scared, especially if this wasn't planned. Just remember, so is she. So be there for her. Hold her hand. Be whatever she needs from you at that moment. Just… be there for her. She's going to need you every step of the way."

"I'm not leaving her side," I say with conviction, because that's the only thing I know to be true. I might be scared. I have no idea what's about to happen. But I know Gabi will not be alone in any of this. Not because I think it's my duty. Not because I have to prove to myself that I'm better than my father. But because, even though I haven't said these words to her yet, I love her. I love the baby that might be there. And I can't imagine my life missing a moment of anything.

"Then the rest you two will figure out together."

I hear the slight crack in his voice at his words, and my heart breaks for the guy.

"Thanks man," I say. "It's…"

"Exactly," he says, slapping my back with his free hand. "Now, how about we put some of these back. Save your money for diapers."

"Good call," I say as the two of us start getting to work. Even Adalyn joins in the fun and puts back a few on the bottom shelf.

"Gallagher? Did you really get an ovulation test? You know those are for before you get pregnant?"

I laugh. "At that point I was getting one of everything. Bases covered you know?"

He laughs as he puts it back on the shelf for me. "You don't know it yet, but I have a feeling you're going to be just fine."

"Gabi? I'm back."

Before I left for the pharmacy, she gave me her keys so I could let myself into her apartment. I didn't know if I would see her in the living room, but she's not here, and I don't hear anything coming from the bathroom. Which I don't know if that's a good or bad thing. The problem is, I don't hear anything else.

Wondering if she's fallen asleep? I know how tired she's been over the last few weeks. Which should've been my first clue to this being a possibility. There were signs: Her random nausea. How I noticed her boobs were a little bigger, but I thought it was my imagination.

I gently tap on her bedroom door that's ajar, which inadvertently pushes it open a little farther.

My heart drops to my feet when I see her lying on her bed. But it's not the visual that gets to me. It's the faint sound of her crying.

I don't say a word as I take two huge steps to get to her bed, dropping the bags at the foot. I want to scoop her into my arms and hold her, but before I can, she's sat herself up, trying to wipe away the tears as if she did it quick enough, I wouldn't see them.

Joke's on her. I notice every single thing she does.

"I'm sorry I took so long. I—"

"It's okay," she cuts me off. "Did you get one?"

"Something like that."

I reach over to the end of the bed where I dropped the bags, now suddenly curious if the five I ended up buying were too few or too many, but I'm trusting Asher on this one. Part of me wants to tell her about how I almost got her an ovulation kit, figuring maybe a story about me being a dumbass would help ease the tension. Though judging by the worried look on her face, I'm not sure a joke is appropriate right now.

She's silent as she pulls a few out of the bag, reading them quickly before deciding to take the one where the words pop up. "I guess I should go do it."

I give her hand a squeeze as Asher's words from the pharmacy roll through my mind.

Be there for her.

Hold her hand.

Be whatever she needs from you.

"Do you need anything? What can I do? Do you need any help?"

Gabi turns to me, her eyes squinting and her eyebrows are raised. It's a "what the fuck" look if I've ever seen one.

"Why are you looking at me like that?"

"You asked me if I needed help."

"Yeah. I want to…" I trail off, realizing that my wording probably wasn't the best for what she's about to do. "Oh…"

Gabi walks in front of me. "Maddox. I appreciate you wanting to help, but I have the peeing thing under control."

I feel my face flush, hating that I'm fumbling this already. "I'm sorry. I wanted to offer…"

"I know," she says as she places her free hand on my cheek. "I know you're trying to help, and you are, believe me. I'm just… I'm nervous and I'm scared. And when I'm done doing this, I'm going to need you exactly right here because I'm going to fall into your lap and likely break down. But what I don't need is for you to watch me pee. In fact, let's make it a rule that never in our lives are we going to see the other do that."

Now she's the one with the jokes. "Deal. And I'll be right here when you come back."

"Thank you," she says, replacing her hand with her lips for a soft kiss. "Here goes nothing, right?"

I smile at her attempt at a joke. "Something like that."

I don't know how long I sit on her bed, and it's only a few minutes, but it feels like time has stopped. I haven't moved. Not a muscle. I think I breathe. I may blink a few times. I know for a fact I stare at the carpet so long I think I can count the fibers.

What the hell is about to happen? I know in my heart of heart's she's pregnant. And I want to be excited. I'm going to be excited. I'm already picturing a little girl with Gabi's green eyes, or a little boy who is going to drive his teachers crazy with his devilish smile like I did. The thought brings a blast of warmth to my heart. But as quick as it hits me, the thought I've been trying to keep out all night barrels right through:

Am I my father?

I know I've said to Gabi, my therapist, and the select few friends I confide in that his leaving did shape me into the man I am today. Whenever I have a dilemma in life, I ask "what would Dad do," and I do the opposite. It's served me well so far.

But will that change when I become a father? I want to say it won't, but I can't see the future. Yes, our circumstances are completely different—he and my mom were married, had two children, and the stress of him bouncing from job to job on top of having a family was too much for him to handle—but being a father is a pretty universal thing, right? Is it going to be too much for me? Am I going to be able to handle it? I know Gabi hasn't brought it up yet, but I know she's going to come in at some point and wonder if a twenty-four-year-old guy is ready to be a father? And honestly, I'm asking the same question. I don't know if I'm ready.

I just know I have to be. I will be. There's no other choice.

I know in my brain time has stopped, but I also know it hasn't, and Gabi has been gone for a lot longer than I expected her to be. I know she told me to wait for her, but I'll ask for forgiveness as I get up and walk across the hall to the bathroom.

Surprisingly, the door is open, which is how I see Gabi sitting on the edge of her bathtub.

"Everything okay?"

She doesn't look up at me, but I can tell she's holding the pregnancy test in her hands. I don't remember how long that specific one said it was going to take to show the results, but as Gabi slowly looks up at me, her face as white as the tub she's sitting on, I know the answer. But I still need to hear the words right now. "Is it?"

She nods. "We're having a baby."

A mixture of excitement, panic, worry, and about fifteen-thousand other emotions run through me in a nano second. But prevailing through all of that noise is the words from Asher earlier tonight:

Be there for her.

"Come here," I say, sitting on the toilet and reaching out for her, bringing her onto my lap. She doesn't fight me, test still in hand, as she sits on me, wrapping her arms around my waist as I pull her in tight.

"I've got you," I say, doing my best to sooth her worries. Except at this moment, and unlike other times she and I have been like this, I'm not sure if my words are enough.

CHAPTER 20
GABI

"Gabi dear? Can you grab me a scone to go? I'm taking it to my boyfriend."

I raise an eyebrow to Phyllis. I know I've been out of it the past few days, but I feel like I should've known this. "Since when do you have a boyfriend?"

"You're not the only one around here who can bag a youngin'," she says. "John is a ripe seventy-five and he can still drive. Hottest guy in the home."

"She stalked him for months," Kitty adds. "He finally gave in last week."

"And I'm just finding out about it?" I say as I deliver the to-go pastry.

"We've barely seen you," Phyllis says in a semi-chiding way "Between how busy you are now, and you taking off early the last few days, I feel like we haven't seen you in ages."

"I'm sorry," I say, truly feeling guilty. "The last few days have been a lot. I needed some time to sort some things out."

If that's not the understatement of the century, I don't know what is. Because "sorting some things out" really means buying pre-natal vitamins, crying a lot, freaking the fuck out, and throwing up.

So much throwing up. Whoever coined the term "morning sickness" had to be a fucking man. Because no way a woman gave a title to something that is *that* misleading.

I feel like it's all I do. From the time I wake up to the time I go to sleep, I'm battling so much nausea I can barely get out of bed. Every once in a while in the middle of the day I'll think, "Wow, I'm done."

Wrong. Five seconds later, I'm making a beeline to the bathroom and thanking the architectural heavens I have a bathroom in the back so I'm not throwing up in the customer restroom. Because if Phyllis and Kitty were to have seen me ten minutes ago, they'd be asking questions. And I wouldn't put it past them to figure me out before I'm ready to say the words "I'm pregnant" out loud.

Which I haven't yet. To anyone.

"Are you feeling okay?" Kitty asks. "You look pale."

Damn, she's good…

"I'm fine." I wave her off, making sure to also turn around so she can't analyze my sickly appearance anymore. "Do you want a bear claw for the road before I close up?"

"I'm good," she says. "Plus, I only saw one left. Save it for that hunk of a man of yours."

"You mean the man we haven't seen this week?" Phyllis adds. "Is everything okay with you two?"

"Yes. Fine. We're fine," I assert, though probably a little too quickly.

"That doesn't sound fine," Kitty says. "You two just started dating. The honeymoon shouldn't be over yet."

"She's right," Phyllis adds. "You're still in prime bang like rabbits time."

Oh for fuck's sake…

"Schedules aren't aligning. Don't worry. Everything *is* fine."

At least, I hope it is. Then again, if it's not, it's completely my fault.

As I go to say something out of my ass to get these two to

stop asking me questions, the bell above the door rings, and I almost faint from surprise when I see the brown hair walking through it.

"Shelby! What the hell?"

I run over to my best friend, nausea be damned, and hug the crap out of her. "When did you get into town?"

"Came straight from the airport," she says, patting my back as I squeeze the life out of her. "Figured I'd surprise you."

"Why didn't you tell me you were coming today?" I ask. "I'd have picked you up."

"I needed to rent a car anyway, so this is better." Shelby links her arm in mine and walks us deeper into the bakery, straight to my favorite pair of ornery customers. "You two must be the infamous Phyllis and Kitty I've heard so much about."

"In the flesh," Phyllis says. "And you must be one half of the duo who took our girl here to Vegas."

"Guilty as charged," she says. "I'm Shelby."

"Nice to meet you, sweetheart," Kitty says. "Unfortunately, we have to get going. Can you make sure Gabi here eats something and gets to bed at a good time tonight? She hasn't been feeling herself."

"Tattle tale," I say to Kitty. "No more bear claws for you."

"I'll chance it," she says. "Phyllis. Let's go. Your boyfriend is outside with our ride."

Phyllis stands up slowly and slips on her long trench coat. "Damn right he is. He knows he better be on time if he wants any tonight. Wednesdays are blow job nights."

I slap my hand to my forehead, thankful they're the only two in here right now. But Shelby? I think she might pee her pants laughing.

"Phyllis, I want to be you when I grow up," Shelby says as she wipes tears from her eyes.

"Then always have a man ready to go," she says. "Never settle for one, and keep the one you do have on their toes."

"It's like you're a prophet."

"Better than all the shitty male ones who start cults," she says. "Bye, you two. See you tomorrow!"

Shelby is still laughing her ass off as I fall into the seat just abandoned by Kitty. "Proof every story I tell you about them is real."

"If anything you didn't tell me enough," she says. "But back to what Kitty was saying. Are you feeling okay?"

Lying and hiding my symptoms to a few regular customers and my part time employees is one thing, but lying to Shelby? Impossible. Doesn't mean I'm not gonna try.

"Yeah, I'm fine."

As if my stomach wants to scold me for lying, I'm flying out of my seat the second the words are out of my mouth. Thankfully this isn't a long bout. And in the grand scheme of what my body's put me through over the past few days, it's not even in the top five worst. But it's enough for my conscience to punish me for being a damn dirty liar.

I'm not fine. In so many ways.

I quickly splash some water on my face and rinse my mouth out the best I can before making my way back out to where I left Shelby. When I'm back in view, I watch as Shelby turns off my "open" neon light and locks the door. When she turns to me, her arms are crossed, and I know I'm about to get scolded.

"How far along are you?"

"What?" I ask, playing stupid. There is no way she could know.

"You're pregnant, aren't you?"

"I'm...that's...why would..."

I splutter my way into silence and stare at her. I didn't expect her here, so it's not like I rehearsed how to tell her. Plus, I thought I had more time to figure out how I was going to tell *anyone*. But like most of my life over the past few years, this is not going as planned.

Shelby doesn't ask again as we both take a seat. She reaches for my hand and gives it a comforting squeeze. It's funny how that one little action relaxes me and provides enough strength to say the words out loud for the first time.

"Yes. I'm pregnant."

I look down at the table, letting the words hover in the air. I thought saying it out loud would make me cry. I mean, I've cried every time I've thought about it, so it would've tracked.

I cry thinking about it. Then I cry because I'm crying. Then I feel even worse for crying, and cry some more. I'm basically a clusterfuck of emotions.

"Hey," Shelby says softly. "You tell me what you need me to be right now. Am I excited to be Auntie Bee, or am I making a few calls? No matter your answer, I ask no questions and will make zero judgments."

God I love this woman. Considering how much she hates Nashville, I know whatever's brought her into town isn't making her happy, but I'm so fucking thankful she's here.

"I'm...I don't know if I can make myself be excited yet. But I'm keeping it. That I know. The rest? I have no fucking clue."

I spoke too soon. Cue the tears.

Without hesitation, Shelby gets up from her seat to move one closer to mine, making it easier for her to wrap me in her arms. My best friend isn't an overly touchy-feely person, but man, does her hold right now feel good.

"That is all understandable. I remember the first time you told me you wanted to start trying, but the douche canoe talked you out of it. My heart broke for you. And now you're starting this new phase of your life, and bam! Baby. It makes sense to feel a shit ton of emotions. You wanted this for so long, just not this way."

I love this woman for knowing me so well that she perfectly articulated every thought going through my head. Justin and I had been married for thirteen years. And yes, I know most of that was spent with him in med school, and then his residency, and I was okay with working to take care of us. But I'd always wanted a family. And like so many other things during that part of our marriage, it was always with the caveat of "soon."

Soon…when he was done with his residency.

Soon…after I started the bakery.

Soon…after the economy recovers, because it's too expensive to have a child.

Obviously that was another soon that never happened.

Then again, maybe it was a small favor from whoever controls my fate that we never got pregnant. Custody and child support would've made the divorce even worse than it already was. Now, he can be cleanly out of my life, and I don't have to see him every other weekend at drop-off.

But having a baby now? At this stage of my life? And with Maddox? A twenty-four-year-old man I just started getting used to dating? This isn't how it was supposed to be.

"I want to be excited," I say honestly. "This just…the timing is…"

"Shit?"

"That's one way of putting it," I say through a huffed laugh. "I don't know if I'm ready for this. If I can handle it. The bakery is still getting on its feet. I was looking forward to being my own woman. Traveling. Doing every single thing that I wanted to do in this city that I never got to do when I was married.

"And then there's Maddox…"

Oh sweet Maddox. The man who didn't leave my side the entire night when we found out. The man who didn't say a word and simply held me as I fell asleep. I wanted to cry…God I wanted the tears to flow, but I couldn't do it in front of him. I didn't want him to think I wasn't happy. I also couldn't make myself pretend I wasn't a little sad. I didn't know what I was feeling, and I wasn't ready to say things because I didn't know if they were true or gut-check thoughts.

"How's he doing?"

I shrug. "I haven't talked to him since we found out. I told him I needed some time to clear my head and think about things."

"How long ago was that?"

"Three days."

Shelby's shoulders slump. "Gabi."

"I know," I say, instantly feeling like a horrible person. "It's just...It's too much, Shelby. We just started dating. We hadn't even put a label on it. I didn't even think I could be pregnant until he came over and he was the one who figured it out. It was too much, too fast, and I needed some time to process."

"And did you?"

I shrug. "A little. Not as much as I'd like, but I feel like every day I'm coming to terms with it a little more."

"What was Maddox's reaction?"

"I think he wanted to be happy."

"Think?"

A fresh tear rolls down my cheek as I think back to the little smile he had when I told him it was positive. The one he quickly put away when he realized how freaked out I was. "He's good at noticing things. He saw my panic, so he swallowed his reaction to be there for me."

"Sounds like the young one is a pretty good guy."

I let my head fall to the table. *Dammit.* I've done this all wrong.

"I'm a horrible person, aren't I?"

"What makes you think that?"

I look up at her, wondering why I need to follow that up. "Because I'm selfish."

"Do tell."

At least she didn't say "doth" this time. "My reaction to begin with. Maddox wanted to be happy, but because I was a mess and breaking down, I spoiled that moment for him. And don't even get me started on the guilt I'm feeling. Something I wanted for years is finally happening, but I feel like it's ruining my plans. All I can think about is how this was supposed to be a time where I could really focus on me. No more 'soon.' And now I can't be happy about 'now.'"

There, I said it. The most self-absorbed thoughts I've had since Maddox and I found out.

"You're not selfish. You're human."

"It doesn't feel like that," I admit.

"In your defense, you don't know what you're feeling because you're feeling everything."

If that doesn't hit the nail on the head…

"Let me see if I can help untangle some brain webs."

"Please do. Because every time I think I've got it all figured out and under control, I think of something else, start crying, or have to puke."

"I'd really like it if you didn't do that last one again while I'm here," she says. "But let's start with this place. What are you worried about in terms of the bakery and the baby?"

"The time," I answer immediately. "Am I bringing the baby with me? Daycare? I've been working twelve-plus hour days every day since I opened, but it's what I've needed to do to get this place off the ground. And it's finally here. Yes, I had some help along the way, and I've been able to add permanent part-time help. But it's not at the point where we can afford someone full-time to manage it all, or add another baker. So what does that mean for Sugar and Sweets? The baby? Because there's no way I can do both."

"Who said you're doing this by yourself?"

I let out a sigh. "You know what I mean, Shelby."

"Actually, I don't, but now I'm starting to see the root of our problem," she says. "Listen, I might hate your brother and everything about him, but do you really think he wouldn't shell out the money to hire another baker to help you right now?"

My stomach drops. I hadn't even thought about Beau and how I'm gonna tell him this, but that's future Gabi's problem.

"I know he would, but I don't want to ask him to."

"I have a feeling once he finds out, he's not going to give you a choice."

"You're probably right," I agree. "I just hate— This was always supposed to become mine. Beau never wanted to own a bakery. And we were getting there. Finally, after all this time, it was on the horizon. But now? How could I own a bakery and raise a child?"

"And that's valid…"

I wait for her to add the rest of her thought, but the words dangle in the air.

"What?"

"When you were talking about where the baby would go, or what you would do, or that you couldn't own a bakery and raise a child, not once did you bring up that Maddox could, and I'm hoping would, be helping. You said all of these hypotheticals like you are completely independent in this. Why is that?"

I sometimes forget that while Shelby was in college on a golf scholarship, she majored in psychology.

Sometimes, I kinda hate her for that.

But I kinda hate my next admission even more. "I don't know."

All that gets me is one raised eyebrow. "Try again."

I open up my mouth to talk, but nothing comes out. And that's only because words, and these feelings, are hard to say out loud.

"Okay, I'll start," she says. "Let's pause the bakery talk for a second. I have a feeling your bigger worry—and an important person in this equation—is Maddox. What's your status? Besides the fact that you haven't talked to him in three days."

"I'm not deflecting when I say I don't know," I admit. "We've had two dates, and one was interrupted by a pregnancy test."

"But you like him, don't you?"

Leave it to my best friend to see right through me. "I do. I didn't expect him. Or these feelings. Lord knows I fought them off for how long? But I do like him. He's sweet and kind and he makes me smile. He makes me laugh. He's present and he—"

"Fucks you properly?"

I couldn't keep the smile off my face if I tried. "He's a good guy, Shelby. And I…I feel like…he didn't ask…he seemed happy but…I don't…"

I feel Shelby's hand on my wrist as I stutter for what I'm trying to say. "Are you worried he might not want this?"

I nod, the tears coming back. Sure, I think I saw a smile, but did I? I'm not sure of anything anymore.

"Has he told you that?"

I shake my head. "He says he's gonna be here for me. That he's gonna be here for us. But…"

"Aw! There it is," Shelby says. "Your trauma is back. And here I thought you were all healed."

Fucking psychology major.

"I feel like I'm ruining his life," I finally admit. "He's twenty-four. He has his whole life ahead of him, and here I come along with a baby that beat the odds of a condom. I know he's going to be there. If there's one thing I've learned about Maddox—if he says he's going to do something, he does. And I don't think this is different."

"Then what's the problem?"

I take a deep breath, finally ready to admit my truest fear. "That he's going to regret me. Us. This baby. That he was in the moment and made a promise, and because he's a good guy, he's going to follow through. But as we go down the road, I'm going to feel like I robbed him of what could've been."

I know my best friend isn't a big "there, there" kind of friend. She's the one who tells you straight up what she's thinking. Never ask her a question if you don't want the honest truth. But I'd appreciate it now if she wasn't looking at me like I have two heads.

"What?"

"I'm not invalidating your concerns," she says. "But…and I

don't know…hear me out for this crazy notion. Maybe instead of ignoring him, maybe you call him and talk to him. Ask how he's feeling. Express your concerns. Or you could keep avoiding him and letting all of this fester. Your choice."

I narrow my eyes at my best friend. "You know, no one asked you to come here."

My sarcastic quip earns me a smug smile. "I know. But I'm glad I did, because you needed to hear that. Gabi, I'm so happy for you. You're going to be the most amazing mom in the world, and I can't wait to be Auntie Bee to another little nugget. Look, I know it's scary and not one damn thing you've wanted has gone to plan, but it's here. And when this settles, I know you're going to be over the moon."

"I have a feeling Maddox will be too. But you need to talk to him. You need to be honest and up front with each other and express every fucking fear and worry you have. It's the only way the both of you are going to be able to navigate this together."

"You're right," I say as I move closer so I can hug my best friend. "Thank you so much."

"Anytime," she says. "I'm glad I was here."

"Me too," I say as I feel one more stray tear fall down my cheek. "Now, why are you here? It's not because you had a twisted intuition that I'm pregnant."

"What! You're pregnant?"

Shelby and I jump apart at the booming sound of my brother's voice. Damn him for having a key and always using the back door.

"Beau…uh…hi…"

Shit, shit shit! This is not supposed to be how he found out. Granted, I didn't really have a plan for how it was going to be, but it definitely wasn't going to be like this.

"You're pregnant, Gabi?" he says again, making short work of the distance between us and the kitchen door he came through. "Who? When? How?"

"How? Have you gone that long without sex that you don't remember how babies are made?"

The sound of Shelby's voice—and maybe the realization that she's here—stops my brother in his tracks.

"Shrew."

"Dick head."

If someone walked in right now and saw my best friend and my brother staring each other down like this, they'd probably call the cops in anticipation of a blow up. I know better.

They're going to stand here and stare at each other, subliminally willing the other to crack first. Whoever does is going to blame the other for making them, they're going to call each other names—most of them unsuitable to be said in a family dining establishment—and one of them is going to leave because they physically can't be in the same room together.

Welcome to my entire life with Shelby and Beau.

Actually, I take that back. This didn't happen until we were in high school. To this day, I still don't know why they started hating each other. I just know this has been my life for the past twenty years.

Yay me.

"Okay you two, as much as I love revisiting the classic hits of Beau and Shelby, I need to speed this up." I walk over and place myself between the two of them. "Shelby, put away the claws. Beau, yes, I'm pregnant. And before you ask any other questions, here are the highlights: I just found out, I'm keeping it, and Maddox is the father."

Shelby gives him one more narrowed glare before taking a step back. But Beau? I watch as his face morphs from the hate he's sending to Shelby, as it softens as he focuses on me.

"Are you okay?"

"I am," I say, and for the first time in three days, I don't think that's a lie. "It's been a lot. I'm still figuring a lot out, but I think it's going to be okay."

"It is," Beau says as he brings me into his arms. "If you're happy, I'm happy for you."

I nod against his chest, a fresh wave of tears hitting. Only now, they're of the happy variety. "I am."

"Good." Beau kisses the top of my head. "And don't you worry about a thing with this place. Whatever we need to do, whatever money we need to spend, people we need to hire, it'll be done. Full stop."

"See! I told you the asshole would step up."

I laugh at Shelby's comment, and not because she was right. But because even in a sentimental moment, these two still can't keep from going at each other. I wonder… Maybe if I make them the godparents to my child they'll get along. Then I internally laugh, because I don't think anything—even a priest—could ever make these two like each other.

"You're laughing at that?" Beau chimes in. "She called me an asshole."

"And I meant it." Shelby walks over and grabs my hand, pulling me away from my brother to give me a hug. "I need to get going. Call me tonight after you talk to Maddox."

"I will," I promise. "Thank you."

"I'm here for you. Anytime." She gives my hand one more squeeze before turning to scowl at Beau. "As always, it's not a pleasure seeing you."

"Oh darlin'…why does it have to be like that?"

"Don't call me that."

If I didn't know them better, I'd think they were angry flirting. But then I remind myself Shelby was once asked to say one nice thing about Beau, and all she could tell the interviewer was "he's alive."

"Oh this is going to be fun," Beau says, a new twinkle in his eye he only gets when he's getting under Shelby's skin. "I heard I'll be seeing you around more?"

Shelby grabs her keys off the table, not answering Beau, but turning to me. "Call me, okay?"

Before I can say I will, my best friend storms out of the bakery, leaving me all sorts of confused.

"Care to tell me what that was about?"

Beau shakes his head. "She will when she's ready."

That's not vague and annoying at all...

CHAPTER 21
MADDOX

never thought those two words would fill me with such dread. Or hope. At this point, it's a coin flip.

I mean, it could be "just you" in the sense that she's planning on ending things and doesn't want me making a fuss over her because this is going to be a quick visit. She could've decided she doesn't want the baby, that she's not in a place for it in her life, and with that, she thinks it's best there's no more us. And she'd have every right to do that. Her body. Her life. Her choice. And I'll support her in that decision.

She could also want to keep the baby but put a pause on us. I'd hate that too, but I'd understand it.

Or! Or maybe "just you" is relaxed and she meant it like, "I need you Maddox because I love you and you being in my life will make everything feel better and we're going to have a baby!"

I guess I'll see once she opens the door.

When she does, she doesn't jump into my arms. Then again, even if she wanted to, I wouldn't be able to catch her. It's not like I was going to show up empty handed, no matter what her text said.

"Maddox..."

I had to know that was coming. I mean, I'm standing here with ginger ale, caffeine free Coke Zero, and crackers.

"Gabrielle..."

God it's been too long since we've had one of our standoffs. I've missed it.

I've missed her.

"I told you I didn't need anything."

Those are the words she said. But I relax the second I see the hint of a smile at the corner of her pink lips. "And if you think by now I'm not bringing things, then you don't know me at all."

She steps out of the way, letting me through to her living room. I know I was here a few days ago, but it feels like a lifetime.

When I left that morning, she was honest that she needed some time and space to think about things. I told her I'd give her as much of both as she needed. And that was the truth. While it was killing me to stay away, I knew that's what I had to do.

I needed time to think too. Sure, I thought a lot about things in rapid fire when I went out to get the pregnancy tests, but once it was real, I needed a solid game plan.

So I made notes to call my financial planner to talk about money, as well as my insurance person to talk about upping my life insurance. Football is a dangerous game so I've already had a will drawn up, but now I need to get with my lawyer to change that around. I also made notes about items to look up in terms of strollers, cribs, and everything else baby that I don't know anything about. Oh, and of course preschools. My kid is going to be whatever they want to be, and it's going to start off by making sure they're in the best preschool in the area.

Am I ready to be a father? Who the hell knows. Probably not. But that doesn't mean I'm not going to try my damndest. Because like so many other times in my life, I'm going to do the exact opposite of what my father did.

"I need to start off by apologizing," Gabi says as we take a seat on her couch. I sit next to her, putting my phone and keys on her coffee table. "I knew I needed to think, and thank you so much for giving me that space. But I shouldn't have gone radio silent for that long. That wasn't fair to you."

"Thank you, but you don't need to apologize. It was good for me to think too." I take the chance of reaching out and taking hold of her hand. Thank fuck she not only accepts my touch, but intertwines our fingers together. "How are you feeling? Are you okay? Have you been getting any sleep?"

"I've been hanging in there," she says. "Nausea comes and goes all during the day. It's been pretty constant, but that's been the worst part. Luckily, no one at work has noticed my frequent bathroom trips, but I don't know how much longer that's going to hold up."

"I'm going to guess Phyllis and Kitty know, but they're probably waiting to see when you'll spill the beans. After another week when you don't, Phyllis is going to say something out of pocket and then Kitty's going to come clean."

Her smile is what my soul needs right now. "You're right. And then they're going to start knitting baby blankets at the bakery and pick out their grandma names."

I smile at the thought, but then it hits me that she's talking in future terms. I don't want to ask the question, and I'm ninety-nine percent sure I know the answer, but I need to hear it for myself.

"So...you're...we're..."

"Yes, I'm keeping it," she says, pushing back a stray tear as I do my best not to be obvious about the huge breath I let out. "Back when I was married, I'd always wanted a family."

"Let me guess, the asshole gave you a million reasons why not to have a kid."

"A million and two, to be exact."

Gabi pauses for a second, which gives me an opportunity to bring her a little closer. Not too much that I'm invading her space, but enough for her to know that I'm here for her. However she wants me to be.

"I'm not going to lie to you," she continues. "I'm petrified. This was also the last thing I had on my post-divorce bucket list. And it's one of a million things in my life that have happened unplanned. But at the end of the day, this is something I had wanted. That I do want. And even though I'm terrified, scared, freaked out and everything in between, I want this. I want this baby."

I have no words. For a guy who's been voted most talkative in every classroom and locker room I've ever been in, I don't have the words to express the joy, and relief, that is running through me right now.

So I show her in the best way I know how.

I take her face in my hands and pull her to me, kissing her with every excited, nervous, ecstatic, hopeful emotion I have in my body. I can't hold back my own tears, and I don't try to. In fact, there's something poetic about knowing she's crying as well, and feeling each drop of our emotions as they roll down our cheeks.

"Maddox…you're crying. Do you not want…? I know we didn't get to that part yet, but I want you to know, if you don't want this—the baby or me or anything—I don't want to force you or expect—"

She lets out a yelp as I scoop her into my arms, placing her firmly on my lap. "Oh no, Gabrielle, these are the happiest tears you'll ever see. You and me? Having a baby? I don't know how I could be more happy than at this moment."

I pull her into me again, our lips locking in what might be the most truly happy kiss I've ever experienced in my life. I didn't know kisses could be happy. Hot? Sure. Sexy? Without a doubt. Needy? More often than not. But happy? This is a new one.

One I want to experience every day for the rest of my life.

"What are we doing?" she asks as we pull away, our foreheads resting against each other's.

"Apparently, having a baby."

She pulls away slightly, enough so our eyes can lock after my apparent bad joke. "Aren't you scared? Why don't you seem scared?"

"Of course I am. Every fear and emotion you said earlier, I'm those times a thousand. Plus add in a little childhood trauma for an additional kick."

Gabi doesn't laugh at my self-deprecating joke, but her hand runs softly down my cheek. I lean into it, trying to will it into giving me the strength to tell her everything—and every fear—in my mind.

"I'm so scared, Gabi, of so many things. Am I ready? I mean, I have to be, but am I? I don't know. I had to Google last week how to set the clock on my microwave. That doesn't sound like a guy who's ready to raise a human." That pulls a little chuckle from her, so that's progress. And I hold onto it with everything I have as I spill my guts to her. "But I sucked it up and I did what I do best—I went to the store, bought twenty notebooks, and started writing down my plans. Everything I need to do now that I'm about to become a father. I don't know shit about shit, but I have roughly thirty-four weeks to get my act together."

"Because I want to be there for you. I know I'm going to be there for you. But there's this voice in my head reminding me I'm *his* son, and I'm going to get scared and leave. I promise you, I'm fighting it. Every day. Because I'm scared shitless of becoming my father, and I don't want to be anything like him.

"So yes, I'm scared. Terrified is probably a better word. But I am going to be ready. I'm going to be here. The best partner and father I can be. There's going to be a million and a half things to worry about until November first, but none of those are going to be whether or not I'm in this with you. Because I'm in, Gabi. I'm all in."

Her blinking picks up, and while I think I delivered one hell of a monologue, her curious look is making me wonder what I said wrong.

"You know our baby's due date?" Her voice is soft, but wavers a bit, almost like she's about to cry.

I feel my cheeks flush, because I didn't even remember dropping that date in there. "I went on a baby website. Punched in the conception date. Pretty memorable day for me, for numerous reasons. The internet can be a great place. Also, in case you haven't looked it up yet, tiny tot is the size of a sweet pea."

And, crap. I see the tears pooling back in her eyes. She's definitely gonna cry.

"You looked things up?"

"Of course I did. I might be scared shitless, and might've YouTubed tutorials on how to change a diaper yesterday, but I also bookmarked eighteen baby progress web pages, and I'm damn sure going to know my kid's birthday. I'm going to know everything."

She takes my face in both of her hands as she leans back down into me. "I didn't know your father. I don't know why he left or what his reasoning was for staying away. But I can promise you this, you're nothing like him. I know that for a fact."

She closes off the distance between us, kissing me with such sweetness I might cry again. I've heard of sympathy pains—okay, I read about them during my research—but are there sympathy emotions? Because I'm all over the place tonight.

The feelings quickly turn from happy and emotional to heated and needy. I don't mean to turn the kiss into something more, but there's no stopping it. It feels like weeks since I've held Gabi in my arms, and between her needy lips and her soft skin under my fingers as they trail up under her shirt, I can't help myself.

Apparently, neither can she. She lifts her arms above her head, allowing me to pull off the fitted T-shirt she's wearing. The second it's gone, my face is buried between her tits. God, I missed these. My lips don't know what to do, so they kiss and suck as I make quick work of her bra, needing her nipple in my mouth like I need air to breathe.

"Holy shit, Maddox!" She screams, so loud so that I pull away. "That…I'm so sensitive…it…"

I pull back for a second, letting my tongue swipe over her peaked nipples. "I'm sorry, gorgeous. Do you want me to stop?"

She shakes her head. "No…just…softer."

I kiss the tip of her nose. "I can absolutely do that."

Taking a breath, and reminding myself I'm not a horny teenager sucking on his first boob, I do as she asks. Instead of sucking and nibbling, I kiss and lick. Massage with just enough pressure to make her hips roll down onto my hard dick. Make her hands grip the back of my neck so hard her nails leave a mark.

"Wait," she says, pulling back from the kiss, but not from her position. "We're forgetting something."

"I don't think we need a condom anymore. Per my research, you can't get more pregnant."

That earns me a playful slap to my chest. "Not that. It's just… this…us…I know we've slept together before, and it's probably stupid to have this talk, but…are we…together? Not that we couldn't do this if we weren't, but my brain is already going a million different directions, and I'd really like to not have to wonder about one thing in my life. I'm pretty sure of what page you're on, but I do better in non-assumptions."

I don't know if I could smile any bigger than I already am. "Reach back for my phone."

That makes her eyebrows raise. "Your phone?"

"Yes, my phone." She twists her body to grab it from where I put it down, but I can read the confusion on her face. Oh, yeah. This is gonna be good. "Pass code is 031301."

"You're giving me your passcode?"

"I'll give you my social security number and my bank account information if you ask. Just scroll through the texts until you see something that catches your eye."

I can tell she's slightly hesitant. Bet her dickface ex never let her scroll through his messages. I know she's not going to see anything incriminatory—I haven't texted a female other than her, Ainsley, and my family since we met. I'm also not a cheating asswipe.

After a very assessing stare, she finally does as I ask, and I lay back against the couch, watching the woman I'm crazy about, the woman who's carrying my child, slowly scroll through my phone while sitting topless on my lap. I didn't know this was a moment I needed until now, but I know I'm not going to forget this picture for a very long time.

My eyes are trained on her, watching every little nuance and waiting for the moment she sees it.

And there it is.

Her eyes double in size. Her jaw drops a little. Her cheeks flush. And the look she gives me? Priceless.

"Future wife? When did you save my contact as this?"

"The day Linc gave me your number."

Her eyes are now fully threatening to jump out of her head. "Maddox, I didn't even know if I wanted to date you then."

"I know."

"And you still saved me as that?"

I coyly shrug. "I was very confident in my abilities of persuasion."

For a second, her eyes start to water, and I think she's going to cry again. But just as quick as I saw that, she's tossing my phone on the couch and her lips are crashing into mine.

"Take me to bed Maddox. Right. Now."

"Gladly."

I kiss her again for good measure before sitting up, getting ready to carry her down the hallway to her bedroom. But as I'm about to stand up with Gabi in my arms, I hear my phone vibrate on the couch cushion.

"Do you want me to get it?" she asks, her lips now trailing kisses down my neck.

"Only if you want me to break it."

"You should check it," she says, pulling back from me slightly and climbing off my lap. "I need to freshen up anyway."

I'm about to protest that she needs to do nothing of the sort, when it starts vibrating again.

"For the love of everything!" I scream. "I just want to have sex with the mother of my child!"

She laughs and gives me one more kiss. "You will. Many times tonight. But you answer that. And then, meet me in my bedroom. I promise it'll be worth the wait."

The groan I let out vibrates through her apartment as I reach over for my phone, fully ready to tell whoever's texting me to kindly go fuck themselves.

BEAU

We need to talk.

Okay, maybe that's not what I'm going to tell him.

Fucking hell… He knows…

I remember what Beau looked like when he saw me in the kitchen of Sugar and Sweets. And that was just him having a hunch that we slept together. Now if he knows she's pregnant? From my penis? Maybe I need to update my will sooner rather than later.

MADDOX

Okay.

> Tomorrow. Sugar and Sweets. 8 p.m. Do not tell Gabi you're coming.

What the hell?

"Everything okay?"

I turn to my left, pulled toward her voice like a moth to a flame. And, fuck me. I didn't know I could get harder. But it turns out, I can.

Standing in the hallway, wearing nothing but the T-shirt she took from me in Vegas, is the woman I'm head over heels for.

"Everything is perfect."

I stand up and stalk toward her, which only makes her giggle as we all but run to her bedroom.

Sure, I might die in a bakery tomorrow. I might be murdered with a rolling pin and my body stuffed in a walk-in cooler.

But tonight, I'm going to fuck the mother of my child while she's wearing my shirt, and that's not a bad way to spend your last night on Earth.

CHAPTER 22
MADDOX

don't know how one gets into a fight club—you know, because one doesn't talk about fight club—but I'm pretty sure that's what I'm walking into.

Or a cult. It's up in the air at this point.

I do as Beau instructs, making sure my head lights are off and parking next to the dumpster. I'm the only car in the Sugar and Sweets parking lot, which also has me on edge. Is he here? I completely understand why Beau wants to have a chat with me, but all of this seems excessive.

Then again, I'm not about to piss off my future brother-in-law, so I do as he says, lock my car without the fob, and walk to my doom.

Knock.

One Mississippi, two Mississippi.

Knock.

One Mississippi, two Mississi…shit that's hard to say right in a row.

Knock.

Am I saying Mississippi too fast? I never thought about the speed of my Mississippis.

Knock.

Fuck it. Here goes nothing.

I take a step back after my final pound on the heavy back door. My stomach is completely tied in knots as I wait. It's more than a little ominous back here, with only the moon and the security light above the door illuminating the space. I hear the turning of a deadbolt, which makes me suck in a breath, unsure of what I'm about to walk into. But I swear to everything that's holy and my unborn child, if I walk in and people are wearing robes with candles lit all around, I'm out. I've seen that movie. It doesn't end well.

"Come in."

The voice is deep, and I can't make out whose it is, but I do as it says and start slowly walking through the back hallway. There's barely any lights on inside, and the only sounds are the refrigerators and freezers that are always running.

When I turn the corner, I nearly jump out of my skin. Standing in front of the massive prep table are two larger than life figures. I can't make out their faces in the dark, but I can tell that their arms are crossed, and I don't think they're smiling.

"What is going on?"

I jump again as I feel a hand on my shoulder. "Maddox Gallagher. Welcome to Poker Club."

As if on cue, every one of the lights comes on in the kitchen. I immediately have to squint, the brightness too much for me to handle.

"Oh that was fucking cool…"

The voice standing next to me said that, except now it's not as deep as it was before. I rub my eyes, needing to be able to see what the hell's going on. When I start to regain sight, I see that Beau is in front of me, one of the shadowed figures. And he's standing next to...Asher Reed? Not sure how he got here, but I'm even more confused when I turn to my left and see the starting center fielder for the Nashville BlueBirds, Theo Lawson.

"What the fuck?"

"Here, take a seat," Theo says, ushering me toward a stool at Gabi's prep table in front of a waiting bottle of water. "Sorry if I scared you earlier. I was doing as I was told."

"Oh shut it, you volunteered," Beau chimes in. "But I need to know, were you scared? I feel like you were scared."

"Of course I was scared," I say to him. "I thought I was about to get murdered!"

"I mean, you did get his sister pregnant," Asher says. "Also, if I would've known when I saw you that night it was Gabi that you were going home to, I would've taken a lot more pleasure in our interaction, and given you a lot more shit."

"Good to know," I say, still trying to get my wits about me. "Can we back up like...I don't know...twenty steps? What the hell is going on? What kind of poker club meets in a bakery?"

I have a million more questions, but I have to start here. I also notice the table is suspiciously devoid of a deck of cards, chips, or anything to do with poker. All I'm seeing are three professional athletes, along with bags of flour and other assorted baking ingredients.

"The kind that isn't poker at all." Theo steps up to me, reaching out his hand. "We haven't formally met. Theo Lawson. The founding member of the Poker Club."

"Will you quit with that shit," Beau says. "You can't be the founding member when the three of us came up with this together."

"No, Asher wasn't there," Theo defends. "He came after. The idea was mine and you agreed to it. The sooner you come to terms with that, the sooner we can stop having this fight."

I chug the bottle of water as I watch two of the biggest sports stars in Nashville argue about who started a secret club that might or might not have anything to do with poker. What the hell is my life right now?

"Guys, you're confusing Maddox," Asher says. "Take it easy on him. He's going through a lot right now."

"Thank you," I say. "Can we back up? Like…so far back it would probably be called a prequel?"

"Yes, but there's one thing we need to clear up first," Beau says. I take a deep breath, because I know what's coming. And actually, thank God it is. It's the only thing that's going to happen tonight that I would've even remotely predicted. "I know about the baby."

I nod as I make sure to look him in the eye. I don't want him to think for a second I'm not confident about me, Gabi, or the tiny tot. "I figured you did."

"I talked to her today," he says. "So I know you two had a heart-to-heart last night."

I smile, thinking about what happened after the heart-to-heart. Which probably isn't my best move in front of her brother. "We did. We're on the same page."

"And you're ready for this?"

Now that makes me laugh. "Is anyone ready to become a father?"

That only earns a loud "ha!" from Asher.

"I'll tell you what I told her—I'm going to be ready. I'm going to do everything in my power to be as prepared as possible, and be the best partner I can for Gabi. And really, I think that's all anyone can do."

"See, Devereaux, you don't have to kill him."

I laugh at Theo's statement. "Was that a possibility?"

"He talks a big game," Asher says. "But at the end of the day, pretty boy would never get his hands dirty like that."

"Excuse me for not getting in a fight every day," Theo says to Asher. "What's your total up to this year?"

"You mean what's his total up to in the fight jar his daughter implemented?" Beau adds in. "Has she got the puppy yet? You know that's what she's saving for."

That makes me snicker, remembering Adalyn's swear jar I've already contributed to.

"Don't you fucking worry about it, and it's not everyday," Asher grumbles, throwing up a middle finger for added effect. "But can we get back to business? We properly freaked out Gallagher. You gave him your 'what are your intentions with my sister' spiel. Can we fucking bake now?"

Can we what now?

"Did you say can we bake now?"

"Damn straight we are," Theo confirms. "Here's your apron. Let's get to mixing."

I'm slightly slack jawed as Theo hands me an apron that says "Poker Club" with little chips around the swirly script. "So you call this the Poker Club, but you...bake?"

"Genius, right?" Theo says, his fully tattooed arms tying his apron around his waist. "Though I can't take credit for that one. That was all Asher."

"Only because I refuse to tell my babysitter I'm leaving her with my child to go bake."

I know they just told me a bit of what the hell is going on, but I'm still really fucking confused. "Remember when I said we needed to start back at the beginning? Maybe we need to go before that? Because I still feel like I'm missing a few chapters."

"We'll fill you in, but first, what's your baked good of choice?" Theo says. "We'll get you set up."

"I've only ever made cookies," I say. "But how about tonight I observe. This is...a lot."

"Wise choice. Especially since it's a free bake night," Beau says as I watch him start to knead a ball of dough.

"Free bake?"

"We meet twice a month," Asher says, keeping his focus on the egg whites he's separating. "Usually we can find a night where none of us are playing, or traveling, or taking a kid to dance class, or doing some crazy-ass trick shot with a golf ball."

"Hey!" Beau chimes in. "That trick shot series made me a million dollars in sponsorships."

"We know," Theo groans. "He tells us that all the time. Be ready for it."

"Okay…" I'm still very confused, which apparently Beau can tell.

"Where do you want us to begin?" he asks.

"I couldn't even begin to tell you where."

"That's fair, considering we did try to make it look like we were kidnapping you," Theo says. "It all started last year at one of those boring parties Ethan makes us go to."

It hits me at this moment that Theo is also signed at West Athletes. "Ethan? As in our agent Ethan West?"

"The very one," Theo continues. "You know the type of events he makes us do. Dinners for sponsors so we can have face time and kiss ass. Fancy foods you can't pronounce. Tuxedos that choke us. The savior of an open bar with expensive liquors."

"I'm familiar," I say. "Did you say last summer? I don't remember having to go to one at that time?"

"It was during your training camp, so all the football guys got out of it," Beau says. "Unfortunately, that was the one weekend I wasn't at a tournament, and Ethan conned me into putting on the tux and showing up."

"Oh, you act like it was an inconvenience," Asher interrupts. "Something to know about this guy"—he tips his head at Beau—"if there's an excuse to put on a tux, he's doing it."

"It's not my fault I look like I could be the next James Bond."

Both Theo and Asher roll their eyes. All I can do is laugh. "You mean, minus the accent. And I don't think any James Bond ever had a beard."

My joke hits the mark as Beau narrows his eyes at me.

"Watch it Gallagher. There's still time for me to punch you for getting my sister pregnant."

"Noted," I say, turning back to Theo. "So, sponsor gala. Fancy food and drinks. What happened next?"

"Good transition," he says. "Anyway, Beau and I here had never really talked more than pleasantries at any of these functions. Which is common for most of us. But in this particular case, we found ourselves standing near the bar, only the wall holding us up, as one of the servers brought around a tray of these tiny desserts."

"Mini pavlovas," Asher adds.

"They tasted like shit, and I made my feelings known," Beau says.

"And I agreed," Theo says, fully comfortable in his role right now as storyteller. "Next thing I'm learning is that Beau here is quite the baking show binger."

"It's good television when I'm traveling. The British one is my favorite."

"And little did Beau know that I have wanted to learn to bake since I was a child. But no…I had to play baseball."

I look over to Asher. "And where do you come in?"

He doesn't make eye contact with me, carefully concentrating on filling a piping bag with icing instead. "I was making my way to the bar when I heard these two idiots going back and forth about what was wrong with the desserts. They both knew they tasted like shit, but they couldn't figure it out. After overhearing them going back and forth for five minutes, I grabbed one from a passing tray to taste it for myself. It was the vanilla. The vanilla was off. Which I let them know before making my way back to whatever boring conversation Ethan was making us have."

"When he said that, our jaws went slack," Theo continues. "But it got Beau and I talking. Turns out we both enjoyed baking, or the concept of it, but neither of us ever really dove into it."

"Really?" I ask Beau. "Gabi said she baked as a kid. You never did with her?"

He shakes his head. "A few times. But if it was light out, I had a golf club in my hand. Or I was finding something to make into a putting green. Plus, that was her thing with Mom and Meemaw. I just reaped the rewards of fresh chocolate chip cookies."

"Her cookies are delicious." I really meant it as the actual cookies she makes for the bakery, but apparently by the look Beau is giving me—and the snickers coming from Asher and Theo—he clearly thinks I'm speaking in innuendo. "The chocolate chip variety. And the oatmeal cookie. The edible ones."

Beau chuckles. "Oh it's going to be fun fucking with you."

"Anyway," Theo drawls. "I didn't think about it again, until the three of us were cosmically put together as judges in a charity pie competition."

"No fucking way," I say with a laugh. "It's like the world was telling you this needed to happen."

"Exactly, my football playing new friend," Theo says. "When we went back to deliberate, the three of us were very judgmental, while the fourth and fifth judges didn't seem to care at all that the meringue on their top pick was runny."

"No fucking fluff," Asher says, shaking his head. "I was pissed and left. Told them that they had my vote and they could figure the rest out."

"After he stomped out, we convinced the other two nimrods the wildberry crumble pie should win," Beau says. "During all that, I also happened to mention to Theo that I recently opened a bakery for my sister, and that I had keys."

"And then I happened to mention that I wouldn't mind starting to learn to bake, and that we should get together and do it. Which is why I say I'm the founder."

I look over to Asher. "Then how did you get added into the fold."

He finally looks up to us with a sigh. "I didn't have a choice."

"Yes he did," Theo says. "He makes it seem like we took him hostage. We've only done that to you."

"In reality," Beau adds, "I saw him a few weeks later—coincidentally, in the baking supplies aisle at a grocery store—and floated to him what Lawson and I were doing. He was here first for the next meeting."

"And thus, the baking club was born."

I laugh as I take this all in. Here I am, standing in my girlfriend's kitchen with three superstar athletes. More specifically, three *additional* superstar athletes. Because I know I'm no slouch. But these guys? Next level.

Beau is at the top of the golf—and social media—world. He's the oldest in the room in his late thirties, yet, here he is, lining cellophane on the counter for easier cleanup.

Asher is the one I'd never expect to see in something like this, had I known something like this existed. He's so gruff and so isolated. At least that's what he shows the public. Him being here tells me this is a group of guys you can tell secrets to. Confidants. And every person—pro athlete or not—needs that.

I know Theo the least, which is saying something since I barely know Asher and Beau. From what I've heard around town, he's a good dude. Stud player for the BlueBirds. The closest in age to me. The tattoos give him a little edge, but I can already tell he and I are going to get along just fine.

And while I don't know any of them well, I do know Gabi would trust Beau with her life, and that's good enough for me. If he's bringing me here, sharing this secret with me, rather than calling in his squad to take me to task for getting his baby sister pregnant? I'm not about to look that gift horse in the mouth.

"Poker club," Asher corrects me. "Because if anyone found out the three of us were meeting twice a month to bake, we'd have a lot of explaining to do."

"Have to keep up the appearance," I say. "I mean, what would it look like if it got out that one of the biggest enforcers in professional hockey knew how to pipe icing like that?"

He narrows his eyes at me, and for the first time tonight, I'm more frightened of him than I am of Beau. "Adalyn's preschool has a bake sale this week. And I'm not going to send her to school with some store-bought chocolate chip shit."

I laugh as he goes back to piping out smiley faces on sugar cookies. Which is something I never thought I'd see from Asher Reed.

"Okay. So this is baking—I mean poker club. Can I ask where I fit into this?"

Beau puts down what looks to be a ball of bread dough and brushes his hands down his apron. "When I found out Gabi was pregnant, I called both of these guys. Yes, I had some feelings I needed to vocalize—and though they weren't completely against you, your name did come up. Asher suggested we invite you. That you might benefit from a support group like this."

I look over to Asher. "Did you tell him at that point you already knew?"

He shakes his head. "No. I saved that for earlier tonight so I could see his reaction. It was fucking priceless."

I laugh. I bet it was.

"Thanks…I mean…yeah…there are some guys on the team who have a kid, but not any in my immediate friend group. And I'd be lying if I said I didn't feel like I was paddling like hell to keep my head above water, while also telling the lifeguard I'm not drowning."

"And that's why you're here," Theo says. "Me? I'm not going to be much help until it hits the time where you need help putting shit together. That's my forte. Otherwise, I'm here to bring the vibes. But baby questions? Asher's your guy. Need help deciphering the Gabi dictionary? Who better than her brother."

"Speaking of my sister," Beau says. "She doesn't know about this. That night I saw you two here after hours? That's why I freaked out. These two were on their way."

Things make a lot more sense now. And explains why he was

so jumpy. I assumed it was because of my existence in Gabi's life. "You know she wouldn't care, right? Hell, she'd probably help."

"Which is why we're not telling her," Beau continues. "This is just for us. A way we can get away from the stresses of our sports and responsibilities. Where we don't have to keep up appearances of being these big-time athletes. Where we can get together, do something we all enjoy, unplug for a bit, talk about random shit, and be…"

"Normal." I finish his sentence, loving the sound of that. "A place where you can just be yourself."

"Exactly," Theo says. "So no one knows. We use the bakery after hours. Beau orders our supplies separately so nothing of hers goes missing. We clean up and don't leave a trace behind. Are you good with keeping that secret?"

I think about it for a second, because in theory, I hate to keep anything from Gabi. Then again, if I tell her that her brother invited me to join his twice monthly poker night, I don't think she'd suspect anything.

And I need this group. I need guys to lean on. Guys who have my back in ways my teammates can't. Plus, I did say I wanted to take up baking…

"I can do that," I say. "So when do we meet again?"

"Two weeks," Beau says. "It's macaron night."

CHAPTER 23
GABI

For the first time in weeks, I can actually say that not only am I comfortable, but dare I say, relaxed.

Welcome to the second trimester.

Yes, the bath I'm currently taking absolutely helps. And that my morning sickness has finally curbed. I'm not as tired as I was, which is great because I'm now awake for more than two non-working hours a day. I know Maddox is excited about that. Except the other night I'm pretty sure he was wondering why we weren't in bed by seven.

Mind you, it was seven-fifteen and we were in bed twenty minutes later. My boyfriend is newly twenty-five going on sixty.

Boyfriend. I don't know what's harder for me to wrap my head around—the fact that I'm thirteen weeks pregnant, or that Maddox Gallagher is my boyfriend.

Honestly? It's a tie. As much as I can't believe it, as the days go by, it's becoming harder and harder to imagine what I'd be doing right now if I wasn't here. Well, not physically here, as I'm currently in Maddox's huge bathtub. But here in general.

Here with a successful bakery, where I'm in the process of hiring another baker to help me with the workload. Beau says we can afford it without him chipping in any extra of his own money, and he wouldn't lie about that.

Here with my professional football player boyfriend. A man who shows me daily what it's like to not only be loved, but to be in a relationship that's a true partnership.

And here as an expecting mom. Now that I think about it, this wins the baffling trophy.

Getting divorced in my mid-thirties, I figured the odds of ever being in this position were pretty much slim to none. I didn't even know when I was going to be ready to date again, let alone start a family. Guess slim had better odds than none.

My hands absent-mindedly go to my stomach, where the slightest baby bump has started to show. We had our first doctor's appointment two weeks ago, and hearing Tiny Tot's heartbeat was the most surreal experience of my life. I was crying, Maddox was a mess, and the doctor was all smiles as she pointed out different things on the ultrasound. I heard most of them, but I forgot them as quickly as she said them. Because all I could do was look at the monitor and stare at what I've come to think of as my little souvenir.

The one I didn't know I wanted.

The one that terrifies me every day.

The one I already love so much.

I feel the water start to chill and take that as my cue to start getting out of the bathtub. Except when I open my eyes, I notice I'm not alone.

"Hey gorgeous."

I could say the same to him. Because Maddox Gallagher wearing nothing but drawstring gray sweatpants, leaning against the doorframe, his arms crossed over his broad chest, giving me the perfect view of his trim waist? I don't know if "gorgeous" is an adequate enough word.

"Hey," I say softly as he starts walking toward me. "I didn't hear you come in."

"I didn't know if you were sleeping or not, so I made sure I was quiet." He leans down to place a kiss on my forehead. "Have a good night?"

"So relaxing," I say as I fight the urge to sink back down into the tub, and maybe pull Maddox in with me. "How was poker?"

"Really fun," he says. "We…I made some money."

"There you go," I say as I start pushing myself up. It's either get out now or I'll be here for the night. "Help me up?"

His smile turns wicked. "Gladly."

I give Maddox my hand as I brace myself on the edge, not wanting to lose my balance or slip. As I step out, Maddox reaches over for the towel that I placed on the counter, and begins *thoroughly* drying me off. He pays special attention to my chest—that's not a surprise—but he also makes sure to travel down my body, having me lift a leg so he can dry off each. But then, just as I think he's done, he takes the towel and dries my growing stomach.

Sigh…

"Were you good tonight Tiny Tot?" His lips hover over my stomach, and he places a lingering kiss just above my navel. "If you weren't, you're grounded. If you were, I'll give you ten dollars."

"Tiny Tot was perfect," I say with a laugh, already picturing a conversation like this when our son or daughter arrives. "No upset stomachs, no weird cravings, all and all, a peaceful night."

"That's good." He stands up, kissing me gently but deeply once he's at his full height, and wraps the towel around my body. "I'm glad I went to poker, but now I'm jealous that I didn't get to enjoy this bath with you."

"There will be plenty of chances for that. I'm glad you've joined Beau's poker game. You know, the one I didn't know he even had."

"Me too," Maddox says, and maybe it's from the lingering steam in the bathroom, but I swear his cheeks are turning a little red. "They're good guys."

"I'm biased on my brother," I say as I bring my hair up into a towel. "I can't wait to meet Asher and Theo."

"I'm sure you will at some point," he says, sneaking in for another kiss. "How about this? You finish in here, and when you're ready, I'll be in bed waiting for you with a surprise."

I quirk an eyebrow. "Is the surprise your dick? Because that's not a surprise at this point."

He takes my hand and rubs it against his already hard length. "That's not the surprise. That's just the bonus."

I laugh as he kisses me one more time before leaving me alone in his expansive bathroom. Between the double shower, the separate bathtub that can hold me and him easily, and the double vanity, it's hard to go back to my apartment on Sundays. We've fallen into a groove of staying at my place during the week—simply for logistics as it's easier for me to get to the bakery in the early hours. Which means most weekends we spend here. I knew tonight was poker night, but I asked if I could come early and take advantage of the bathtub while he was gone. I know he wasn't opposed, but asking while I was giving him a blow job didn't hurt.

I hurry and brush my teeth, moisturize in all the right spots, and take my hair out of the towel before slipping on the clothes I laid out. When I walk into the connecting bedroom, Maddox is laying on the bed, head propped up with his fist, and something conspicuously not baby or sex related in front of him on the bed.

"Is that a bag of white cheddar popcorn?"

He nods and holds out his hand like he's a spokesmodel showing off a product. "Not just *a* bag. Six bags."

I laugh as I walk to the bed, and yup, all right in a row, six bags of white cheddar popcorn. Why six bags? Because I mentioned once last night that they sounded good, and the rest is because he's Maddox Gallagher.

"I don't know if you needed to bring them all to bed," I say, putting five of them on his dresser but keeping one bag for me. Because they do sound really good.

"I thought it added to the effect," he says as he opens the bag and grabs some for himself. "Then again, I also pictured throwing every bag off the bed when you walked in here naked."

That makes me laugh. "Sorry to disappoint you. It felt like a T-shirt and sweats kind of night."

Of course not just any T-shirt and sweats. Maddox's Fury gear. Also known as the set from Vegas that I now consider mine. And my favorite thing to wear.

"Not disappointed. You know I think you're sexy as hell in my clothes."

"Good to know a football T-shirt and sweatpants do it for you," I say as I crawl into bed with him.

"Everything about you does it for me."

And just like that, all thoughts of popcorn, and my clothes being on, are out the door. I mean, I should've known. I did know. I've spent the night with Maddox enough times to know that when he's walking around in his fuck-me sweats—yes, that's their new name—or I'm within touching distance of him, more often than not we're going to have sex.

Not that I'm complaining. I never will. The man makes me feel things I didn't know were possible.

Like the way I always feel seen and heard. I didn't realize your heart can literally expand just from having a partner who not only listens to you, but values your opinion. And those tingles that go through my body every time he touches me? And I do mean every time. Plus, what he just did in the bathroom? Taking care of me like I'm a precious gem? I almost cry every time he does it.

Then of course there's the sex. I never knew I could actually have multiple orgasms. I used to struggle with singular. Turns out it wasn't a me issue. I wish I knew that years ago—it would've saved me over a decade of frustration and self-defeating thoughts wondering what was wrong with me when it came to sex with Justin. Newsflash: There was nothing wrong with me.

I've discovered I really enjoy reverse cowgirl, too. It's fun. Turns out, you *do* learn new things every day.

I'd heard that second trimester hormones were a real thing. That my sex drive was going to go way up. So I don't know if these thoughts are because of those, or because of how ridiculously sexy Maddox looks in bed eating popcorn.

I'm gonna say it's about fifty-fifty.

"Can I have a piece," I say as I crawl over to him.

"Gladly." He places one delicious bite on my tongue, and I swear his eyes dilate even more when I close my lips around his fingers before pulling slightly away from him.

"Mmm." I make sure to over exaggerate the noise, and by the swallow of his throat, I'm pretty sure it did the trick. "Now…is there anything else you want to feed me?"

Popcorn kernels go flying through the air as he throws the bag off the bed, rolling me over to straddle me, each of his hands holding my wrists above my head. My laughter is quickly swallowed by his mouth crashing into mine, kissing me like he hasn't in days instead of hours.

"Does my gorgeous girl want my cock?" he asks as he inches away the barest amount..

I lick my lips, knowing what I need. "Yes please."

"I love how you ask so nicely." Maddox rolls us over, taking my chin in his fingers to give me one more soft, yet charged, kiss. "Take me in that sweet mouth Gabrielle."

He lifts up his hips so I can pull down his pants, and luckily for me, Maddox conveniently forgot about his boxer briefs when putting on his fuck-me sweats.

I can't hold my moan as his cock springs free, my hand starting to stroke his length as I lick my lips. Except when I lean forward, ready to lick the precum from his tip, his hands cup my face, stopping my movement.

"Is there a problem?"

He smiles at my playful words. "Never gorgeous. But you're forgetting something."

"And what would that be?"

His hands trail down to my shoulders. "Shirt off. I want to feel those tits against me as you take me down your throat."

Never, and I mean never, did I think I was the kind of woman who would respond, or even get turned on, by a dirty mouth. Yet here I am, sitting up to strip off a T-shirt like I'm under a spell.

"That's it," he says, giving himself a few strokes as I take my time, slowly pulling the fabric over my body. "Are you going to let me fuck them later?"

I smile as I squeeze them together, knowing—and feeling—how much it turns him on. "Possibly. But I get to have my fun first."

"Please do," he says as he lays back. "Show me how much you want me."

I don't waste another second. Lowering my body to his, I slowly, yet ever so deliberately, lick his cock from root to tip. I know Maddox loves it—the noises he makes when I do it are addicting to hear—so I make sure to start off with that every time.

And that has turned into quite a few times.

That's come as a bit of a shock to me, to be honest. Blow jobs with my ex were always more of a chore than mutual foreplay. A way for him to get pleasure that was never reciprocated. A means to an end so he could get off quickly and have an excuse to not have sex with me.

But with Maddox? I would suck this man's dick every morning, and every night. And if he came into the bakery in the middle of the rush and asked for it, I'd put up a temporarily closed sign.

The difference? Maddox. How he holds my face while I do it —reverently, not controlling. How he's always touching me, making sure I know he's in the moment with me, not just lying back and reaping the pleasure. How he'll whisper dirty and delicious words to me, or sweet ones that turn me on just as much. But it's also knowing that no matter how it ends—because sometimes he refuses to finish in my mouth—what I just did to him will pale in comparison to what he's going to give back to me.

And that's what comes with being with a secure and giving man.

"Look at me. Let me look into those eyes as you're sucking my cock."

I do as he says, loving how each of us are still in control in our own ways. When Maddox and I were together in Vegas, I honestly thought the brazen and bold woman I'd turned into was just a product of the night. But the more I'm with him, and the more we learn every little thing each of us likes, the more confident I am in myself.

I've realized that Vegas Gabi was actually me, I just didn't know it yet.

I love telling him what I want, and I love how he reacts to it. He's not scared when I take charge. In fact, he loves it. The way his eyes dilate when I tell him to fuck me? Or earlier, when I told him to feed me his cock? That's a rush I never thought I'd want.

But not only do I want it, I've become addicted to it.

I adjust my angle, allowing my free hand to cup his balls as I work him in my mouth. I feel his body tense underneath me, signaling that I am seconds away from making this man lose his mind.

"Gabrielle...fuck...I'm about to—"

I don't falter. I don't even pretend to let up. Instead I take him farther, opening my throat so his hips are hitting my face as I feel him empty himself into me. The sounds he's making are earth shattering, his hands holding onto my head like he needs me to keep him grounded.

"Goddammit woman," he moans, lifting my head as I swallow the last drop of his cum. "Get up here."

He pulls me up to him, fluids and sweat be damned, and

holds me to his chest like I might disappear. Sure, that might've been my default a few months ago. But now? Now I'm wondering if I'm ever going to leave.

"Have I told you how perfect you are?"

"You've alluded to it."

He kisses my forehead before rolling us to our sides, my leg naturally wrapping around his as he holds me in his arms.

"How was your day?"

I smile, because of course we could just share an intensely intimate moment, then easily fall back into the mundane seconds later. But even talking about things as boring as our days, it's still special because I'm doing it with him. Funny how a person can feel that way when she knows her partner actually listens and cares.

"Fine. A little slow for the weekend, but honestly, I didn't mind. I had a ton of things to catch up on, so I was able to close right on time and then head back to my apartment to grab things for tonight and tomorrow because I forgot to this morning."

"I hate that, you know."

"Hate what?"

"You going back and forth."

"I know, but it's easier right now," I remind him. "My apartment is two miles from the bakery, and I hate navigating traffic here each morning. Especially during the week."

"I know," he pouts...but just as quickly as his lip juts out, I watch his eyes get wide. "Wait. I have an idea."

"Why do I feel slightly nervous?"

"Don't be," he says. "What if I buy you a house?"

I know we're each coming down off of sexual highs, but the man isn't thinking straight. "You want to buy me a house?"

"Yes. But for us," he says with all the conviction in the world. "For you, me, and Tiny Tot. For our family."

Every time he calls the baby "Tiny Tot" my heart flutters just a little. And by just a little, I mean a lot. But I need to ignore the flutter to let the father of my child know that right now, he's being insane. Romantic, but insane.

"Maddox…"

"Gabrielle…"

I had to know it was coming, but I'm not backing down. I'm so determined to be taken seriously about this that I sit up to have this conversation—because serious conversations can't happen mid-cuddle.

"I love that you want to do that for us. But, is it practical? Where would we live? Are you just paying for it? Am I contributing at all? There's a lot to think about. Also, I know it doesn't feel like it—probably because we did things all out of order—but this is new. We're new. Who moves in with their significant other, or buys a house with that person, when they haven't even been dating for two months?"

"I don't know? My Aunt Jane moved in with my Aunt Becky after two dates."

"I'm being serious Maddox."

"So am I. They're the happiest couple I know."

Maddox sits up, putting us at eye level. "Counterpoint?"

I smile because how can I say no to his determined look. Also doesn't hurt that he's tracing circles on my thigh right now. It's making me want to forget talks about living situations and see if he's ready for round two.

"The floor is yours."

He stops tracing circles, but only to take my hand in his. "When I told you that I was all in, I meant it. And I'm not just talking about financially or making sure that I installed the car seat correctly. I saw a future with you from the moment you walked up on stage with me. I want to delete the word "future" from "wife" one day in my cell phone. I want to find your dream home with a huge back yard and a swimming pool and the biggest bathtub we can legally install."

"That's a big-ass bathtub."

"And I'll get it for you. No questions asked." He cups my

face with his hands, bringing me in closer. "Yes, this might be fast. It might be out of order. But it's in my plan. And I hope it's in yours too."

Damn this man and his puppy dog eyes and his good heart.

But he's right. I might've been late to the game on everything in terms of us. But I can't deny what I feel for him. What he makes me feel. That when I think of my life in five years, it's of me, him, and our kid, all together at a pee wee football game—either as a player or a cheerleader.

I didn't plan for this. I didn't even think I wanted this. But here I am, falling in love with Maddox Gallagher.

"Okay."

The smile starts slowly forming on his face. "Okay?"

"Yes, okay." Maddox starts to pull me down onto him, but I put my finger in front of his mouth. "But I have a few rules."

He takes my finger in his and quickly kisses it before moving away. "I wouldn't think anything less."

"I'm serious Maddox, we have a—ah!"

I can't get another word out, because before I can tell him rule number one, I'm on my back and he's pushing my legs apart, bringing my sweatpants down soon after.

"You think of your rules. I'll just be down here celebrating."

My laughter trails off the second his tongue hits my center.

But he's right. We can talk later. We have plenty of time for that. Right now, I'm going to enjoy my boyfriend fucking me with his tongue while I fantasize about a house with my dream kitchen that also comes with a pool and, most importantly, him.

CHAPTER 24
MADDOX

On our way to the doctors office. It's gender day, baby! Final predictions. Winners get to pick next week's baking challenge.

Girl. And I hope she has a thing for athletes so you get a taste of the medicine you had for so many years.

Also girl. But mostly because I need a fellow girl dad. Braiding hair is for the fucking birds.

Beau? Care to take a stab?

You're both wrong. It's a boy. I already sized his golf clubs. So get ready to lose gentlemen, next week we're making sourdough cinnamon rolls.
I'll bring my starter.

You mean Dough-gy?

BEAU

That's not its name and you know it. I would never name my starter after a bad golf score. Bad juju.

ASHER

Apologies to Betty.

BEAU

Thank you. Put some respect on her name. RIP to my favorite Golden Girl.

THEO

You mean the longest relationship Devereaux has ever had?

BEAU

Fuck you both.

MADDOX

I'm so glad I'm in this group.

laugh and put my phone back in my pocket as Gabi and I wait in the doctor's office. I wish she knew her older brother was a sourdough expert. The man makes one hell of a cheddar and jalapeño loaf. Sugar and Sweets would make a killing if he sold it there.

"Does it feel like this is flying? Because I swear we just found out yesterday," I say as the nurse calls back another couple.

She looks over to me, her head falling to my shoulder as she rests her hands on her growing baby bump. "It's somehow going so fast that I'm freaking out that we have nothing ready, but I also feel like I've been pregnant forever. And we're only at the halfway mark."

Today is twenty weeks to the day that Gabi has been pregnant, which means we're set up for the big gender reveal. And when I say big, I mean her and I. Knowing her ex has exhibited tendencies to stalk her social media, and that anything I post goes immediately viral, we both agreed that keeping it off of the internet was best. Our families and friends know. Most of my teammates, coaches, and my agent know. And now that she's clearly showing, the regulars at Sugar and Sweets know. Phyllis and Kitty—who of course claim that they knew she was pregnant way before we did—are already knitting baby blankets.

On the same note, we decided against a big party. Would I have liked one? Sure. I'm always down for a party. But we're under limited time with me a few weeks away from training camp and Gabi starting to hire and train more people to help once she's out for maternity leave. Then there's my grand idea of house hunting in between all that. With all of those factors, it was an easy decision to keep the gender with just the two of us. And, of course, the doctor when we find out in roughly thirty minutes.

"We have some things ready," I say as I put my arm around her, giving her a better angle to rest her head on my shoulder. "I mean, we did get a house."

That brings a huge smile to her face. "Not just a house. Our perfect house."

A little known fact about professional athletes is that the real estate market moves fast between us. Players are always getting cut or traded. Which means players are always moving in and out of the city.

That next morning after Gabi sucked me off so good I decided to buy her a house—zero regrets on that decision, in case anyone was wondering—we started putting our wants together. How many bedrooms and bathrooms. Ranch or two-story. How far out of the city we'd consider moving. If a commercial baking kitchen could be installed so Gabi doesn't have to head into the bakery on her day off to make one thousand cookies for the local bake sale. Or if the Poker Club needs a new location. You know, the important things.

After we settled on a four-bedroom, three-bath house that's no more than ten miles outside downtown Nashville, we went on and made our wish list. Things we'd love for it to have, ranking from "really, really, want" to, "I mean, it would be nice."

And yes, those are the actual names of the columns Gabi wrote down in my new homeowner notebook.

For her, it was a big kitchen, complete with a massive center island that could also serve as a breakfast bar, a wrap-around porch, and an oversized bathtub. I wanted a swimming pool and a bonus entertaining space, so that way I could have my teammates over. Some of our veteran guys do that, and I love how it always bonds us. As I grow through the organization, I know one day I'll be a veteran, and I want to keep that tradition alive. Oh, and a big back yard for Tiny Tot and, of course, my hypothetical—but we're totally getting—dog, Sir Barkley.

When we looked at the list, we wondered if we could ever find anything that would even come close to matching our dream home. We considered the possibility of building, but we wanted to be in before the baby comes in November. And then fate said hold my beer, and the BlueBirds traded a veteran left fielder who happened to live in our perfect home.

In the blink of an eye, I was writing one of the biggest checks I've ever written, and we were signing roughly eighty-thousand pages of paperwork. I was all smiles once I scribbled my name on the final line. Poor Gabi looked like she was going to pass out. But she recovered, and walked away with keys to our new house —one we're going to start moving into after training camp in August.

"Can I admit something to you?"

"Depends. Is it gonna be one of those times where you tell me I'm right? I really love those times."

She playfully slaps my chest. "Unfortunately, yes."

"Then absolutely. Do tell."

"I know I made a stink about you hiring movers, and insisting they pack for me. But knowing I don't have to, and that's one less stress I have to worry about…"

Gabi trails off and I just give her a smirk. "Just say it, Gabrielle. Say the words. Three little ones. So easy to say."

She narrows her eyes at me. "Keep talking like that and I won't."

I lean in and kiss the tip of her nose. "Yes you will. Just whisper them. I'll love it even more."

She gives me a mini eye roll before a reluctant smile. "You were right."

I let my head fall back and pump my first in triumph. "Victory!"

"I really shouldn't have said it."

"Too late, gorgeous. It's out in the world. No backsies."

Gabi's state of shock after leaving the realtor's office lasted until we walked into her apartment. Then she promptly started freaking out. She was pacing in circles, wondering how she was going to pack her apartment, run her shifts at the bakery, and finish training the baker she just hired. When I suggested hiring movers—the kind that packed your house for you—she immediately scoffed. She didn't need them. She could do it on her own. She just had to figure out a schedule.

I said her name.

She said mine back.

I stepped into her space and pressed against her, letting her know I wasn't budging. That I was going to do this for her. That in case she forgot, I just signed a multi-million-dollar contract and there was still money left over in the account even when the house check cleared.

Then I kissed her.

I won.

And I just won again by hearing her say those three little words.

"Say it again," I whisper.

"I hate you."

"Wrong three words."

She lets out a groan. "You were right."

"There we go. Was that so hard?"

She smiles and leans back into me as another couple is called back. While those three words are amazing to hear, so would another three. Yet, as much as I want to hear them, I'm not worried in the slightest that neither of us has said them out loud. I know we love each other. We show it to each other every day. Maybe five months ago I would've thought I'd need to hear it, but I don't now. I love this woman. She loves me. And one day we'll say it out loud. Until then, we'll be here waiting to hear the most important word of the day—boy or girl.

"Gabi Devereaux."

We follow a nurse back into an exam room and Gabi takes her position on the exam table. After the standard questions and checks, the nurse excuses herself, leaving us alone to wait for the doctor.

"You ready for this?"

I detect a little bit of uncertainty in her question. "I am. Are you?"

She nods, but I see her eyes swirling. "Gabi?"

"I'm fine," she says with a shake of her head. Probably because she's not fine.

"I don't know why you're lying to me right now." I stand up and take her hand in mine. "Talk to me. Whatever you're thinking or feeling, I'm here."

As far as Gabi has come with her trust issue, and voicing her opinion over the past few months, there are times she reverts back to staying quiet. But hey, that's healing. Sometimes it's not a smooth path. All I can do is be there for her, assure her that she can tell me whatever she wants, and then make damn sure her feelings are not only heard, but seen and acted on.

"I'm not sure I want to find out the gender."

I try to hide my disappointment, but I don't think I do a particularly good job of it. "Oh...I thought..."

"No! That's not what I mean!" she quickly says. "I do want to find out. Just not here in the office."

"I thought you didn't want a big reveal?"

She shrugs. "I don't want the big part, but I think I want the reveal part."

Okay. I can work with that. "What were you thinking?"

Before she can tell me the idea that's putting a spark into her green eyes, her OB comes into the room.

"Ready to find out if we have the next big star for the Nashville Fury in there?"

We share a look, nothing but love in our eyes, as we nod.

"Yes," Gabi says. "But I have a favor to ask you."

"Ermygod, Gabi. These are fucking amazing."

Both of us laugh as Theo is all but drooling as he eats one of the many desserts Gabi and her staff made for today's gender reveal get together.

Not a party. A party is big. A get together is more intimate apparently. At this point, whatever my future wife wants to call it is fine by me. I just know that almost everyone she and I love are here today, and we're finally going to find out if Tiny Tot is a boy or girl.

Emphasis on finally. It's a good thing Gabi gave the envelope to her newest baker, Josie, so she could make the reveal cake. Otherwise, I know for a fact I wouldn't have been able to resist opening it. I was the same way with Christmas presents as a kid.

I'm thinking girl. She's convinced boy. We might or might not have a friendly wager of oral sex on the line for this one. It's a bet I don't care if I win or lose.

"I appreciate that," she says with a warm smile. "I'd never made them before, but they felt fitting for a party like this."

"No doubt," he says, swallowing the last bite of cupcake. "What's your secret? I've never had one this fluffy."

Gabi gives him a curious look. "Are you an undercover baker or something?"

"No," Theo says a little too quickly. "Just an appreciator of good desserts."

I have to turn my head at that one to fight off my laughter. This dude is the worst liar in history.

"Then I can safely keep my secret," she pats his shoulder. "A baker never tells."

"I thought that was a magician?"

"Same thing," she says before giving me a quick kiss. "I'm going to go talk to Hannah and Shelby. You okay?"

"Of course," I say, pulling her in for a better kiss. "Reveal in twenty?"

"Sounds good."

Our hands stay held until we can't reach each other anymore. When I turn back to Theo, I realize the rest of the baking—I mean poker—club has gathered around him.

"Thank you guys again for coming," I say. "I know it wasn't the easiest to schedule."

Beau gives me a pat on the shoulder. "We wouldn't have missed it."

Once Gabi told me her idea, we immediately started planning. And we quickly realized scheduling this was going to be a nightmare. We did the best we could to coordinate everyone's schedules for our Vegas-themed gender reveal, complete with cookies decorated as playing cards, cake bars shaped like microphones, and the grand attraction—a two-tiered cake that, when we cut into it, will tell us if we're having a boy or girl.

Oh, and of course a healthy amount of bear claws. For obvious reasons.

"It was no trouble," Asher says as he takes a quick glance to get eyes on Adalyn, who's currently coloring with my niece. "I'm in offseason mode. Fucking love July."

"Speak for yourself," Theo says. "This month I swear is the longest fucking month of the season. I've never been so happy to get a rainout game as I was today."

"Mother Nature and her fucking rain can go fuck herself," Beau says with a grumble.

"Yeah, sorry about that," I say, glad Adalyn's across the room. She'd have a field day billing him for all the f-bombs. "Last weekend was tough."

Last weekend was the first time I watched Beau play in a major tournament—and apparently it's one of two he's never won. Gabi and I were glued to our televisions all weekend as Beau took the lead into the final day. Unfortunately though, the skies opened up and rain came down hard and fast on the back nine. Because there was never any lightning, play continued.

Beau ended up losing by two shots.

"Fucking bullshit is what it was," he groans. "They should've stopped the tournament for inclement weather. It was a fucking major, not some podunk bank's invitational."

"Aww… is someone still upset they lost? Doesn't matter if he's thirty-five or fifteen, poor Beau Devereaux still can't handle losing."

I watch as Beau's eyes turn to fire as Shelby walks in front of us, mocking him the way I've learned only she can. I've only been in a room with them one other time, but I swear, if I didn't know from Gabi that they vehemently hate each other, I'd put money on them being three seconds away from fucking.

I watched *General Hospital* growing up. I know that look before the enemies become lovers.

"Rich coming from the woman who withdrew from a tournament last month because of a toe injury."

"Fuck you. It wasn't a toe, it was my finger. How the hell am I supposed to grip a golf club with my finger double in size?"

"You wouldn't hurt your finger if it wasn't always stuck up your ass."

Now it's Shelby's turn to narrow her eyes. As for myself, Theo, and Asher? We just take a step back, and I think we all wish we had some popcorn.

"Fuck you, Devereaux."

"You wish, darlin'."

"Shrew."

"Asshole."

The two stare at each other for a few more seconds, before Shelby spins on a heel and storms back to Gabi and Hannah. Beau doesn't say anything else and bolts off in the other direction, leaving the three of us slackjawed.

"We're asking him about this next Poker Club, right?" Theo asks. "Because there definitely was a thing there."

"Fuck yes we are," Asher says just as Adalyn starts sprinting across the bakery. "Adalyn! No! No more candy!"

Theo and I share a laugh before we part ways. Since I'm by the cookie table, I do a quick once over to make sure nothing needs replacing, when I feel an arm come around my waist.

"I can't believe my baby boy is going to be a dad."

I smile as I turn to my mom, wrapping her in a tight hug. "Believe me, neither can I."

When Gabi and I were planning this, we wanted to do it quickly. Even though it was killing both of us that we didn't know, we also wanted to make sure we had time to get our families and friends here. Unfortunately for Gabi, her parents couldn't make it as they had a summer-long travel schedule that they were in the middle of. They did say they'd reroute through Tennessee on their way back to Louisiana to make sure they were here for the baby shower, though.

Yes, Gabi was disappointed, but both Shelby and Hannah were able to make it. The three of them had a girls' night last night, my only duty being to bring them pizza and refreshments before seeing myself out. Which was fine. I hadn't seen my mom, sister, or niece in months, and it gave us the time we needed to catch up.

"I'm proud of you," she says as Hannah starts gathering everyone together for the reveal. "You did good."

I laugh. "That wasn't your tune when I told you what happened."

She shrugs. "I've had time to process. And meet Gabi. That helped a lot. She's wonderful, Maddox."

"She's one of a kind," I say, smiling, as Gabi winks at me from across the room.

"She's the one for you," Mom says. "And that's what matters."

"Even if she's the one you warned me about all those years?"

She laughs. "I'm just glad it happened after college."

Since my dad wasn't around, all of the big "talks" in my life came from my mom. The one that no teenage boy of a single mother will ever forget is the sex one. And in her case specifically, the importance of a condom. I remember her words like it was yesterday.

"Just please. Use one. Every time. The last thing you need is a child you didn't ask for with a woman who might or might not be only using you for a potential chance of being a pro football wife. Just...wrap it up. Please, Maddox. For the love of God."

The irony of it happening while I was wearing a condom is not lost on me.

But once Mom met Gabi, every one of those fears of her son getting the wrong girl pregnant—or the worries I know she had when she heard that Gabi was nearly eleven years older than me—melted away. She saw the woman I'm in love with. The mother of my child. They laughed and shared stories. Mom told embarrassing tales of me as a kid, and Gabi made her bear claws and a strawberry pie that sealed the deal.

"Thanks for being here, Mom," I say, giving her a kiss on the head. "Are you ready to find out if you get a grandson?"

"Absolutely," she says, patting my chest. "And if it is, I

already have a list of things ready to give to Gabi. Raising a mini Maddox isn't for the weak."

I laugh and give her one more hug before I meet Gabi at the table with the cake displayed on it. We each say a few words before taking a champagne flute in our hands that we're going to use to scoop out the cake.

"Ready?" I ask, the anticipation about to boil over.

"So ready."

We share one emotional but relatively chaste kiss before silently counting to three. We do our best to keep looking at each other, not wanting to accidentally see what the filling is. Except I see it. She does too. And I immediately burst into the happiest tears of my life.

CHAPTER 25
GABI

"First I want to show you this stroller I saw. Every review is amazing. Completely top of the line. All the bells and whistles. It's also apparently so strong it can survive being hit by a moving train."

Now that gets my attention. Not for the reason Maddox probably thinks, though.

"Our stroller is going to survive being hit by an actual locomotive?"

"Yeah. It's really durable."

I stop him before he can start pushing the buggy through the all things baby store. "Maddox…"

Instead of his normal "Gabrielle," I'm just met with a blank stare. Bless his heart.

"Maddox. Father of my child. The man I'm about to share a bathroom with on a permanent basis. Let's back this up. While I appreciate such a sturdy piece of equipment for our unborn child, I need to know in what universe are we letting go of the stroller where it rolls far enough, and fast enough, away that it could be hit by a moving train? Why are companies testing these on moving trains? Also why are we that close to operating train tracks? On that note, if it were to happen, I'm not sure if the stroller gives much protection at that point."

"Hmmm…you're right," Maddox says. But just when I think he's back to Earth, he continues. "I could have the kids down at LaunchPoint build a bubble for the stroller. I feel like they could do it."

"First, we're not using child labor to build us things. Second, do you really want our son to be riding around in a bubble?"

His shoulders sag for a second, and honestly, he's too cute right now. Ridiculous. But cute.

"Listen," I say as I place both of my hands on his chest and lean up for a quick kiss for reassurance. "I love how excited you are. And that you want to spend your last day of the off-season shopping for baby things. But how about we just focus on furniture for the nursery today like we planned?"

He nods and leans in to give me a quick kiss. "You're right. But what if—"

"If we pass the strollers, you can absolutely show me the one you want."

"You're the best."

Maddox gives me one more kiss on the cheek before we make our way through the store, heading straight for the baby furniture. I know both of us are going to get sidetracked. I'm going to see baby clothes and get a little too excited, and Maddox is going to find that stroller and geek out. But we have a mission—buy every single furniture item we need for the nursery.

It's now or never. I'm nearing the end of my second trimester, we're moving into the house slowly but surely over the next few weeks, and Maddox starts training camp tomorrow where he'll be gone for a month. Then when he gets back, it's football season. So now that we know it's a boy—and that we've decided to go with a blues and whites theme for the nursery—we can start furniture hunting.

"Are you absolutely sure you don't want a football theme?" I ask as we pass by a section of Fury merchandise, complete with

Fury onesies. "I'm fine with football if you want it. This isn't the hill I'm going to die on."

He shakes his head as his eyes wander down the technology aisle. I have a feeling we'll be stopping there and checking out monitors before we go.

"No. If my kid wants to play football, it'll be because he fell in love with it all on his own. I don't want him to think we have this expectation for him because he was literally sleeping around footballs since he was born. Sure, there'll be team gear and clothing, and at least one mini football he'll play with. But I just feel like if that's literally all he grows up around, it could put some sort of weight on him that I don't want. He can be whatever he wants. A football player. An engineer. A baker because he inherited his mom's talent. An astronaut. A singer. A dancer. Sky's the limit, and I want to let him find it out for himself."

I stop walking, needing a second to take all of that in. I know for weeks I couldn't get past Maddox's physical age. And I think there will always be times when I'm reminded just how far apart our birthdays are. But then there are moments like this when he says things that are so mature, so wise, so thoughtful, that I'm reminded that age is actually just a number. And if a man says, does, and thinks things like Maddox does every day? Then fuck the number. It doesn't mean shit.

"Everything okay?"

I nod and take his hand, pulling him into an empty aisle. Sure, people are still probably walking by, but Maddox can't say things like that—especially when my hormones are raging like they are—without me kissing him.

His surprise at my reaction lasts the better part of a second. Then he's wrapping his arms around my waist and turning me around so my back is against the shelving, as he brings me in as close to him as I can be. Damn baby belly.

"You're killing me, Gabrielle," he says, his lips leaving mine, but just so they can move up to my ear. "Is there a dressing room we can slip into?"

I moan, loud enough that if there are people in the aisles to either side of us, they have to be wondering what we're doing. But in my defense, Maddox's tongue is swirling at my pulse point, and lately that's a one-way ticket to an orgasm.

"We're at a baby store."

He replaces his tongue with his lips, leaving a wet kiss that I can feel down to my toes. "You started this. You don't want me to finish it? I bet you want to. I bet if I felt you right now, you're already wet for me."

The moan I let out says "yes." But I need to say no, even if he's right. "In my defense, you said the sexy things first. How was I supposed to resist?"

"I love how turned on you get when I talk about the least sexual things possible."

"What can I say? You just do it for me, Gallagher."

Our eyes stay locked for another second before Maddox leans in and kisses me hard—but quick—then steps away.

"You go start looking at the changing tables. I'm going to go look for this stroller, but mostly because I need a second."

I can't help but smile knowing he's just as affected as I am. "I can't wait to see it."

I give a glance down to his cock then back up to his eyes, and hear him let out another groan as I saunter away.

I'm all smiles as I let myself browse through the baby clothes Maddox had to know I wasn't going to be able to resist. I don't know what it is about baby boy clothes, but I've become a little obsessed. I mean, the little overalls? Ironic onesies that say things like "Mr. Steal Yo' Girl?" Little Fury football jerseys? I want them all. Luckily for me, I have a partner who is just as excited for everything as I am, and doesn't bother looking at price tags.

Every day I'm getting better at coming to terms with Maddox being the bread winner in our relationship, and that it's going to be a few years until I'm the owner of Sugar and Sweets. Because of the pregnancy—and Beau insisting every penny I earn goes to me and his nephew—we've agreed that he's going to stay the owner for the time being. This way, he can still pay me a salary, and I can make sure everything I need is taken care of. At first, I wanted to be stubborn about it. But he's right. If I bought the bakery now, no way would I be able to handle the stress.

So yes, I technically could afford all ten of the baby outfits I just picked up, but I know Maddox won't let me pay for a single one of them. The strange thing is, I don't mind. And it's all because of who Maddox is. He's not holding his paycheck over my head. He's not reminding me of how much he makes on a daily basis, emphasized with the knowledge that he just bought a million-dollar home for us. He's not telling me every day how his career is more important than mine.

And I love him for that.

I love him for a lot of things.

I just…love him.

I do. There's no denying that anymore. I probably have loved him for a lot longer than I realize, but hey, it's always taken me a little longer to see things that have been right in front of my face.

I should tell him. I've been meaning to. But saying those words again when I've only said them to one other person not related to me is hard. They mean something. I thought they meant something last time. And for a while, they did. So I've wanted to be sure. Not just say it because it felt like I should. I want it to mean something.

And it will. I know that in my heart of hearts.

With a smile on my face for a non-sexual reason, I put back a few of the outfits, but keep seven of them, as I make my way over to my original destination. I already found the changing table I want on the store's website, but there's something about seeing furniture in person to make sure it's really the right one, so I head that way. I'm searching for my phone in my purse, and completely miss the fact that I'm not the only one looking at baby changing tables.

"Pleasssssssssse, Daddy. I really want this one. And so does the baby. Don't you want to get it for us?"

"What I want is to not spend my entire month's salary on baby shit," the guy with her grumbles.

Daddy? Really? I mean, to each their own. Not my cup of tea, but I'll never knock anyone's yum. Though judging by his response, I don't think this is a kink thing.

Not being able to resist the curiosity, I turn to look at the couple who are now arguing about cribs.

That's when I see who "Daddy" actually is. And puke a little in my mouth.

"Justin?"

His name is out of my mouth before I can think to keep it inside.

"Gabi?"

The two of us stare at each other, because this is the *last* place I ever thought I'd run into my ex-husband. I haven't seen him since the last divorce mediation when the final agreements were set in stone and I walked out a free woman.

Since then, I've wondered a few times what he was up to. Not in a "want him back" way. But in a curiosity way. I assumed he and his secretary were off living their new fabulous life.

Turns out I was wrong. Because the woman standing next to him—who I guarantee is younger than Maddox and is clearly more pregnant than I am—is not his secretary.

"What are you doing here?"

Is he confused? Does he not know what store he walked into? Judging by his tone, I feel like he's confused. And of course mad, because it's my ex and that's his default mode.

"I think the same thing you're doing," I say, nodding to the woman's belly as she drapes herself onto him. "I guess congratulations are in order."

"Thanks," she says happily, clearly having no idea who I am. "Daddy and I are so excited."

"Oh I can tell," I say, eyeing Justin, whose face is the polar opposite of happy. "*Daddy.*"

His eyes narrow at me, my sarcasm already getting to him.

Mediocre men… so sensitive.

"I'm Gabi by the way," I say, extending my hand to…

"Kaila. With an I," she says, like that makes any difference to me.

"Good to know."

We awkwardly shake hands, and Justin's face is becoming increasingly red by the second.

"You okay over there? You look a little upset? Having a baby is supposed to be a happy time!"

I don't know if it's my sarcasm or nonchalance that's getting to him, but I must admit, it's fun.

"How far along are you?" he asks with a bite.

I put my hand over my stomach and act as if I'm offended by his question. "I don't think that's any of your business. I'm not sure if they covered this in medical school, but I haven't had sex with you in over two years, and a baby's gestation is only nine months. Now I know you've never been as good at math as I am, but you don't have to worry, it's not yours."

"You two had sex!" Kaila cries out. Does she seriously think she's the only woman he's ever slept with? Now that's hilarious. "Who *are* you?"

"Oh. My apologies. I'm his ex-wife."

She snaps her head to glare at Justin, who looks like he wants to murder me right now. And honestly? I can't stop smiling. This is the best fucking day ever.

"Is she for real, Daddy? Were you married to her?"

Before I can hear his answer, Maddox steps up next to me. Impeccable timing.

"There you are gorgeous. Everything okay here?"

I'm not sure how much Maddox overheard or saw before he walked up, but I'm guessing by his dramatic arm over my shoulder, the twinkle in his eye, and the way he made sure to call me gorgeous, he heard enough.

Oh this is about to be *so* much fun.

"Oh my God! You're Maddox Gallagher!"

I have to swallow my laughter as Kaila's mouth drops to the floor.

"I am. Nice to meet a fan."

"She's not a fan." Justin scowls as he pushes back the hand Kaila tries to extend.

"But I am! I saved every one of his photos from his *Men's Health* shoot last year."

"Weren't they so hot?" I say to Kaila, because she's clearly oblivious, and this might be the last time I'll ever get to piss off my ex. "And guess what, not a thing was Photoshopped, if you know what I mean."

"For real?" Kaila-with-an-I decides to take that moment to eye my boyfriend up and down. She even bites her bottom lip as she stops at his crotch. I know I basically egged her on to do this, but no one stares at that dick but me.

"Sorry," I say, stepping in front of Maddox. "You can't have this one. You just get my leftovers."

I hear a low growl coming from Maddox's throat before Justin rudely interrupts it.

"Seriously, Gabi! What the fuck!" Justin's voice carries through the store, and I'm not sure how many other people are shopping now, but they have to know there's something happening in Aisle 10.

"Oh Justin, calm down," I say. "We're adults. I've moved on. So have you. Apparently a few times. We're both where we want to be."

"Really, Gabi? You're with *him*? The dumb jock? And you're having his baby!?"

"Damn right she is," Maddox says. "I'm sorry, who are you? I didn't get your name. And since you know mine, it's only right."

"You fucking know who I am."

"I promise you I don't."

I don't think I've ever seen my ex so mad. "I'm Justin."

I glance up to Maddox, and based on his smirk, I know he's about to have a lot of fun fucking with my ex-husband.

"Hi, Justin. And how do you know Gabi?"

Yup. Maddox is totally fucking with him. If I didn't love him before, I sure as shit do now.

"I'm her ex-husband." Justin spits out.

"Oh! Justin!" Maddox says dramatically. "My apologies. I *did* know your name. We just don't talk about you, and Gabi never thinks of you, so you were easy to forget."

My eyes go wide. Kaila's jaw drops. And Justin? I'm pretty sure he wants to punch Maddox. He won't, because he's smart enough to know he'd lose, but oh man does he want to. Instead, he turns his eyes to me, trying to intimidate me.

"This is who you want?"

I look up to Maddox, the three words I haven't said yet ringing loud in my head. "He's everything I've ever wanted."

I hear Kaila let out a romantic sigh as Maddox kisses my forehead. Justin is trying to grab her hand to pull her away, but not before Maddox speaks up.

"Hey man, you know, I'm glad we ran into you, because I've always wanted to thank you."

This seems to throw Justin for a loop. "Thank me?"

"Yes. Actually, this is all because of you," he says, taking my hand in his and giving me a quick wink. "Gabi was in Vegas because you cheated on her. She was there celebrating her divorce from you, and frankly, I'm glad she made that decision. Because even if she didn't end up with me, she clearly deserves better than you. But because you're a piece of shit and don't know how to treat women, I met the love of my life. I met the woman who's going to have my child. And it would've never happened if you weren't a complete and total fucking failure as a man. So, thanks. I owe you one."

I'm not sure if this is real, but I'm pretty sure I hear a slow clap from somewhere in the store. Maddox looks down at me, the smirk on his face so fucking sexy. "You ready to get out of here, gorgeous? I couldn't find the stroller."

"Please." And without a look back to Justin or Kaila, Maddox and I walk out of the store hand in hand. Our chins are held high, and I'm on cloud nine. Because not only do I know for a fact that I made the best decision of my life by leaving Justin, I truly picked the best man to truly be with for the rest of my life.

Because if I didn't know it before, I know it now: I'm one hundred percent, head over heels, in love with Maddox Gallagher.

CHAPTER 26
MADDOX

"God…Gabi…I…fuck!"

I'm white knuckling the steering wheel after nearly driving us off the road a mile or so back. Though, if that would've happened, I already had my entire story ready for the first responders.

"My apologies. I'm sorry I caused a pile up. My future wife was mid celebratory blow job on me because we just told off her ex and his sugar baby and it was hot as fuck. And see, the woman I'm in love with? She's really good at giving blow jobs. I mean really good. I bought her a house once after one of these. So please, forgive me this once, because it was really fucking good head…"

Yeah, I'm sure that would make a few headlines around Nashville.

Thank God we're about to pull into her apartment parking lot, because I don't know how much longer I can last. And after what just transpired at the baby store, I am not finishing in her mouth. No, I'm fucking her until we both scream so loud her neighbors are begging us to bump up the move out date.

The second I put the car in park and get my hands to let go of the wheel, I hear that telltale popping noise as she pulls her mouth off my dick like it's the best lollipop she's ever had.

"Gorgeous, you have a five-second head start to get upstairs and get naked. Wherever I catch you, that's where I'm going to fuck you."

She leans over the console, her hand stroking me a few more times as she leans into my ear. "Is that a threat? Or a promise?"

I place my hand over hers, stopping her motions. "There's only one way to find out. Five…"

She smiles and gives me one more kiss before hustling out of the car. Well, hustling as quickly as she can at this point. She's just about to hit the third trimester, and her stomach is getting bigger by the day. Every night when I lay down next to her, my hand resting on it, I'm in awe of the fact that this woman—this gorgeous, breathtaking, smart, funny, amazing woman—is growing a whole fucking person inside her. And not just a person. My son. The one we didn't plan for, but the one I already can't imagine my life without.

Or without his mother.

I put my dick back in my pants as I watch her make her way up the stairs to her second-floor apartment, loving every movement of her body. She puts a little extra sway in her hips, and looks back to me with a wink before she lets herself inside.

"Oh, Gabrielle…you better watch what you're asking for."

I turn off the ignition and take my time getting out of the car. Sure, I could be up the stairs in the blink of an eye, but I want to give her time to settle. Let her go where she wants. Get comfortable. Because I meant what I said—wherever I find her, that's where it's happening.

At least round one. Because there's going to be multiple rounds. I start training camp tomorrow, which means I'm gone for a month. Between that and the interaction we just had with Justin and his plaything, I have no intentions of being dressed again until I have to leave in the morning.

There have been numerous times over the past six months that I didn't think I could be attracted to or love Gabi more. The number one being the moment we found out we were having a son.

I might need to reconsider that list after today's events.

The way she bragged about me, while also showing a bit of a possessive side? The way she boldly stood next to me, telling Justin I was the one she wanted? The one she was going to have a family with? The loving and heated way she looked at me after I told Justin what I thought about him? Frankly, I don't know how we left the store without me finding a dressing room and showing her just how much I love her. And judging by her actions on the way home, she definitely feels the same way.

I wanted to say that I loved her right there. But I didn't want her to hear those words for the first time in front of her ex. She works daily on moving on from him and what he put her through. She deserves memories that have nothing to do with him. So as far as I was concerned, he didn't get to share that moment with us. If I have my way, today is the last day either of us are ever going to think of him again.

Figuring Gabi has had enough time to do what she needs to do—and I've softened enough that I can walk semi comfortably to her apartment—I make my way inside. She's not in her living room, which I didn't expect her to be. I know she's going to be in her bedroom, but what I see when I open the door has my jaw on the floor.

"What the…"

I'm speechless. My eyes blink twice then go impossibly wider as I take in the vision before me. She's kneeling on her bed, looking like a fucking wet dream in forest green see-through lingerie, accompanied with matching lace panties. There's a small bow just under her tits, but the material is so thin, I don't know how they aren't spilling out. Under the tie it opens to show Gabi's rounded stomach, which frankly, makes me hard every time I see it. But surrounded by sheer and lace? I'm a fucking goner.

"Is your silence a good thing?"

I can tell by her smirk that she knows every ounce of blood that was in my head is rushing to my dick.

"I actually don't have words." I kick off my shoes and strip down to my boxer briefs before meeting her in the center of the bed. I let my fingers gently trace around the cups, giving her goosebumps as I feel her heartbeat pick up. "When did you get this?"

"The other day when you were working out with Linc. I did a little baby shopping."

"This doesn't look like it's for the baby."

She shrugs in an ever-so-sexy way. "I meant to shop for the baby. But I walked past a store and saw this in the window... and...I don't know...it called to me."

"I'm so glad it did," I say as I hook a finger in the barely tied together bow and unravel it, letting it spill open. Once her breasts fall from the fabric, I'm like a man possessed, shoving my face between them.

The only sounds coming from me now are the feral moans I let out as I bury my head between her tits. I've been obsessed with her—and these—from that first night. But pregnancy tits? Holy shit that was a new kink unlocked, and I'm not mad about it.

"Maddox," Gabi cries out, her hands immediately grabbing onto my shoulders as I lick a line straight up between her breasts. "That feels so good."

"You are so fucking sexy," I say as I pull one of her peaked nipples in my mouth. I don't mean to moan into her skin, but once my free hand travels down to her pussy, which is absolutely already soaked for me, there is absolutely no holding it back. "How long have you been this wet for me?"

Her breathing is heavy as I work my finger in and out of her, her voice a low rasp as she answers me through the pleasure. "Since the car."

"Did sucking my dick like that make you wet?"

"Yes," she sighs out, her legs nearly giving out as I add a second finger. "I wanted you so badly."

"You were sucking me so good, gorgeous." I don't stop working my fingers, but I make sure to keep my other hand around her waist, wanting her to stay upright for this, ensuring our eye contact never breaks. "You couldn't stay away from my cock could you?"

"I couldn't…I didn't like her looking at you like that."

"Was my gorgeous girl jealous?"

She shakes her head. "I didn't like her looking at what's mine."

Mine. One word. One syllable. But that's all I need to send me over the fucking cliff for this woman.

Because she's right. I am hers. And she's mine. In every sense of the fucking word.

I crash my lips to hers harder than I have probably ever kissed her before in my life. The force of it knocks both of us down on the bed, but neither of us mind. Her hands are in my hair and down my back, leaving marks as I kiss every inch of skin I can find. I do one more pass down her body, resisting a prolonged pit stop at her peaked nipple. Not that I couldn't spend all night there, I just have somewhere else I'd rather be.

I push off my boxer briefs as I move down, making sure to pay special attention to my favorite parts of her. Which is basically every part. But I love watching her writhe as my tongue circles her belly button, feeling her twitch as my hands graze her waist. Hearing her sigh as I place open-mouthed kisses on each hip. This close, I need to taste her more than I need air to breathe.

I glance up to see her back slightly arched and her eyes hooded, already feeling every sensation between us as my fingers toy at her opening. My plan was to lick up every last drop of Gabi—craving her taste on my tongue—but with her words running on repeat in my head, I can't wait another second. I do take one long lick, curling my tongue at her clit and giving her just a taste of the sensations she now knows so well, before I crawl back on top of her.

"You're mine, Gabrielle."

"Yes," she says as she runs her fingers through my hair, holding my head close to her. "Yours."

Our eyes stay locked as I glide into her with ease, harmonized groans leaving our bodies as I sink into her. I mean to take this slow, I really do, but I can't help myself. Between looking at Gabi's pregnant body taking my cock like only she can, the word "mine" on loop in my head, and the fact that I, without a doubt, am head over fucking heels in love with this woman, I can't control myself.

"Do you know how magnificent you are? Every time you take my cock all I can think about is how perfect you are."

"I love taking it. You fuck me so— Ah!"

There it is. That spot that flips her switch every time, always guaranteed to give her a toe-curling orgasm. "Yes, Gabrielle. Scream it. Scream how much you love taking me."

"I...love...taking...your...cock."

Every word is more breathless than the last.

"Fuck, Gabrielle," I say as I grab one of her legs, bringing it up and around my hip to help her lower back. "I love you."

My eyes widen and I let her leg fall when I realize what I said. And before I can wonder if I actually said it, or if I can take it back—because what kind of fucking jackass says I love you for the first time during sex—Gabi stops moving.

"Gabi...I..."

I'm scrambling, trying to figure out how to take it back—I seem to do that a lot with this woman—but I can't get another word out.

Because Gabi's hands are around my neck, and she's pulling me into her so hard I think I might crush her.

I quickly roll her to her side so we're facing each other, knowing how uncomfortable she's been now that her stomach is really starting to pop, but our lips never disconnect until Gabi slightly pulls away.

"I love you, Maddox. I love you so much it's crazy."

Those are the last words either of us speak—well, the last coherent words—because with her admission, the dam breaks. Our kisses become hard, but not desperate. It's like we're trying to make sure we seal our words with a kiss so intense, so passionate, that neither of us will forget this moment.

Like I ever could.

"Come here," I mumble out, scooping her into my arms so I can adjust us to the end of the bed. "I need to feel you under me."

"Yes," she moans as I stand on the floor with Gabi at the edge of the bed, adjusting her legs around me.

"Are you okay? Do you need a pillow?"

She shakes her head. "No. I just need you."

Those are the final words I hear before I bury myself inside her. Her back arches slightly as I start thrusting in and out, her hands grabbing onto my biceps so hard they'll leave a mark. Good. I want her to mark me. I want to take that with me into camp. That way, when I see her nail marks on my skin, I'll think of this. I'll think of our eyes connected, never wavering as I fuck her with every ounce of love and feeling I have for her. I'll remember her tits bouncing and her stomach hitting mine. I'll remember how it took me a matter of minutes to send my girl, and me, into orbit.

But most important, I'll remember hearing those three little words for the very first time.

"So, what are the next few months going to be like?"

I thought Gabi had fallen asleep on my chest, and I was two seconds away from joining her. "In terms of?"

"Football. Your schedule," she says, her fingers tracing absentmindedly on my bare chest. "Wait, am I a WAG now?"

"Damn right you are," I say as I kiss the top of her head. "Speaking of, I need to get you a jersey."

"Maybe get it in a size up," she says as she rubs her stomach. "I swear, every day a new pair of pants doesn't fit."

"I'll get you every size you want. And one in every baby size for Tiny Tot."

That makes her smile. "Put that in your baby to-do notebook, but for after camp."

"Noted," I say. "But the season is actually pretty predictable. Camp is a beast in itself."

"And I'm really not going to see you for a month?"

"Except for when I FaceTime you, which is going to be every night," I say. "The Fury used to stay in town for camp, but players wouldn't take it seriously. When Coach McAvoy got hired, he moved camp to a college campus a little bit outside of town so we have to stay in a hotel the Fury rents out for the month. Some guys apparently hated it at first, but it's worked really well. We bond together. Focus completely on football. It's part of the reason why we're the best."

"Then that's what you do," she says as she leans in for a kiss. "And the season?"

"Season is the easy part. Games, mostly on Sundays. Off on Mondays. Light days that consist mainly of meetings on Tuesdays. Full practices Wednesday and Thursday. Light day Friday. Travel or meetings and a walk through on Saturday. Game Sunday. Rinse. Repeat. The only way it deviates is if it's a bye week or if we play on Thursday or Monday."

"Good to know," she says, but I can tell by her telltale bouncing eyes that something is going on in her head.

"Gabrielle…"

She knows she's been busted by the tone of my voice. "You know I'm not the person to bug you for every little thing."

"I do. I wish you'd bug me more about things. I don't know if you've realized this about me, but I'm a pretty make-things-happen kind of guy."

That makes her smile. "I was just… What happens if you're at practice, or traveling, and I need you for baby purposes. And just to let you know, we're talking about a major emergency. I'm not going to try and get a hold of you just because I want those cajun fries you got me addicted to. I'm talking if—God forbid—something bad happens. Or, the more real possibility, that I go into labor and you aren't here."

Shit. In all the things I looked up and wrote into the baby notebook, it didn't even dawn on me that I could be away from here when she goes into labor. "In meetings we can have our cell phones, so always text me first. But like, with a code word."

"Considering I never came up with a code word for when I wanted to sing in Vegas, I'm not sure that's our best plan of attack."

The memory makes me smile. "I nearly forgot about that. How did you remember?"

She shrugs with a coy little grin on her face. "I remember a lot from that night."

I groan into her neck, which fills the room with her laugh. "What do you remember the most?"

I can tell she's trying to keep her composure, but the open mouth kisses I'm leaving on her neck aren't helping.

"Focus, Gallagher. But it's the way you ripped my dress when I was pinned against the door."

"Fine…" I say as I'm already planning a babymoon in my head where I can recreate this for her. "We'll figure out a word. Or a signal. Or just text me in all caps MADDOX IT'S TIME. I'm going to find someone on staff who will always have their phone with them and make them your emergency Fury contact. An equipment manager or someone from the social team. That'll be the first thing I do tomorrow. And if I don't respond to your message in four seconds, you call them."

Her smile softens as she runs her hand down my cheek. "I love you."

I place my hand over hers. "Not nearly as much as I love you."

We come in for a kiss, and I refuse to rush it. Every year before I leave for camp, I'm always excited like it's the first day of school. That another season is starting. But for the first time in my professional life, there's a little bit of sadness. Because I now have someone I'm leaving. Sure it's only for a few weeks, and I'm going to talk to her every day, but…it's hitting me that this is not just about me. It's about Gabi. My son. Our fam—

"Oh! He's kicking!"

I pull away as I hurriedly put my hand on her stomach. I swear I miss it every time.

"Where? I can't feel it."

Gabi moves my hand to the right, and the second she does, Tiny Tot gives me a good one.

"Oh…that's…oh my…"

I couldn't keep the tears from my eyes if I tried. It's like he knew I needed to feel this before everything changes.

"We're having a baby, aren't we?"

She chuckles as the tears come for her too. "We're having a baby."

CHAPTER 27
GABI

The sound of Maddox's text pulls me from my deep concentration as I'm about to add a peanut butter drizzle over a batch of chocolate peanut butter brownies. I've never had them on the menu until today and that's only because I was craving them.

Owning a bakery and having massive pregnancy cravings is a win-win situation if there ever was one.

You love me.

I do. Wait. I didn't think I was going to get to talk to you until tonight?

We're finishing up lunch. I only have a few minutes before I have to go back to playing football. Blah.

Don't pretend you aren't having a blast. You were a kid skipping out of the apartment today on his first day of school.

You're right. I am. There's an energy here today. Everyone came to camp in amazing shape and ready to go. I can't describe it. And it's not because we won last year. It's something different. I have a good feeling about this year.

I love that for you. And the Fury.

Thanks. Doesn't hurt knowing that you're going to be in the stands this year.

Pregnant as hell scarfing down nachos.

So fucking hot.

Go back to playing football with your friends. Be safe. Love you.

Love you too.

The smile on my face is ear to ear as I set down the phone, doing my best to try and get comfortable on the stool that I now use every day when I bake. I mean, what's there not to smile about? My pregnancy has been as smooth as it can be, despite the early sickness I felt in the first trimester. We have the keys to the new house and move in is going to happen once Maddox gets back from camp. And the best news that I didn't think I'd be as excited about but I am? Beau forcing me to hire that second baker. Josie—a.k.a. my angel—has become my godsend. Not just for her baking skills. But because she asked to work the four a.m. shift.

I love her almost as much as I love Maddox and these brownies.

"What's the pregnancy craving of the day?" Josie asks as she tosses her apron into the laundry hamper I keep near the office. "Oh! Brownies!"

"Not just any brownies," I say, holding up my piping bag so I can give her a little taste of the drizzle. "Chocolate peanut butter brownies."

She takes a lick of the peanut butter sauce off her finger and the sound she makes is one I hope all women in their lifetime make—but not from brownies. "Those are fucking amazing."

"Why thank you," I say as I set them aside. "You taking off?"

"If that's okay?" she asks. "I'd like to run a few errands before school pickup."

"Absolutely," I say as I wave her away. "And you're one thousand percent, absolutely sure, you're good with coming in at four each weekday?"

"Are you kidding me? It's the best schedule I could ask for," she says as she digs for her keys out of her massive purse. How she doesn't lose them in there I have no idea. "It helps me get my eight-year-old to bed at a decent hour, especially with summer coming to an end. And since I live with my mom, I won't feel guilty about not being there for the mornings and I'm back in plenty of time to pick him up. It's wins all around."

"I'm glad," I say as one of my favorite songs of all time comes on over the Bluetooth speaker. That's the other great thing about Josie—we share the same musical tastes. She might be a few years younger than me, but it's nice to have someone who appreciates my millennial music. It makes for fun mornings when I get in around nine and we have a few hours baking away together. "Again, I know I've thanked you—"

She holds up a hand. "I should be thanking you. Seriously. I was suffering at my last job waiting tables. The schedule sucked and the money was worse. Being able to do a job I love and not feel like I'm the worst mom in the world? It's more than I could ever ask for."

"Damnit Josie," I say, wiping a tear away. "You know I'm not stable enough for words like that."

"Sorry boss," she says, walking behind me and giving me a small hug. "I'll leave now so you can stop crying."

"I appreciate it."

I turn my attention back to the brownies, which are ready to be cut and plated, as another one of my favorite songs comes on. My playlist isn't missing today. Before I realize what I'm doing, I hear myself singing along. Not loud. The walls aren't that thick and I'd hate to interrupt anyone's experience with my renditions of 2000s pop ballads. But how loudly I'm singing isn't the point. It's that I am.

Because I'm happy. Happier than maybe I've ever been in my life.

I stand up to get a better angle to slice into the brownies when my phone vibrates on the counter.

I forgot to ask you! Can you take a video of Phyllis and Kitty when they come in today? Especially if they're extra spicy. A few of the guys don't believe they exist.

You're talking to your teammates about Phyllis and Kitty?

Of course! And you and the bakery and Josie and the rest of the workers. I'm telling them everything.

Why?

Because I love you. And the bakery is part of you. And I want everyone to know about it.

I think I'd be crying now even if I wasn't overly hormonal.

How did I get so lucky? How did I go from a man who practically hid me away from the world to a man who's shouting about me from the rooftops?

I love you. So much.

Not nearly as much as I love you.

"How was practice?"

The moan Maddox lets out could be confused for another kind of moan if I didn't know what he went through today. Add in the wince on his face and I can tell it was a rough day. "It's days like this when I question why I chose this career."

"Because you love the game?"

"Yeah… there's that."

I laugh as I sit back against the headboard of our bed, ready to shut my eyes the second Maddox and I hang up from our nightly FaceTime. He's been at camp now for almost two weeks, and this part of the night is always my favorite. After their nightly position meetings and dinner, Maddox heads back to his room so we can have a few minutes of phone time, just the two of us. Even though the call usually comes around eight, I'm always a few minutes from falling asleep, my body tired from the day and carrying around a baby that's somehow on the weight track to be a lineman rather than a safety like his dad. "But you said it wasn't full contact, right?"

"It's not, but that first day a player hits you, even in the controlled setting we're in, it always reminds your body of what it hasn't been feeling for the past six months, and what you're about to feel for the next six."

"I can't imagine," I say as the baby decides to kick me with his full weight. "Then again, I feel like I was tackled from the inside by your son, so maybe I can."

"Just like his daddy."

I shake my head with a smile. "Do you know one thing we haven't done yet? Or maybe you have and you haven't shared the notebook with me yet?"

A terrified look comes across his face. "What did I forget?"

"You didn't forget anything," I say, trying to reassure him. "I was thinking that we've never talked about names."

He lets out a breath, but he's still slowly blinking. "Are you trying to remember if you have a spare notebook to start jotting down names in?"

My observation takes him back a bit. "How did you know?"

I shrug. "You're not the only one who notices things Gallagher."

Maddox is the king of noticing the little things. And not just noticing, but then acting on it. He never asked what my favorite soda was. He's never asks what my current cravings are, yet I'm always supplied with whatever it is. So getting a chance to do this for him, to show him a little of what I feel every time he does it, hits me square in the heart.

"I did have a spare, but then I used it today. And you know I can't mix football notebooks and baby notebooks."

"Of course you can't," I say. "But did you find the one that's in the front of your suitcase?"

This takes him aback. "The front of my suitcase?"

I smile as I slide down into my bed, needing to take the pressure off my lower back. "Go check."

He carries the phone with him as he walks across his room. I hear him open the zipper and I'm so glad he kept the phone to his face, because his reaction is priceless.

His face is lit up like a kid on Christmas Day. His eyes are wide and his jaw is dropped.

"You got me notebooks?"

The little hitch in his voice gets me a little choked up. "Surprise."

"When did you do this?"

"I slid them in when I left for the bakery the morning you left," I say as I grab my best friend—also known as my pregnancy pillow. "I know you had some, but I thought you might need a few extra."

"Gabi." His voice is in awe as he opens the first one. "Wait. Did you…"

"Read it."

He looks up to me, then back to the inscription, tears pooling in his eyes:

Number #35 on the roster.
Number one in our hearts.
Love, Gabrielle and Tiny Tot

"Gabi… I don't know what to say… thank you."

"I know it's cheesy," I feel myself quickly saying, but Maddox cuts me off before I can finish the thought.

"It's perfect. You're perfect. I love them. Thank you."

I let his words run through me, hating that even after all these months of healing, from time to time I fall back into habits. But that's the process, right? As long as it's two steps forward, and only a step back every once in a while, you chalk that up as a win.

"You're welcome." I say, but a yawn follows right behind.

"Get some sleep," Maddox directs.

"No I'm good."

The second yawn I let out says otherwise.

"Get some sleep. Plus, I have a long night of notebook filling to do."

"No weird names. And I'm not naming him Maddox Junior."

"Noted," he says. "But I'm going to say I love you and hang up before you realize you didn't take Maddox the Second or Maddox 2.0 off the table."

It takes me a second to realize what he said. "Wait. What?"

"Night, Gabrielle! Sweet dreams! Love you!"

Oh this man…

What are your feelings on alliteration?

Out of all the text messages Maddox has sent me since we met, this has to be the most random of all. And that's saying something. Especially because it's the second week of camp, which I've been told is a big week in terms of play installment. Whatever that means but yay football!

In the right scenarios, the double letters scratch the right itch in the brain.

Good. So you aren't opposed to baby names starting with the letter G?

Are you spending your lunch break thinking of baby names?

Yes. It's a free country and this is my free time.

You're sweet. I'm taking it you have a list already?

Oh gorgeous. Do I ever. Hold please.

"Are you texting your baby daddy? Is that why you have that shit-eating grin on your face?"

"Yes," I say to Josie. "Sorry. I never know when he's going to get a few minutes to text each day, so I try to make myself available when he does."

"No need to apologize to me. If I was dating a Fury player you'd have to start a no cell phone rule in the kitchen."

I don't know Josie's story. I know she's a single mom with an eight-year-old. I know she had to have him young because she's closer to Maddox's age than me. But I know there's no ring on her finger and in the near month she's worked here, I've never heard her talk about a partner of any kind.

"You know I can arrange that," I say, acting like I have any idea who any of his teammates are other than Linc and Wyatt. "Not all the Fury players are in relationships, you know. Oh! He has a camp roommate. New in town. A rookie who got drafted this year. Maybe we can set you up?"

That makes her laugh. "Sure. Tell Maddox—who by the way you need to tell me sometime how you snagged the hottest player in the league—that a single mom who's twenty-six going on forty is looking for her happily ever after, but comes in tow with a chaos gremlin child."

I wave her off. "The important question is do you like karaoke?"

That wasn't the follow-up question she was expecting judging by her confused look. "Sure. Why?"

"That's all I need to know." I smile and furiously start texting Maddox. But before I can tell him my idea, I realize that during my conversation, he's sent me a laundry list of names.

Okay, the first one are G names. The others are ones that are my current favorites. Please respond back to which ones you hate and/or love. Those ones will go in the notebook and advance to the second round:

Gabriel, Gunner, Gus, Garrett, Gary (ew no.), Garth (double no), Graham (Oh I like that one)

Non G names:

Baker (current favorite for obvious reasons), Liam, Levi, Shawn, Shaun, Sean, Buster (eh), Lincoln (guess who suggested that)

I have every intention of trying to play match maker for Josie, but right now I need to swoon. And use my veto powers.

All of those were off the top of your head?

Some. And I took a poll around the locker room today for suggestions. Those were the best of the bunch.

I like a few of them.

Yeah? Care to tell me which ones?

Let's get rid of the bad ones first. All of the Shawns. Went to school with a Shaun. Justin's best man actually. He was an asshole.

Noted and crossed off.

Also not a huge fan of Gunner.

Really? Why not? Sounds like a badass. "Coming onto the field, wearing the number his dad made famous for the Nashville Fury, Gunner Gallagher."

I thought we weren't forcing him to play football?

I'm not. But a guy can still dream, right?

Of course he can. Or maybe Sugar and Sweets will become a family business and our son will be the next great baker and franchise it out all over the country. Which is why I don't know if we should name him Baker. Feels like we're forcing him.

True. He needs a name that allows him to be whatever he wants to be.

Except named Gunner or Shawn.

Noted.

What about Noah?

You're in your last day of camp and you're texting me baby names still? I thought we were talking about this when you got home tomorrow.

We are. But I thought of that one and I didn't want to forget it because I left my baby name notebook in my room.

You could've made a note.

True. Or I could text it to you so I know if it deserves a spot in the notebook.

I like it. Maybe a little too popular, but it can definitely go on the short list.

See. This is why I messaged you. And because I love you and miss you.

See you tomorrow? You'll be home around noon, right?

Eleven fifty-five if I have my way. I can't wait.

Same. I love you.

Love you more

"I'd roll my eyes if I wasn't so happy for you."

"Oh shush," I say to Shelby as I heave myself up into her SUV. "Shouldn't you be happy that not only did I listen to your advice, but your advice has me in a healthy and loving relationship?"

"I should, and I am, but I didn't know it came with all this lovey-dovey, hearts-in-eyes, shit."

"Well you better get used to it since you're officially moving here!"

I do a happy dance—as much as I can do at twenty-nine weeks pregnant. I know I still have a ways to go, but holy shit how can I get bigger?

"Yay… I'm moving to Nashville…" I don't know if Shelby could've said those words in a more dead-panned tone. "Get ready, Music City. Here I come…"

"Can I ask you a question?"

She turns out of the parking lot of the department store we were shopping at for cleaning supplies for her, and baby clothes for me. "Is it about me moving here?"

"Partly."

"Then no."

"Too bad," I say, adjusting myself so I can watch her answer. Shelby plays things close to the vest, even with me and Hannah, so getting any read on her always helps when I know she's going to want to hold back. "Why do you hate Nashville so much?"

It's a question I've wanted to ask her for years. I remember when I told her I was following in Beau's footsteps and going to Vanderbilt, I remember the scowl that crossed her face like I ran over her driver.

Which is a big deal. It's her favorite club.

"I don't hate Nashville per se," she says, her knuckles becoming white as she grips the steering wheel. "It's… the people."

I wasn't expecting that answer. "People? Who are people? Because I thought the only people you knew here were me and Beau?"

"Out of those two you're the only one I like," she says.

"Wait. Are you telling me that you don't come here because of my brother?"

Her shoulders slump and she lets go of the wheel with her right hand to reach over and take mine. "I love you. I love you like the sister I never had. And it's because of that love why I haven't come here."

"You're going to have to explain yourself because I'm not following."

She takes, then releases, a deep breath. "One day babe. I promise."

I know Shelby well enough to know that I can keep prodding, but that's only going to make her tell me less. "Are you going to tell me why you're moving here at least?"

The fact that Shelby's been so cagey with this reason has been driving me bonkers. I didn't press it before when it was still only a maybe that she was leaving Las Vegas, but now that she's bought a house on the grounds of a premiere country club—and coincidently next door to my brother, though I don't know if she knows that yet—I need to know.

"Let's just say that me moving here can be classified under the category of desperate times calling for desperate measures."

"That's not cryptic at all."

She shakes her head as she turns down my street. "The longer I don't have to say it out loud, the longer I can pretend this isn't my life."

I drop the subject and Shelby and I sit in silence for the last few minutes of the drive. I wish she'd confide in me—lord knows I've trauma dumped on her plenty of times over the years —but I know how she gets. She's guarded. Always has been. And rightfully so. Her mom died when she was a baby and her father was a piece of work, and that's the nicest way to describe him. I know she'll tell me when she's ready. Whenever that may be.

Shelby turns the corner into my apartment building—the one that isn't going to be mine after next week—when I notice something, or should I say, someone, standing in front of my car.

"What the…"

I sit up on the edge of my seat, the seatbelt struggling to keep me back, as I stare at Maddox, leaning against my car, holding a teddy bear and a dozen roses in his hand and wearing the biggest, and sexiest, smile I've ever seen.

"He wanted to surprise you," Shelby says as she turns into a spot next to Maddox.

"Wait! You were in on this?"

"Of course," she says with a soft smile. "You think I wanted to go shopping? When was the last time that ever happened?"

I unbuckle my seat belt so I can better wrap my best friend in a hug. "I know you aren't happy about it, but I'm so glad you're here now."

"Yeah, yeah," she says, patting my back. "Now get out of here. Go get your man."

I kiss her cheek, which makes her roll her eyes, before I grab my bags and start to open my door. But before I can, Maddox is opening it for me.

"Hey gorgeous. Miss me?"

I don't say a word, instead I launch myself into him. How he catches me—belly and all—I'll never know. All I know is the last thing I hear from Shelby is her laughter, the door shutting, before I kiss Maddox to make up for thirty days of not kissing him.

As he sets me to the ground, and our kiss that probably should've been saved for the privacy of my apartment, ends, all I can do is smile. Because I'm happy. So fucking happy.

I have Maddox and the baby.

I have my brother who gave me my dream.

I'm going to have my best friend with me for the first time in our adult lives.

I have everything I could ever want.

CHAPTER 28
MADDOX

"I'm back! Did you guys miss me? Because I missed all of you."

I'm not saying that I expected to walk into Sugar and Sweets tonight to a full-on party. We have enough to clean up every time we meet before adding in streamers and balloons. But I thought maybe a little fanfare. Instead, I'm greeted by my three newest friends looking at me like I grew a second head while I was away at training camp.

"No party?" I ask, making sure I'm not missing something. "Nothing?"

"Sorry to disappoint you Gallagher," Beau says. "Being away for training camp—a.k.a. your job—doesn't warrant a welcome back party."

"That sucks," I say as I take the apron that Theo is holding up for me. "Did you guys miss me at all?"

"Not really."

"Ouch," I say to Beau's response, holding my hand over my heart. "You know, you can lie to me. Or at least let me know before you throw the verbal brick in my face."

Theo claps me on the back as he passes by on his way to his

station. Looks like he's trying to tackle macarons—the one thing none of us can get a handle on. "What he means to say is that this is the first Poker Club meeting since the last time we saw you."

"Really?" Doing the math that it was more than a month ago, right before the gender reveal. "Schedules not lining up?"

"Been busy as hell," Beau says. "I've had three tournaments and a week in Los Angeles finalizing a new offseason streaming deal."

"Really?" I ask, fascinated by how Beau's made a career not only of golf, but also through social media. "Gabi didn't say anything."

"Because she doesn't know," he says as he prepares his dutch oven to preheat for his loaf of the day. "I'm still finalizing things, so I didn't want to say anything."

"You? Not want to say anything?" Asher chimes in. "I didn't get the memo that pigs were flying today."

"Fuck you Reed," Beau says as he gets his raised dough, ready to score it. I didn't know that term before Poker Club, and now I know a little too much about it. My future brother-in-law will talk your ear off about the different techniques if you let him. "Plus, what has you so busy this summer? It's your fucking offseason. Yet the only time I asked if you wanted to get a drink you said you were busy."

"I was," he defends. "I had to take Adalyn to dance class."

Beau's raised eyebrow means he doesn't buy it. "And that took all night? I thought you went to a studio where you dropped her off?"

"Normally it is," he trails off like he's gearing up to tell us the deepest, darkest, secret of his life. "It was bring a special friend to dance night."

Theo's eyes nearly jump out of his head. "Are you telling me, you attended, and participated, in a dance class with your three-year-old and none of us were there to document it?"

"Exactly," he says. "I wasn't telling you fuckers a thing."

"Please tell me there are pictures," I say. "And please, please, tell me that there was a tutu involved."

"There wasn't, but just you wait." He points a finger at me. "Once your kid is here, if he wants you in a tutu, or throw a ball, or build some crazy-ass contraption, you'll do it. No questions asked."

He's right. I would. Hell, I'd probably come up with half the ideas myself.

Because that's what a good father does. What my father didn't do, and probably never would have done even if he'd stayed. He wasn't like Asher who's learning to french braid and going to a dance class. He didn't go the extra mile. I doubt he ever left straight from his job to come home and paint a nursery. But that's what I did today. Went directly from football practice to the house to throw on a coat of paint in the nursery before coming to a baking club to make his partner the brownies she's craving.

I never really knew him, but he'd never have done that.

But I did.

I will.

At least, I hope so.

"Quit stalling, are there photos and video?" Beau asks, bringing me back to the conversation.

"No," Asher says gruffly. "At least… I don't think so."

"So you're saying there's a chance!" Theo proclaims. "Don't worry guys, I'll make some calls. We'll have evidence by midweek."

"Doing the Lord's work Lawson," I say as I start getting situated at the spot I've seen Gabi make countless deserts in the time I've known her. "And what about you Theo? How was the July-August slate of games?"

"Exhausting," he says. "I don't feel like I had a minute to myself. It was either a plane or a game."

"Not true," Asher says without making eye contact. "I seem

to remember you having time to help Ellie with her wedding arch."

"Ellie? Who's Ellie?" I ask, feeling, yet again, I'm way behind the eight-ball. "Did Lawson get engaged while I was gone? I didn't even know he was dating anyone."

"He wishes," Beau says as he takes a seat, the insinuation laced in his tone.

"We're just friends!" Theo shouts, and it takes me aback. I know I'm only getting to know Theo, but he's never struck me as the kind who loses his cool. Or maybe he only does when a certain woman is named? All I know is that he's trying to even his features, but he can't stop the redness from covering his cheekbones.

"Sure…" Asher and Beau say in unison.

"We are."

"Yup. Totally," Asher says. "Because I know for my best friend's wedding I agreed to be a bridesmaid while helping her build a wedding arch even though I've been in love with her since I was five."

"I'm a brides-man. Get it right."

Beau laughs under his breath. "If that's the only thing you're denying then you're in a heap of trouble."

Theo flips off Beau before turning to me. "Ellie is my best friend. We grew up together and by the fate of the baseball gods, she works for the BlueBirds on the social media team. She's also getting married next year. And since I'm a good guy, who happens to be pretty handy, I told her I'd help build some things for her wedding to save her money. On my off days I go to her house and work on some projects. That's it."

"You left out the part where you're madly in love with her and you're pissed as fuck that she's getting married."

A ball of dough that Theo was working on goes flying across the kitchen, missing Beau by less than an inch.

"Next time it's going to make contact," Theo says. "I don't know how many times I need to tell you that we're just friends."

"You need to keep telling yourself that."

"I will. Just like you keep telling yourself that you're not feeling some sort of way about Shelby LeBlanc moving next door to you."

The two stare each other down and I don't know where to look as I lean in to whisper to Asher. "I know I thought this was my welcome home party, but this is so much more entertaining than any party."

"Wait till you've been here a little longer," Asher says as he starts loading sticks of butter into a stand mixer. "I've heard this fight more times than I can count. Frankly, I'm a little tired of it."

Tired of it? I don't know how anybody could get tired of this. It's a stare down. A fuck-off off. It's who's going to admit first that they're secretly in love with people that they refuse to admit their feelings for. I live for this shit.

"Why would you think I'm happy that Shelby's here?" Beau asks. "I hate her. She hates me. That's how it's been our entire lives."

"Do you though?" Theo asks. "Because every time you two are together, I always have to question whether or not you're gonna fight or fuck."

"My bet is that they fight then fuck," Asher adds. "Makes more sense."

I've never seen Beau's face as red as it is right now. "I will never—emphasis on never—fuck Shelby LeBlanc."

"I'll take that action," I chime in, making every face turn to look at me. "What? He said never. I believe in never say never. So I'll put down a few bucks."

I take my wallet out of my back pocket, and I just so happen to have a hundred-dollar bill at the ready that I dramatically set on the table.

"I like where the kid's head is at," Asher says, taking out his own bill. "I'm in."

"What the fuck?" Beau says, rubbing his hand down his jaw.

"I'm not going to fuck her. If anything, y'all need to make sure I don't murder her."

"With your dick," Theo says, adding to the pile. "The odds aren't in your favor, old man."

"Fuck you all," Beau says, bringing out his wallet. "Want to know how sure I am that nothing is ever going to happen between me and Shelby? I'm going to see each of your bets. The way I see it, this will be the easiest double-my-money situation ever."

Beau walks over and slams his three hundred dollars on the table before turning to me. "I liked it better when you were scared of me."

I wave him off. "Nah. This is more fun for everyone."

Beau shakes his head as he walks back to the oven and pulls out his preheated dutch oven. "Weren't we supposed to be talking about you and training camp? Or maybe my future nephew? Or the new house? How did this conversation turn to me?"

"Because somehow as the guy about to start a season and welcome a new baby, I'm leading the boring life," I say. "Now spill. What I want to know, and what the rest of the room wants to know, is why you and Shelby hate each other?"

"The room doesn't want to know this," Beau points over to Asher. "He definitely doesn't want to know it."

"Actually, I do." Asher says as he turns on his stand mixer. "I've heard you grumble about her since I've known you. I'd at least like to know the reasons."

"Yes," Theo says, taking a seat and leaning forward on his elbows. "Please tell us everything."

"That's not happening," Beau says as he puts his bread in the oven. "We grew up playing golf together. She was my little sister's best friend. She was annoying then, and she's only become worse as we grew up."

The three of us look at each other, none of us believing that's the whole story, before Theo speaks up. "You don't call somebody the names you call her just because she is your sister's annoying friend."

"Agree," I say. "My sister was older, but she had annoying friends. But I've never once accused them of having a nine-iron up her ass."

"Fuck you all," Beau says before storming out of the kitchen toward the back door. A second later we hear it slam behind him.

"I really need to thank you two," I say with a huge smile on my face.

"For what?" Asher asks.

"I said I wanted a welcome home party. And this didn't disappoint."

"Maddox, is everything okay?"

"Yeah, Mom. Everything's okay."

Is it? I mean, the short answer is yes. But the gnawing feeling in my stomach that has been festering for months—and became a full-on stomachache tonight after I left Poker Club—says otherwise.

I had every intention of going back to Gabi's apartment after leaving Sugar and Sweets. But I knew she wasn't going to be there—she was over at Shelby's so I just started driving. Poker Night was much needed. Yes, I have my teammates, but having a different perspective from guys who understand the pressures of being a professional athlete, while also giving a slightly outside point of view, has been invaluable.

But after our conversation that sprung up memories of my father—which led to thoughts of what kind of father I'll be—I needed to clear my head. Yes, I've thought about these since the moment I realized I could be a dad. But they always went away. Tonight's didn't. Before I knew it, I was on the interstate before driving up to the new house. When I let myself inside, I went straight to the nursery, feeling like it was the only room I could go in to help me process these thoughts. I sat here for twenty minutes before I pulled out my phone to call the one person who could help me sort through my head space.

"Are you sure? Doesn't sound like everything's okay. Is it the baby? Gabi?"

"No, Mom, they're fine," I say, holding a plush football between my hands. The one I took off the shelf above my son's crib that rested next to a picture of Gabi and I from the gender reveal. A football that looks like one my dad gave to me when I was little. Before…

"I'm just... I don't know…"

I don't even know how to start this conversation. The topic of Dad was always an awkward one. When she filed for divorce after he'd been gone for nearly a year, he didn't contest. He didn't ask for custody. She didn't even try for child support knowing he wouldn't pay it. It was like one day he was there, and the next, me, her, and my sister were trying to rebuild our lives. No one has seen or heard from him since.

"I know Maddox."

"How? I haven't even told you why I called."

"Because Maddox. I'm your mother. Mothers know things. And I've been waiting to get this phone call for the past six months. So just ask Maddox. I promise I'm ready for it."

My mother is a both a witch and a saint. "Am I anything like him?"

In her years of shielding me and my sister, Mom made it a point to bring up my father as least as possible. Looking back, I have a feeling it was because she didn't want to remind us of what we didn't have. That also means I don't know much about him. I was only four when he left. I've seen pictures, so I know I have his hair color and build. My eyes look nothing like my mom's, so I assume I got them from him. But other than that, everything I know are stories from Mom or long faded memories that I don't know if they're real.

"You're so much like him that sometimes it scares me."

That's not the answer I wanted to hear. "Mom, I'm—"

"Let me finish," she interrupts. "You *are* like him, but the version of him that I fell in love with. The boy who at sixteen years old lit up every room he walked in. Had a smile that every girl wanted to be flashed her way. I remember when he first moved to our school district, every female had hearts in their eyes, especially when they found out he was the next star running back. And somehow, I'm the one who caught his attention."

"Not somehow. You were, and you are, the most beautiful woman in the world."

"You're sweet Maddox." She trails off and I can picture her sitting in her recliner, looking up at the ceiling as she tries to find the words. "When times got hard, before he left and I wondered who the man standing in front of me became, I tried to remember that boy. The one who took me to prom. The one who gave me his letterman's jacket. The one with the brown eyes that I could get lost in."

I swallow down the anxiety that's building in my chest, though this is what I called and asked for.

"But people change, Maddox. Your father changed. The boy I fell in love with was not the man who left us with barely a note saying goodbye. His eyes weren't the same. His smile had faded. I still don't know why he thought leaving was the best plan, but I know he wasn't happy."

Tears prick at my eyes, fighting to get loose, as I think about what could ever push someone to that decision. How could a man who made a vow to my mom, a woman he at one point loved, who gave him children, could up and leave like that? And not just leave her, but us. His entire fucking family. He knew he'd never see us again. He'd never watch me and my sister graduate from high school. He'd never see me play football. He'd never get to hold his grandchildren.

But the scariest part of everything my mom admitted is that she doesn't know why. If I knew why, then I could prevent myself from doing the same thing. But like she said, I'm the guy with the dazzling smile. What if I don't know my why yet?

"I remember the first time one of your teachers talked about your smile," Mom continues. "She said it lit up the room. Was a little mischievous. I smiled through her words, but it hurt knowing that your father was the reason for your smile. And he'd never see it for himself."

"If it makes you feel better, this smile has got me out of a lot of potential trouble," I say, trying to lighten the mood. "Your sanity should thank you."

She laughs slightly. "Oh, I know it did. But that's not why I bring it up, or to say that you better watch out for my grandson if he's anything like his dad."

"Then why did you?"

"Because, you haven't lost your smile. If anything, it's shining brighter than ever."

I get what she's saying—in theory—but I'm still a little confused. "When did Dad lose his smile?"

I hate asking this, knowing it's probably bringing up a painful memory, but I have to know.

"The day I told him I was pregnant with your sister."

And that proves my suspicion...

"We weren't necessarily trying, but we weren't preventing, either," she says. "I was happy when we got the news. Surprised, but I was ready for something more in my life. I was working a retail job that didn't mean much to me. Your dad had a job at one of the plants in town. It wasn't much, but we made it work. We'd talked about having kids one day, so I was excited for this. Your dad, however..."

She pauses to take a breath, and I find myself now sitting in the middle of the nursery, clutching the football like it's a lifeline as I wait for the rest.

"It was the last day I saw the sparkle in his eye, but even before then, it was slowly burning out," I hear her push back a tear, and I hate that I can't dive through the phone and hug the woman who's given everything for me. "It came back for a second when we found out about you, and that you were a boy. But even the potential of you one day following in his football footsteps wasn't enough to keep him around. He bounced from job to job. He never found his footing. And he never took to fatherhood. Though as the years have passed, I realized nothing was going to. He did what he had to do, and I've made peace with that."

"I still don't know how you did."

"Some people aren't meant to be on the paths that they start on. Your dad? He wasn't cut out for family life. Me? I can't imagine a better one than being you and your sister's mom."

Fuck... how am I supposed to stop the tears now?

"But am I like him? You were married. You talked about having kids and you thought he was on board. He was happy at one point. How do I know if I'm going to do what he did? That I'll panic and flee?

"Because you're ten times the man your dad was at your age, and most importantly, like I said, your smile has only gotten brighter since you and Gabi saw that pregnancy test."

"Mom, you've seen me once since then."

"But I saw his. I stared at his for years. Yours is the polar opposite. The way you looked that day? How your eyes sparkled when you looked at Gabi? Your reaction when you saw that blue filling? That's a smile your dad never once had in his life."

"Mom, I appreciate the words, but a smile can't—"

"Maddox Jacob Gallagher."

Fuck. Full government name?

"What's going to happen if one day Gabi comes home and

says that the bakery has to shut down and she needs you to support her?"

I know this tone. This is her "I've asked you three times to take out the trash," tone. I better start listening or else she's going to make me fly back to Iowa and *actually* take out the trash.

"Then I do."

"What do you do if your son takes after you and never wants to sleep and cries all night?"

"Gabi and I come up with a schedule and a system."

"And what would you do if, God forbid, you have an injury? Football is done. How do you support your family?"

I hate thinking about it, but I have, and I have a whole notebook called Plan B. "I use the degree I got. I become a high school science teacher and coach football."

"And at any of those points do you foresee the situation where you'd leave Gabi and your son?"

"Of course not. That's ridiculous. Why would…"

Oh.

I get it now.

"If I had asked your dad any of those questions before they happened to us, he would've said the right things, but it wouldn't have been with the firmness you just did. He would've stumbled through an answer or tried to change the subject. And that Maddox is how I know you're nothing like him."

I let her words hang for a second when I nearly jump at the sound of the nursery door creeping open.

"Maddox? Is everything okay?"

I don't know how Gabi found me, or why she's here, but I've never needed her more than I need her now.

"Thank Mom," I say as I stand up and turn to face her. "I love you."

"I love you too Maddox."

I hang up the phone and drop it on the floor and take one step into Gabi, hugging her as tight as I possibly can. I press my lips to her stomach, needing the connection between the three of us.

"Hey," she says as she strokes my back. "It's okay. I've got you."

She does. In every way. She has my heart. She has my soul. She has my world. Now and forever.

Always.

CHAPTER 29
GABI

"Where did I put the..." I trail off because not only don't I remember where I put it. I don't know what *it* is.

Welcome to the final stretch of pregnancy...

I want to say that my inability to find the *it*—seriously what the fuck was I looking for—is a product of that I've only been in this kitchen for a week and we just finished unpacking it yesterday. In my defense, this kitchen is bigger than my whole apartment was. And there are so many cupboards and drawers I can't fathom how I'm going to fill them all. Everywhere I look there's a cupboard. The island has cupboards and inside those cupboards are drawers. Even the garbage can is hidden in a cupboard.

The worst part is that I can't find *it* and only half of the cupboards are full. I can't imagine my confusion when all the bottles I registered for—that are all bought from the registry—get here, along with the other baby things. I really won't be able to find shit then.

Oh well. It'll be worth it. It already is.

Realizing that I'm not going to remember what I was looking for any time soon, I turn my attention back to the cutting board that has a spread of vegetables on it. I call out to my speaker to turn on my favorite playlist—appropriately called Kitchen Jamz —and immediately, the playlist doesn't disappoint, playing an upbeat song that doesn't make a lick of sense lyrically, but back in high school, I couldn't stop singing it. I mean, how do you kiss someone through the phone?

The lack of lyrical understanding doesn't stop me from moving my hips—which are as wide as they've ever been—to the song as I start cutting green peppers. But not any green peppers. Ones that I'm using to use to make our first official dinner in our new home.

I hate that every meal we've eaten here has been take out of some sort, but between the bakery, unpacking, and his football schedule, neither of us have had the time or energy. But tonight I'm feeling good, probably better than I have in weeks. Our son, who's still being called Tiny Tot because we can't decide on a name, has been pretty calm today. It's Saturday, so I had the early shift at the bakery. I was home by noon and took a glorious nap that's left me refreshed. I was even able to finish unpacking the last of my clothes. And because Maddox plays away on Monday night to open the season—a rarity in pro football from what I've been told—we have tonight to ourselves before his travel day tomorrow. Just the two of us.

Because before I know it, it'll be three.

I can't wait for Tiny Tot to be here, but at the same time, the closer I get, the more terrified I am. There are the little things— the fact that we don't have a name. Still having no clue what brand of diapers to use. There are the much bigger ones, which all fall under the category of being a mother in general. Breast-feeding, sleep schedules, and keeping a human alive. You know, the basics. I want this. I think I'm ready for it. But that doesn't make me less terrified that I'm going to screw one or a hundred things up.

Then there's the actual birth, which is the fear that has kept me up most nights. Sure, I've already told my doctor to give me every legal drug and pain killer there is, and Maddox has made me a playlist that he's insistent is going to make me think that I'm at a dance party, but that hasn't quelled the worries. Things happen. Plans change. If anyone knows that, it's me.

What if something happens and surgery is needed? What if the baby is breech? What if Maddox isn't there? Shelby is on standby to be in the room with me, but I want Maddox there. I need him there. I love my best friend, but I know if the going gets tough, I'm going to need his strength. The way that he can keep me focused and calm. There are a hundred more thoughts like those that run through my brain daily, and I hope that not one of them comes true.

But again, plans change. Hell, nothing in my life has ever gone according to plan. But maybe, just maybe this time something will, and we'll have the normal, routine, very undramatic but completely exciting birth of our son.

A girl can dream, right?

I take a deep breath and grab a red pepper, giving myself an internal pep talk to stop thinking about the what-ifs, when I hear the distinct sound of crowd applause followed by guitar chords I'd know anywhere.

Our song.

That's what I think of it as now. It used to be the song that reminded me of such a bad place in my life. A day I never wanted to think about again. Yet, with one night, one man, and one dare, I can now listen to it without pain, but most importantly, I can sing it.

I turn it up before closing my eyes, letting the opening chords, and then the male lead's words, run through me. Of course I transport myself back to Vegas. I think to how Maddox looked on stage. So poised. So confident. So handsome. How when he turned to pass the song off to me, the care and gentleness in his eyes was overflowing. He gave me more encouragement in that moment than I had received in years.

I should've known then he was different. Boy how stubborn was I...

Why couldn't I see it? Since the second I met him, that man has never faltered when it came to me and what I needed. He gave me strength that night and with that performance, just like he has every day since we met. He comforted me then when I broke down after the song the same way he did in the bathroom when we found out about Tiny Tot. He brought me back to life in that Vegas hotel room and has continued to do so every day I spend with him.

When the female lyrics come on, I don't hesitate to start singing. And I don't hold back. I put down my knife, take a deep breath, and let the words I know by heart ring out. I'm so lost in the moment that I don't hear anything else or realize that a certain someone has come behind me, wrapping his arms around my very large stomach.

"I love hearing you sing," he whispers, kissing my neck, just underneath my ear.

I think the only thing that could get me to stop singing this song is Maddox Gallagher's lips on me. "Then why'd you stop me?"

Maddox's hips start swaying back and forth, his hands guiding me to dance with him. "Keep going gorgeous."

I listen to the song, doing my best to sing with the lyrics, but I'm having trouble concentrating while Maddox's mouth is doing everything in its power to distract me.

"I'm off the deep..." I can barely get the words out, and they're just above a whisper. Maddox's mouth is hot and the open kisses are now moving down the length of my neck to my shoulders. He pushes down the strap of my cotton sundress as his mouth continues to travel up and down my neck to my shoulder, leaving me hot, bothered, and definitely *not* thinking about singing.

"Do you know how fucking sexy it is to walk into our house

—our home—and see you like this? Your body looking like this? Hearing you sing? Seeing you so happy?"

I shake my head because if he's lying, I never want him to stop. Sexy is the last thing I've felt recently that I've crossed the ten-weeks-to-go mark. Example A is the sundress I'm wearing. It's not a sexy one. It's made of cotton T-shirt material that hangs on me, but between the still-summer heat and my size, it's the most comfortable thing I own. Which means I bought one in every color. I know it isn't the most flattering article of clothing, but Maddox doesn't care. I can feel what I'm doing to him. One would think I was wearing French lace and thousand-dollar lingerie.

His hands reach up, cupping my heavy breasts in each of his hands. "Gorgeous was the first word I thought of when you walked up on that stage. But every day I spend with you I realize that word isn't enough. And every other word that comes to mind doesn't feel strong enough."

If I wasn't horny before, I am now.

I turn around into him and drape my arms over his shoulders. "Then show me."

His eyebrows raise in a question. One downside to becoming as big as this kitchen is that my sex drive has plummeted. Most days I can't get comfortable laying down, let alone trying to have sex.

I know Maddox doesn't care about our little drought—at least if he does, he's the best actor I've ever seen—but I've missed it. Him. That connection. I know we love each other. We tell each other that dozens of times a day. He always kisses me before I leave for the bakery, or he leaves for practice, and it's the first thing either of us do when the other gets home. But for a person who didn't think physical intimacy was a love language I needed to realizing I crave it, it's been a slight shock to not have.

But for the first time in weeks, I want it. I need it.

I need Maddox.

"Are you sure?" he asks, concern pooling through his still heated eyes. "I didn't mean for—"

I put my finger up to his mouth. "I want you Maddox. I want us. Just… maybe not on my back."

Yes, it was a cautious warning, but then I see when my words hit the creative side of his brain. "I think that can be arranged."

Before I can ask any questions, Maddox is swooping me up in his arms, carrying me bridal style to the living room.

"Maddox! Put me down. I'm the size of a whale."

"Don't talk about the mother of my child and the love of my life like that," he says as he pecks a kiss on my cheek as he walks me to our finally furnished living room. "Plus, you forget that I'm a professional athlete. Every part of my day is lifting weights. You think I'm doing that to tackle grown men? Ha! What are these muscles for if I can't carry my girl across the house?"

I giggle as Maddox sets me down in front of the expansive sectional that was delivered a few days ago. It seats twelve, takes up a large part of the open-concept first floor, and is by far the most comfortable piece of furniture I've ever laid on. Now I guess we see how it holds up to whatever Maddox has in mind.

"Arms up," he instructs, and I do so without question. He quickly gathers the hem of my dress, lifting it over my head, leaving me in the ugliest pair of panties along with a cheap bra I bought because my boobs have never been this big before, and I don't want to spend money on something I know I'm only going to need for a few months. Again, the blaze of heat in Maddox's eyes can't be faked as he unhooks the bra from the back, kissing below my ear, moving down a little more to let his tongue circle at my pulse.

He peppers open-mouth kisses across my collarbones, before lingering at the swell of each breast. If my body wasn't trembling already from the sensation of his mouth, it would be from his fingertips brushing across my hips. The soft rasp of his knuckles trailing up and down my sides before dipping into the waistband of my briefs and slowly sliding them down off my legs.

"Sit down. Make yourself comfortable. I'll take care of the rest."

I don't have to question what he means. If I know one thing about this man, it's that he'll put my needs first. He has since the first night. And I have a feeling he'll do this for the rest of our lives.

I do as he says, situating myself on the chaise end of the couch, grabbing a few pillows in case I need them for whatever he has in mind. Maddox takes the time to strip off the shorts and T-shirt, and if I thought his body was sexy before football started back up, I'm in awe right now. He's been working with a few of the trainers to put on more muscle, wanting to add some bulk to his frame while also not taking away from his speed. And the results? I don't know what it's going to translate to on the football field, but the definition in his abs, combined with how his biceps flex even more than they did before when he takes off his shirt, is something that is making my mouth water.

"Are you going to spread your legs for me?" he asks as he kneels in front of me.

"I wasn't sure you wanted me to."

He raises his eyebrow at my teasing tone. "If there's a day in our lives when you hear me say that I don't want to eat your pussy, then have me committed. Now come here. Hold on. I'm fucking starving."

I push myself forward like he asks, and my arms nearly give out from the moment his tongue is on me. I do my best to push myself back up again, knowing I'll be uncomfortable if I'm on my back, but it's nearly too much. His tongue is swirling around my center, determined to lick up every drop that was waiting for him, before he begins to flick my clit. The rapid-fire motion has my body shaking long before the orgasm releases.

"Fuck Maddox! I… can't hold myself up…" I cry out, the pleasure too consuming. I don't know what the solution is—I don't want him to stop but I also can't think straight when his tongue and fingers are working in tandem to make me have the hardest orgasm of my life—but apparently Maddox can multitask.

One more thing to love about him.

"Come here," he says, sitting me up so he can put his mouth on mine. I can taste myself. It's hot and a little dirty and it makes me want to taste him. Except as Maddox places his hands on my hips and starts turning me around, I don't think a blow job is on his agenda.

"I know you said you can't hold yourself up, so let me do it for you," he says as he sits down on the edge of the couch. "Now sit on my cock Gabrielle and fucking ride me."

I bite my bottom lip as Maddox situates himself, lying back on the chaise and positioning himself on the end. His cock is hard and leaking and for a moment, I consider saying fuck his plans, lowering myself to the ground so I can feel him in my mouth. But I can do that anytime. I don't know how many more times in the next two and a half months I'll be up for this, and I'm not about to waste a single opportunity.

"That's it. Climb on top of me. Let me watch your ass bounce on my cock as you ride me."

For a split second I think about if the logistics are there for the couch to hold both of us, but that thought is out of my mind the second Maddox starts stroking himself.

Oh, I'm going to make this work.

I slowly turn around, keeping my eyes on him as long as I can, as he takes the precum from his cock and coats himself with it.

"That's it gorgeous. Just like… that…"

Maddox squeezes my hips as I lower myself down onto him, his fingers resting on my hips as I take a second to make sure I'm comfortable. There isn't an ounce of pressure on my stomach, which allows me to feel every inch of Maddox. I'm tilted forward slightly, my hands clinging to his thighs as I slowly start moving up and down, his hands guiding my movements.

"You are so fucking sexy," he cries out before swallowing whatever he was going to say next as I shift my hips, seeing how deep he can fill me. "How are you so fucking perfect? So beautiful. So fucking mine."

His words spur me on, and as much as I wanted this to last, I had to know that was never going to happen. My movements speed up. Our breathing is ragged. His hands are digging into my skin in the best way possible. I feel him sit up behind me, his defined chest coming flush against my back as each of his hands wrap around to my front, one tweaking one of my nipples as the other rubs perfectly pressured circles on my clit.

"Maddox. I'm so close."

"Me too gorgeous. Oh fuck!"

His cries and one last pinch to my nipple is all I need to send myself over the edge with him. If he wasn't now holding onto me with every ounce of his strength, I think I'd fall off the couch. I'm lightheaded. Sated. Filled. And more in love than I ever thought I could ever be.

"I love you," he says as he helps me onto the couch, where I lay against him, my back to his front.

"I love you too," I say back, gently kissing the corner of his mouth before resting my head on his shoulder.

Neither of us move, even to put our clothes back on, and I feel his breath slow down with mine. I know he must be exhausted. Training camp was no joke and practices have been long all week leading up to the season opener. I take advantage of the stillness as he holds me close, letting my heavy eyes fall shut.

I might fall asleep. In fact, I think I might've been one step away from a REM cycle when I snap my eyes open.

"Oh! I remember!"

Maddox jolts awake, clearly a little dazed and his voice a bit groggy. "Remember what?"

"What I was looking for before you got here."

"Huh?"

"A plate! I was looking for a plate!"

I push myself up, because if I don't go get the plate immediately I'll forget again. Pregnancy brain is a real thing. I should also put on a shirt.

"Is this a good thing? The plate?" Maddox asks. "I want to make sure I'm appropriately excited."

I smile and kiss the tip of his nose. "I love you, you know that right?"

He gives me a lazy smile as he pushes a stray piece of hair behind my ear. "I do."

CHAPTER 30
MADDOX

I have a definitive order of ranking my favorite kinds of football games to play solely based on atmosphere. They're listed into regular season games and playoff games because you can't compare the two.

And yes, they're written in a notebook.

The honorable mentions of my regular-season rankings are the classics—rivalry games and revenge games. There's a different vibe in the air when you know you're going to be facing an opponent you hate, or they hate you. But in my rankings, there are better games.

Third place is when you clinch your playoff berth. Home or away, doesn't matter. That feeling of relief when you know your season's going past New Year's, and that you have the chance to be the best in the league, is something only players know.

The second best is the home opener. No matter the kind of season you had the year before, the first game in front of your home fans always has an energy that can't be beat.

Which means the only thing better than a home opener, is a home opener when you're raising the championship banner.

Fucking best game ever.

The atmosphere here today is insane. Normally, the champs

will have the first game of the season, but weird scheduling snafus meant we opened on the road. Doesn't matter to us. All that means is now we're 1-0 after a dominant Monday night performance, and the fans are bringing that energy here tonight. People give Nashville a lot of shit for being a town full of transplants—which it is. But when you have a good team that fans can rally behind? Our town shows up and shows out. Just like they are today.

This is my third championship banner game, and each of them is special. But without a doubt this has personally been my favorite, and that's because of who's here today.

My girl. Wearing my jersey.

I take my eye away from the game for a second to glance up to the suite I know she's in—a few of the WAGs get one every year to be away from the crowds and they made sure to bring Gabi in there today so she would be more comfortable. I don't even try to hide the smile on my face as I look up at her. The jersey I got her would normally have been swimming on her, but it's the perfect size to hug her bump. Her face is glowing as she talks to a few of the other wives and girlfriends. Ainsley is standing next to her, wearing a similar jersey, only that one I know says Kincaid on the back. The two are talking to Lucy, our quarterback Bryce's wife, who is balancing a toddler on her hip. It warms my heart that Gabi is already fitting in. Like I knew she would.

"You know we're going to have to go make a final stop. Think you can take your eyes off your girl for that long?"

The words come from Austin Keller, the rookie linebacker who was my roommate through training camp and has gotten a good amount of reps in today. Not many rookies do, but this guy is the real deal.

I give one more look to Gabi before bumping shoulders with Keller. "Let's go put this fucking thing away."

As if on cue, our defensive coaches call out for us to assemble as the punt unit runs off the field. Our offense has done a good job for most of the day of getting us in scoring position, but Cincinnati is no slouch. They were a playoff team last year for a reason, which is why the game is as close as it is. Our defense has bent but hasn't broken, and we need to do that one more time to make sure we're 2-0 going into next week, when we head to Philadelphia to play the Kings.

"Do you have one more drive in you?" The question comes from my head coach, Hunter McAvoy.

"You know I do."

He slaps me upside the helmet, a classic move by all football coaches. "Don't get a penalty. Keep them out of the end zone. And whatever you do, keep your man the fuck in bounds. Make them burn their last time out."

"I'll do you one better, Coach. I'll just pick it off."

The look my coach gives me says all I need to know—quit being a cocky asshole. But also, go intercept up the fucking ball.

He knows by now I can be both.

I run back on the field, Keller next to me as we head into the huddle. Our defensive captain reminds us of our scheme before we break apart, much earlier than the offense across from us does. Cincinnati has one timeout left and there's a minute and thirty left on the clock. They're back on their thirty-five-yard line, meaning they have ninety seconds to try and make it sixty-five yards. But like I told Coach, they won't be going anywhere.

I look at how Cincinnati is lining up, and they're playing with an empty backfield, knowing they have to pass on every down to have a prayer of winning this game. They have three receivers to the right, a receiver to the left along with the tight end. He's who I've had to keep my eye on for most of the game, which I've done and done well. But I don't think he's the first option. Cincinnati runs this formation a lot in their two-minute drill, but the beauty of their play is that it never goes to the same receiver twice in a row, so it could be going anywhere.

The quarterback starts his cadence, everyone waiting to jump off the line the second he calls the play. That is, everyone except me. As a free safety, I'm in the back and looking. Trying to figure out where he's going to throw it. Again, I don't think it's going to be the tight end. He's not a downfield receiver and they need yards. I also don't think they're going to go to their top receiver. He has more than a hundred yards today, but we're choosing to double team him, and they aren't going to like those odds.

When I look to my left, I see that it's their number two receiver lined up next to the tight end. The guy can make plays. He's a veteran in the league. He might've lost a few steps, but he can still ball. And because our defense overloaded on the right side, it means he's going to likely be the most open.

That is until I get over there.

The quarterback snaps the ball and it's a flurry of motion as everyone runs their lanes or routes. I'm cheating my way to his side, more confident than ever that's where the ball is going to go. When I see the quarterback turn to his right, my left, I know I've made the right call.

Which is when I take off.

Part of being an elite safety is all about timing. Many players can pick off a pass. It's part of the job. But perfectly timing the ball so the receiver doesn't see you coming? That's an art. One that I've perfected.

The pass is in the air as I pick up my speed.

The receiver doesn't see me coming. He's too worried about making sure he catches the ball and staying in bounds.

Too bad that's not going to happen.

I pause for a half second before making my move.

Step.

Step.

Jump.

Grab.

Interception.

I keep my eyes open as I fall to the ground. I would've loved to get a few yards, but as I was securing the ball, I fell to the ground, and Cincinnati quickly piled on top of me.

Sorry guys. Ball is mine. And with less than two minutes on the clock, we're about to win the fucking game.

2-0.

"Maddox! Your first interception of the season, and a pretty big one at that. How'd you feel out there?"

"It always feels good to pick one off, but when it seals the game, it's a little sweeter," I say to the reporter. "But more than that, I'm glad we got the win. It was a total team effort out there today."

I'm standing in front of my locker, the media scrum enclosing me in, as reporters shout their postgame questions. This is typical for postgame. A few cameras are around—one being the team's camera as they air each of the interviews live. Usually, I don't mind fielding questions. I know I'm a favorite sound bite because I generally don't hold back, while also pleasing our media and PR team by giving canned answers as well. But today, I'm anxious to get out of here. I have my girl waiting for me at home—our home—and hopefully I'm greeted by her wearing nothing but that jersey.

"Maddox!" I point to a reporter I'm friendly with, who's covered the Fury for a few years now at the Nashville Banner. "Are the rumors true? You have a little one on the way?"

It was only a matter of time before the pregnancy became public. Gabi didn't come to any of the family days at training camp. Not that she didn't want to, but because it didn't line up with her schedule at the bakery as she was still getting Josie settled in at the time. But with the season starting, and anyone who had eyes could see her in the suite today wearing my jersey, I knew I could get this question.

"That's right folks! Maddox Gallagher is going to be a dad!"

I get a few congratulations from the reporters, as well as some cheers from teammates who can hear the interview, before the reporter has a follow-up. "When is she expecting?"

"November 1. And it can't come soon enough. Gabi and I are both ready for our little guy to get here."

A different reporter throws up her hand. "November 1 is the rematch against Miami. Do you know if you're going to be traveling with the team or are you going to stay at home for the birth?"

Gabi and I haven't explicitly talked about this, but I've discussed it with my coaches. "If she's in labor, or if it's anywhere close, I'm going to be there for her. Would I like to be with my team? Absolutely. But my family is going to come first. Always. Plus, I have a feeling Miami doesn't want anything to do with me. Last time they faced me it didn't go well for them. I'm pretty sure they'd fund my son's college education for me not to play them again."

That gets the laugh I was hoping for as the scrum moves on to go talk to Linc. I take the break to head to the showers, where I quickly wash up so I can go home and not completely smell like I played a three-hour football game.

When I get back to my locker, it's only the players left, which allows me to fully relax.

"Great game today," I say to Linc, patting him on the back before I take a seat next to him.

"Same to you," he says. "Ainsley and I were going to go out to dinner later. You and Gabi want to come with?"

That could put a damper in my postgame plans.

"Yeah... I can... let me see if..."

Linc laughs at my stumbling. "Our reservations aren't until seven. You'll have plenty of time for whatever you're planning."

"How'd you know?"

"I've been in your shoes before," he says as he stands up from his seat. "That first game when you see your girl in the jersey? It does things to you."

Ain't that the truth.

I grab my phone, but before I can send the message to Gabi, I see that I have one.

FUTURE WIFE

Straight home. We need to talk.

"Oh shit."

Linc looks over to me, confused by my outburst. "What happened?"

"I don't know," I say, holding my phone to him. "But I think I fucked up."

"You were playing a game. How could you do that? That's impressive, even for you."

"I'm not sure. Any idea what it could mean?"

Linc reads it and even looks closer for a second read. "I have no clue. But I'm going to go on a limb and say that you're not coming out with us."

I rack my brain, trying to figure out what I did. "What do I do?"

"I don't know. But whatever she's craving recently, get it before you go home. A text like that? You're going to need as many brownie points as possible."

Armed with brownies from the bakery that she had in the cooler, a cheeseburger she asks for at least once a week, and the sour candy she's started buying in bulk, I cautiously walk into the house from our garage entrance, which leads into the mudroom before I hit the kitchen. The house is silent, which is strange. There's usually some kind of noise. Music. The television. An appliance running. The eerie quiet makes me even more nervous.

"Gabi?" I call out as I kick off my shoes.

"Living room."

I really am in trouble. I spent the thirty-minute drive home going over every word I said to her last night, the texts I was able to send her before the game, and then, what I said postgame in the interviews. Nothing is sticking out to me, which is maybe worse than knowing that I fucked up. But even with my pitstops, I can't figure out what I did or said. I slowly walk across the kitchen, and when I first get eyes on her, a cold chill goes down my body.

She's sitting on the edge of the couch, legs spread because that's what's comfortable for her right now, and her crossed arms are resting on her stomach. Her eyes are intense and staring right at me, waiting for me to walk into the room. She still has my jersey on—I'll take that for a small win—and I don't see her bags packed. Second win.

But otherwise? Gabi is *pissed*.

"Whatever I did or said, I'm sorry," I say as I hold out my peace offerings. "I was wrong and you were right. I also brought you snacks."

Not even a hint of a smile. I'm cooked.

"What the fuck was that?"

I set the food down on the coffee table in the center of the room and pull up an ottoman so I can sit across from her. "I want to answer you, but I can say for certain I have no idea what I did."

She gives me a "really" look, complete with a disapproving head tilt. "Your press conference?"

My press conference? I rewind what I said to the reporters for no less than the tenth time since I left the stadium

Interception… got the win… oh! The pregnancy! I didn't talk to her about us announcing it. That must be it.

"I'm sorry I told them about the pregnancy. They knew and—"

"That's not what I'm talking about."

Damn. I thought I had it. Okay, so after that was…

"Are you mad about what I said about traveling to the Miami game?"

"Yes, I'm mad!"

Wait… she's mad I want to stay with her? For the birth of our child? "You're mad that I said I was going to stay with you?"

"Yes!" she yells, like I should realize this. "You're not missing a game!"

"If my son is being born, yes, I am."

She gives me a raised eyebrow. "Maddox…"

"Gabrielle…"

Many times in our stubborn standoffs, I've relented. Sure, I love the build-up, but most of the time if it's going to make her happy, I'll stand down. This one I won't. Because I love this woman who will one day be my wife, but I'm not quite sure what she's thinking right now.

"You're going to miss the biggest game of the season?"

"It's not the biggest game of the season," I defend. "The media wants to make it out to be the biggest game of the season because it's a championship rematch but it's not even in my top five games notebook. In reality, Miami did a fire sale after the championship last year. They're going to be lucky to win six games. If we can't beat them because I'm not there, then there's bigger problems in our locker room."

"Still," she says, but I can tell she's already scrambling. "You only have so many games a year. You shouldn't miss one."

"Yet I'm going to." I sit back for a second and watch her eyes jumping. Her tell. Between that, and the way she's grabbing at words makes me know this is bigger than just where I'm going to be on November 1. My first instinct in the moment was to think she didn't want me there for some reason, but she's said out loud that she's nervous for the actual birth, so I don't think that's it. No. This is something deeper. Something that's been festering.

I lean in to take her hands in mine. "Can I ask a question?"

She tries to put on a stubborn face, but I can also tell by how her shoulders slightly slump, she knows she's going to lose. "Yes."

"Don't you want me there? In the room with you when you deliver to help support you?"

I know those narrowed eyes. I'm about to be right, and she knows it. "Yes…"

"And don't you want me to have the experience of being there when our son is born?"

"That's two questions."

"Humor me."

"I hate you. And of course I do."

I laugh as I realize that everything is going to be okay. "No you don't. But it's cute you think you do."

I rub my thumb over the tops of her knuckles. Even though I have a feeling I know what this is about, I want her to tell me in her own words. "Talk to me Gab. What's going on in that head of yours?"

Gabi isn't one to pick fights. In fact, this might classify as our first official one, and I'm not even sure it counts for that. But I do know her well enough to know that this didn't come out of the blue. And if I'm right, this has been building since we first saw those magic words on the pregnancy test.

"Remember when I went radio silent for three days when we found out?"

I nod. "Longest seventy-two hours of my life."

Her eyes shift down and she takes my hands in hers before she goes on. "One of the things I was wrestling with was that I felt like this baby was going to be a burden on your life. That we were going to be a burden."

"Gabi. I—"

"Please Maddox, let me finish." She takes a deep breath before turning her eyes back to me. "You did nothing wrong then. And you're doing nothing wrong now. I just hate that, every once in a while, something in my brain wants to try and tell me that this isn't something you signed up for. That you're going to be giving up so much for me and the baby. And when I heard you say that you weren't going to one of the biggest games of the season, all I could feel was like this was the first of many things I was going to be taking away from you. I don't want to be that person. I don't want you to resent me. Ever."

I pull my hand away but only to use my thumb to brush away the tear that slowly moves down her cheek. "I love that you think about those things. That you're thinking about me. But you need to know that every natural disaster could hit Nashville simultaneously and I'd still find a way to be at the birth of our child."

"Well that's not safe."

"Don't care," I say. "I had already talked to Coach McAvoy, which I should've told you about. He understands. He has two kids and he said he would've done the same thing I'm doing. If you're in labor, and it's time to get on the team plane, then I'm messaging them and saying that it can take off without me. I'm staying right here."

"Can I make a request?"

"Maybe."

"If I'm not in labor. If I'm feeling fine. No contractions. Not dilated. All signs pointing to "I'm fine," will you please go to your game?"

I let out a breath, because I don't like the sound of that, but she has a point. I can't sit at home and do nothing while I wait for Tiny Tot to make his arrival. "I'll say yes, but only if you agree to call me the second any of that changes."

"Deal." She cups my face, bringing me in for a slow, but too quick, kiss. "I'm sorry. I wasn't trying to keep you away. Or make decisions for you. I heard that and flew off the handle."

"Thank you, but you don't apologize," I say. "Thoughts can conflict. We can want one thing while wanting another that can't happen if the one exists. It's being human, Gabrielle."

She slightly smiles. "Wise words from a man who got carded for beer last week."

"I'm wise beyond my years." I move to my knees, wanting to be as close to her as possible. "I can see why you want to make sure I'm not missing out on my life. And I love you for that. But you're my life. The baby is my life. And there are going to be many other football games. More than you're going to be able to keep track of. But there's only going to be one birth of our son, and I'm going to be there for it. Come hell or high water, wild horses couldn't keep me away."

She leans forward, her forehead tapping mine. "I'm sorry I got so mad. Can I blame it on pregnancy hormones?"

I laugh as I run my thumb over her lip. "You can. But I'd also like to point out that this could be considered our first real fight."

She smiles, her tears coming to a stop. "And since I started it, I'm guessing I need to make it up to you."

"I'm not going to argue," I say. "But one request."

"Anything."

"However you want to make it up to me, the jersey stays on."

CHAPTER 31
GABI

"And you're sure you don't have any pains? Any symptoms? The coaches know I'm a phone call away from not going."

I love this man with every fiber of my being. But if we need to go over this one more time I swear it's going to be much longer than six weeks postpartum before we have sex again.

"For the hundredth time today Maddox, I'm fine," I say, as I bounce on my medicine ball—also known as the most comfortable piece of furniture in the house. "You were with me at the doctor's the other day and I'm barely dilated. Yes, I'm uncomfortable, but I'm thirty-seven weeks pregnant. That's to be expected."

"But it's really close and I'm out on the West Coast," he says as he throws his toiletries into his travel suitcase. "The doctor even said we are in the window. The window Gabi!"

"She did," I say as I rub a spot on my stomach that Tiny Tot has been pushing against all day. "But what else did she say?"

He pretends to think about it for a second. And I know he's pretending because he's not making eye contact with me while also looking like how I imagine our son will look when he tries to convince me that the dog we're supposedly getting named Sir Barkley ate his homework.

"Maddox…"

I don't get the customary "Gabrielle." I get slumped shoulders. "She said that she'll contribute to his college fund if you have him before Monday."

"Exactly," I say. "Now come here."

He throws in a few pairs of socks before doing as I ask. He leans down so he's eye level with me, which is perfect, because that's where I need him to bring him in for a kiss.

"I love you."

He lets out a breath and kisses me one more time. "I love you too."

After our fight about Maddox traveling to away games—a fight I fully admit picking because I got scared in the moment—we had a long talk about logistics and his football schedule with our doctor. That was after I said I was sorry in the form of a blow job and sex in his jersey, which honestly was fair for the way I reacted.

Luckily, we had an appointment the next day, so Maddox talked to our doctor about his wanting to be there for the birth. And because she's a huge Fury fan, and a kick ass doctor, she looked at the baby's measurements, and mine, before saying that we would be able to safely induce labor the Monday before the Miami game. That way, he'd be with me during an off day and he'd be fine to rejoin his team for Thursday's practice. And then, the week after is their bye, which means he has a whole seven days at home helping to get me settled in. It's the best situation for two people who unknowingly decided to have a baby in the middle of football season.

Now, the little guy—still nameless—needs to hang on until then.

Two more weeks. Give us two more weeks.

"I need to go on record saying that I fucking hate our

schedule for sending us to fucking Los Angeles this weekend," he says. "Could they have picked a farther game?"

"Technically yes," I say. "You could be going to Berlin. Or London."

"Thank fuck I'm not," he says, giving me a kiss on the forehead before leaning down to kiss the top of my stomach. Something he now does every time before he leaves for anything. "Now, what are you going to do if you feel labor pains?"

"I'm not calling you because of a little pain," I say. "We went over this."

"Fine. But! What are you going to do if you're going into labor?"

I know I've also gone over this with him a hundred times, but I can see the stress in his eyes for having to leave for a West Coast game. The least I can do is set him at ease before he gets on the plane.

"I'm going to call you first in case you happen to have your phone. Then when you don't answer, because you probably won't, I'm going to call social media extraordinaire Tatum, who always has her phone on her. If Tatum doesn't answer, the next call is equipment manager Keith. If he doesn't answer, then I call Coach McAvoy's wife, Sadie, who has press credentials and will literally walk down onto the field and pull you away."

"Now that's what I call a plan!" Maddox says, clapping his hands like he's leaving the huddle.

"Question? Why am I not calling Sadie first? It sounds like she's a get shit done kind of woman."

"She is," Maddox says as he zips up his suitcase. "But Coach says she has to be the last resort because the media will realize something is up when she pulls me off the field in the middle of the game, and they'll be outside the hospital before Tiny Tot is even out."

I never thought of that. "Okay. So you, then Tatum, then Keith, then Sadie."

Maddox lifts his suitcase off our bed and comes back over to me, only this time he kneels down with a more serious look on his handsome face.

"I love you," he says before kissing my stomach. When he stands to come eye level with me, my heart nearly bursts from the pure adoration I see in his eyes. "And I love you, so much."

He brings me in for a kiss, this one much longer than the one from a few minutes ago.

"I love you too," I say, squeezing his hand. "Please call me when you land."

"I will," he says as he helps me up off the ball. "And text me every hour please?"

I laugh. "Every hour?"

"Yes, every hour. I want updates. How you're feeling, if anything is bothering you. If you need me to order you food. Doesn't matter."

"You know Shelby is coming to stay with me for the weekend, right?"

"While I'm glad she is, I still need to see the name 'Future Wife' pop up on my screen every hour on the hour."

Now I'm laughing. "I can't believe that's still my contact name."

Maddox pulls me in as close as he can. "Only because I'm waiting for the day that I get to change it to 'Wife.'"

His words warm my heart. And I know it's not my never-ending heartburn. "Let's have a baby first. And maybe name it. Then we can talk about that."

He kisses the spot where eventually a wedding band will rest. "Deal."

"Are you sure you're okay?"

"I'm fine," I say to Shelby as I wince a little bit at the slight contraction—emphasis on slight—I just had. This one was not as slight than others I've had, so much so that it caused me to hold onto my bathroom vanity to get through it. "He's very active today."

"You look like you're in a shit ton of pain. Chalk this up to reason number two-hundred-and-twelve why I will never have a child."

"We're only at two-twelve?" I ask, breathing through the last of the pains. There. Better.

"It's probably more, but I've lost count. Now get your ass to bed."

"I'm washing my face."

"You can go one night without washing your face Gabi. I promise you're not going to get wrinkles from one night of neglect."

"I'm almost done. And I'm fine." I am. I'm fine. Everything is fine. I can still wash my face. I can still take five minutes out of my day to feel human. Plus, this is serving a secondary purpose. In my mind, if the contractions are close enough that I have two in the time it takes me to wash my face and put on my moisturizer and eye cream, then it's probably time to go to the hospital. "See. I'm done."

"Good, now lay back down so your baby daddy can quit texting me asking why you haven't answered him."

I smile as I waddle—yes waddle—my way back to the California king-size bed in my master suite. "He's just worried."

"I hope there's a play call called 'Blue Baby 88' or some shit like that tomorrow, because I'm pretty sure that's the only thing he's going to respond to," Shelby says as she rolls out of the bed. "You okay if I use the bathroom?"

"Yes of course," I say as I do my best to get comfortable. "Despite what you and Maddox think, I can be alone for a few minutes at a time."

"I don't know about that. I left you alone in Vegas and you ended up pregnant."

I want to argue with her, but I can't. She's right. So I do the only thing I can think of and throw my pillow at her.

"Go."

She laughs at me as she closes the door to the en suite before I turn on the television and take my phone off the bedside table.

GABI

Were you bugging Shelby?

MADDOX

Yes. You missed your check-in.

I was in the bathroom.

And…

Maddox…

Gabrielle…

I love you. I'm fine. Nothing different from what I told you last hour. I was washing my face.

Shelby says you're in pain. Are you in pain?

"Shelby! Are you tattling on me?"

"Damn right I am," she muffle yells as she pops out of the bathroom, toothbrush in her mouth.

"I'm so glad you moved here," I grumble sarcastically as I type again to Maddox.

I'm fine. Yes, I've had some discomfort. But you're not getting on a plane.

You're not lying to me?

I'd never.

I should tell you, I have access to a plane.

How the hell did you get access to a plane?
Like the team plane?

No. A private one.

Please tell me you didn't buy a plane.

I didn't buy a plane. I was talking to Linc today,
and his future brother-in-law has a plane.

That's handy.

Right? He told him to keep it ready.

Let's hope you don't need to make that call.

I know. I have to go to our position meeting.
You sure you're good?

I'm great. Now go be a football player.

Text me before you fall asleep.

Yes sir.

I kind of like you calling me sir.

Head out of the gutter Gallagher.

Love you.

Love you more.

"What the fuck is that!"

"What is what?" I ask Shelby, because I don't know what she's talking about. The only position I can get comfortable in is laying on my left side, which means I can't see half the room. For all I know, Big Bird is sitting in the corner wearing a sombrero.

"On the television."

I lift up slightly and start laughing when I see my brother on the television, explaining to a sports commentator how he plans on breaking the world record for lowest score on an eighteen-hole golf course. The world record is 55, and Beau is insistent he's going to beat it this season.

"Hey, at least with him trying to do this, he won't be at home much," I say, turning slightly to hopefully put off a little pressure. "How has life been living next door to my big brother?"

"Horrible," she says as she sits on the bed next to me. I told her to sleep in the guest room, but turns out, my best friend is more of a helicopter than my boyfriend.

"What has he done?"

"Nothing."

If anything is going to make me figure out a way to turn my head to look at her, it's that. "Clarify."

"I haven't seen him. But I know he's there."

"And how do you know that?"

"Because every morning there are fucking golf balls in my yard. Golf balls I didn't hit. Name brand I don't even play. But you know who does?"

"I'm going to guess Beau Devereaux for a hundred please."

"Ding fucking ding. Also! Why does he play golf shirtless? No one needs to be on a putting green shirtless."

"I thought you didn't see him?"

"I don't."

"Clearly you do if you're seeing him, and looking at him, shirtless." Fucking with Shelby is something I rarely get to do. It's pretty fun. "If I saw someone I hated, I'd make sure I did everything in my power to ignore them."

"He's right there! How can I ignore him!" she screams, which makes me snicker. "What are you laughing at?"

"Doth protesting a whole lot…"

"Fuck you," she says, taking a pillow and smacking me on the shoulder. "Go to bed so we can stop talking about this."

On cue, I let out a massive yawn. "Fine. Sweet dreams. About Beau…"

"You're making me regret moving here."

I shrug and slide back down to the bed, readjusting my pregnancy pillow. "You love me."

"You know I do."

We each say goodnight as I make sure to do one last check-in with Maddox.

> Signing off for the day. Going to sleep. I'll text you when I wake up.

> Okay. I love you. Remember about the plane.

> Like I could forget.

I put my phone on the bed and adjust myself one more time, hoping to get comfortable.

Except I never do.

CHAPTER 32
GABI

3:22 a.m. Central Time / 1:22 a.m. Pacific Time

Why in the actual hell can't I get comfortable?

I've felt a few what I'd call mini contractions. I've read enough books, talked to enough moms, and watched enough videos to know this can't possibly be "real" labor.

Though if this isn't real, I was right to be nervous about actual labor.

Because this fucking sucks.

"Gahhh…." I try to moan as quietly as possible into my pillow, doing my best not to wake Shelby. She should get some sleep. It's not like she can do anything for me.

I swallow down my groan as I see my phone light up on the nightstand.

MADDOX

Everything okay?

Did the man already install the baby monitor in here? I wouldn't put it past him.

GABI

I'm fine.

Please don't call me out on it… please don't call me out on it…

But you're answering a text at three in the morning?

And you're texting me at one a.m. your time.

I couldn't sleep. Worried about you.

You're sweet, but I assure you, I'm fine.

I'm not giving the order to gas up the plane?

Stand down. I'll send you the signal.

Gabi, we're really bad at coming up with code words and signals.

It'll be easy. I'll send "GET ON THE FUCKING PLANE."

Clear and to the point. I like it.

Get some sleep. You have to play football tomorrow.

Technically it's later today.

Semantics. Go to bed Maddox.

Only if you're sure you're okay.

I'm fine. I love you.

Love you too.

I set my phone down and promptly turn my head back into the pillow. It's not a contraction but fuck… something is going on with my body.

But I'm not in labor. And that's what matters.

5:58 a.m. CT / 3:58 a.m. PT

"Gabi?"

I've been trying for hours not to wake up Shelby. Around 4:30, I moved into a spare bedroom so I could moan without alerting her that anything was wrong.

Apparently, that didn't work so well.

"Go back to sleep," I say, though my voice is gritty as I fight off a contraction. But it's fine. My last one was maybe six minutes ago? Sixteen? Fifty-six? Who knows at this point, because really, what is time?

"Are you in labor?"

"I'm not in labor," I insist. "My contractions are way too far apart, and in no way consistent."

"You've been tracking?"

"Yes." It's not a complete lie.

"Gabi…"

"I swear I'm fine, Shelby. Go back to sleep. I'll wake you up if anything changes."

I feel the bed move as Shelby lays down next to me. "I'm not going to sleep."

I shake my head. "I'm fine. Please, one of us should get some rest."

"Do I need to text Maddox?"

"Absolutely not," I insist. "I promise you if my contractions get closer, we can text him. But right now, the closest one was twenty minutes apart. That's not labor. I'm sure this is going to pass."

Shelby gives me a heavy side eye. "Are you sure?"

"Positive. Now get some sleep."

9:14 a.m. CT / 6:14 a.m. PT

"Fuck me!"

And not in the good way. Then again, "fuck me" is how I'm in this situation.

"Gabi."

Shelby's stern voice has me looking up from my spot that I've created on the medicine ball, my arms gripping onto the bathroom counter.

"Yes?"

"Can I text him now?"

"No. It's four a.m. in California. Plus, I'm not in labor."

"You're not?"

"No," I say, tossing my phone to her. "I looked it up."

She takes my phone and reads it, but I don't think she's believing my highly vetted baby blog source. "At what point are you in labor? Because this sure as shit looks like labor."

"When my contractions are consistently less than ten minutes apart, and even closer to six minutes. Or my water breaks. Neither of which are happening."

Shelby gives me a side eye. "And you're going to tell me when you're there?"

"Yes. I'm going to tell you."

"And you're going to let me text Maddox."

I let out another groan. Hopefully she thinks it's because she's annoying me. "And then I'll let you text Maddox."

12:02 p.m. CT / 10:02 a.m. PT

"Why are you not at the hospital?"

I look up from my odd positioning half on the bed, half on the medicine ball, to see Beau storming into my bedroom. "Hey big brother. What brings you by?"

"Shelby called me," he says.

Shit. I must be worse than I thought if she did that. "You did?"

"Believe me, not the call I wanted to make," she says. "But you're being hardheaded and not listening to me, so I had to bring in backup. As much as it pained me to do so."

"And I'm glad she did," he says, looking back to Shelby with… wait… is that a little bit of care in his eyes? Wait! Is this it? Is my child already performing miracles by getting these two to not hate each other? "How could you not drag her ass to the hospital? Clearly, she's in pain."

I thought the thought too soon…

Shelby immediately gets defensive. "I don't know Beau. Maybe because I'm not about forcing people to do things against their will."

"She's in labor!"

"She's not in labor. Believe me, that was the discussion about six hours and three coffees ago."

"This has been going on all night?"

"Yes. It has. And I didn't sleep at all making sure she was okay and the contractions didn't speed up."

"And you didn't think to call me?"

"I'm sorry, what were you going to do? Nothing. It was the middle of the night. There was literally no sense in calling you."

"You don't think I'd want to know? Classic Shelby. Her way or no way and God forbid you lean on someone for help."

"I'm sorry I didn't call Beau to save the day. In a situation he couldn't do anything for."

"Stop!" I scream, and good timing too because a minor contraction hit at the same time. "Y'all, I love you both, but I really need you two to cool down the 'Beau and Shelby Hate Each Other Show' today. I just… I can't."

The two share a look and then give each other slight nods. It's not saying I'm sorry, but it's silence, and I'll take it.

"What can I do?" Beau asks, kneeling on the floor next to me. "And can the answer be to take you to the hospital?"

"No, I'm…" I swallow a hiss, and whatever I was about to say next, as another very minor, nothing to worry about, contraction hits me.

"Those were two pretty close together," Shelby says.

"I thought I hid the last one."

"You didn't. Now can we go to the hospital?"

"I'm going to say something I never thought I would, but I agree with Shelby."

She starts to reply—likely of the smartass variety—but Beau puts up his hand. "Just let me agree with you and maybe she'll go."

She swallows her words and gives him a glare, before sitting down on the bed next to me. "Please Gabi. Let's go. Sure, they could send you home. I know that's a possibility. But let's have that peace of mind?"

"Fine," I grumble as I let both Shelby and Beau help me to a sitting position. "But please, don't tell Maddox yet."

"Maddox doesn't know!" Beau yells. "How could you not tell him?"

"Because I didn't want him to worry, and he's two hours behind us," I defend. "I wanted him to get sleep for the game and to not worry about me when there's nothing to worry about."

"But he's awake now and probably hasn't gone to the stadium yet. This is the time to pull him away before his game begins."

I think about it for a second, remembering his face and how upset he was during our fight about him traveling around the time of the birth.

"I know that, but when it's a false alarm—because it's going to be—then he's distracted. He's going to have a horrible game and it's going to be my fault."

"You need to call him," the two of them say simultaneously. I know they're serious because neither makes a remark to the other about stealing their thoughts.

"And I will. When there is something of note, or anything to worry about, I'll alert the Emergency Maddox System. But we're not going to need to do that. We're going to go to the hospital, they're going to check me out, and then they're going to send me right back home."

3:05 p.m. CT / 1:05 p.m. PT

"Gabi, your doctor wants us to admit you."

I look to the emergency room nurse, who I clearly heard wrong. "Excuse me? I think you said the wrong words."

The nurse clicks a bunch of buttons on her rolling computer. "Nope. Getting you ready now. There's a bed upstairs and you're even getting the VIP treatment as one of the nurses from labor and delivery is going to personally escort you there."

The only relief right now is that I know that nurse has to be Ainsley. Thank God she's working today.

"I'm in labor?"

"I don't want to say for sure. It's better for your doctor to answer those questions, who's on the way."

When I reluctantly look to Shelby and Beau, they're sending me the same look. It reads "we told you so." They're even standing the same way—arms crossed, eyes narrowed.

"All it took for you two to get along was for me to be wrong?"

"No, all it took was for you to be an idiot," Shelby says. "Now can I call Maddox? Please."

I look up at a television from my bed in the emergency department. The Fury's defense is running on the field, and like the world is sending me a signal, the camera zooms onto number thirty-five.

I'm not going to hold back on him. I want him here. I'm going to need him here. But, I want to make certain.

"You said the doctor is on her way?"

"Talked to her myself," she says. "By the time you get to your room, she should be there waiting for you."

"Then we wait," I say to Shelby and Beau. "It's not going to be much longer. At this point, what's the difference of twenty minutes?"

3:35 p.m. CT / 1:35 p.m. PT

"Bad news, you're in labor. Good news, at least for you, is that I'm contributing to your child's college fund."

"Fucking told you!" Shelby yells.

"Not now," I scold her before looking back at my doctor. "I'm really in labor?"

She nods and makes a few notes as Ainsley gets me situated. "You are. Now, the second piece of good news is that it's early. But it is active. Ainsley here is going to be doing checks for me every hour, and you call her if you need anything."

"And I'm not leaving until this little one makes his entrance," she says. "I don't care if it takes all night."

"Shit!" I yell out, looking panicked to Beau and Shelby. "I didn't bring anything. I thought I was going home. My bag. The baby stuff. It's—"

"I've got it," Beau says. "Tell me everything you need."

"Already taken care of," Shelby interrupts, stepping a little bit ahead of Beau. "I put it in my car hours before you agreed to come. That way it was ready."

"Look at you, Bell. Planning ahead." Beau says.

Shelby glares at Beau. "Don't call me that."

"What? You did a good thing. That's a good name. I was trying to be nice!"

"Enough you two," I say as I take a few deep breaths, the weight of the situation suddenly crashing in on me. I'm so overwhelmed I don't even take a second to truly process that Beau used the nickname he used to call Shelby when we were kids. "How much time do you think I have, Doc?"

"It's going to be a while," she says. "Then again, I didn't think I'd be here with you this weekend. So what do I know? I'm only the doctor."

Her humor isn't appreciated right now as Shelby takes my hand, and the floodgates open. "I fucked up…"

Like he knows I'm talking about him, I look up at the television through my tears to see Maddox leap through the air and pick off a pass. He jukes around one player, makes another one miss him, and then he's off toward the end zone for a touchdown.

"Make the call," I say to Shelby. "Tell him to get his ass on the fucking plane."

CHAPTER 33
MADDOX

4:15 p.m. CT / 2:15 p.m. PT

"That's what I'm fucking talking about!"

I nearly skip off the field, loving how this first half has played out. We're up by twelve going at halftime —one of those touchdowns compliments of me and a quarterback who basically told me his target in his body language—and if we keep this momentum after halftime, I might not even play the fourth quarter. And the best part? We're about to start the season 6-0.

"Good fucking half my man," Linc says, patting me on the back.

"Can say the same to you." Linc is having himself a game today, already catching for sixty yards. It's like Los Angeles forgot we have one of the best catching tight ends in the league."

"Now we need to keep the pressure on," Coach McAvoy says as we all step into the locker room. "Great first half gentleman. But we're not about to let up now, are we?"

A chorus of "nos" echo off the locker room walls before he continues. I go to check my phone, because I might've been in game mode, but I need to make sure Gabi is okay, when I hear

Coach McAvoy stop talking. My eyes look up to see what's going on, but I can't make it to him, instead seeing the woman standing at the door of our locker room.

Sadie Kincaid-McAvoy.

That's when my heart drops into my stomach.

Coach McAvoy's wife steps into the locker room, but doesn't look at her husband. She doesn't have her normal reporter's notebook, but she does have a serious look on her face. And it's pointed straight at me.

"I've been told a very specific message to give you Maddox," Sadie says before she shows a knowing smile. "And that's to get on the fucking plane."

It's a moment of silence before an eruption of applause hits the Fury locker room. I never told my teammates our code word, because I didn't think I'd need to, and before I know it, I'm being mobbed by my peers who instinctively knew what the message meant, a few of them throwing out the term "Daddy Gallagher" before I step away.

"Coach? You need me for the next half?"

Coach McAvoy smiles and shakes his head. "Not at all. Congratulations Maddox. Now get home to your family."

My family… holy shit I'm about to become a father…

I panic and freeze for three seconds before I start tearing off my gear. My teammates give me space as I strip faster than I ever have before. I throw on shorts and a T-shirt because it's the first thing I see. I don't even shower. There's no time for that. I need to get on the fucking plane.

"Fuck! Linc!" I yell out. "I need—"

"Already taken care of brother," he says as he holds up his phone. "The call has been made. Plane happened to be on the West Coast. It'll take a bit to get to the private airport, but it'll still be better than flying back commercial. I'll text you the address."

I bring Linc in for a hug, so grateful for him and the family he's going to one day marry into. "Thank you. For everything."

"You're welcome," he says, patting me on the back. "Now get the hell out of here. We have a game to win and you have to go meet your son."

5:45 p.m. CT /3:45 p.m. PT

Where. The fuck. Is. The God. Damn. Plane!

I'm sitting at the private air strip that Linc told me to go to, my knee bouncing in anticipation as I wait for the arrival.

Yes, I know that I'd be waiting even longer for a commercial flight. I know this because I looked it up, wanting to make sure. There's only one nonstop flight tonight out of L.A., and that doesn't leave for another three hours. And with the time difference, that doesn't get me back until closer to midnight. That's way too long for me to wait. Sure, I might be waiting now, but from what I quickly researched, private planes travel faster.

Not knowing how long I'll be waiting, I take my phone out and hit Gabi's contact. I've texted her on my way here, but I still haven't talked to her. It only rings once before I see her face, and I breathe a little easier.

Emphasis on little.

"Gabrielle..."

Gabi tries to give me a smile, but I can tell she's grimacing through the pain. "Hi Maddox."

I see her try and get comfortable in the hospital bed, and someone—I'm assuming Shelby—helps situate the phone so Gabi doesn't have to hold it.

"How are you feeling?"

"Fantastic," she says, though her sarcasm isn't landing.

"Not the time gorgeous."

Her shoulders slump a bit. "I'm better now. They gave me the epidural. Last night was… rough."

"Last night?" I bark out, but then immediately feel bad because I don't want her to think I'm mad at her. Even though I am. A little. "Why didn't you call me?"

"In my defense, I tried to make her," Shelby says as she steps in front of the camera. "I want that on record."

Gabi swats her away. "You're no help Shelby Lynn. Didn't you say you were hungry? How about you go find that food."

"Fine," she says before stepping in front of the camera again. "Whatever she's about to tell you, I was Team Maddox in everything."

"That's why you're my favorite."

"Damn right. Just don't tell Hannah." I watch on as Shelby kisses her forehead before I presume she exits the room.

"Now tell me everything. Even if I'm not going to like it."

And I don't. Not one word that comes out of her mouth. I hate how much pain she was in. I hate that I wasn't there for her. I hate that she let her stubborn self take over and waited as long as she did. I hate that I'm not there now.

Seriously, where the fuck is the plane?

"I'm sorry," she says as a tear falls down her cheek. "I really didn't think I was in labor. My contractions were—"

"You don't need to apologize," I say. "I hate that I left you."

"And I don't want you to do that. That's why I didn't call until I had to. We didn't know. I promise it didn't start until well after you left. They didn't even start until after I went to sleep. There was no way we knew this was going to happen this quickly."

I nod and bring down my phone, letting my elbows rest on my legs. "What has the doctor said?"

"That I still have a while," she says. "She's keeping me here because I progressed so fast. She wants my water to naturally break, but if the pain continues, and hopefully once you're back, they'll break it for me if it's what's best for me and Tiny Tot."

I feel the tear in the corner of my eye. "I'm hurrying back. I promise."

"I know," she says. "I love you."

"I love you. So much." I look up to see a plane coming down onto the air strip. "I think my ride just got here."

"Okay. Get back safe."

"Wild horses, Gabrielle. Wild horses."

6:30 p.m. CT /4:30 p.m. PT

"Mr. Gallagher? I'm sorry, but we have a problem."

Of all the words I want to hear from a pilot, those have to be the last ones. "What is it?"

"The plane is grounded."

"Is it in trouble?" Yes, it's a bad joke, but if I didn't crack a joke, I was going to go off on this guy. And that won't do anyone any good.

"Something like that. It's the steps that collapse to let you on and off the plane. They're broke."

"Broke?"

"Yes, broke. They won't retract."

"How did you get down?"

"They weren't broke then."

"But they are now?"

"Yes. They're broke now. We can't take off."

"Okay, let's fix it!" I stand up and clap my hands. "I'm not handy per se, but I can help. How do we fix it and get this plane in the air and off to Nashville."

His face turns more serious. "We don't."

"I'm sorry. I don't think I heard you right. Did you say we don't?"

"I'm sorry Mr. Gallagher. We don't have the parts needed here since this is a private air strip. I know it seems silly, but it's a deeper issue I'm seeing. It would take a day for me to get the part I need here."

"I don't have a day."

His shoulders slump. "I'm so sorry. I wish—"

I hold up my hand to him as I grab my duffle bag. "I know you are. And I'm not mad at you. I just need to get to a fucking plane. The love of my life is in labor with our son and—"

"I understand," he says, typing something into a phone. "Mr. Matthews, the owner of the plane, normally uses a car service that isn't located too far from here. Let me call you a ride to the airport."

I let out a sigh of relief. "Thank you. I'm sorry if I snapped."

He finishes typing in his message. "Don't apologize. Let's get you back to Nashville."

From his mouth to God's ears.

7:45 p.m. CT /5:45 p.m. PT

"I'm sorry sir, I can't help you."

I shake my head at the ticket counter agent, who's sporting a spectacular mustache, because I had to have heard him wrong.

Yes, I know that when I searched on my phone on the drive over that I couldn't find a flight, but I assumed that was a user operator error. Surely, he has to have *something*.

"You can't help me? As in you're going on break and I can move one window down?"

"No. As in, I can't help you get you back to Nashville tonight."

"Can someone help me get back to Nashville tonight?"

"No sir. No one can."

I don't want to scream, but it's out of my lungs before I can swallow it back. "You've got to be fucking kidding me! This is fucking LAX. A huge fucking airport. How are there no flights tonight to Nashville?"

"I'm sorry sir. There's nothing direct for the rest of the night."

"What about with a stop?"

He looks, but his face isn't hopeful. "There are, but with the time difference and layovers, you wouldn't be there until morning."

I take a breath, because I know this guy doesn't make the plane schedules, but you've got to be fucking kidding me right now.

"I know. I'm sorry. It's just that my girlfriend is in labor with my son and I really need to get home."

It's at that moment that Captain Mustache realizes the emblem on my warm-up jacket. "You're Maddox Gallagher!"

"I am. What's your name?"

"Pete."

"Nice to meet you Pete. Now how close can you get me to Nashville before midnight. I don't know how long I have."

8:20 p.m. CT /6:20 p.m. PT

"You're flying where?"

"Memphis," I say to Gabi as I sit down at the gate. "It was the best Pete could do."

"Who's Pete?" she says through a wince.

"The gate agent. Helpful guy after I yelled at him. Don't worry. I apologized."

My humor isn't doing much for Gabi now, who still looks miserable as I FaceTime her to keep her up to date on the change of plans.

"Would it be quicker if you waited on the team now?" she asks. "They have to be leaving soon, right?"

"I thought about that but no. I'm boarding in ten minutes, and the team plane doesn't leave for another hour and a half. It always has a late call in case we go into overtime."

Gabi takes in a deep breath, and slowly lets it out, and a stab of pain hits me in the chest. I should be there with her. Holding her hand. Getting her ice chips. Rubbing her back. Dancing and singing like an idiot to take her mind off the labor. Whatever she wants. I should be there.

But no, I'm sitting in an airport hundreds of miles away, before I drive another three hours to get to her. My estimated time of arrival right now is after three in the morning in Nashville. It's not as quick as I wanted, and I'm praying to every God I've ever heard of that I get back to her in time.

"Shelby still with you?"

She nods. "She went to grab some snacks and drinks for the overnight shift."

"And Beau?"

"I sent him home. He was on call to come get you from the airport, but I guess that's not needed now. Wait! How are you getting here from Memphis?"

"I'll rent a car," I say. "Shit. I hope someone is even working at the rental car counter since it'll be after midnight by the time we de-board."

"Did you say Memphis?" I recognize Ainsley's voice before she comes into the frame of the FaceTime. "My brother is there on business. He can give you a ride back."

"Ainsley, that's nice, but—"

She's texting before I have the words out of my mouth. "But nothing. You've never met my brother, but he's the world's biggest Fury fan. He also likes fixing things and being the hero. When I tell him that he needs to drive you to the birth of your child? He'll change every plan he has to help."

"He doesn't have to do that."

"Too late," she says, putting down her phone. "I texted you his phone number. Keep him in the loop. Doesn't matter what time your plane lands, he'll be there, bells on, and willing to drive ninety miles an hour to get you back to Nashville."

I'm so glad Linc ran into Ainsley at this very hospital. Because damn she's one of the good ones. "Thank you Ainsley."

"This is what friends do," she says. "Now, I'll take care of everyone here. You get back. Deal?"

"Deal."

Now beginning to board, flight 383 from Los Angeles to Memphis.

"Text me before you take off," Gabi says. "I love you."

"Love you more," I say as I stand up and grab my backpack. "I'll be there before you know it."

CHAPTER 34
MADDOX

8:43 p.m. CT /6:43 p.m. PT

adies and gentlemen, we're so very sorry, but we're going to be delayed for a few minutes. The pilots need check a few things before we're able to take off. No need to panic, we'll be in the air soon."

I sit in my seat—a ridiculous expensive seat that isn't even in first class because beggars couldn't be choosers in the situation I was in—and try to think positive thoughts. At least I have the row to myself.

I'm on a plane. That's what matters. I'm on my way home. I got a text from Shelby that she's progressing slowly, but there is movement. I'm going to focus on the word slowly, because I need every minute.

MADDOX

On the plane. Delayed a few minutes. They said not to worry.

FUTURE WIFE

What's a few minutes at this point?

> Exactly. Have I said how sorry I am that I'm not there?

> You have, but I feel worse that I waited so long to tell you.

> But would it be us if this baby came with a normal birth story?

> Not even a little bit.

The little bit of humor we add makes me smile and relax for a second. That is, until I hear the pilot over the speakers.

"Folks, I'm very sorry, but it's going to be another few minutes. No need to panic or deboard the plane. Just taking a little longer than expected. We'll be in the air to Memphis in no time."

9:26 p.m. CT /7:26 p.m. PT

"I'm sorry again folks. I didn't think it was going to come to this, but we're going to need you to exit the plane. We can't fix what we thought we could, and we're going to need to wait for a new one. Good news is that it's about twenty minutes away."

I'll believe it when I see it...

I do my best to regulate my breathing, because what the fuck kind of bad luck is this? The worst part? Is that the Fury team plane I know has taken off, so my idea of meeting back with them is now not a possibility. No one can have this much bad luck when it comes to airplanes in a single day. But I can't do anything about it now except grab my duffle from the overhead compartment and make my way off the plane.

"Are you Maddox Gallagher?"

I turn back and see a kid, maybe around eight years old, behind me with a man who I'm going to assume is his father. "I am. What's your name?"

His smile is big and toothless. "Gunner."

I laugh at the irony. "I wanted to name my son Gunner."

"What's his name?"

How in the world is the fact that we don't have a name for our son not even in the top ten things to panic about today. "He doesn't have one yet. He's about to be born."

"I heard that on the television today," the dad says. "Says you had to leave the game to head back to Nashville."

"That was the plan," I say as we make our way through the jetway back to the gate. "Forces are keeping me away."

"That sucks," he says. "But if you're like when this guy came, my wife was in labor for twenty-four hours before he came out."

That would be great. Except that if we're counting how long Gabi was in pain last night, she might already be nearing the twenty-four-hour mark. I can't imagine what she's going through. "I'll get there. There's not another option."

"Absolutely not," he says. "Good luck."

"Thanks." I go to walk in hopes of finding a semi-private place where I can call and update Gabi, but I hear whispers from my two new friends.

"Maddox?" Gunner whispers with a nervous smile.

"What's up buddy?"

He holds out a hat he's wearing that has nothing to do with football. "Can I have your autograph?"

"Absolutely," I say as he hands me the hat. I might be in a shit mood. I might've yelled at two people today who were trying to help and had to tell me bad news. And I might now live at LAX. But I'll always take time for a young fan. Who knows? Maybe my act of kindness will be smiled upon by the airline gods. "Wait, I have something better."

I kneel down as I start digging through my duffle bag. I always carry a marker for this exact reason, and I'm pretty sure I have the pair of gloves I was wearing today. In my crazed exit from the stadium, I threw them in here instead of leaving it for the equipment managers. "How about one of my gloves? Keep that hat nice and crisp."

Gunner is wide eyed and speechless as I sign the glove for him. "Thanks Maddox!"

"Anytime."

When I stand back up, the dad is holding out his hand. "Thanks for that. And good luck."

Passengers of flight 383 to Memphis, please be advised, your new flight time will be departing at 8:30 local time.

"Was that good luck about fatherhood or about getting out of Los Angeles?"

The dad laughs. "At this point? I honestly don't know."

10:20 p.m. CT /8:20 p.m. PT

"You're on the plane?"

"I'm on the plane. Again."

Gabi's eyes are hopeful. "And it's taking off?"

I smile as I sit back into the seat. "As far as I know."

I haven't been told it's not, and after the quickest boarding process in the history of airline travel, everything seems good. Though after the events of today, I hate to get my hopes up too much.

"Oooohhh…" she lets out, biting her lip as I contraction rolls through her.

"Breathe, gorgeous. One…two…"

I continue doing the exercises we practiced together so many times, only, I'd hoped to be doing them next to her, holding her hand or rubbing her back. Not sitting here watching her through my telephone.

I really need this plane to take off…

"I'm good," she says as she sits back against the pillow.

"What's the update?"

"I'm at five centimeters, according to Ainsley."

"Five!" How have I not asked her about this up to now? This should've been my first question. "That means you're moving at one centimeter away from being at the stage where you dilate at one to two centimeter per hour! I'm going to miss it."

"Which baby notebook is that in?"

"The one where I write down all the numbers I needed to watch out for. That one got a lot of pages devoted to dilation centimeters and what they all mean."

Somehow my panic is making her look more relaxed. Which at this point, anything I can do to help. "You're not going to miss it. I've been at five for hours. You're fine. Just breathe."

"You're telling me to breathe? That's not how this goes, Gabrielle." I want to tell her more about how I'm about to freak the fuck out when I hear the engine of the plane rev up. "I'm hurrying home. I promise."

"I know you are," she says. "I'm going to try and sleep. You have a safe flight. And a safe drive."

"Okay," I say as the pilot tells us that it's finally time to take off and to turn off our devices. "And Ainsley's brother is still good to drive me? I feel horrible how late it is."

"He's more than ready," she says. "His name is Simon. He says you'll know him when you see him."

"What's that mean?"

"I'm honestly not sure."

2:01 a.m. CT

I'm that guy. The guy who, as soon as the plane lands, stands up, grabs his stuff, and cuts in front of everyone trying to deboard.

I hate that guy.

In my defense, everyone on this flight has given me the green light to do so.

During the three hour and thirty-one minute flight to Memphis, I made friends with about everyone on the plane. Once the flight attendants found out I was onboard, they did everything they could to make sure I had everything I needed. The elderly married couple who sat across from me kept my mind off how long the damn flight was by asking every detail of how Gabi and I met. Gunner and his dad, who wound up in the row behind me and slept for most of the flight, were a great reminder of what I have to look forward to. I also yapped with three lovely women who were sitting in the row in front of me who live not too far from Nashville and can't wait to come try Sugar and Sweets.

Every one of them heard the story of how Gabi and I met, and of how freaking in love with her I am. Each one gave me a piece of parenting advice they wished they had when they were young. One even gave me an idea for a name for Tiny Tot. One I think could stick.

And most important, every single person told me to make

sure that I was the first person off the plane. So maybe I'm not an asshole. I'm just a guy trying to get home, with an unexpected squad making sure it happens as quickly as possible.

"Good luck Maddox! You got this!"

I don't even know who yelled that, but I hold up my hand to wave as I begin my full-on sprint through the Memphis airport. I quickly sent a text to Gabi and Shelby the moment the wheels hit the tarmac, knowing the second I could leave, I couldn't bother messaging. And I'm glad I did, because I'm running faster now than I did in my game today. Yesterday? What day is it even?

Considering the hour, the airport is empty, and it's easy for me to be at full speed. There's not an option of *not* running. I don't even stop to go to the bathroom. All I can do is focus on signs that say "baggage claim" where I'm meeting a man named Simon. Now it's just an escalator and a three-hour drive home separating me and my family.

Family. Fuck. That one word has me turning it up another gear. I'm exhausted. My legs are jelly and I can feel the adrenaline starting to fade away. But I can't let it. Not yet. I can when I get in the car. There's nothing else I can do as a man named Simon drives me across the state.

Because I need to get to Gabi. My son. My family.

I do my best to quickly jog down the escalator to baggage claim, and I'm halfway down when I see a man holding a sign that says, "The Dad to Be," and wearing a full chauffeur suit.

"Simon?"

Did he buy that? Did he have something like this at the ready? Who is this guy?

"The one and only!" he says, way too loud considering we're one of four people in this entire area. "Any bags?"

"Nope."

"Perfect, I left the car running. It's right there."

"Thanks man," I say as I walk up to the BMW. "You didn't have to do this, but I really appreciate it."

"Nonsense!" he says as he opens my car door for me. He's

really playing up that chauffeur thing. "You're a friend of Linc—who's currently sitting at the top of my brother-in-law rankings. You're a Fury player—great interception today, we're going to be talking about that during this drive. And of course, in a few hours, you're going to be the newest member of the Dad Squad. Of course I was going to do this. Now get in the car! Let's fucking go!"

This man has said a lot in five minutes. And this coming from a guy who always has a lot to say. "Dad Squad?"

He hands me a cigar and a blue button that says "Dad Squad" on it. Does he have these laying around? Does he keep them with the suit?

"We have plenty of time to talk. Now buckle up. Let's get you the fuck back to Nashville!"

CHAPTER 35
GABI

2:30 a.m. CT

"Gabi?"

I open my eyes, even though I wasn't really sleeping, as Shelby taps me on my arm.

"Maddox?" I ask but instead of him walking into the hospital room, she hands me my phone.

"Hey gorgeous."

I let out the biggest breath and for the first time in a full day, I'm a little more relaxed. "Hey you."

I've talked to Maddox plenty of times tonight. He's kept me updated during every step of his disastrous travel day. But seeing him in a car, which means he's in Tennessee, makes me feel so much better.

"Where are you?"

"We left the airport about twenty minutes ago," he says. "We're going… fast."

"You know you don't do me any good if you get into a car accident."

"We're fine!" I hear the voice of I'm assuming Simon before Maddox turns the camera. "Hi Gabi. I'm Simon. Nice to meet you. Don't worry, we're going to get him there by four thirty safe and sound."

I look at the clock and double check the time. "But Memphis is more than three hours away. How are you doing that?"

"No one's on the road and I'm an excellent driver."

"Are you factoring in the time you'll need when you get pulled over?"

He waves a hand at me. "I won't get a ticket."

"How?"

"I know a guy. It'll be fine. Ask Ainsley. There's nothing to worry about."

"Clearly you haven't met me."

"Listen, all I need you to worry about is being comfortable. How far are you dilated? If you tell me beyond a six I'll take it up to ninety-five miles per hour."

"She should be," I hear Maddox say before he begins to tell him every update I've given him over the past however many hours. I look up to Shelby, mouthing a "what the fuck is happening" as my boyfriend and a friend's brother talk about my cervix.

That wasn't on my delivery bingo card.

"Am I needed for this conversation?" I ask.

"Oh sorry. I'm here."

I can't help but laugh at this ridiculous, yet amazing, man. "It's okay. You have fun on your road trip. I'll be here preparing to birth your child."

"I love you," he says, all playfulness gone from his voice. "I love you so fucking much."

"I love you too. Get here safely, okay?"

"I promise."

3:20 a.m. CT

MADDOX

Updates?

GABI

Eight centimeters. Things are moving.

GPS says we're getting there around 4:50.

Please don't die.

We won't. Oh! Did I tell you that Simon has the same stroller we bought? We're stroller buddies!

Love that for you.

You aren't as excited as I am, are you?

I am. You just can't tell because I haven't slept in twenty-four hours and I've decided we're never having sex again.

That's fair.

I'm going to go have a contraction now.

I wish I was holding your hand.

You say that now. Shelby might have to go to rehab after what I've done to her.

I'll pay for it myself.

Get here safe.

Love you.

Love you kind of.

4:28 a.m. CT

"Fuck… fuck… fuck!"

This is the oddest feeling. I should be in pain, but I'm not. Not really. But the pressure. Oh God the pressure…

"Breathe Gab, I got you," Shelby coaches out, doing her best to be here for me without ever taking a single class or reading one word of a book on childbirth. But like with most things Shelby does in life, she's killing it.

I do the best I can as I let the contraction pass through me. Once it does, I fall back against the bed, spent and tired from now officially more than twenty-four hours of pain.

"Did I hear a big one?" my doctor says as she walks in my birthing suite with Ainsley.

"They can't get worse, right?" I ask hopefully. "Like that was the max?"

"Sure," the doctor says in a tone that's anything but sure. "Let's have a look at you."

The doctor does her thing and I close my eyes for a second, taking advantage of the few minutes of silence.

"All right, nine centimeters, but ten is almost here," she says. "It's almost baby time."

"No!" I shout. "Maddox. He's almost here. He's less than an hour away."

The doctor looks at the clock before looking back at me. "I'll wait as long as I can. But we're checking on you frequently. This baby is coming soon, and as much as I want Maddox to be here for this, and for you, I'm not going to put you or the baby at risk."

"I understand," I say, but her words have sent my anxiety through the roof.

"Everything will be okay," Ainsley says as she wipes my forehead with a washcloth. "He'll get here. I know Simon. He won't fail. Especially for something like this."

She gives my hand a squeeze before leaving the suite.

"Shelby? I'm scared." It's the first time I've said those words out loud, but I can't keep them in anymore. "I know he's on his way. But I feel like things are coming fast now and he's not here yet and I already feel another one coming on and…"

"Hey," she says, leaning down and tapping her forehead to mine. "No matter what, you're going to do this. Whether it's me or Maddox standing next to you, you're going to do this. Hard things are petrified to see you coming. No matter the obstacle, you've always overcome it. And what you've done this past year? Starting your life over? Divorcing the douche bag? Running the bakery? Finding love again? Some people can't do that in a lifetime. But here you are, adding giving fucking birth to that list. I know it's hard. I know you're tired, but if anyone can do this, it's you Gabi Devereaux."

I feel the tears on my cheeks, but don't have the energy to wipe them away. "Thank you. For everything."

"What are best friends for? Though I would've liked to have known when we became friends that one day I'd have a front row seat to you pushing a human out of your vagina."

"Would you not have been my friend if you knew that?"

She shrugs. "I would've had to consider it more."

I'd throw a pillow at her if I had any energy. "I love you."

"Love you too," she says as she picks up her cell phone.

"What are you doing?"

"Messaging your baby daddy," she says. "I'm here for you. But now that I think about it, I really don't need to see my nephew being born."

CHAPTER 36
MADDOX

4:35 a.m. CT

think that name is fucking perfect!" Simon says, slapping his steering wheel.

"Thanks," I say as we pass a sign that says we're thirty miles away from Nashville. And one that says the speed limit is sixty-five miles per hour. A sign Simon is clearly ignoring. Though he's at least not going ninety anymore. "You said you have a daughter?"

"Yup. My Lainey. She's two and a half. My pride and joy and the reason why I've embraced the salt and pepper hair."

"That's amazing," I say as I look out the window. Simon has tried to keep my mind off things, but I can't help but worry every time the conversation stops.

Am I missing it? I haven't heard from her or Shelby in nearly an hour. What's happening? Is she okay? Why haven't I heard? Should I call? Am I a bother to call? Are they not calling because it's happening and they don't want me to feel bad? Are they not calling because nothing significant is happening? The not knowing is killing me. I feel like I'm failing her already and Tiny Tot isn't even here yet.

"Let me guess. You feel like shit because you aren't there and you're worrying yourself to death that you're a horrible father already and the kid isn't even born yet?"

I look over to Simon in awe. Is he also a mind reader?

"How did you know?"

"I had that look approximately two and a half years ago," he says as he weaves past a car. "Charlie, my wife, wasn't due for a few weeks and my friends took me out for a stag party, but for babies. Golf, beer, a diaper haul, the whole nine."

"That's amazing."

"It was until one of my best friend's teenage sons, who was our designated driver, had to pull my ass out of the bar because she was in labor."

"You're kidding me," I say with a laugh. "Your kid was born and you were drunk?"

"Hungover," he corrects me. "Nothing sobers you up quite like your person screaming at you and squeezing off your hand."

"I can only imagine," I say as my hand inadvertently starts opening and closing in a fist. I wonder if someone can get put on the injured reserve because they're laboring wife broke it?

"I'm telling you this because I remember feeling like dog shit for being away from her. But life happens. Nothing goes to plan. And it's not going to go to plan once your son gets here. In Lainey's entire life, there has not been a day that hasn't gone to shit somehow."

"That makes me feel better."

"Listen, being a parent is fucking hard," he says. "But just be there for your kid. Be there for your woman. Just be there and everything is going to work out."

Be there.

Two words. Short, simple, and to the point. Asher told me the same thing. Maybe it *is* that simple? And exactly the reminder I need every day to make sure my worst fears don't come true.

"Wise words from a wise man."

"Why thank you." He doesn't take his eyes off the road as he grabs his cell phone. "Actually, can I record you saying that? I have a few people I'd like to play it for."

"That's the least I can do."

I hear my text notification, and my heart drops when I see that it's Shelby.

SHELBY

She's at nine and the doctor says ten is around the corner. Hurry the fuck up Gallagher.

"Fuck!" I yell. "She's almost at ten centimeters."

I don't know if he has a turbo charge, but somehow, he hits a button and we're going faster than should be legal. "Screw the speed limits. It's fucking baby time!"

5:02 a.m. CT

"I'm here! I'm here!" I yell, holding onto the door frame as I swing myself into Gabi's room.

Gabi looks up to me with relieved, yet scared eyes as she grips Shelby's hand. "You made it."

I step on the other side of her, taking her free hand as I bend down, needing to kiss her more than anything in the world right now. "I made it."

For a moment—a few seconds in time—the world stops. It's just me and Gabi. After the crazy last however many hours. After a half of a football game. After three planes and a thrilling car ride. After meeting strangers on a plane. After Gabi having to navigate the last day of pain. We're here. Together.

Be there…

And I will. Always.

"I think my work here is done," Shelby announces, breaking us of this moment.

"If you want to stay, and if Gabi wants you to, you don't have to leave," I insist. "I don't know how I can thank you for everything you've done."

"I love you both, but no one is happier you're here than I am." She kisses Gabi's forehead before walking around to me. "I'm going to be the best Aunt Bee I can. I'll buy him booze when he's eighteen and I'll sign tests when he fails them. But I do not, and I repeat, do not, need to see him being born."

We all laugh as she gives me a kiss on the cheek. "Take care of my girl, okay?"

I pull her in for a hug, maybe the tightest one I've ever given someone. "Forever."

We let go and Shelby steps out of the room as Ainsley pulls me aside to get me gowned up.

"You ready, Daddy?"

I nod and give her a hug because I'm so grateful for the women in our lives that were here for Gabi when I couldn't be.

"I am," I say as I walk back to Gabi. "Let's have a baby."

CHAPTER 37
GABI

"And then she walked up on stage with me, and let me tell you Tiny Tot, she was the prettiest girl I ever saw."

I have no idea how long I was sleeping, but I open my eyes enough to watch as Maddox sits in the recliner in my hospital room, our son to his bare chest, as he talks to him in what I assume is the story of how we met. He hasn't noticed that I'm awake, which I'm glad. Being in this moment, seeing this interaction between him and our son, has me intrigued like it's something I didn't live through.

"And then she danced with me. On stage in front of a huge crowd. It was so exciting. She moved like she didn't care that there were hundreds of people watching. She was living in the moment, and I got to be a part of that. One day you'll learn about love at first sight. I didn't think it was real until I met your mom. But I promise you it is."

Love works in such mysterious ways. Here's Maddox, who says he's loved me from the first moment he met me. If it were anyone else on the planet, I'd tell them that they were crazy. That no way someone could fall in love with a random woman who hijacked the stage with you in Vegas. Especially when it wasn't love at first sight for me. No, to me, he was going to be a good time. A hot time. A way to start the new chapter of my life. Little did I know…

"And then she sang with me. My man, there are going to be times in life when you meet a girl, and she does something that might not work for other guys, but it's going to make you fall in love with her that much harder. And that was what happened when I heard your mom sing. Wait until you hear her voice. I can't wait until the first time she sings you a lullaby. You're going to want her to sing to you every night."

Well now I'm crying. Which, it wasn't going to take much for that to happen. I can already feel the hormone swing and I've been not pregnant for roughly eight hours. But hearing Maddox talk to Tiny Tot right now? I think I'd cry no matter what.

"Then after we sang together… well I can't tell you about that, but you'll figure it out one day when you can do math and realize when your birthday is. Also, when that happens, I'm going to talk to you about condoms and how they aren't always effective."

I know I said I didn't want to make a sound, but how do I not laugh at that? I try to keep it under my breath, but I watch as Maddox turns his head to me, a dazzling smile on his face from ear to ear.

"I'm sorry. I know you were asleep—"

"No," I interrupt. "I liked hearing it."

"I don't know if he did," Maddox says as he stands up and walks over with our son and sits next to me. "He slept the entire time. Of course, now he wakes up."

I laugh as I take our son from Maddox and position him for another feeding. "Or maybe your voice relaxed him so much that he could close his eyes and take it all in."

"Let's go with that."

Maddox helps me sit up a little more as I do what I need to do to feed this little guy. We've already done it twice since his arrival this morning, and the fear I had about not being able to breastfeed was quickly dispelled when this guy latched on like a champ and has every single time.

I couldn't help but notice the proud look on Maddox's face the first time he did.

"How are you feeling?"

"Weird," I say, not truly able to come up with another word. "My body is my body again, kind of, but not really. There's some pain. I'm wearing a diaper. But somehow, I also feel good."

"You look beautiful," Maddox says as he kisses my cheek.

"You're biased."

"So what if I am? I also forgot to say that you're strong. Your body is able to feed our son, which might be the most impressive thing anyone can do. You were a fucking rockstar during all of this. And I'm not going to tell you this nearly enough in our life, but I'm amazed by you."

I tilt my head so it can rest on Maddox. I know I did those things, and I don't want to downplay them, but I do wonder how the hell I did it. It almost seems surreal. How a body can endure that type of pain and trauma, and a few hours later, be sitting upright? It's baffling.

I also know that I'm lucky. Tiny Tot's birth, despite the hours of labor leading up to it, was seamless. He waited for his dad to get there, and an hour after that, he was born. At least one person in this scenario got the memo about a non-dramatic birth. His mom and dad on the other hand? Not so much. If anything, it's going to provide years of good story telling about the day that he came into the world.

"Is it time?" I ask as I maneuver him to burp. "I don't think we can put off the name anymore."

We were asked immediately if we had a name, which of course, we didn't. In our original birth plan, we were going to use the time that I was in labor and waiting for him to arrive to decide on that. Clearly that didn't happen.

"It's time," Maddox says, not moving from the bed.

"Did you bring the notebook? I remember most of them, but I don't want to accidentally forget one."

"I have it, but I want to add another contender."

"A late addition?" I ask as our son lets out the cutest burp. It's probably not cute, but he's mine, I made him, and therefore everything he does is adorable. "When did you come up with this?"

"Last night."

"Was this on the plane, the train, or in the automobile?"

"The plane, and there was no train, though that would've been kind of fun. But in the car ride, my new best friend Simon approved it."

"Well then if Simon approved it…"

"Listen, you'll really like him," he adds. "And! His wife owns a restaurant in Rolling Hills, which is like a half an hour from us. I got her number for you so you two can connect when you're back in bakery mode."

Even in the most panicked situation, and when this man was being driven by a virtual stranger at ninety miles an hour, he's still doing the littlest things for me.

Yeah… I think I'm going to keep him.

"That sounds amazing. Now, can I hear this name?"

"Oh! Yeah. So anyway, I was talking to people on the plane."

"Of course you were."

"Shush. This is a good story."

"My apologies," I say as I bring Tiny Tot down off my shoulder, positing him in my arms against my chest. "Continue."

"After I was done telling them about you, and us, someone asked what we were naming the baby. I, being the honest man I am, said that we didn't know. So, I whipped out the notebook, figuring we had nowhere to go so I might as well crowd test some of our contenders."

I can picture everything he's describing. A jet in the air flying over the Midwest, and there's Maddox in the emergency exit line, holding court with his notebook calling out baby names.

"And what were the results?"

"Our favorites got great reactions—Graham, Noah, and Levi. Oh! There was a kid named Gunner on the plane, so I know you're going to veto it, but I need to put it back in there for him. And they told me not to sleep on Baker, and I told them that we'd throw it back in the mix."

"If that's what the people want, who am I to deny the people?"

Maddox picks up on my sarcasm. "Quit teasing! Do you want to hear your son's potential name or not?"

I can't keep in my giggles. Watching this man get so excited is still one of my favorite things. "I won't interrupt again."

"Thank you. Now, where was I? Oh! Yes! Then, out of the blue, someone said a name, and I think it's my favorite."

If I could sit on a seat properly right now, I'd be on the edge of it. "Well don't hold back. What is it?"

He smiles down at the baby before looking back up to me. "Ace."

I let it process for a second. I never would've thought of that, yet somehow… it's perfect.

"What do you think Tiny Tot? Are you an Ace?"

The child has no idea what we're saying, but like he does, he takes that time to sneeze. Which, considering he's less than twelve hours old, I take as a sign of communication.

"Ace Gallagher." Maddox leans in closer, his fingers gently trailing up and down our son's—Ace's—cheek. "If he ever does decide to play football, it's a hell of a name. It's unique without being out there, which is what we were going for. But most important, it gives an ode to Vegas. The place that changed our lives forever."

Cue the tears.

"It's perfect," I say as I prop him up a little. "Ace Jacob Gallagher."

"Jacob?"

Now it's Maddox's turn to cry, which I expected. My man is

not afraid to show his emotion. "I know I wasn't a fan of juniors, or two-point-ohs, but maybe one day it will become a family name that he can pass down."

"Fuck I love you," he says, taking his fingers to my chin and bringing me in for a kiss. "But can we take him home before you think about marrying him off? We have a lot of years left with this guy."

"Absolutely."

"It's my turn to hold him!"

Beau turns away from Shelby, covering Ace's head like he's shielding him from an attack. "You've had plenty of time. And I'm his blood, remember?"

"How could I forget. You only remind us every day!"

"Because it's true," he looks down at Ace, his face gentler than the looks he was giving Shelby. "Don't listen to mean Aunt Shelby. Whatever she tells you about me is a lie."

Shelby starts to fire back some sort of insult before she, and this fight, are gladly interrupted.

"Actually, I'm going to take him." Phyllis walks right between Beau and Shelby and takes Ace out of his arms. "He needs time with his great auntie Phyllis. And you two need to go bang it out."

"Phyllis!" Shelby cries out. "How could you say that? You know I hate him, right?"

"There's a thin line," Kitty says as she sits next to Phyllis and Ace. "And you two are walking a damn tight rope."

Beau and Shelby share a look before each turning on their

heels, storming off in separate directions of the bakery. Beau charges back to the kitchen. Unfortunately for Shelby, she doesn't have very far to go, but instead of admitting defeat, she decides to walk out of the bakery.

She'll be back. I think. I hope. We made her favorite dessert—carrot cake—and we haven't even cut into it yet.

"Thank you for inviting us," Kitty says as I step behind her, because apparently, I'm incapable of being out of reach of my child for more than five minutes. "We already love this little guy."

"He's easy to love. And like I could have a baby welcome party without you two."

"You really couldn't," Phyllis says. "Oh! And let us know when you're going to be back to work. We have booties for him."

"You two already got us gifts. You didn't need to do that."

"We would've brought them today, but they aren't ready."

I'm confused. "What do you mean they aren't ready?"

"It's a hundred pairs of booties," Kitty says. "Oh! And some blankets."

I had to have heard them wrong. "A hundred?"

"We asked the girls at the assisted living facility to start knitting. They got a little carried away. The last sewing meeting is next week to finish them all up."

I laugh because that's too sweet. But also, what the hell am I going to do with all of those? "Thank you. I'll make sure we send you guys back with treats for everyone."

"See! I told you!" Phyllis says as she smacks Kitty's arm. "She didn't believe me that I thought we could work on trade. Booties for bear claws."

"Now that sounds like something I can get behind," Maddox says as he steps behind me, wrapping his arms around my midsection. "I hate to interrupt, but the little guy is being requested. Asher's daughter really wants to hold him."

"Oh absolutely," Phyllis says as she gives Ace to Maddox. "Now, let's talk about this trade deal."

"Never mind her," Kitty says. "You go enjoy your party. And thank you again for inviting us."

I give each of them a hug before stepping back and looking around my bakery, and inside it is every single person I love.

Mom and Dad flew to Nashville the day after Ace was born and were able to come back now three weeks later for the official welcome party for Ace Jacob Gallagher. Maddox's mom, sister, and niece were also able to fly down from Iowa, and even Hannah got away for a day to be here. I believe her words were: "The kids and husband can fend for themselves. I need to meet my nephew."

Of course, our Nashville contingent is in attendance. Josie, who helped prepare everything and has been my rock while I've been gone on maternity leave. Shelby, if she ever comes back after her dramatic exit. Beau, Theo, and Asher, and of course, his daughter, Adalyn, who looks adorable right now in her pig tails and blue dress as she holds Ace with the help of Asher supporting his head. We have Linc and Ainsley, and obviously, we had to invite Maddox's new best friend, Simon, and his wife Charlie. They brought their daughter, Lainey, who has fit right in with Adalyn and Maddox's niece.

It's a sight to see. And I love every minute of this.

"Everything good boss?"

"Quit calling me that, at least today," I say as I nudge Josie's shoulder. "Your work is done. Just enjoy it now."

"That I can do," she says as she picks up a chocolate peanut butter brownie. "I get why you craved these. They are *really* good. Did you do something different though? There's something different about them?"

"I didn't bake them," I say. "I thought you did?"

"Me? You know I can't get the peanut butter sauce right," she says. "Whoever did it, I'm glad they're here. Because I can't make them, but I sure as shit can eat them."

Maddox sends me a wink like I'm supposed to know what

that means. Wait, is he signaling me to the brownies? He didn't make these. He couldn't have.

Right? Right.

Maddox laughs and I make a mental note to talk to him later about whatever that was. Josie went all out when I told her that I wanted to have everyone at the bakery to officially meet Ace. And she didn't disappoint. Cookies, cupcakes and mini cheesecakes. Scones, cherry danishes and apple tarts before they go out of season. Carrot cake for Shelby. Cinnamon rolls for Beau.

And of course, bear claws for Maddox.

The dessert that started it all.

I felt bad I couldn't help her more, but I did try a little. It's been three weeks since Ace came into the world, and while I know I'm not ready to come back to the bakery full time, it has been nice to get in here every once in a while to remember the life I have outside of feeding, changing diapers, and washing bottles.

Seriously, how does a baby who now weighs a whopping eight pounds, three ounces go through so many diapers? I was ready for it—at least I thought. It only took me two days to realize I vastly underestimated how many diapers we'd go through in a day.

And how many outfits he'd wear.

And how many showers I thought I'd take.

But I wouldn't trade any of that for the world. And neither would Maddox.

With the timing of Ace's arrival, Maddox was able to miss a few days of practice before he reluctantly went back. Luckily, it was a home game, and Coach McAvoy gave him a waiver to spend the night with me and Ace instead of the team hotel that Saturday. I'm so glad he's with a team that values family like the Fury, because I don't know what I'd do if he hadn't been there with me that first week.

I can't ever believe that I had a single worry that Maddox wouldn't want to be part of this child's life. I know we're only a few weeks in, but no way could you ever convince me that this man won't be one-thousand-percent in our child's life in any way he can.

And I think he's starting to believe it, too.

I know he was worried that he could be like his dad. That when the baby came, he'd be scared and eventually panic and leave. That couldn't be farther from the truth. Maddox regularly takes the nighttime feedings, even if he has practice in the morning, and always takes care of bath time. When I told him once that I could do it if he wanted to relax after practice, he told me to go lay down and rest. It was only after I walked past the bathroom and heard Maddox talking to Ace—like he did the day he was born—that I understood why.

It's their time. The time for the two of them. I know something like that only goes on for so long, but I hope they always have something like that.

Because if there's one thing I haven't underestimated is how much Maddox is not like his father. Not even close.

"You okay?"

Maddox's arms snake around me, his lips next to my ear before he kisses my cheek.

"Yeah. Just taking it all in."

Maddox stands with me, doing the same, as we watch our family and friends love on our little guy. Theo is holding him now, and I laugh as Kitty and Phyllis are literally drooling over the tattoo-covered baseball player holding a baby. At some point, Shelby has come back in, her eyes going from loving when she's looking at Ace, to daggers when she's looking at Beau.

And sure, there might be a touch of hatred between my best friend and my brother, but it doesn't outweigh the love that is in this room. Nor does it cover the love I feel every day from the man standing behind me.

"How did we get so lucky?" Maddox says as I fall back into his hold. "Sometimes this doesn't feel real."

"I ask myself that every day."

And I do. Maybe not that exact phrase. But each morning when I go to feed Ace, I look at him and think about how much my life has changed in less than a year.

At this time last year, I was in the middle of an ugly divorce. The bakery had just opened. I was trying to decide what I wanted to do with my life. I didn't know what was next.

I surely never expected this.

Having a thriving business. Being with a man who loves me endlessly. A son who will one day call me "Mommy."

Who knew all I had to do was go to Vegas, take a dare, and put on a sequin dress, for the rest of my life to come into shape.

"Oh fuck!" Shelby yells and we quickly turn our attention to her. At some point, it looks like she took hold of Ace, who has his "yup. I pooped" face. And judging by Shelby's reaction? It's a blowout of epic proportions.

"Shelby! Bad word!" Adalyn yells, which makes Beau laugh harder than he ever has.

"Make her pay Adalyn!" Beau says. "Actually, she called me a *really* bad name earlier. Can she pay for that too?"

"Oh fuck you Devereaux," Shelby says before walking over to us. "Here. Take your child."

Maddox takes Ace from Shelby. and yup, upon further inspection, our son ruined another onesie.

"This is our life, huh?"

"Damn right it is," Maddox says, giving me one more kiss on the cheek. "And I wouldn't change it for anything."

Neither would I. Not one bit.

EPILOGUE

MADDOX

~~ Five Months Later ~~

Vegas is much different from the last time I was here.

Yes, both trips were for sporting events. A year ago, it was the championship game. This time I'm a spectator, because you better believe I wasn't going to pass on the opportunity to watch Shelby and Beau playing together, as a pair, in a mixed-doubles tournament. To an outsider, they probably look like they're just playing a round of golf. And going into the final day of play, they're in second place. But to Gabi and I who know them as well as anyone on the planet? We can tell they're one snide comment away from trying to murder the other with their drivers.

It's epic. And we weren't about to miss a single second of it.

Plus, a return trip to Vegas felt right. Especially for what I have in mind when it comes to the love of my life.

"I need another ten minutes," Gabi calls out from the bathroom.

I look down to Ace, who's currently on my lap and finding his plush golf ball very entertaining. "Do you think Mommy's going to be ready in ten minutes?"

My little guy laughs at my question. Sure, I'm bouncing him on my knee—one of his favorite things—but I like to believe it's because he's agreeing with me.

"You're good," I say as I look over to the clock. "We have plenty of time."

That's true. The reservation I made for us at a rooftop restaurant in Las Vegas isn't for another hour. I'm dressed and ready in a white button down and black pants. I have my suit jacket waiting on the back of a chair. Classic. Easy. And hopefully, an outfit that won't give too much away from my motives for tonight's date.

I don't think she's suspicious. At least, she's not acting like it, and I think I've done a pretty good job of keeping my surprise under wraps.

It wasn't hard to convince her to have a date night while we were here. I told her we were celebrating a year of knowing each other in the place it all started, even if it's about a month late. And when her parents decided to come—they also weren't missing front row seats to the Beau and Shelby Show— the childcare piece of the plan was secured. Now, Gabi thinks they're going to watch Ace then head back to their hotel room when we return at a reasonable hour—because we're parents of a five-month-old who like clockwork is up three times a night.

That's where she's wrong.

Her parents are going to stay here overnight. And us? If all goes well, by the end of the night, Gabi will have said yes to the most important question I'll ever ask, and we'll be celebrating in the hotel room I booked two floors up.

"What do you think Ace? Do you think she's going to say yes?"

He doesn't respond to my whispered question as he's too busy deciding which toy to keep him occupied as I put him down on the play mat we brought. One thing about parenthood no one warns you about is why when you're traveling anywhere, it's like bringing the whole house with you. And a trip to Vegas? We needed two suitcases just for him.

Pack and play. Toys. Bottles. Clothes. I mean, his clothes aren't that big. How did we need so many for a four-day trip?

But I wouldn't have missed coming back here for anything. It's the perfect circle back to what started it all. And what will hopefully start our next chapter.

"Almost ready!"

"You're good!" I call out as take that moment to slip the ring —a three-carat pear-shaped diamond that Shelby swears Gabi's going to love while also thinking it's too much—into the pocket of my suit jacket. I check myself in the hotel mirror one more time, suddenly feeling nervous for the night. But somehow, that all melts away when I catch a reflection of Ace in the mirror, playing with his plush football, letting out the best sound in the world.

His giggles. They get me every fucking time.

There's nothing to be nervous about. This is everything you want and more. Things at this time last year you didn't even know were on the horizon.

The past five months have been a blur, while also being the best five months of my entire life. On the football field, it was as close to a perfect season as a team could have. I wasn't wrong that first day of camp when I said there was something special in the air. We put up a season like no one could imagine. Pundits said we'd be dominant, but we even shocked them. One loss. Records set for scoring and defense—which never happens in professional football. No team is dominant on both sides of the ball. We could've gone unbeaten—the media and fans sure as hell wanted to see it—but we had bigger goals, and that was to win our fourth championship in five years. We rested every starter in our final game of the regular season. We weren't taking any chances. The scary thing was that our backups and third-string players nearly got the win.

A little more than a month later, we were hoisting the championship trophy again. The championship game was in Miami this year. No, there wasn't a championship rematch. That would've required the home team to make the playoffs.

But we were back. And we won again. Only this time now instead of celebrating by myself and surrounded by teammates, I got to kiss my girl after the win as the confetti rained down from the sky. Ace was there, looking fucking adorable in his little jersey and wearing a custom pair of baby Fury headphones. It was one of the best moments of my life.

Well, not the top one. That was the day he was born. Number two I'm reserving in the notebook for when Gabi and I say, "I do" and she officially becomes "wife" in the cell phone. Number three was when I found out I was going to be a dad. But that championship win with my family there to celebrate with me? It gets a solid fourth place.

Which considering the top three? Isn't bad at all…

Since then, my life has been all things Gabi and Ace. Gabi is back to work and we've found our new normal. Sugar and Sweets is thriving. Beau still technically owns it, and while the goal is still for Gabi to take over one day, he's not in a rush to sell. For obvious reasons to me but unknown ones to her. Yet, even though one day she wants it to be her business, she's more than happy running the bakery, working a mid-shift where she doesn't have to open or close so she can still be part of the creation of the desserts, and guide the menu to where she wants it to go, without having to miss too much time at home.

Since it's the offseason, I'm a proud stay-at-home dad, and I fucking love it. Honestly, I don't understand why some men think it's beneath them to be at home and take care of their children? Every day is a new adventure. We make sure to go visit Mommy at work at least three times a week, which also lets Ace see his great aunties. But we quickly learned that one of us always needs to be around. Not for safety concerns. More for what our child is hearing. The other day when Kitty was holding him so I could use the restroom, I came back to Phyllis talking to him about the importance of pleasing women and making sure they always come first.

And people were worried about me as a father…

I mean I was, but not for that reason. How could I not be the best at it when I have the best fucking kid in the world? He sleeps on a tight schedule that has allowed Gabi and I to get into a rhythm for feedings. He's hitting every milestone like a fucking champ. And he's a happy baby. Always smiling—my mother has said that my smile has made it to the next generation —and for the most part, very good natured. Sure, he's starting to get a tooth and he's not a fan of that. But who would be?

Sometimes I don't have words for how much I love him. I was told by every man I know who's a father that you don't know love until you hold your child in your arms, and fuck if they weren't right. That moment I first felt him against me, I felt my whole world shift.

It was also in that moment that I knew for a fact I was never going to be like my father. Because leaving him? Gabi? This life? Never in a million fucking years.

"Okay, I'm ready!"

"Here we go," I whisper to Ace before I gently kiss the top of his head, picking up my suit jacket at the same time.

I stand up and turn around, and my jaw is immediately on the floor. "When… where… fuck Gabi, you look stunning."

I had no idea what Gabi was wearing tonight—my only instructions to her were that we were going to an expensive dinner before a night on the town—but never in my wildest dreams did I expect to see her walk out of the bathroom in a sequins dress.

The sequins dress.

"Where did you get this? I thought…"

"I bought another," she says with a shrug and a sly smile on her lips. "I have very fond memories of that dress in this town"

"As do I."

I pull her into me, hoping like hell that I'm not going to ruin her makeup, but also not caring. I need to kiss her. Taste her. Let my hands feel the roughness of the material as I trail them up her body—just like I did that night.

"We better stop," she says, her lips barely away from mine. "Or we aren't going to go out."

I groan, because she's right. Any other night I could've been convinced to cancel the plans. But tonight? No. Not tonight.

"I need to warn you," I say as a promise before quickly kissing her one more time. "That dress might suffer the same fate as the last one."

"I'm counting on it."

I groan against her throat, allowing a laugh from her as I pull myself away so I can throw on my suit jacket. The only problem with that is for a second, the jacket goes upside down, which causes the very important contents of the jacket to fall on the ground with a thud.

Fuck… fuck fuck fuck…

I'm wide-eyed as I look at the ground where a light blue ring box is staring at me. I look up to Gabi, who sees it too.

"Maddox… is that?"

Fuck, fuck, fuck, fuck, fuck shit fuck…

What do I do? I had a whole night planned. Dinner. Dancing. Karaoke (obviously). Then a grand proposal with champagne and roses and the whole nine yards.

I could pretend she didn't see it. Or that I didn't see it. That we're both seeing things.

But that's not me. That's not us. But what is us? Doing things the completely wrong way.

"This isn't how I planned it." I scramble to try and remember what I wrote down to say in my "all things engagement" note-book, but the words are escaping me. But as I look at Gabi, who has tears filling in her eyes, it hits me that it doesn't matter what I say. I need to tell her how I feel.

That I can do. I've been doing it since the moment I met her.

"Gabrielle, nothing in our journey has gone according to

plan. Neither of us thought we'd meet each other in Vegas. Hell, that night I didn't even know if I'd get to see you again, and that's before you went back to my hotel and changed my life in so many ways. Then there was the time I tried to ask you out and didn't have the words and sent you the cringiest voice note known to man."

"I still have it by the way."

"Of course you do," I say with a laugh. "But every word in that message, all of those first conversations, there was one thing I knew. And that was you were it for me."

I feel bad that her tears are going to ruin her makeup before we even leave the suite, but judging by the smile on her face, she doesn't care.

"I didn't plan on falling in love with you at first sight. I didn't plan on being put in the friend zone and then somehow falling more in love with you. But I did. And I was going to wait Gabi. I would've waited forever."

As if on cue like he's a paid actor in this scene, Ace lets out a sneeze. We both look at him, and swallow our laughs because the little guy looks like he scared himself with that one.

"Then there was the joy I felt when we found out about him. And the day he came into this world." I pause, reflecting back to that whirlwind day. How the hell I made it there in time still baffles me. The MVP of that journey is forever Simon Banks, who I'm going to see if I can get the approval to join the Poker Club. I have a feeling he'd fit right in.

"What I'm trying to say is that there have been so many times in our relationship that were unplanned. Unexpected. I don't think a single thing we've tried to do has gone according to plan."

She knew it was coming, but she still lets out a gasp and covers her mouth when I go down on one knee.

"Gabrielle Devereaux, I had this big idea to go back to the karaoke bar tonight. We were going to sing again, and then I had the same room reserved upstairs that we spent our first night in together. I was going to do this, only better, and ask you to be my wife. But here we are, in a regular hotel room with your parents walking in any minute and our son probably needing a diaper change, but the question is still the same. Gabrielle, will you marry me?"

She shakes her head, but the smile on her face doesn't mean she's saying no. "You didn't need to do all of that. You could've asked me on the airplane here. Or in the kitchen last week. No matter where you would've asked, the answer would still be the same. Yes Maddox. I'll marry you."

My tears are out before I can think to hold them back as I take the ring out of the box and slide it onto her finger. Shelby got her ring size for me, but I still breathe a sigh of relief when it slips right on perfectly.

I'm standing up and embracing her in an instant. I'm holding her so tight that I end up spinning her around, our laughter filling the room. Apparently, this is quite the show, because I hear laughter from Ace join in.

"You like that?" I ask as I put her down, both of us sitting on the ground next to our son. "Do you want to be a ring bearer at Mommy and Daddy's wedding?"

In true five-month-old fashion, his only response is letting out a sound so loud, and so disgusting, that you can't help but laugh.

"A blow out? Really?" I ask. "Couldn't have waited for Grandma and Grandpa to get here?"

"I got—"

"Absolutely not," I say as I pick Ace up, the smell immediately sending a shot of disgust to my stomach. Another thing no one fully warns you about with parenting—they might be little, but their smells aren't. "You think you're going to change our son in that dress? Take the chance of ruining it? Not on my watch."

She smiles and stands up with us. "You go change him. I'll

get his bottle ready for my parents. You might've sped up the proposal, but I'm still counting on that date night."

I lean in for the kiss that I forgot to give her when she said yes. Of course, it's not as deep as I'd like considering I have a squirming baby in my arms, but it's perfect, nonetheless.

"I love you."

"I love you too."

"Hey," I say, turning around one more time. "You're sure you're okay that I proposed this way? Followed by the grand finale of our kid stinking up the room?"

Gabi walks over and presses a kiss on Ace's cheek before taking my chin in her fingers, turning my lips to hers in the most perfect kiss to seal the moment.

"I wouldn't have wanted it any other way."

ABOUT THE AUTHOR

Known for her witty sense of humor, Chelle Sloan is a former sports editor who after completing her Master's degree in journalism, decided to become a romance author. You know, because that's the normal path to writing happily ever afters.

An Ohio native, she's fiercely loyal to Cleveland sports, is the owner of way too many — yet not enough — tumblers and will be a New Kids on the Block fan until the day she dies. She does her best writing at Panera in her magic booth. When she's not writing, she's trying to learn to bake, fixing up her condo (badly and by watching YouTube videos), or falling in love with a book.

As for her own happily every after? Maybe one day...

Stay up to date with all things Chelle & join the VIP Squad!

ALSO BY CHELLE SLOAN

THE NASHVILLE FURY, PRO FOOTBALL SERIES

Off the Record: A secret office romance

Off Track: A surprise pregnancy romance

Off Season: A second chance romance

Off Limits: A sibling's best friend romance

LOVE ONLINE SERIES

Thirst Trap: A social media romance

Match Maker: A fake dating romance

Run Run Rudolph: A celebrity, holiday romance

ROLLING HILLS

The One I Want: A single dad / nanny romance

The One I Need: An accidental marriage romance

The One I Love: A friends to lovers romance

The One I Hate: An enemies to lovers romance

GUIDE TO LOVE SERIES

Runaway Bride's Guide to Love: A brother's best friend, age gap
romance

Single Mom's Guide to Love: A billionaire, marriage of convenience
romance

Roommate's Guide to Love: A small town, single dad, romance

Good Girl's Guide to Love: A fake dating, pro football romance

GUIDE TO LOVE WORLD

Vixen's Guide to Christmas: A rivals-to-lovers, one bed, holiday
romance

www.ingramcontent.com/pod-product-compliance
Lightning Source LLC
Chambersburg PA
CBHW051752050726
47598CB00006B/2258